Before you begin reading the "Detroit Thorn Birds" series, you may want to order a FREE eBook of an introductory novella setting the stage for entering the mafia underworld in Detroit.

Detroit was a fast-growing boom city in the 1960s. But unknown to most, under the surface corruptive forces including the Italian, Greek and Black mafias and many gangs were at work. The *Gloom and Doom* novella is a synopsis of the tough life in the inner city of Detroit in the years after the 1967 riots. It was a violent time. The new historical fiction series, *Thorn Birds of Detroit* begins in the late 1970s. Les Cochran weaves a tale of the underworld and the effort of citizens to fight back from a state of anguish and despair.

Get Your FREE eBook at:

http://lescochranblog.com/gloom-and-doom-2/

ACKNOWLEDGEMENTS

In researching and writing the Detroit Thorn Birds series, I became acquainted with two men — Oscar Westerfield and Scott Burnstein — who made a significant difference in my ability to bring authenticity to the novels. Each brought their own expertise to the series that allowed me to narrow the line between fact and fiction.

The interviews with Oscar Westerfield, who was the Supervisory Special Agent of the FBI Detroit Division during the time of the series, were particularly rewarding. He provided countless experiences and insights that helped bring a sense of reality to *BLIND PIG*.

Scott M. Burnstein's two books — *Motor City Mafia* and *Detroit True Crime Chronicles* — were of immense value in providing the context for my fictionalized characters. His in-depth research on and knowledge of the Detroit Mafia brought a powerful perspective to *BLIND PIG*.

A special thanks to Oscar and Scott for their willingness to share their experiences and expertise; they are the finest professional colleagues an author could have.

And guess what? I have Lin and LinDee on my side. I appreciate their meaningful assistance and ongoing support.

My wife Lin, spent countless hours reading each word, giving me feedback and providing "constructive criticism." She devoted hundreds of hours reacting to the storyline, raising questions to clarify and amend, and editing each chapter one more time, even after I thought it was completed.

The precise work of my editor LinDee Rochelle, Penchant for Penning, whose attention to detail and questions complemented her tedious task of editing and critiquing. Thanks to her for inserting a little levity into the painstaking process.

And thanks, to my readers — I listen — I hear what you say; I'm encouraged. I take your advice seriously.

Keep sending notes to LesCochranBlog.com, making comments on Facebook (Les-Cochran-Fiction-Author), and tweeting me @AffairsByLes. You're helping make my novels better!

BLIND PIG

DETROIT THORN BIRDS DEFY MAFIA

MAFIA WORKS # 2

BY

LES COCHRAN

www.bookstandpublishing.com

Published by
Bookstand Publishing
Morgan Hill, CA 95037
4572_3

ISBN 978-1-63498-599-4

First Edition

Printed in the United States of America

ii

PREFACE

The Celtic Legend of the Thorn Birds

There is a legend about a bird which sings only once in its life, more beautifully than any other creature on the face of the earth. From the moment it leaves its nest, it searches for a thorn tree, and does not rest until it has found one. Then, it impales its breast on the longest, sharpest thorn. But as it is dying, it rises above its own agony to out sing the lark and the nightingale. The thorn bird pays its life for that one song, and the whole world stills to listen, and God in his heaven smiles, as its best is brought only at the cost of great pain.

Colleen McCullough, author of "The Thorn Birds"

In each of us there is something that cannot be denied. Maybe it's a desire to be the best we can be — the best mother, teacher or banker — it doesn't matter what, as we strive to climb the highest pinnacle, solve a complex problem, or live one more day.

In our society most individuals are not thorn birds; they are people who go on their merry way, day-by-day without giving serious thought to their actions, quietly shadowing others or doing what they're told. They are the followers, the rank and file — the essential ones who get the job done.

Like the thorn bird who sings its own song, some individuals strive to play the most beautiful music of all. They are the doers; the leaders — the people who make a difference. They are thorn birds. They work their hearts out without fear of failure, reprisal, or dying. They're driven, sometimes blindly, to accomplish a goal; they're on a mission. And so it is with the thorn birds of Detroit; they're driven against all odds to take back their city.

Blind Pig Defined

The prohibition era stimulated a growth of blind pigs and speakeasies nationwide—blind pigs were typically smaller establishments located in lower class neighborhoods; speakeasies were far glitzier and catered to the upper class in their hey day, during the twenties and thirties.

Originating during the mid-1880s, the term speakeasy referred to a place where unlicensed liquor was sold—patrons were asked to "speak quietly, speak easy" so as not to alert the police or neighbors. The term blind pig evolved much later, referencing the large number of corrupt police officers who "looked the other way" and did not report the illegal activity.

For the most part, speakeasies disappeared at the end of prohibition, but blind pigs continued, particularly in the poorer areas of some Midwestern cities, chiefly Detroit, Milwaukee, and Pittsburgh. The opening of the Windsor-Detroit tunnel in the 1930s provided a direct smuggling route to Detroit. Over the following decades the Mafia exploited this opportunity and built a network of blind pigs, sometimes including gambling and prostitution. As a result, the term blind pig is still well-known and commonly used in Detroit.

Clark Phillips grew up on the Southwest side of Detroit. As a kid he walked the Scotten/Vernor Highway beat with his dad, Lewis, a long-time police officer. Following a summer job with his uncle at the Cadillac Plant on Scotten, he knew he'd become a Detroit cop.

CHAPTER ONE

THE DETROIT NEWS

August 2, 1979

MAFIA-CONNECTED FRONTMEN CONVICTED IN ALADDIN CASINO SCHEME

A Detroit federal jury convicted four men of conspiring to conceal the identity of the real owners whom exerted control of the Aladdin Casino in Las Vegas, Nevada.

General Manager James Abraham, bail bondsman Charles Goldfarb and Casino boss Edward Monazym, were given two years of probation. Local businessman James Tamer was sentenced to three years in federal prison for his role in the skimming operation for the Detroit Mafia.

Repeated references to Mafia Boss, Jacob "Jake" Nicolette, resulted in no actions or charges being filed against him.

FRANK "Nitti" USHER GUILTY
OF TRIPLE MURDER

Detroit Kingpin Francis "Big Frank Nitti" Usher and hit men Robert "Bobby the Animal" La Puma and James "Red" Freeman, were found guilty of the triple murder at a local social club on July 18, 1978.

The bodies of William P. Jackson, 41; Joanne Clark, 33; and William J. McCoy, 33, were found in a van outside the club. Their heads and hands were placed in brown plastic garbage bags lined up side-by-side.

***

An extremely attractive black woman sat handcuffed on a straight back chair in the middle of the back room of a boarded-up grocery store on Detroit's east side. Its best days long gone, graffiti marred the faded green walls, plaster and paint chips littered the floor. An early spring breeze from an unboarded alley window, twisted the loose plaster hanging from the broken lath above and ruffled the tattered curtain.

Sitting stoic behind a rickety four-foot long rectangular table, her wrists handcuffed behind the chair, the woman refused to wince at the telltale musty air assailing her nostrils. A light blue short-sleeve blouse hung loosely from broad shoulders and just met the top of her designer jeans. Long raven hair invited to be touched, atop a lovely, sculpted face dominated by large black eyes. Her eyes darted around the room pensively, as she searched for a sign that might suggest her future.

The back door creaked open.

Eight black gang members marched in, single file and circled her — their tongues waggling innuendos and vulgarities — their body language sending chills up and down her back. Showing off his muscular build, one of them stepped in front of her, stroked the back of his fingers suggestively around her face, leaned over and whispered something in her ear. Cringing inside, she took a deep breath so as not to convey an unwanted response.

Like many of the twenty-five hundred places looted and closed during the '67 riots, nearly thirteen years ago, the store was part of a block filled with decay. Not much remained of the vibrant neighborhood business district that once spawned active lives for hundreds of hard working people. Several burnout stores and half a dozen boarded-up stores lined the street. Only a pawn shop across the way and a liquor store with barred windows on the corner remained.

Tossing a gaze to the left, where gang members had taken position, the woman caught the eye of the tall one.

He eyeballed her.

Her skin crawled.

Acting like the most important dude in the world, he strutted forward as if sent by God Almighty — a half-buttoned yellow shirt showed off his black hairy chest, laden with layers of gold chains conveying the message — I've got everything you want!

Moving closer, he stroked her silky hair.

She sat stiff as a stone statue, unwilling to give him the pleasure of a glance. He scoffed, spit on the floor and walked back to the malcontents, still lined against the wall. Casting a disdainful glimpse her way, he muttered something to the miscreant next to him. The guy laughed and spread the word to the one next to him who passed it on. Chuckles rolled down the line.

The woman inwardly recoiled as the drug-ridden crew members stood — evil on their faces — a motley group of do-rags, ripped tee-shirts, torn tops and ragged pants. Each one ogling her, hoping he'd be the one to mount her tonight. She cringed and took a deep breath, trying to slow her pounding heart.

The door behind the henchmen opened.

A short, skinny black man, five-foot-five at most, with long, greasy, slicked-back hair, entered. Smartly clad with gold rings on each finger, he paraded in like a peacock and stopped arrogantly between her and the table. Taking his time, the man studied her narrow nose and flawless complexion, then moved his attention slowly down her well-proportioned body and back up again, his hormones sparked. He took a half-step back and slid his small frame onto the table in front of her; it wobbled a little. Leaning back with his legs dangling loosely, his eyes narrowed in an unmerciful glare at her.

She shifted uncomfortably; her hands moistened.

"Who do we have here?" the kingpin asked.

Glowering at her, the tall lieutenant spat out her name. "Nicole Weatherspoon."

The boss scowled, his lips turned down. "What the hell does she want?"

The number two man pointed toward the front door. "She appeared out front an hour ago, said she wanted to talk with Lonnie 'Hollywood' Williams."

Hollywood's ego peaked. "Why does she want to talk to me?"

"She wants to make a deal so there aren't any problems around her convenience stores." He flipped four fingers up. "Four of them are in our territory."

Nodding his head slowly up and down, Lonnie finished a contemptuous inspection of her. "What kind of deal are you willing to make?"

"One like I made with the Mafia," she said, meekly. "I talked with the man in charge and he agreed to stay out of the area around my stores."

"Huh." Lonnie flung her a punitive glance. "You the one heading up that neighborhood watch crap?"

"It's not crap, it's…"

"Shut up," he shouted, cutting her off. "If I say it's crap, it's crap." He turned in a huff to his top man. "Bring me the Bowie."

The tall guy stepped forward and laid a black-pearl handled knife on the table.

Staring at the long blade, Nicole's eyes bulged as if ready to pop out of their sockets.

Picking up the Bowie, he eased off the table and flashed the sixteen-inch blade back and forth in front of her face, swiping the air with the blade like a Kung Fu master might.

Her anxiety rose, fearing he'd cut her face or harm her in some other way.

Lonnie brushed the flat side of the blade against her left cheek, around her chin and down one side of her neck.

Holding her breath, Nicole swallowed hard.

He laid the Bowie on the table, rubbed his crotch with both hands, and asked suggestively, "What are you offering?"

She took a deep breath and sighed. "I paid the Mafia fifty dollars a month per store. I'm willing to do the same with you," she fibbed.

Lonnie burst into laughter. He lifted a huge gold rope chain with a gold, diamond-encrusted medallion from his neck. "See this, it's worth fifty grand. Do you think money is important to me?" Twisting his head toward his crew, he mumbled a lewd remark, then turned back to her and ran his hand around her lips, and caressed her chin. "You can do better than that."

Sensing the implied sexual message, she turned her head away without saying a word.

"Something wrong?" Lonnie jerked her head up by her hair, forcing her to look at him.

Unable to restrain her anxiety, Nicole's lips quivered.

A sneer slid across his ruthless face in total disregard for her feelings. "You nervous?"

She nodded unconsciously and squeezed her hands tightly, trying not to shiver visibly.

"I like that." A broad smile split his lips, exposing the large gap between his two gold-capped front teeth. Turning to the side, he picked up the Bowie and gently slid it down his arm, shaving off every hair it touched.

Nicole shuttered; her heart raced, moisture popped from her upper lip.

Using his free hand, he circled his index finger around and between her lips. "Let's hear it… one more time."

Nicole's mind swirling, unable to speak, she was at her wits-end.

"What's wrong?" He laughed. "Cat got your tongue?"

Moisture oozed from her pores, glistening her skin, as a queasy feeling gripped her stomach. She felt faint.

Waving the Bowie in front of her face; he lowered it and with the flip of his wrist clipped off the top button of her blouse. "You ready to deal now?"

"I-I-I could pay a hundred dollars a store," she squeezed out.

He turned to his crew. "Whataya think guys?"

Laughter filled the room. The hoods stomped their feet loudly to a jive beat — the stifling noise vibrated against bare walls.

"Check her out, boss" the tall one urged.

"Yeah," the gallery echoed, clapping and chatting even louder.

Hollywood shot them a sneer. "My exact thoughts." He slid the blade down the front of her blouse snipping off the remaining buttons — her blouse fell limp — exposing her décolletage held firmly in place by a silky black bra.

A euphoric expression jumped from his jaw; his urges fired.

Gawking from the gallery, the gang members closed in, forming a tight semicircle around her, for the boss's next move. Barking like a pack of wolves, the beat accompanied their howls and pounded louder than ever.

Hollywood eased the Bowie up her sleeve, slicing through the neckline — the blade dividing the cloth like a knife cutting hot butter — the left side of her blouse fell loose.

Squeezing in closer, the group cheered.

Hollywood gave them a thumbs up and cut through the top of the other sleeve — her blouse dropped to her waist — bare shoulders and bra visible to all. Beads of perspiration ran down her cleavage.

Jubilation filled the room. The gang members' shouting rose to a deafening rhythmic beat.

"Let's hear about the deal!" Lonnie shouted more forcefully than before.

"I don't understand," she said, knowing full well the thoughts he had in mind.

He tossed her a cunning glance. "You don't understand?" his voice blistered. "Let me make it perfectly clear." He placed the Bowie under the left strap of her bra and sliced it in half. Stepping to the other side, he split the other strap with a flick of the wrist.

Her bra held firm.

Reaching forward, he ran his hand over her bare shoulders and down to the bulging top of her bra. The guys sang the chorus line from Queen's "We Will Rock You." Hollywood gestured like a maestro leading an orchestra, encouraging them. With the Bowie in the other hand he placed it between her breasts and cut the centerpiece in half.

A trickle of blood ran down her chest as her bra fell loose, displaying her large, full breasts. Nicole swallowed hard; her half-dollar-sized nipples and perfectly shaped breasts inviting all to see.

The troops shouted and cheered, louder than before. Cat-whistles shrieked.

Lonnie's face brightened; a rush came over him. He placed the side of the blade under her left breast and gently lifted upward. "Hmm, firmer than I thought." With a sense of ownership, and with pride beaming his pleasure, he slid onto the table and cocked one leg over the front edge.

An expression of excitement filled his face. "Four weeks."

A deep furrow dug into her brow. "Four weeks, I …"

He cut her off. "Sleep with me four weeks, one week for each store, and I'll protect your stores for the rest of the year."

"And?" she asked, weakly.

"Four more weeks and you get another year."

Trying to compose herself, Nicole took in a deep breath. "How do I know you can deliver?"

Lonnie's face turned sober. He leaped off the table in anger, picked up the Bowie, and flung it into the table — the tip plunged deep into the top, directly in front of her, the handle quivering like a bowstring. "Ask any one of the guys." He motioned to his gang members.

"Ha." She gave him an eye, showing surprising strength, considering her precarious circumstance, and fired back. "That's a fine group of references."

Lonnie's sour face curdled, embittered by her disdainful suggestion. He reached into his hip pocket and pulled out a small black book. "See this, it's a list of my dealers and suppliers on the east side. Ask any one of them."

Her demeanor softened, like she'd flipped a switch. She gave him a seductive grin, her eyes moved slowly up and down his slight frame. She paused for a long moment at his bulging jeans, moved past his gold chain, and parked on his face.

"Well," he stated impatiently.

"Well, I'm ready." She pushed her shoulders against the back of the chair, elevating her breasts. "Take off my handcuffs. We might as well get started."

Surprise raced across his forehead; his eyes brightened, *desire* pulled his lips into tight, cocky smile.

"Well …" She raised her right shoulder, flaunting her breasts with a scintillating shrug. "I need more than talk."

His enthusiasm spread, ear to ear. "Take the cuffs off," he said to the tall guy.

The lieutenant moved in front of Nicole, taking in a close-up view. He slipped behind her and unlocked the cuffs.

Nicole rubbed her wrists, took a deep breath and stood. Towering nearly a half a head over Lonnie, she pulled him off the table, slapped her left hand on his butt, wrapped her right arm over his shoulder, and planted a heavy wet kiss on his lips.

The guys squeezed-in tightly, stomping, clapping, shouting. "Go for it man! Take her now! Spread eagle on the table!"

Lonnie placed his hands around her bare back, pulled her breasts into his chest and sealed her lips with a long French kiss.

The gang members cheered with delight.

The front and back doors burst open. "Hands up, you're all under arrest," Clark Phillips shouted.

DEA agents crashed through the back door and shoved the gang members against the wall. "Hands against the wall! Don't anyone move!"

Clark ripped off his cardigan and handed it to Nicole. Slipping it on, she buttoned it quickly and released a deep sigh. Clark placed his arm around her and eased her shivering body close to him. Her body fell limp against his firm six-foot-two frame.

"Geezs," she gasped. "I can't believe what he did; it was awful."

"At least it's over."

"Thank God.

"That's the problem with gangs, you never know how they're going to act. I'm sorry I had to wait so long, but I had to make sure we had the goods on him."

"I knew you were coming. I just kept pressing forward, pushing the bad thoughts out of my mind. I don't know how much longer …" Nicole broke into tears.

Clark pulled her tighter. "I can't imagine the kind of thoughts that ran through your mind. The best thing is it's over." The city's top detective whispered in her ear. "I'm so proud of you. You were terrific."

"Thanks." She sucked in a deep breath and cracked a partial smile.

Clark turned his attention to Lonnie.

Earl Walker, Clark's six-foot-four assistant, stepped across the room and stopped in front of the tall fella. The two black men stared, eye-to-eye, for the longest moment. Earl spoke in a firm tone. "Turn around and put your hands against the wall."

Without making a move, the creep sneered, as if to say *make me*.

Earl snapped his shaven head up and jammed his Beretta 92 into the guy's gut. "Turn around."

Slowly, the creep turned around and placed his hands on the wall.

Cuffing and frisking him, Earl pulled a switchblade knife and two bags of white powder from his pockets, but no I.D. He swung the thug around. "What's your name?"

The egomaniac sneered. "None of your business."

"Okay, none of your business, you have the right to remain silent. Anything …"

"Billy Fletcher."

"Billy Fletcher, you have the right to remain silent. Anything you say or do can and will be used against you in a court of law. You have the right to an attorney. If you cannot afford an attorney, one will be appointed to you. Do you understand these rights as they have been read to you?"

"Hell no!"

Earl stepped forward, nose-to-nose. "Do you understand your rights?"

Billy stared at Earl then spit to the side. "Yeah."

Earl tightened his grip and shoved him toward the DEA officer standing a few feet away. "Take him away."

After reading Lonnie his rights, Clark turned him to the side to cuff him.

Lonnie lunged for the knife.

Nicole grabbed it from the table and slid the Bowie under his crotch. "I wouldn't move if I were you."

He gave her a smug sneer. "You don't have anything on me. It'll be your word against mine."

Nicole leered. "We'll see about that." She held the Bowie in the air, then laid it on the table. "Aggravated assault with a deadly weapon." Raising her left hand, she held the black book she'd slipped from his pocket. "The names of your drug network on the east side." She loosened her belt, reached inside her of jeans and pulled out a wire. "You shoulda looked below my breasts, you idiot. Your confession has been recorded."

His face wilted like an un-watered flower.

Earl cuffed him and read him his rights.

Turning to Nicole, Clark spoke softly, "You doing better?"

Still dazed from her horrifying experience, she nodded. "I think so."

Clark gave Lonnie a spiteful glare. "You're going away for a long time."

"Huh." Lonnie returned with a malicious scowl. "I'll get even with you and your slut."

***

THE DETROIT NEWS

March 17, 1980
Section D

EASTSIDE GANG MEMBERS ARRESTED

Gang leader Lonnie Williams, his top henchman Billy Fletcher, and seven other gang members were arrested yesterday in the raid of an abandoned building on East Warren. The sting operation was set up by Clark Phillips, head of the city's Special Crimes Task Force, in coordination with the DEA.

Williams, an acknowledged leader of notorious Young Boys Inc. is the first high-ranking member of the leadership council to be arrested. The organization reportedly controls over 80 percent of the city's drug traffic.

CHAPTER TWO

Three years ago Police Chief William Hart appointed Clark Phillips to head up the Special Crimes Task Force composed of Detroit's best police officers. With most of the Detroit police force on the take or tied to the Mafia, it was essential that Clark's team works independently of the DPD. In a short period of time, his team had made significant inroads into curbing the power of the Detroit Mafia. A feather in his cap, Clark saw it as one more job that needed to be done. Those who know Clark were not surprised; they know he works hard and plays hard.

Reflecting from a far corner booth of the Sax Club on Six Mile/McNichols Road, Clark ran his fingers through his thick crop of sandy hair. *We're starting our fifth year of playing poker on the first Friday of every month. Before going upstairs, the guys used to sit with me on the bar stools directly under pole number one, where my girlfriend performed. That was until one afternoon when I betrayed her. How dumb could I be? Caroline was smart as a whip, had a great personality, and could hold a conversation on any topic with anyone. Now she's out of my life and I'm relegated to the booth farthest from her. Shit, I still get turned-on when she's on the center pole.* Tonight was no different.

Renzo and Carlos slid in, one on each side of Clark. The three of them had grown up in the same southwestern neighborhood. Clark had graduated from Detroit Western High School and his two buddies had attended Detroit Holy Redeemer High School, just down the street. Both men were highly successful small business entrepreneurs — Renzo Ricciuti, a local remodeling contractor whose father was from Sicily, and Carlos Montes, a Mexican-American, had several used car dealerships in the inner city.

Earl Walker eased in next to Renzo. He'd been with the poker group just over a year, having replaced Alsye Weatherspoon, Nicole's husband, after he'd been killed by the Mafia. A basketball teammate of Clark's, Earl had set several Detroit city high school-scoring records before blowing out his knee in college. A slight limp was barely noticeable.

Arriving late, as usual, was Ted Moomau, a self-described gypsy who owned five apartment buildings. Ted had stopped his philandering ways since becoming engaged to Laverne Belk — a tall, blonde, pediatrics doctor at Wayne State University's medical college.

A well-endowed waitress showed off her ample breasts as she placed two new pitchers of beer and another bowl of pretzels on the table.

Before sitting down, Ted asked the question that was on everyone's mind. "How in the hell did you figure out Barbara Nash was involved in the bank scam?"

"It's crazy," the usual tight-lipped detective admitted. "At the sentencing of her husband, Huston, my girlfriend Sharon saw a woman standing behind him. When Huston turned toward her he sneered. It was not like I'm sorry dear; his eyes were as vindictive as hell."

"I wish I could have seen that," Carlos interjected.

"It was surreal." Clark said, taking a sip of beer. "Sharon remembered seeing the woman's picture in the paper a few years earlier when Huston Nash had held a press conference to announce the reward for the murder of his grandson."

Renzo leaned closer. "Shit man that was two years earlier. How in the hell could she recall something that long ago?"

Clark shrugged his shoulders. "A women's thing, I guess. She remembered Barbara's glacial smile."

"Her smile" Ted said. "I've been there. Women are born with steel-trap minds."

Clark ignored the innuendo. "Sharon continued to watch her. Next thing I know, she nudged me and nodded in Barbara's direction — she was cozying-up to Angelo Travaglini in the hallway outside the courtroom. He was the number two man in the Mafia. That's when the bells went off — Huston's expression of disdain moments earlier tied in with his wife playing kissy-face with Angelo. It didn't take long to figure it out — one plus one makes two — Bingo! The two of them had set up Huston and he was taking the rap for her. 'Damn,' I said to myself, 'we convicted the wrong person.'"

Carlos smiled, finding ironic humor in Clark's remarks. "Lucky for you."

Clark nodded in agreement. "You're telling me. We had no reason to expect anything like that. Huston had pleaded guilty; it was over. Had Sharon not picked up on Mrs. Nash's look, the two would have gotten off scot-free."

"It's interesting how one piece of information can unravel everything," the stocky Mexican-American observed. "Anything else happening with you?"

"Not much …" Clark paused. "Our task force is establishing priorities for the second half of the year."

"I bet you have plenty of cases to pick from."

Clark gave him an expression of wonderment. "Hundreds of penny-ante stuff; we're trying to zero in on a couple big ones."

Earl sat his half-empty mug down. "If we could clean up another major case this year, that'd be something."

Ted emptied the last drop in the pitcher. "Ready to play cards?"

"I can hardly wait." Renzo jabbed Ted in the side. "C'mon, let's go upstairs."

***

Father Dominic "Dom" Repice greeted the guys as they filed into the small poker room upstairs — a round table in the center of the room with a broken fan above, two windows without curtains to the left, positioned over the alley below. And, a beat-up six-foot rectangular table filled with bowls of chips and dip, M & M peanuts, cashews, and a row of subs, stood invitingly under the windows. Clark's old Detroit Tiger's cooler sat on the floor to the right, loaded with ice and bottles of Stroh's.

In his mid-sixties, Father Dom had changed little since he was the principal when Renzo and Carlos were in high school at Detroit Holy Redeemer. After that he'd been promoted to the headquarters of the Catholic Archdiocese of Detroit located on State Street, not far from Clark's office on 1300 Beaubien. The four had played poker in one location or another for almost ten years.

Renzo plopped down and shuffled the cards, waiting patiently for the others to finish their gabbing. It wasn't long before he gave up and flipped the cards to the vacant chairs. "Dealer's choice," he called, and when the first ace landed in front of Ted's chair. "It's your deal,

Ted," he called to the squared-jawed hipster with black slicked-back hair.

Not your typical Detroit guy, Ted had been as loose as loose could be. The five-foot-eleven loner suffered the brunt of the group's jokes because he had a *big one*. Several women had said he was hung like a horse; he'd been known to *service* eight to ten different women a week in the apartment buildings he owned. Jokingly he had called himself the maintenance man. That was, of course, before becoming engaged to Laverne. In his fourth year at the poker table, wedding plans played in his future.

"Hold your horses," Ted replied, adding a heaping pile of chips onto his plate. "Five-card stud, read 'em and weep," he called, sat his plate on a TV table and squeezed into his chair. Picking up the deck cut by Clark, he flipped the cards around the table. And with that, the poker marathon was on.

An hour passed without a word spoken other than poker lingo.

Glancing at Renzo and Carlos, Ted broke the conversation code. "The two of you ever get things sorted out with the mob?"

Carlos grabbed a couple of potato chips. "Yeah, I guess."

Ted curled his brow. "Yeah, I guess. What the hell does that mean?"

"I agreed to their demands," Carlos admitted. "I'm providing them with four cars a month like they wanted — each one, two hundred dollars under wholesale."

Father Dom perked up. "You're loosening eight hundred dollars a month just for protection?"

"I don't have much choice, father." Carlos flipped his palms in the air, in dismay. "Eight hundred bucks spread over five lots ain't so bad. At least I don't have to worry about gangs and vandals tearing up my places."

"Sounds like a rationalization to me." Ted raked in the chips and glanced up at Renzo. "Did you cave too?"

Renzo glanced toward the back windows. "Yeah, I remodeled one of their blind pigs last year at the discount rate they wanted, haven't heard a thing since then."

"Remodeled? What kind of work did you do?" Father Dom inquired.

Renzo's eyes opened wide, recalling his surprise. "It was supposed to be a small job. I ended up gutting the inside of a two-story building. We ripped out a couple of walls on the main floor, tiled it, and covered the walls with red shag carpeting."

"You put carpeting on the walls?"

"Yeah, the old walls were pretty scuzzy so we carpeted them. They are surprisingly attractive."

Father Dom twisted his head to the side. "Guess I never thought about doing that."

"How about outside?" Ted asked. "Did you make a lot of changes to the exterior?"

"Nope, not a thing. The outside is totally boarded up. If you drove by you'd think the place was vacant." He chuckled. "Except from two to six o'clock in the morning the street is packed with cars."

"Are all of the blind pigs like that?"

"No. This one was special. The Mafia is setting up different types of places all over the city — some for the high-rollers, others for the guys from suburbia. Most of them are neighborhood bars with maybe a prostitute or two hanging around and a card game going on in the backroom. The Mafia either runs them or takes a piece of the action."

A frowning Carlos waited patiently for Renzo to finish. "Back to the point you mentioned, have you heard from the mob since Clark turned down the heat?"

"Not really." Renzo counted on his fingers. "That's four, maybe five months."

"Funny" Carlos scowled. "I haven't seen a thug for over a year."

Earl picked up the cards, ruffled the deck. "Interesting, Clark cleans up the Kingston case and the Mafia backs off."

Clark gave Ted a sideways glance. "Did you agree to house the prostitutes as they wanted you to do?"

"No. I drug my feet, told them that I had year-long contracts and a published waiting list. After that they backed off."

"Sounds like more than coincidence," Father Dom speculated. "When Clark's investigations were over you guys were out of the picture."

"You're right, Father," Clark said, one hand smoothing back his hair.

Earl shook his head and cracked his million-dollar smile. "Two of you caved and the other found a loophole. I don't get it. Nicole

meets with Blackie Giardini and she comes back with a free pass —
twenty years of protection with no fees. Am I missing something?"

Renzo and Carlos stared blankly.

"It wasn't a loophole," Ted asserted. "No way would I *ever* cave
into those bastards."

Clark stood and headed for the beer cooler. "Not only did Nicole
finesse Blackie, she was something else during the last week's sting."

Father Dom frowned quizzically. "Could you tell us more,
Clark?"

"Sure," Earl jumped in. "It's all been in the press. She's
superwoman, a Detroit thorn bird."

"I agree." Carlos shook his head. "Sounds like it from what I've
read."

"You wouldn't believe her tenacity," Earl went on to describe in
detail, the entire operation.

Questions flew on each point as he worked his way through the
episodes.

"I can't believe it — her inner strength — sitting there while this
creep cuts off her blouse and bra. And then she has the tenacity to take
him on." Earl stopped, realizing his fifteen-minute testimony was more
about Nicole than he'd intended.

"Seven cards, deuces wild." Clark called; saving the day for
Earl, who he knew had more than a passing fancy for Nicole.

"Maybe you guys should take a lesson?" Earl said, unable to
stop singing her praise.

***

Blackie Giardini sat in the elevated corner booth in his favorite
neighborhood bar, as he had for the past ten years. His black outfit and
large black sunglasses were barely visible in the dimly lit lounge. Next
in line for the Street Boss position, the number three slot in the Detroit
Mafia, Blackie had earned respect of all, particularly Boss Jake
Nicolette.

His right-hand man Joey Naples lifted a pitcher of beer and filled
his glass.

Vicky Cromwell, Blackie's attractive mistress, slid her glass
across the table.

Joey filled it to the brim and eased it carefully back to her.

She smiled and took a sip. Bearing a striking resemblance to Cher, one of the top singers of the day, some said Vicky could pass as her twin — her long black hair, narrow face, high cheekbones and large black eyes made the case. Whenever someone drew that comparison, Blackie quickly announced, "There is a big difference. Vicky is extremely well-endowed."

Blackie took a slug of his brew and turned to Joey. "Something is going on out there. I can tell — it doesn't smell right. Something is in the works downtown."

"Do you think it's Clark Phillips?"

"Hell yes. It's always Clark Phillips; everyone else downtown is on the take."

"Whataya think we ought to do?"

"I'll lay you ten to one that will be the same question Jake will raise at our next meeting."

Joey stared at Blackie. *He has an amazing ability to pick up on the subtleties, process them and come up with a solution that's always right on target.*

"Nicolette has to be thinking the same thing. I'm making a call to Philly to see if 'Red' is available."

"Red?" Joey responded quickly; maybe a little too quickly. He recalled her body with pleasure, then masked his thoughts with a nonchalant comment. "If anyone can get to him she can."

Raising her hand, Vicky said, "If all of that is settled, I'd like to say something."

Blackie turned her way, realizing he had not included her in the conversation. "Yes of course, sweetheart."

She fidgeted with her napkin. "August 7th will be our third anniversary."

"Yeah," Blackie interrupted. "I've been thinking about doing something special."

Pausing for a moment, she spoke with strong resolve. "I've been thinking about it too." She flipped her long black hair over her shoulder. "It's time for us to go our separate ways."

Blackie's face went blank. "You can't do that, darling," he said in a low sexy tone, snuggled close and slid his hand up her thigh. "We've never talked about another type of a relationship. You know I …"

She cut him off, "I've thought about that too. I can envision a wonderful life we might have together. One I'd never thought possible. But I'm thirty-two, figure I have five, maybe six years to make something more out of my own life."

"Sweetie."

Raising her hand, she shut him down. "I've been contacted by the Cherokee Nation in Tahlequah, Oklahoma, to play a major role in the revival of our people."

Blackie leaned back, without an inkling of what she might say.

"My great grandparents were forced to walk from North Carolina to Oklahoma; hundreds of those who walked with them died. That was one hundred and fifty years ago."

Blackie's eyes glazed, waiting for her to get to the point.

"In commemoration of that horrible event, the Nation is undertaking a national campaign to restore our rights and they've asked me to severe as one of the spokespersons. I can't turn my back on them. I have to go."

***

Clark sat in a black leather club chair in the Ghostbar at The Whitney on Woodward Avenue, just south of Wayne State University. A landmark since the 1890s, the bar inside the restaurant had become a regular stop for Clark. He enjoyed the ambiance; the bar's arched, painted ceilings, wood-crafted backbar, and tastefully done wallpaper, all combined to make it a perfect place to unwind and chat with an old acquaintance.

Clark stared into his beer, lost in thought about the last few years. While his task force had made progress, resulting in his award of the Detroit Police Medal of Honor for Excellence, the city had failed to slow its downward spiral — adverse signs of the city's future were apparent.

The auto industry had suffered major setbacks — Japanese and German carmakers were grabbing market share.

Downtown leadership was passive.

The mass flight after the '67 riots of over two hundred thousand people (mostly white) to the suburbs in the following three years, had supposedly ended. Unfortunately, the exodus continues today fueled by corruption downtown, approval of unrealistic employee contracts, ongoing legal issues, and resulting negative press.

The opportunity to fix the problem passed. The deeply segregated city was a hopeless case with few solutions.

Admiring the street lamps hanging upside down, as light fixtures, Clark glimpsed Nicole out of the corner of his eye. He rose and extended his arms. She fell into his embrace and the two hugged as good friends might.

He pulled back and shook his head. "I still can't believe how well you pulled it off. You were terrific!"

"Pulled it off?" She laughed, sliding into a barrel chair across from him. "I was scared to death. That Bowie knife seemed like a meat cleaver."

"I can imagine."

"When he snipped off my bra … I thought I would die. I was so embarrassed I didn't know what to do … I remembered how strong Alsye had been, facing the mob. I said to myself, 'square your shoulders, Nicole, and take charge.'"

"You did more than that. We've already arrested eighty-four members in Lonnie's drug ring, most of them connected to the Young Boys Inc."

Nicole wrinkled her brow.

Before she could ask, Clark went on to say, "YBI is a black organization that controls most of the heroin business in the city. We estimate they're taking-in over $250,000 per day."

"Per day! No wonder Lonnie said money wasn't a problem."

"It's unreal." Clark understood her perfectly. "Lonnie's little book connected him to drug-kingpins Raymond 'Baby Ray' Peoples and Dwayne 'Wonderful Wayne' Davis, and one of the Mafia's drug distributors Harry 'Taco' Bowman."

"That's wonderful," she said, turning her lips down in distaste. "I used half a bottle of Listerine to wash my mouth after he French kissed me." She sighed and tossed Clark a pleasant glance. "Thanks to you my stores are now gang-free."

"Me? The credit is all yours. It was all about you." Clark flipped a hand in the air. "Still, I'm sorry you had to go through all of that. I had no idea Lonnie would do anything like he did."

Nicole shrugged her shoulders. "You warned me black gangs operated spontaneously. Guess you were more prophetic than you realized."

"Still, I hated it."

Reflecting for a moment, Nicole said, in a more resolute tone, "Well, it's over now."

"Could I order you a drink?"

"Yes," she said, without hesitation. "A glass of Chianti."

Clark's eyebrows rose. "Chianti, what happened to the sodas?"

Nicole shot him an embarrassed grin. "The women corrupted me. I've been meeting with them over lunch at the Roman Village for the past two years. I have a glass of Chianti every time, sometimes …" she bit her lip, "I have two glasses."

"Good for you." Knowing a couple of Tanqueray gins was nothing for him, Clark laughed. "You better be careful, you'll become a lush."

"I don't think so." She leaned back, her lovely face more attractive than ever.

The barmaid delivered her wine and Clark's usual, Tanqueray on the rocks with three olives.

"Here's to your continued success." Clark toasted. *She's an amazing woman. When Alsye died at the hands of the Mafia two years ago, she could have folded the tent and moved back to South Carolina. Instead, she's become a dynamo, managing their eight convenience stores, running several neighborhood-watch programs and raising two boys.*

Nicole waved her hand, shunning his admiration. "Thanks, and here's to your continued success in rounding up the bad guys."

Running his hand through his Robert Redford hair, Clark asked, "You have any new projects?"

He listened to her reply thinking Nicole seemed so much happier; her voice revealing a normal positive tone.

"I have a long list," she stated without hesitation. "My first priority is to clean up the neighborhoods around my stores."

Clark glanced in wonderment. "Beyond the watch programs?"

"Yes, we need new streets, sidewalks and lamp posts for all of the shops, like the city did for my main store. I want to set up a program that attracts investors.

"Investors … for what?"

"To construct buildings in the vacant lots and where burnt-out stores still stand. We need to make the neighborhood whole again — a continuous block with no vacant stores."

"Wow." Clark's eyes opened wide. "How many years do you think that'll take?"

Nicole's broad smile turned into a laugh. "That's *this* year's plan." Fluffing her hair, she raised a hand. "We have to start construction … there's no time to waste."

Clark dawdled over his gin, recalled Alsye's remark "whenever she decides to do something, I take a backseat. There's no stopping her."

Nicole downed the last of her wine. "Thanks, again, for all you did for Alsye. You were his closest friend. I only wish he would have followed your advice one more time." She pulled a tissue from her pocket and patted the moisture on her right cheek.

"Alsye was one great guy, so easy going. I really miss him." Clark glanced at the tapestry wallpaper then turned back to her. "Who knows why terrible things like that happen," he philosophized. "Hopefully things will work out for the best."

"It's still hard," she sobbed and dabbed her left cheek. "Darn, I hate it when …"

Clark interrupted her. "There's no reason to feel that way. We're good friends. A tear now and then is only natural. You can't keep it locked inside."

"I know," she said, a sound of relief in her voice. "I'm so pleased you agreed to see me."

"Hey, Alsye was my best friend. I'd do anything for him and I'll do anything I can for you."

With a serious tone, the firmness of her resolve made Nicole's commitment clear. "I want to get even with the Mafia."

"Nicole … I …"

She reached across the small table and placed her index finger on his lips. "People don't stand up against them. Mobsters come and go as they please around here. They're like the slave masters of the past — beating up, killing people, and stealing from them — reigning with terror. I'm not going to kowtow to them. My boys are not going to live in fear of them. They've sucked every last penny out of this city. It's time to say enough is enough."

Sitting dumfounded, Clark stared at her, *her will; her fervor flashing*. He rummaged his brain for the right words. "Nicole, I understand how you feel …"

She cut him off, "Clark, I'm going to do something that will change the minds of people and motivate them to resist the Mafia. We have to force people to take action. It's *our* city *not* theirs."

Clark reached across the table and squeezed her hand. "I know how you feel Nicole. I want the same thing."

"These are not just words, Clark." Her focus sharpened. "Sometime in the future I'm going to need your help."

"You know I'll do anything you want." Clark took a sip of gin. "How can I help?"

"Not now." She waved her hands in front of her. "Just knowing you'll be there is enough." She glimpsed at the backbar and turned back to Clark. "I don't know when, but when the time comes I'll know."

Shaking the ice to make sure he'd gotten the last sip, Clark finished his drink. "You name it and I'll be there."

She leaned across the table and pecked him on the cheek. "You're such a good friend."

CHAPTER THREE

Downtown Detroit, task force members waited in the FBI-assigned conference room atop the McNamara Building. The decision to create Clark's seven-member team had been hugely successful. They'd made significant inroads into the city's criminal activity, including the firing of countless policemen. Not only did the move provide a convenient location where the team could work freely, without fear of being compromised by the corrupt police department, they had formed a strong working relationship with their new FBI colleagues — a stark contrast to most police departments. Agency personnel had a history of being reluctant to share sensitive information with local officials. Plain and simple; police officers talked too much. And that was certainly the case in Detroit.

Waiting for Clark to arrive for their bi-weekly meeting, John Ralston and Will Robinson, the two senior patrolmen of the group, gazed out the twenty-sixth floor window. John, a long-time friend of Clark's father, Lewis, pointed to the Ambassador Bridge. *Just two blocks east of where Clark was raised.* He laughed to himself. *Those were the days. Lewis and I talked late into the night, two or three times a week. Fran didn't seem to care; she always had a pleasant smile and something hot coming out of the oven. Lewis puffed on that damn stogie of his and I sat across from him in the same wicker chair, every visit. Thank goodness the breeze usually blew in the opposite direction.* Ralston pointed south. "You can see Windsor clear as a whistle today."

"Let me see." Earl Walker squeezed between them. "Yeah, and over there is Western High where Clark and I went to school."

"I seem to recall that," Ralston jested. "Lewis and I saw every basketball game the two of you played."

"Yeah, Lewis was always on the refs."

"I guess, how could I forget? He shouted louder than anyone in the gym. At Northwestern I thought he was going to get us a technical foul."

"He should have." Earl pointed down Vernor Highway a few blocks. "Guess you know what those two buildings are?"

"Detroit Holy Redeemer High School and Holy Redeemer Church," Ralston announced with pride.

Earl smiled. "We almost got our butt beat there, one night."

"I remember Clark threw up a last-second prayer from downtown."

Placing a hand on his forehead, Will Robinson shielded his eyes from the sun and pointed into the distance, off to the right. "There's the Rouge."

Ralston's nod confirmed. "Home to thousands of Ford workers."

The senior black patrolman pointed west toward Dearborn. "The old city shows off pretty well from up here."

"Maybe from here, but it's not so good at ground level," Eddie Grissini, the team's Mafia expert, spouted from across the room.

Glimpsing at him out of the corner of his eye, Earl gave him a quirky grin. *Now there's a special breed. Half Sicilian — his skin nearly as dark as his black curly hair — he should be working for the mob. His Greek mother's side wasn't much more flattering; his broad nose smashed between dark beady eyes.*

Sitting at the end of the table, Max Cumberland, the longtime precinct captain, chewed on a PayDay candy bar. In striking comparison with Eddie, his blonde hair and blue eyes made him seem like a Godsend. That is, except for his pudgy face and two hundred and forty pounds stuffed into a five-foot-four frame.

"You're damn right. The east side is boarded up; it's plain out ugly."

Pulling up a chair next to Max, Eddie asked, "Hey John, you've worked with the FBI Strike Force more than anyone … have an impression about them?"

Nodding his head, the forty-year patrolman produced a huge smile. "They're real pros; they have highly skilled experts for every task. Whenever there's a need for a particular skill that isn't available locally, they fly a person in from Washington—it goes like clockwork — smooth as silk." Ralston flipped his hands in the air. "With the Detroit police force I can't get an officer to walk across the street."

"The feds are the best," Kimberly said, chiming in from across the table — her rosy cheeks needed no introduction. Neither did her large breasts, a point often made by Max. "I've been impressed by the way they work together and have welcomed us; we make a seamless team."

"Ha," skin-and-bones Nancy Sterling from Narcotics added. "That's because you have the hots for that undercover agent."

"So I asked if he was married. Big deal!"

"I saw you hitting on him the other day."

A secretary stuck her head in the doorway. "Clifford said it'll be another fifteen to twenty minutes before Clark and he are finished."

Weston turned to her well-endowed colleague. "Are you finished working with the FBI team on the Nash case?"

"Yes, I updated Clark on Friday." She glanced around the room. "If you want I can fill you in while we're waiting for him."

"Might as well," Ralston said, motioning for the others to join him at the table.

"Clark figured out the case several months ago," Eddie whined. "I can't believe it's taken legal so long to indict Barbara Nash."

Flashing a smile, Kimberly thought that over for a moment. "It may seem like that, but it was important to get it right. One loose end could unravel the whole thing."

"I suppose," Eddie acknowledged.

"Anyway, here's the scoop." Kimberly flipped open her notebook. "The entire scam was orchestrated by Angelo Travaglini, the Mafia's number two man, and Barbara Nash."

"Can we nail him too?"

"Hmm, I don't think so. Everything with him is speculative and circumstantial; his signature is not on one piece of paper."

"Damn, they've done it again," Eddie moaned. "How do the top guys in the Mafia always seem to get off scot-free?"

Max's interest peaked; he tossed an empty Tootsie Roll wrapper in the ashtray. "I suppose the same is true for the other guys on the boards for the banks."

Kimberly gave him a double-thumbs down. "They weren't so lucky."

A quizzical look crossed Eddie's face. "Why? Not so lucky, I don't get it."

Having his attention, she took a deep breath. "A year ago, five of the former bank board members were alive; all of them upstanding men in the community."

"In addition to Angelo?" Eddie asked.

"Yes. Somehow, each of them died over the past nine months."

Shaking his head very slowly, Will Robinson asked, "How can that be?"

Kimberly cast him a friendly smile. "The coroner recorded each one as an accident."

"An accident," the short curly-haired detective shouted. "That's bullshit!" Eddie kicked the table leg. "Those sons-of-a-bitches rubbed them out."

"My exact feelings." Losing her smile, Kimberly continued. "I went through each one of the coroner reports. There was nothing. Each death was ruled accidental."

"Accidental my ass!" Eddie slammed his hand on the table. "They killed them; they were liabilities."

John Ralston raised his hand. "I guess that means that Barbara Nash is the big loser?"

"Absolutely," Kimberly said forcefully. "Her signature is on every document — as secretary, and when she forged Huston's name — the handwriting experts all agree on that."

Will rubbed his bald head. "How did she pull it off?"

"Not only was she banging Angelo; she was getting information from him on where and how to invest the money."

"I bet that's where Atlantic Offshore Drilling comes in," Eddie interjected.

"Right." Kimberly gave him a wink. "The money-laundering scam was on — they'd wire transfer the money to Bermuda, pay off the bank examiners, and pocket the profit."

"How did she pull it off?" Ralston asked.

"That's the best part. She'd place a stack of papers in front of Huston and he'd sign them. He thought everything was on the up and up — profits were exploding and his personal wealth was booming." Kimberly let out a long sigh. "Barbara would shred his copy and forge his name on an illegal set of transfers. He didn't know a thing about the scam."

"Poor guy," Eddie lamented. "What's likely to happen with her?"

"She'll be indicted next week; will likely get twenty years."

"Huh," Eddie grunted disgustedly. "Angelo will have the mob's best lawyers on her case. Want to wager? Three to five years at the most." He glanced around the table. "Any takers?"

Not a head moved.

"How about the twenty-year sentence Huston got?"

"The judge has already commuted part of it, and his time served will be deducted."

"I've heard enough about the mob for one day," Max said sharply. "Let's talk about the FBI. I've really been impressed with that Clifford McGill, the new head guy around here."

"Agree," Eddie nodded. "But, you can't beat that Oscar Westerfield. He was a real down to earth type of a guy. Out of a hundred and fifty agents in Detroit he was the best. I'm going to miss him."

Clark rushed in. "Sorry, I'm late. Clifford and I were finalizing our plan for the rest of the year."

"Guess there'll be no resting on our laurels," Max jested, shoving another Tootsie Roll in his mouth.

Clark expressed his mood with a little excited laugh. "You're right about that. We're taking on race fixing at Hazel Park and the Detroit Race Course."

"Race fixing?" Will Robinson gave it to him straight. "That's been going on at the DRC for years."

"Which is why we're taking it on. It's time to end it." Clark rolled up his sleeves, taking his time, one sleeve then the other. "I want everyone except Earl to spend the next month at the DRC and Hazel Park. You can work alone or as teams; just make sure your collective efforts cover both tracks."

"Is that all?" Max jested.

Clark grinned back at him. "As a matter of fact no."

The group came to attention; heads turned quizzically toward Clark.

"McGill is snowed and needs help. Washington has other priorities than us, so I volunteered Will and John to lend him a hand."

Not a word came from either officer; they waited for the other shoe to fall.

Clark nodded to the two. "You'll be heading up the background investigation on Jimmy Quasarano and Peter Vitale."

His dad's old friend raised a hand as he wondered aloud, "I thought they were indicted last fall."

"That's the point, John. No one has cracked their file since last November when indictments were handed down by the federal grand jury. With a legal counsel like William Bufalino in the wings, Clifford feels the case needs to be beefed-up."

"I thought it was a slam-dunk. The jury recommended each of them receive twenty-year sentences for using threats of violence to obtain control of a company in Wisconsin."

"You're right. The two of them extorted two hundred and seventy thousand dollars from the owners. But nothing is for sure when there's an attorney like Bufalino around."

"Hell, he could get them off with a slap on the hand," Eddie reminded the group. "Review his record. Bufalino will put on one of his flashy suits and chew up the prosecutor like he's going out of style."

Clark shook his head. "That's why Clifford wants us to help him out. See what you can find out. We'll meet again in three weeks."

***

THE DETROIT NEWS
APRIL 15, 1980

SOCIALITE CHARGED IN BANKING SCAM

This morning Federal Judge Henry Limbaugh heard one hundred and twenty-three counts against Barbara Nash for tax evasion, money laundering, banking fraud, and racketeering. The charges stem from a six-year period when she served as secretary for two savings and

loans. Her next court appearance is scheduled for July 8, 1980.

Two years ago, her husband Huston Nash was sentenced to twenty years in the federal prison for his role in the swindle. Yesterday, Judge Limbaugh reduced his sentence to five years and lessened that by the time he's already served.

***

"Mom, I'm sorry I'm late, had to get gas," Clark shouted as he burst through the front door.

Fran pointed to the pie. "It'll be five minutes before the apples are cool."

"Whew, guess I lucked out on that one." Clark headed for the freezer. "I'll get the ice cream. Is dad on the porch?"

"Where else … smoking that damn Corona." She turned to cut the pie. "Sounds like that Nicole friend of yours is quite a woman."

"She's a superwoman, mom."

Fran's eyes brightened. "A real thorn bird if you ask me."

"Yeah, that's a great description. One or two scoops?"

"One for me, two for your father."

Clark fixed his mom's plate, added a couple of scoops on the other two, and headed for the slider.

Fran scurried ahead. "I'll get the door."

Clark paused and kissed her on the cheek. "Thanks for baking the pie."

"Shoo." She waved her hand. "Talk to your dad, he wants to hear all about the sting."

Seeing the ice cream and pie, Lewis snuffed out his stogie. "Sounds like you've been busy." He chuckled. "That sting was some operation. C'mon son, give me the details."

Clark handed him a plate and eased into *the chair — John Ralston's chair — nothing new, it'd been a tradition forever. Dad would sit in that old wicker chair, pull out a Corona — bite the tip off, wet it, light up and take a couple puffs — smoke rings floated to the ceiling. When I was a kid, John Ralston would sit in the matching chair and the two police officers would commiserate about the Detroit Police Department. When I got older, I took John's place and received my lectures, sitting right here.*

Between bites of pie and ice cream, Clark spelled out the strategy of using Nicole to set up the black gang, and how the FBI had gone on to organize the bust. His dad listened intently; at every turn, he asked relevant questions and hesitated at the end. "That Nicole Weatherspoon is quite a woman."

Clark drew a grin. "Mom calls her a Detroit thorn bird."

"She's right," Lewis said. He placed his empty plate on the end table. Picking up a couple of newspaper clippings, he asked, "Did you read last week's story the *Free Press* did about historical achievements in the city's police department?"

"No. I have a stack of unread papers piled on my dinette table. What did it say?"

"It's very interesting." Lewis settled his reading glasses on his nose. "In 1893, the department hired the first black officer and the first female police officer."

"Wow, that was really progressive."

"Yeah, and in 1922, the department was the first one to use radio dispatch technology to patrolling automobiles."

"Sounds like the force was on top of things."

"It was, but by the time Coleman Young took over in 1972, over 90 percent of the officers were white. It was a good ol' boy system."

Clark thought for a moment on the fact. "Guess we lost a lot of ground in fifty years." He hesitated. "Yeah, and most of them were on the take."

His old man glanced over the top of his glasses. "Can't argue with that." He paused. "At least now we're well on our way to reaching the Mayor's fifty/fifty race-composition goal."

Clark perked up. "Wouldn't that be something? That'd be close to matching the city's demographics." Clark thought about his dad's earlier point. "Did that article give any recent statistics?"

"No, but a second article did." Lewis reached over and picked it up. "The homicide rate has gone down in each of the past three years. We're now below forty homicides per hundred thousand."

"That's really good." Clark nodded. "Back in the early seventies, it was really bad."

"Bad? It was awful. We topped seven hundred murders in one year." Lewis leaned back in his chair. "In the early seventies, it seemed like a mobster got knocked off every day."

"Give me that article with the statistics so I can share it with my team."

***

Clark hustled around his apartment, finished off the final touches, turned on WDZH soft jazz, arranged the bouquet of yellow roses on the dinette table one more time, and dimmed the lights. Glancing around his small apartment, he checked his watch — 6:10, *twenty minutes before Sharon arrives for a weekend stay.*

He tasted his mother's homemade spaghetti sauce for the third time, removed a plate of assorted cheeses from the fridge, added crackers, and placed the tray on the coffee table in front of the sofa. Heading toward the kitchen to open the wine, he heard the phone ring.

Assuming it was Sharon, he hurriedly grabbed the receiver. "Hello."

"Hi Clark, it's Abby."

His mouth went dry. *Shit, I haven't talked to her in more than a year. Goddamn whore. She screwed out of me every bit of information I had about the Mafia. Damn, how could I have been so dumb?*

"I know you hate me, but I still love you so much. I've transformed my life and have moved back to Detroit. Can we meet, over coffee or a drink? I'll do anything to see you. Please Clark, give me a chance."

Clark hesitated; his mind whirled. "Ah, I … I'm tied up right now."

"Of course, I understand." She hung up.

Shuffling over to the window, he leaned against the frame and stared blankly outside, for the longest time. *For six months we'd eaten at fancy restaurants, gone to Tiger games, talked well into the night, spent a weekend on Mackinac Island, and had great sex — she was fantastic.*

The doorbell rang.

Trying to shake his memories, Clark walked briskly to the door and slung it open.

Sharon stood in front of him, stunning, in black leather pants and a low cut purple sweater — a small diamond pendant hung in her cleavage. Looking better than ever, Clark stared, his mind unable to switch gears.

Her head cocked sideways in a curious look. "Well, aren't you going to invite me in?"

"Yes, of course … please come in," he said, coming to his senses. He pulled her close and planted a wet kiss on her lips. "Welcome to my abode."

"Well, aren't you something?" Stepping inside, she gazed at the romantic atmosphere. "Clark, it's wonderful. How did you come up with all of this?"

"I hired a design consultant." He laughed, trying to settle his nerves. "Seriously, I thought all about how I could make you happy."

She pecked him on the cheek. "Aren't you the lovey-dovey one?"

"The hors d'oeuvres are on the coffee table. We'll dine on spaghetti and meatballs shortly. I'll open a bottle of Chianti if that's alright."

"Perfect." She fluffed her shoulder-length brown hair. "Can I do something?"

"No, just make yourself comfortable." He pointed toward the sofa. "The Caesar salad is in the fridge. All I have to do is warm the French bread. Help yourself to the appetizers."

"Sounds like a gourmet dinner," she said. Sitting down on the sofa, she picked up a couple pieces of cheese and added some crackers to her plate.

Clark filled the wine glasses, thinking about the many times the two of them had been together. They'd been a thing — off and on — for the past four years. While they had much in common, their backgrounds were as different as night and day. He was an inner-city guy and she was a farm girl from Stevensville on the coast of Lake Michigan. They'd had some fun together — spent a week in Aruba, gone to Piston's games, attended jazz concerts — made love all weekend. She could do it all; cook, bake and hold a conversation on any topic you could imagine.

Stepping in front of the sofa, he handed her a glass of wine. "Here's to you, darling."

She tipped her glass to her lips and took a sip. "Thanks, you're the sweetie."

Clark slid onto the sofa next to her.

The two talked over appetizers, munching on cheese and crackers and enjoying a second glass of wine. Sharon sat her half-full glass on the coffee table and snuggled her head on his chest. "I'm so relaxed when I'm with you. I could kiss you all over."

He considered his normal comeback, but thought better of it. "I feel the same."

Tilting her head slightly, she kissed him lightly on the cheek and placed her hand on his thigh.

Clark swallowed softly. *An inch or two more and she'll be ...*

Her urging eyes met his. "Spaghetti is always better warmed up," she ventured.

Picking up on the message, Clark jumped up. "I'll turn the burner on simmer."

He rushed into the kitchen and returned in no time. Joining her on the sofa, the two lovebirds made love, slow and easy, for the longest time, before Sharon's burning desire crested. Moving slowly to the radio's sensuous melodies, she seductively pulled him into the bedroom.

CHAPTER FOUR

Clark turned his Mustang down the alley and flicked off the lights. Driving slowly by the light of the moon, he pulled behind the garage where he'd parked for the practice sting sessions many times — tonight was the real thing. He slipped out and double-timed it to the back door of the white-framed house. It sat directly across Elmira Street from Freddie Salem's, where the dice game was underway. *The lady who owned the place had been most cooperative, agreeing to make her home available to serve as the FBI's surveillance center.*

Glancing around the main floor, he noted the difference in attitude from the practice sessions — this is crunch-time — everyone was on alert. A dozen or more agents stood behind the worktables their eyes glued to the box-sized computer monitors; others with headsets listened to every word. Clifford McGill, the lead agent for the sting operation, stood poised with his bulletproof vest tightly secured. *Nothing new for the long-term FBI veteran of thirty years. And he looked the part — a six-foot-four no-nonsense type of guy in cowboy boots and a white Stetson hat.*

In the far corner, Earl tightened his vest and wiped the moisture from his upper lip. He'd been involved in several small-time busts before, but this was the real thing — a direct hit on a Mafia operation.

"Glad to see you," Clifford said, handing Clark a vest and motioning him near. "Everything is set just like we rehearsed it."

"The place seems different." A hint of nervousness caused a little tremor in Clark's voice.

Clifford chuckled and stepped closer. "It's always different when it's the real thing. It's like attending a Tigers' spring training ballgame with five thousand people in the stands and watching opening-day with fifty thousand roaring fans."

Clark smiled and nodded.

Clifford stepped closer. "The basement across the way is loaded with heavy hitters, a couple of guys from New York and Jersey. Come over here by the monitor." He motioned to Earl. "Over here, I'll show the two of you some of the key players."

The two nudged closer to Clifford, each standing on a side. "We're getting great pictures tonight from the camera hidden in the basement ceiling."

"In the ceiling?" Earl frowned, quizzically.

"Yes, one of them is by the third beam." Clifford pointed to another monitor.

"Oh yeah, I would have never noticed it."

"See the guys in the middle of the room with the sport coat and open white collar? That's Freddie Salem."

"Yeah, I see him," Earl said. "Balding with thin gray hair."

"You got him."

"Over to the left, the heavy-set one is Henry Hilf. He's one of the most prolific bookmakers around. They're best friends and he's helping Freddie tonight. Hilf spends all week dealing with little guys so he really enjoys being in the middle of the action with the big hitters."

Clark inched closer. "Is that Randall behind him?"

"Good eyes. William Randall and Allen Finch are undercover tonight. They'll give us the signal when the coast is clear."

Clifford turned toward the rest of the group. "Okay guys, we're doing everything as practiced. At three a.m. Randall and Finch will come upstairs, slip outside and arrest the two guards standing on each side of the front door. That'll be our signal to storm the place and head downstairs." Sensing Earl's anxiety, he winked. "If anyone is upstairs you can arrest them and bring up the rear."

"Sounds good to me," Earl said with a tone of relief.

"Once we're in the basement, make sure everyone's hands are up. From there it'll be easy — read them their rights and cuff them."

"Any questions?" Clifford scanned the group. "Good, all we have to do is wait for Randall and Finch to appear on this monitor," he pointed to one of the flickering screens.

Tension built in the minutes ahead. Earl wiped the moisture from his brow. Clark took a deep breath and sighed.

Ten minutes passed.

"It's 2:59," Clifford announced. "There's Randall and Finch on the monitor."

Clifford hustled to the front door and gazed across the street. "Any time now." Peering out the front window, he raised his hand. "Randall and Finch are coming out the door. Get ready. They're cuffing the guards and reading them their rights. Okay, let's go."

The leader burst out the door, ran across the street, and took the front steps two at a time then paused at the front door.

The agents closed in behind him. Earl picked up the rear.

Rushing through the door, Clifford pointed to a man standing alone, smoking a cigarette. "Take care of him, Earl."

Earl broke rank, headed toward the guy, and shoved him against the wall.

Clifford ran through the hall and downstairs, Clark close behind. "Hands up!" the two barked. "Hands up!"

"You're under arrest," the gun-wielding FBI agents shouted. "Put your hands on the wall."

Pandemonium reigned for a few seconds as the situation sank into the thugs and hands flailed in the air.

The players stood with their hands against the wall and one-by-one the agents read the cronies their rights and cuffed them.

Clifford pulled Freddie aside and read him his rights. With several arrests under his belt on gambling charges, Freddie was no stranger to the process. He acted casual as if the bust was old hat — held his hands stretched out in front for Clark to cuff him. "See you in court," he said lightheartedly.

After the last player had been led away, Clark stood in front of the table full of the items they had seized — bundles of cash, guns and knives. "This is a real haul, I'd say."

Earl's grin grew into a broad smile. "I can't believe it went so smoothly."

Clark shook his head. "That's what these guys do; they're real pros. It was over in a flash."

Detroit Free Press
April 19, 1980

FBI AND DETROIT POLICE
BUST "THE GAME"

Early this morning a joint team of Detroit police and FBI agents busted Freddie Salem's "big-time" dice game. For years the location of "The Game" had eluded police and federal officials.

Through the joint efforts of Detroit's Special Crimes Task Force headed by Detective Clark Phillips and the FBI's Strike Force led by Clifford McGill, law enforcement officials closed down the north side operation. Close to twenty people were arrested in the raid.

***

Four new Buicks and a year-old black Cadillac pulled slowly into the parking lot and lined up in front of a stucco and brown wood-framed Bavarian restaurant. The well-known German-American eatery, The Little Café at 12601 Gratiot, was a favorite stop for Mafia Boss Jake Nicolette. A quiet and unimposing man of many talents, Jake was smart, prudent, thoughtful, hardworking, and a no-nonsense type of a guy. Early in his career, he'd invested wisely and already had accumulated an impressive portfolio of real estate holdings.

An Italian-American driver stepped out of each car and opened the door for his passenger. In the second car, Underboss Angelo Travaglini, the handsome number two man, slid out and strolled forward. The six-foot two, square-shouldered fellow had an imposing physique that cast an aura of power and respect. A noted playboy earlier in his life, Barbara Nash now held the most important part of his softer side.

Walking slowing behind, aging Street Boss Joe DiGregorio took his time so as not to show the weariness of his failing health. Now the number three man, he'd served the organization in numerous leadership positions for thirty years, and anticipated the day when Blackie Giardini would assume his role.

Dressed in black and wearing large sunglasses, Blackie was next in line to be annotated by Jake. He, too, had earned his leadership stripes and certified a *made-man* while still in his twenties. (A *made-man* was an individual who had killed one or more persons; a prerequisite to holding a leadership position.) He double-timed to the front entrance and held the door.

Blackie waited for the Boss to complete a conversation with Tony Minelli, his top adviser. Officially called the Consigliere — a title that dates back to the early years of the Sicilian Mafia, meaning adviser or counselor — Tony also represents Jake at important meetings in the family and with other families.

Once Jake reached the door, Blackie hurried ahead to the reserved round table in the back, already set with white placemats, red napkins, silverware, and glasses for the beer. Two pitchers of Ritterguts Gose beer sat on each side of the centerpiece. The beer tasted bitter to Blackie, but Jake enjoyed it, particularly its aroma of tart lemon, lime, and green apple.

Leaving vacant the black vinyl-backed chair, with the best view of the front door, the four underlings assumed their places and made light conversation.

Strolling through the restaurant, Jake paused, said something to the owner as he slipped him a white envelope, and took his time nodding and recognizing old friends along the way.

Seeing him approach the table, Blackie filled Jake's glass partway, leaving a one-finger head.

Jake took the remaining seat, picked up his glass high, and toasted the group, "Here's to the best team we've ever had."

"And to the best Boss ever," Angelo Travaglini chipped in.

"Here … here," the group said in soft unison.

Jake nodded and picked up the menu.

In quick order he motioned to the waitress waiting in the corner. She was at his side in a flash. The men ordered their favorite selections of bratwurst, sauerbraten and schnitzel.

Taking their time, they chatted over lunch about important matters — the accomplishments of their children and travel plans with a wife or mistress. Nearly an hour later, Jake pushed his empty plate aside and folded his napkin, readying himself for the discussion of the day.

A trim man of nearly six feet, he was not cut from the traditional mobster cloth. Dressed in a conservative suit and tie, his dark hair combed straight back, Jake and his wife frequented the opera, concerts and other prominent social events throughout the Detroit metropolitan area.

He tapped his spoon lightly on his empty glass — conversation ended around the table. Speaking softly, he asked, "Anything about Freddie Salem's bust we need to be worried about?"

Consigliere Minelli rubbed the gray fringe around his bald head. "I don't think so," he said in a quiet tone. "I talked to Bufalino this morning. As you might expect, he has the entire defense laid out. At most Freddie might get two or three years. The rest of the guys will get off with probation."

"Guess that's as good as we can expect." Jake paused, clearing his throat. "Let's move on … anything new on Clark Phillips?"

Glimpsing blank faces around the table, his dark brow curled down, he spoke softly to each man, "Blackie? Joe …? Angelo?"

Each man shook his head. Jake turned to his adviser. "What do you make of this?"

Tony sucked in a breath. "Phillips runs a tight ship and from the results of the last few years, he hasn't missed a beat." The old man twirled a fuzzy lock with his forefinger. "It's not good when things are this quiet, something is underway."

"I agree." Underboss Travaglini rubbed his jaw in thought. "Phillips has keen insights. I still don't understand how he figured out Kingston's location in Miami."

"You're not the only one." Blackie shook his head. "From the scuttlebutt I've picked up, even the members of his own team think he pulled it out of a hat."

Travaglini turned to Blackie. "Have you heard anything about how he got tipped him off on Barbara Nash's involvement in the bank scam?"

"Hmm, not really. One of our informants said he picked up something in the courtroom."

"Courtroom?" Angelo said, in a sharp questioning manner. "I was there." He wondered what he missed.

Blackie flipped his hands up. "Sorry, that's all we've heard."

Angelo pursed his lips. "Huh, Barbara and I have gone over that day a dozen times. It was a standard sentencing. Nothing stands out."

Jake looked around the table, perplexed. "It still bothers me."

Resting his elbows on the table, the Consigliere folded his hands over his mouth for a moment, then slowly laid them down. "We need more information on the activities of Phillips; it seems like we ought to consider bringing back 'Red' from Philly."

"My exact thought." Jake nodded. "Blackie, you met with her. What's your impression?"

His head bobbed unconsciously. "She's a real pro and has a body that won't quit. If anyone can get information from him, she's the one."

"What do the rest of you think?" Jake glanced at his adviser. "Tony, how about you?"

"I'll go with Blackie's assessment," the Consigliere said.

Glancing across the table, Jake caught a nod from Angelo and Joe. "Done! Blackie, make it happen."

"Will do."

"Anything else for the good of the order?"

Angelo raised his hand for Jake's acknowledgement. "Go ahead."

"I'd like to talk about legal counsel for Barbara Nash. He paused, making sure he had the right words. "My request is not based solely on our personal relationship. She coordinated the bank operations that brought in millions of dollars for us, and when the feds and bank examiners were here she was an excellent soldier. You know, we've been seeing each other off and on for close to fifteen years. I think we should provide legal counsel for her. We should treat her like one of us." Angelo pulled up his napkin and wiped his lips, hoping the Boss would help the *love of his life.*

"No question," Jake said, without hesitation. "I'll tell Bufalino to assemble the best legal team possible."

***

Lying in Angelo's king-size bed in his plush Grosse Pointe Shores home, Barbara snuggled closer. "When I'm with you like this I don't have a care in the world."

He kissed her on the forehead. "It won't be long and it'll be like this forever."

"I hope so."

Angelo placed his hands on her cheeks, framing her face. "Trust me, darling. Jake has assigned Bufalino to your case. There's no need to worry. All you have to do is follow his lead."

Barbara tried a small grin. "I'm sure you're right, but I can't imagine spending one day in jail with those creeps."

"Honey, it won't be that way. Bufalino will take care of everything. He always does."

She buried her head in his chest and sobbed, "It'll be awful."

"Trust me. It won't be like you're imagining. There are places, special places. You'll see. Everything will be fine."

***

Late Sunday afternoon Clark made his regular stop at mom and dad's. Opening the front door, he knew his mother had done it again — something had just come out of the oven. Glancing at the stovetop, his eye caught a blueberry cobbler with her special white sauce.

He kissed her on the cheek and whispered in her ear. "I hope I find a woman just like you."

"Get out of here." She brushed him away, toward the screened-in porch. "Your dad is waiting for you, dear." She filled two bowls with cobbler and added a scoop of vanilla ice cream on each.

"Thanks," Clark said. "Would you get the door?"

"Sure." Fran hustled ahead of him and opened the slider.

Clark stepped through, calling out, "Who's ahead, Dad?"

"Damn Yankees, it's four to one in the ninth."

"Sounds like it's time for blueberry cobbler."

"You're right." Lewis snuffed his cigar, jumped up, flipped off the game and grabbed a bowl from Clark. He gave his son a proud look, "You guys hit a pot of gold last week. Tell me about the Freddie Salem bust."

Clark sat down in *the chair*, took a couple of bites, and took his time to fill his dad in on every detail.

"Sounds exciting." Lewis placed his empty bowl on the end table. "It's been a long time since there's been something like that around here."

"I can't remember any." Clark turned his head away, hoping his dad wouldn't bore him with a series of those old-time stories.

"Who's next?"

With relief, Clark took his time savoring his thoughts. "We're studying our options."

"Anything you can talk about?"

"Not really. You know the process."

"Just as well. Your mother has been fussing all week. She wants to talk to you."

"What about?"

"You're almost forty and not married. She thinks time's a-wasting."

"Dad!"

"Don't dad me." Lewis cut him off. "Your mother has a burr under her saddle and she wants to talk to you about it. Finish up your cobbler and go back in there."

Clark nodded, cleaned his bowl and licked the spoon. "Nice chatting with you." He stood, grinned at his dad, as they both knew what was coming next, and turned for the slider.

"Turn on TV on so I can see if the Tigers rallied."

Clark pushed the black button for his dad and headed back inside. Pausing for a moment, he opened the door and walked through the bright kitchen into the living room.

His mother sat quietly reading.

Plopping down in the Chippendale chair next to her, he asked, "How are things going with you, mom?"

"Fine," she said.

He knew the drill and could tell she had something on her mind. "Want to talk?"

She peeked over the top of the novel. "As a matter of fact, I do," she said, placing a bookmark on her page and closing the book.

Readying for the lecture, Clark braced himself.

Fran cleared her throat. "How serious are you about the woman from outstate? What's her name … Sharon?"

"Sharon Wilson. Why?"

"It won't be long before you'll be forty, and all of the good ones will be snatched up. I'll be an old woman before I see a grandkid."

"Mom, you're not that old."

She grinned to herself, having rehearsed the moment and said to him, firmly. "I'm not talking about *my* age. You're the one I'm concerned about."

"Concerned about *me*, why?" He raised an eyebrow. "I'm fine, mom."

"Is something wrong with Sharon Wilson?"

"No, not at all. She's a M.D. We really hit it off. She's like the girl next door and smart as hell; we talk about everything. She's more than a guy could ask for."

"When are you going to ask her?"

Not knowing what to say, but feeling he ought to say something, Clark hemmed and hawed. "It's not like that, mom. She has her career. I'm working night and day. We've agreed, hmm, maybe it's more me. We're great friends and enjoy being together; that's it."

His words drew silence, like there was nothing more to say.

"That's it?"

"Yes, mom. Really, I'll tell you when I meet the right person."

His mother mellowed; stood and motioned him near. "I know you will, sweetheart." She tugged at his arm and wrapped hers around him. "I just hope it won't be too much longer."

CHAPTER FIVE

Arriving home early Sunday evening after another weekend stay at Sharon's place, Clark picked up the mail and walked slowly to the elevator. Daydreaming about her, he unlocked the door to his apartment, flipped the mail on the coffee table and headed for the freezer.

Pulling out a frozen pizza, he placed it on a baking sheet and slid it into the oven. He popped open a Stroh's, took a swig, and paused for a reflective moment — visions of Sharon naked in the shower, and on top of him, shot through his mind.

Shaking his head, Clark returned to reality.

He hustled into the bedroom, stripped, took a quick shower, and blow-dried his hair.

The oven timer sent Clark hurrying back to the kitchen; he slipped on a pair of padded gloves and pulled out the pizza. Finishing off the Stroh's, he grabbed another, and carried his dinner into the living room.

As he flopped on the sofa, he pulled a TV tray to him, positioning it in front of the television, turned it on, and clicked through the channels.

Hunting for the Sunday night movie — "Caddyshack" — the best comedy from last year, he leaned back. *Chevy Chase, Rodney Dangerfield, Bill Murray — what could be better?* Chuckling to himself, he downed two slices of pizza and half a beer.

A commercial for the eleven o'clock news blasted. The same old news, he thought. *A pile-up on the John Lodge, a robbery on the north side, and a murder on the east side. Crap!* Rubbing his blurry eyes, Clark picked up a cold slice of pizza and gulped it down.

He turned off the television, picked up the stack of mail, and sorted through the advertisement flyers.

Stopping at a four-by-six-inch lavender envelope, he stared at the embossed silver printing — Saks Fifth Avenue.

What the hell is this? I've never even been in Saks. Why am I getting a promotional letter from them? How did they get my name?

His curiosity peaking, he slid his fingers along the back tab and pulled out a matching card. Taking his time to read each word — his mind swirled and went blank.

A fashion show!

What the hell is this?

Who the ... Abby Thompson!

Zeroing in on her name, he read the invite again.

You're Cordially Invited
to
Saks Fifth Avenue
VIP SUMMER FASHION SHOW
2:00 p.m. -- June 21, 1980
Featuring Detroit's Top Models:

| Cynthia Brown | Georgian Keller | Theresa Vasquez |
| Amy Hoover | Abby Thompson | Wanda Ward |

| Second and Lothrop | R.S.V.P. | Invitation for Two |
| Next to the Fisher Theatre | SAKS FIFTH | Coat & Tie Required |

That bitch. A high-class call girl from Philly hired by the mob to seduce me. She keeps saying she's fallen in love with me. That's bullshit! I can't believe she has the gall to send me an invitation. What does she think I am, an idiot?

***

Tossing and turning nightly for a week, Clark barely slept a wink. By Friday afternoon he sat exhausted, looking aimlessly out the window. Deciding to chuck it, he stuffed his week's work in a briefcase and headed for the door.

Earl blocked his way. "Want to grab a brew and burger?"

Looking at his old friend, Clark stared without making a move, dark circles surrounding his eyes.

"C'mon, we can talk about whatever is bugging you. I'll drive."

Clark nodded guiltily.

The two took the elevator down to the parking lot and walked to Earl's car. Not a word was spoken. Earl drove up Woodward toward the Traffic Jam and Snug, parked in the lot across the street, and headed inside. The hostess nodded and the two continued to *their* booth.

Giving Clark a thoughtful look, Earl ordered a couple of drafts. "Wanta talk about her?"

"Her?" Clark said with surprise. "What are you taking about?"

"I've seen you like this before; moping around all week, not tuned-in to what's going on, I figure it has to be a woman. Well …"

Clark took a long sip of beer, pulled the invitation from his shirt pocket, and tossed it on the table, in front of Earl. "Here, check it out."

Earl read the embossed card and shrugged his shoulders. "Pretty fancy, you thinking about taking someone?"

"No, it isn't that. It's Abby Thompson; the name in the middle. She's the one I used to date."

"Oh yeah, the redhead from Philadelphia with the great body. The two of you were into it hot and heavy, and then you dumped her."

Clark brooded for a moment.

"You never mentioned much about her. Wanta talk about her?"

The waitress delivered another round.

Clark lowered his head, deep in thought. "There's so much to say I don't know where to start."

"At the beginning," Earl jested, "that usually works." He picked up his draft and took a slug. "I'm all ears."

Clark stared away anxiously; decided to play it straight — frank and honest. He talked about the places the two of them had gone, the things they'd done and how they'd made love in her downtown luxury apartment.

Earl downed his beer and made a circular hand-motion to the waitress.

"Two Stroh's coming up," she called.

He turned to Clark. "So what's the big deal? She's back in town. Hell, you can bang her all you want."

Clark looked pale. "There's more to it than that."

Earl curled his lip, trying to glean what Clark might say. "You…"

Clark cut him off; his voice cracked, struggling to get the words out. "She was hired by the Mafia to get information from me."

"A prostitute!" Earl's brow rose, along with his hand. "You didn't tell her anything, did you?"

Clark stared unseeing at the vacant booth next to them. "Yeah, I did."

"Shit man, you could be put on leave, demoted, maybe even tossed out of the force."

"I know," Clark said remorsefully. "I don't know what got into me. My dad had lectured me countless times. I have lectured others. Before this I never came close to saying anything inappropriate. It just happened."

"Damn it Clark. Things like this just don't happen. It doesn't matter how many times you didn't say anything. It's about the time you did." Earl paused, catching his breath. "So when and what did you tell her?"

"We were on Mackinac Island. She was terrific."

"I bet she was," Earl replied sarcastically. "She seduces you and you give her the scoop. Bang. Bang. Whoops, I'm sorry." His upper lip tightened. "I don't think so."

"I know it seems bad."

"Seems bad?" Earl's tone sharpened. "Hell, it *is* bad!" He took a long sip. "Okay, Paul Harvey, let's hear the rest of the story."

"When I saw her a few weeks later she got remorseful and told me the whole story about how the Mafia had recruited her from Philly and set her up with a $25,000 monthly salary in a plush riverfront apartment."

"Twenty-five grand? You've got to be shittin' me."

"No, it's true. She told me she'd fallen in love with me and wanted me to forgive her," Clark snarled. "When I started to walk out she told me where Kingston was hiding out."

"Wait a minute. Let me get this straight." Earl pushed his empty bottle aside. "She told you everything about her deal with the Mafia and now she says she'd fallen in love with you."

Clark nodded. "Yep, that's right."

Earl continued. "When you started to walk out, she told you Kingston was hiding in Miami."

"Right."

Earl sounded unsettled, surprised. "I wondered how you'd pulled that off."

He waited, letting the silence lengthen.

"That's it?"

"Well, almost. Over the last year she's left five or six dozen messages. I never responded. Two weeks ago I was in a rush and picked up the phone. She told me she had moved back to Detroit and wanted to see me. I told her I was busy."

"So, *do* you want to see her?"

"Hmm, sometimes. I don't know, I … I can't trust her."

"Shit man, no wonder you didn't sleep all week."

"What do you think I ought to do?"

"Damn, Clark, you're the expert on women. How would I know?" Earl smoothed his bald head, collecting his thoughts. "The fashion show is more than a month away. I'd say take some time. You don't have to decide today."

***

Wendy Ricciuti led the way to their regular table at the Roman Village in Dearborn. Following Alsye's death two years ago, the women had banded together in support of Nicole. Their goodwill had evolved into a monthly event; it turns out the Roman Village was the perfect place to meet. The Venetian mural surrounding their corner table created a pleasing and relaxing atmosphere.

A bottle of Chianti with a red bow tied around the top greeted them.

"What's this all about?" Laverne, Ted's attractive fiancée asked.

"It's from Anthony Rugiero to celebrate the beginning of your third year of meeting here," the short Italian waitress said, popping the cork and filling their glasses.

"My goodness." Rosa Maria Montes, the round-faced Mexican-American flipped her long black hair to the side. "Has it been that long?"

"It seems like yesterday." Nicole raised her glass and toasted the women. "Thanks to all of you. I don't know how I would have managed had it not been for your help. You're the best!"

"Hey, you're the one," Laverne said in a cool voice. "Here's to celebrating your many accomplishments."

Humbled by their compliments, Nicole grinned politely.

Laverne shook her head. "I can't believe you're back into things so fast. Does our resident Detroit thorn bird have another project?"

"As a matter of fact, I do." Nicole's grin broadened into a smile. I don't have time to lie around and mope. I'm making plans for J.D.'s five-year-old birthday parties."

Laverne frowned. "Part*ies*?"

"Yes, in addition to the one I'm planning for you all to attend, I'm hosting one for his little friends earlier the same afternoon."

Laverne rubbed her stomach. "I hope you'll have lots of those water chestnuts wrapped in bacon."

"Don't worry, there'll be plenty," Nicole said. "You're all great cooks. I'm looking forward to enjoying the dishes you bring, too.

Laverne refilled her wine glass and handed the bottle to Wendy. She filled Nicole's glass, and paused. "What do you think about Earl?"

"Ah." Caught off guard, Nicole waffled. "He's nice."

"Nice!" Laverne eye's brightened. "He's one handsome guy if you ask me. He's a stud."

Rosa Maria frowned. "That's not a nice word to use."

"Whatever, he seems down to earth and pleasant," Laverne added.

Wendy stated the point the group had discussed on the phone. "Maybe you ought to invite him over for dinner."

Nicole sounded surprised; acted as if she was having a panic attack. "Ah, I-I-I could never do that."

"You said he was 'nice,'" Laverne reminded.

Nicole broke a small smile. "Well, he is; yes, he's very nice."

"So, why not?"

"'Cause." Nicole shook her head. "Just because."

"Because you're afraid," Laverne interrupted.

Nicole's body tensed; a troubled look flitted across her face. "I'm not afraid."

"I bet you are."

Nicole took a deep breath and sighed. "Okay, why would I be afraid?"

"You're afraid because you might like him. And all the memories of Alsye."

Nicole bit her lip. "I-I don't know if I can."

"Don't give me that 'I don't know if I can' stuff. Hell, you have more gumption than ten women put together. It's time to move on. Get real girl."

"Hmm." Nicole paused for the longest time. "I wouldn't know how to start."

"C'mon, it hasn't been *that* long," Laverne said. "Crank up your engine and show him your stuff."

"Laverne." Rosa Maria's voice hesitated slightly. "Maybe she needs to phase into things."

"Earl is coming to J.D.'s party. Right?"

"Yes. All of the guys from the poker group are coming."

"Well, it's time." Laverne thought for a moment.

"Okay, here's the plan. … We'll tell Uncle Clark to invite him over so Earl can play with the big boys." Laverne paused, letting the intuitive thought brew. "Would that be okay with you?"

Nicole glanced at the wall mural and back to her. "Guess I can't be a stick in the mud forever. Yes, that'll be fine."

"I'll drink to that." Laverne grabbed a second bottle, topped off their glasses and raised hers. "Here's to the future."

Wendy raised an eyebrow. "Tell us about the other party you have planned."

"Good for you," Laverne said. "Special times are reserved for family and friends."

"Funny you said that. Alsye always said the same thing. That's why I'm throwing a party for J.D. and his school friends on Saturday afternoon. J.J. will be with the neighbor lady, so the entire event will focus on J.D."

***

On May 10th a bright-eyed J.D. waited at the door. His school friends were gone and he had lots of new toys. But there were more presents coming! He'd hurriedly changed out of his shorts while Nicole readied everything for her friends.

Dressed in long blue pants, a white shirt and red bowtie, he could have passed for a miniature version of his dad.

Uncle Clark arrived first, right on time at five o'clock. "Wow, a handsome young man."

J.D. flashed the red buttons on the bowtie.

"Perfect." Clark laughed as if he was joking with Alsye. "How would you like a new buddy, birthday boy?"

The little guy's eyes opened wide. "A new buddy?"

Clark pulled a large teddy bear, about half the kid's size, from behind his back.

J.D.'s Magic Johnson smile burst across his face. He hugged Clark's leg. "Thank you, Uncle Clark, I love him!" He turned to his mother. "See what Uncle Clark gave me."

She glimpsed at Clark, mouthing, "You shouldn't have spent that much." Leaning over, she patted her son on the head. "I guess you got your wish."

"It's wonderful. Just what I wanted," he said, running off to his room with his arms around teddy.

The other invitees arrived.

"J.D.," Nicole called. "The rest of our friends are here."

Within seconds he was standing beside her, accepting gifts and politely thanking Alsye's old buddies. Nicole pointed toward his room and the little fellow scampered down the hallway, his arms full of packages. She turned to the guests. "Help yourself to the wine and grab a plate of hors d'oeuvres."

Renzo led the way, followed by Ted, Carlos, Clark and Father Dom. Pausing for a moment, the priest raised his hand and said a brief prayer.

Earl poked his head inside the door. "Sorry, I'm late."

Nicole rushed to his side. "You're right on time," she said in a soft tone and turned toward the hallway. "J.D., Earl is here."

The little tyke came running.

Earl handed him a large square box wrapped in an official NBA (National Basketball Association) paper.

J.D.'s face lit up. He grabbed the box, ripped at the paper, then glanced up at his mother and slowed. Taking his time, he opened the box and pulled out an official NBA basketball. He bounced the ball once, and again. It caromed off the end table and Clark caught the table lamp in midair. Fright filled J.D.'s eyes; he picked up the ball and raced to his room.

Earl walked over to Nicole and whispered something in her ear. She gave him a pleasant smile. He turned and walked briskly down the hallway.

Nicole pointed toward the dining room table loaded with food. "Let the party begin."

It didn't take long before the guys had refilled their plates and had a second glass of wine in hand. The women huddled in the kitchen, chatting and giggling.

Nicole opened another bottle of wine and made her rounds, refilling everyone's wine glass.

J.D. and Earl returned for the lighting of the candles and cutting of the cake; J.D. quickly downed the piece with the most icing. Tugging on Earl's pant leg, he asked excitedly, "Can you go back to my room?"

Earl's glance caught Nicole's nod and he headed for the hallway.

By 7:15 the group was ready to leave.

J.D. and Earl nowhere in sight.

Nicole walked down the hallway and cracked the door. "J.D., it's time to say good night to our friends."

"I'm coming, mom," the little guy said. He picked up his new basketball and ran toward the front door. Stopping short, he turned to Earl.

He gestured for the kid to go ahead.

The little boy took his time, dribbled the ball with his right hand, picked up the ball and dribbled with his left hand. He glanced at his mother. She nodded her approval. The group cheered.

Earl picked J.D. and wrapped him in a hug. "Here's our future NBA star."

CHAPTER SIX

Clark pulled his car in front of Nicole's place and cut the engine. Seeing Earl open the passenger door, J.D. jumped off the porch swing, ran down the steps, and threw his arms around Earl's legs. "I can dribble with both hands just like you showed me."

Earl cast a doubtful eye. "You'll have to prove it to me."

"I will." The little tyke ran toward the front door, stopped, and waved. "C'mon, mom's waiting for you."

Clark gave Earl an encouraging pat on the back. "You made a big hit."

Earl winked. "One down and one to go."

Nicole stepped out of the front door. Dressed in black designer jeans with a loose-fitting teal blouse and black heels — captivating. Earl smiled, then glanced away, afraid she'd think he was staring.

J.D. ran back out the doorway, basketball in hand. "Uncle Clark, look! I can dribble." He bounced the ball a couple of times with his right hand, then switched and dribbled it with his left hand.

Shaking his head in surprise, Clark grinned. "Wow, you're really good."

"Good, he's terrific." Earl motioned for J. D. to toss him the ball. "Here, I'll show you how to bounce the ball from one hand to the other without stopping."

J.D.'s eyes bugged. He tossed Earl the ball.

Catching it with one hand, Earl dribbled the ball with his right hand, his left hand, and then switched back-and-forth, right to left and back. He picked up the pace until the exchange between hands became a blur.

J.D. watched in amazement. "Let me try it."

Earl tossed him the ball. "Take your time."

The kid bounced the ball twice with his right hand. It glanced off his foot and rolled into the grass. J.D. ran over, picked it up and tried again. The ball hit his foot and bounced away.

Earl picked up the ball and slipped behind the kid. "Here, let me help you." Placing his hands on J.D.'s arms, he guided them as if an extension of his own. The two bounced the ball from J.D.'s left hand to his right and back again. "See what a little practice can do?"

Nicole pointed toward her son. "J.D., you're not playing basketball out here. Go to your room.

He grabbed the ball and shot inside.

Clark and Earl followed her into the living room and sat on the sofa. Standing in the kitchen doorway, she asked, "It's Tanqueray and three olives for you, Clark. How about you, Earl?"

"Ah, vodka and tonic will be fine."

"Coming up with a lime, is that okay?"

"Perfect."

Nicole disappeared around the corner. Earl leaned close to Clark and spoke in a low tone, "Do you think I should have asked for a soda?"

"Not at all. Be yourself and you'll be fine."

Nicole popped her head out the kitchen doorway. "Clark, would you carry the hors d'oeuvres? My hands are full with the drinks."

"Of course." He jumped up. "I'm on the way."

"Can I do something?" Earl called.

"We're good." Nicole handed Clark two plates of goodies and whispered, "Earl really looks spiffy in that black Nehru shirt, don't you think?"

Clark grinned at her in a meaningful way. "He's a great guy."

She took his comment without a word, sat the drinks on a small tray and followed Clark into the living room. Placing the men's drinks on the coffee table, she squeezed the stem of her glass of Chianti. "Here's to everyone's success."

"I'll drink to that," Clark said.

"Me too." Earl took a small sip. "How are your neighborhood projects coming along?"

"Wonderfully," Nicole said, trying to restrain her enthusiasm as she eased into the chair across from the two men. "The neighbors around our stores have jumped in with both feet. I'm really excited."

"Sounds like you're on a real roll," Earl said, a sense of enthusiasm and appreciation for her efforts in his tone.

Unable to hold back, she spoke with deep passion. "The city has come through too. We have new curbs and sidewalks, shiny blacktop roads and 1890's streetlamps at five of our locations. The same improvements have been authorized for the other locations in the fall."

"Wow, you ought to receive a medal of commendation."

She smiled with embarrassment. "It isn't about me. My rewards come from the faces on the people in the neighborhoods."

Earl's sincerity was obvious. "I'd like to visit one of your sites sometime."

Picking up on his interest, her voice rose. "Maybe you could stop by after work on Friday and I could show you around."

"That'd be super." He paused before deciding to go for it. "I know a fun place. How about getting a burger afterwards?"

Her mouth quivered as if to open; instead she took a deep breath first. "Yes, I'd like that."

J.D. bolted down the hallway, basketball in hand. "Mom ... Earl, see what I can do." They turned together, eyes on him.

He dribbled the ball back and forth from one hand to another without missing a beat.

***

Nicole and Earl walked into the Traffic Jam and Snug on the corner of Second Avenue and West Canfield Street, a few blocks from Wayne State University. Stopping in the entrance way, she stared at the traffic lights — red, yellow, and green — all shining brightly. Glancing around at the eclectic *Bohemian* décor, she spotted an antique stove, the head of a cloth giraffe, and pointed at a picture on the wall. "Is that you?"

"Ah, yeah," Earl tried to laugh it off. "My senior year in high school, I led the Detroit Public School League in scoring."

"Wow, you must have been really good." She paused and raised her eyebrow. "The basketball uniforms were really short, weren't they?"

"Guess so, I never thought about it," he admitted, then turned to the hostess. "Could we have the booth in the corner?"

Smiling at Nicole, the hostess paused and eyed her one more time. "Right this way."

Nicole leaned closer to him. "You come here a lot, don't you?"

"Since college; it's always the same booth." He pointed at the Vernors clock hanging from the ceiling. "Ever see one of those?"

"This place is amazing. Everything is so unique."

Earl puffed up. "They have great food, too."

Nicole continued to gaze around the place. Pointing here and there at the new discoveries, she eased into the booth across from him.

"Would you like a glass of Chianti?"

She spoke slowly, deliberately. "I'll have what you're having."

Surprise lit his eyes. He nodded and turned toward the waitress. "We'll have two vodka and tonics with a lime."

Nicole's eyes opened wider, showing a sign of interest. "Where did you go to college?"

"University of South Carolina."

"You did?" she said with disbelief. "I went to UC-Spartanburg for three years, majored in social work."

Earl looked at her questioningly. "Weatherspoon … are you related to the big high school football star — William Weatherspoon?"

Nicole cracked a partial grin. "He was my husband's brother. Did you know William?"

"Not personally. Everyone in South Carolina has heard of William Weatherspoon." Hesitating for an instant, Earl wondered. "You said was …"

Nicole cut him off. "He died a few years ago. A drug overdose."

"I'm sorry to hear that."

"My husband, Alsye, died in a fire shortly after that." She squeezed her eyes with an expression of pain, holding back a tear. "It was not a good year."

"Clark told me about Alsye's death, but I never put two and two together. You've gone through a lot." He spoke quietly, gravely. "All of that must have been extremely traumatic."

Nicole's subdued face came alive. "That's why I buried myself in work. I'm on a mission to get even with the Mafia."

"Hmm, I don't know, Nicole." He raised a brow. "They're evil and conniving. You have to give serious thought to that."

Her face seemed impassive; yet, not afraid. "Clark told me how to deal with them."

"Even so, there is a lot to know. They're always calculating; they seem to be one step ahead of everyone." Knowing she was on a slippery slope, but hopeful for her, he gave Nicole a warm smile and picked up his glass. "Here's to you and your continued success on your projects."

"Thanks you so much," she said politely. "Did you grow up in Detroit?"

"All my life. Clark and I were on the same high school basketball team."

"Yes, I recall him saying that."

Earl took the opportunity to get her talking about herself.

She filled him in on her life. The two nibbled on an order of onion rings; their eyes doing most of the talking. Their casual conversation wandered through the early years of their lives.

Nicole took a long sip, the vodka barely touching her lips. "Were you ever married?"

Earl's face sobered. Glancing at his old photo on the wall, he recalled memories of the past — he had dated his wife-to-be in high school. "For seven years. My wife Michele died of sickle cell anemia." He bit his lip. "I watched her body slowly deteriorate; she went through hell. Her death ended up being a Godsend."

"I'm sorry to hear that," Nicole said with compassion.

"No need," Earl smiled. "I've worked my way through it."

"Interesting." Nicole gazed at him, as if his comment had made a point. Leaning back in the booth, she stared at him. "Yes, I'll have something to eat."

Trying not to show his excitement by the tone of her voice, Earl casually handed her the menu. "I've had most everything. You can't go wrong with anything."

A waitress appeared, "Are you ready?"

"Yes." Nicole pointed to the open menu. "I'll have a Reuben."

"That's the best of the best. I'm having one too," He said, then changed the subject, "Tell me about high school and college."

She went down a long list of activities, then countered with questions about his growing up in the inner city.

Time passed quickly.

The waitress stopped by the table. "Would you like dessert tonight?"

Nicole glanced at her watch. "Oh my gosh, it's almost ten o'clock. I told the babysitter I'd be home by nine."

"Don't worry. There's a pay phone up front. I'll pay the bill and get the car.

***

Walking hand-in-hand across the street from the parking lot three days later, Clark opened the door for Sharon at the Traffic Jam and Snug and shot an eye toward *the* booth.

Nicole waved. Earl shifted uncomfortably, like a guilty teenager.

Stepping toward them, Clark asked, "What are you doing here?"

"Same as you." Earl laughed. "Nothing better than having a burger and listening to Jimmy Fender."

"You're right about that." Clark turned to Sharon. "You remember Nicole, don't you?"

"Yes, of course." Sharon tossed a smile Nicole's way. "Last year's Christmas party at Roman Village."

"Yes, it was a wonderful evening," Nicole bubbled. "You had just been appointed to that national committee."

"Right, Clark called you a thorn bird because of your hard work and changes you've made in the areas around your stores." Sharon extended her hand. "How have you been?"

"Good." Nicole turned to Earl. "In fact, very good."

Earl smiled like a kid with a new bike.

Clark winked at him.

The four had burgers and fries and a second round of drinks. They talked like old friends about everything under the sun. Nicole rambled enthusiastically about her many projects. Earl said little; mostly kept his eyes on her. Sharon shared the latest on her research of connecting hair follicles and murder weapons. Everyone wanted to hear more about that, and Sharon couldn't stop talking. "It's the newest line of thinking. It's called DNA."

"DNA?" Earl questioned.

"It's an abbreviation for deoxyribonucleic acid," she rattled off.

Earl's eyebrows raised. "I'll stick with DNA."

The group enjoyed a laugh on him.

Sharon continued, "There's a person in England who's way ahead of the curve. He asked for a copy of my latest report. I'm really excited."

"I can see why," Nicole said.

Jimmy Fender stepped in front of the table, and shot a questioning look to his old buddies. "Hi, how are you guys doing?"

"We're fine." Clark said.

"We can hardly wait for you to play," Earl added.

Clark introduced the slightly built nerdy-guy to Sharon and Nicole. Each one nodded and smiled politely, trying not to stare at his wild, wiry hair.

He grinned, just a little at Nicole. "You picked the best guy around."

She turned her head down, blushing prettily.

"Do you have a favorite artist?" he asked her.

"Fats Domino. Anything would be fine."

"Blueberry Hill, you got it." Jimmy turned and made his way through the packed house.

Easing onto the piano bench, he went through his normal routine, then started his set by playing the venerable Basie standard, "Satin Doll," one of his favorites. Then he attacked the old beat-up Baldwin Acrosonic Console, expanding his range and speed — his juices flowing to the excitement of those jammed around him — the crowd cheered!

For Jimmy it sounded good and felt familiar; he moved into his rhythm and blues repertoire on automatic, banging out Fats Domino's "Blueberry Hill," Herb Hancock's "Watermelon Man," and drove home with James Brown's "I Feel Good."

The patrons went bananas; shouts and applause filled the place, loving the old favorites. Nicole leaned closer to Earl. "He's really good, isn't he?"

"He's the best. He's played backup for Mary Wells, Barbara McNair, Smoky Robinson and most the other singers at Motown. He's already turned away several offers to go on his own national tour."

"Why?"

"I've asked that question myself — he's just a different kind of guy — no stars and glory for him. He'd rather play here than be on stage at some big place. Playing the piano is his life; that's what he lives for."

CHAPTER SEVEN

THE DETROIT NEWS
May 22, 1980

YOUNG BOYS INC. LIEUTENANT—INDICTMENT RESULTS FROM DRUG PROBE

Today the Detroit Grand Jury indicted Lonnie Williams, a high ranking member of the Young Boys Inc. The top lieutenant in the citywide drug network was charged with eighteen counts of selling drugs, possession of drugs, and tax evasion.

Also charged were twenty-six high-ranking members of his eastside drug gang. Authorities say more arrests and indictments are expected within the coming days.

***

Speeding south on the John C. Lodge Freeway, Earl shot off the Pallister Street exit, squealed down the side street and whipped into the visitor's parking lot. Slamming on his brakes, he cut the engine and ran into the emergency room, coming to an abrupt halt in front of the reception counter.

Clark raced down West Grand Boulevard toward Henry Ford Hospital; his mind whirling with despair.

"I'm here to see Nicole Weatherspoon," Earl gasped, out of breath.

"Just a minute, sir," the overweight black volunteer said without a glimpse up.

Earl fumbled for his badge then slammed it on the desk.

Seemingly unimpressed she responded, "Yes, how may I help you?"

"Nicole Weatherspoon … where is she?"

"She's in surgery."

Trying to restrain himself, Earl bit his lip. "Thank you. Anything you can tell me about her condition?"

"I'm not allowed to say."

Cutting her off, Earl shoved his badge in front of her face. "I said can you tell me anything about her?"

The fiftyish woman gave him a disgusting glance, then let out a long sigh. "I'll see if I can find out." She rolled her eyes, turned toward the credenza and slowly rummaged through a stack of papers.

Clark bolted through the double doors and sprinted toward Earl. "How's Nicole?"

"She's in surgery. I'm trying to find out more," he said frantically. Turning back to the clerk, he asked, "Have you found anything yet?"

The woman glanced up at Clark. "Are you a police officer too?"

"Yes." Clark flashed his badge.

"Here's her paperwork." Clark huddled next to Earl at the counter. "She was unconscious upon arrival at 4:18 this morning."

Earl's face paled.

"Do you know anything more?" Clark mumbled.

The receptionist flipped the page. "Here's the initial assessment — CRITICAL CONDITION — her vitals were extremely weak, both arms were broken and so was her left leg. Her face was badly swollen; her nose broken, along with several teeth." The woman took her time turning the page. "She had several broken ribs and extensive internal bleeding. That's all they knew when she went into surgery."

Earl threw his arm over Clark's shoulder and fell against him. "Pray for her, Clark. I can't lose her," he sobbed.

"I prayed all the way here."

Clark gave Earl a bear hug; the two consoled each other.

"You can sit in the waiting area." The receptionist pointed to the grouping of multi-colored plastic chairs clustered in the corner. "I'll let you know as soon as I hear anything."

Earl let out an elongated sigh. "Thank you."

The two men shuffled dejectedly across the lobby. Clark pulled up a green chair next to Earl's red one. "Do you know anything about the crime scene?"

"The store was a shambles." Earl flipped his hands in the air. "It looked like it'd been hit by a tornado; not one shelf was left standing. The freezer and coolers were tipped over. The officer I talked to said someone had taken a 2" x 4" or baseball bat to everything. Nicole was found in a pool of blood behind the counter."

"Why was she working the night shift?"

"I don't know." Earl frowned.

"Was the cash register broken into?"

"No, it was still closed, everything intact." Earl scratched his early growth. "Why would anyone do that?"

Clark took a long pause; his mind narrowed the options. "Robbery wasn't a motive. She had to be the target. Sounds like retribution to me. When we busted Lonnie he said he would get even."

"Why now?"

"The gang probably waited until Lonnie's indictment was over to make sure we got the message."

His face flaming with anger, Earl shouted, "Those bastards." He covered his mouth and whispered to Clark, "Lonnie is in custody. Do you think it was his brother?"

"Maybe, it could be his number two man; you know, the tall one."

"Yeah, Billy Fletcher is out on bond." Clark raked his fingers through his crop of windblown hair. "With the amount of destruction you're talking about, I'd assume the entire gang was involved."

***

Earl sat by Nicole's bedside for the third day in a row hoping for a sign of recovery — she'd been in a coma since the beating and had not moved an inch. He'd taken the week off to be with her. Clark had stopped by every day after work to give him a break. That gave him a chance to zip over to Nicole's neighbors and play with J. D. and J. J. before heading home for a nap.

The women — Laverne, Rosa Maria and Wendy — took turns staying with Nicole from seven to eleven; Earl was back for the overnight and day shift.

Fighting to stay awake early in the morning of the fourth day, Earl nodded off. He stirred, cracked an eye open and checked to see if she'd moved, then dozed a little more. Waking an hour or so later, he stared at her — she lay in the same position. He took a sip of water, poured a dab on his hands, and rubbed the top of his head. Bending down on his knees, he said a short prayer and ended it as he had every night. "Please God bring her back, wake her up."

He eased back onto the chair, held her hand and said another prayer.

As if a miracle, he thought he felt her finger twitch.

Afraid to move, he stared at her hand, hoping beyond hope a finger would stir again — nothing. Wiping a tear from his cheek, Earl wrapped his hand around her index finger and squeezed extra tight.

Her finger moved slightly, ever so slightly.

He firmed his grip. Her finger bent a fraction of an inch.

"Nicole, move your finger if you can feel my hand," he said urgently.

Her finger tightened against his.

"Nurse, nurse," Earl shouted and pushed the call button.

"Yes. May I help you?" came back from the speaker.

"She moved, Nicole moved her finger," he repeated. "She moved her finger."

"I'll be right down."

Within seconds two nurses were hovering over her. "Nicole, wake up … wake up, Nicole," the two kept saying to no avail. The older nurse barked with a loud, raspy voice, "Open your eyes, Nicole."

Her puffy eyelids quivered then cracked open.

"Blink if you hear me."

Nicole's eyes stared upward for the longest moment — her eyelids shuttered — a blink.

"Yes," Earl shouted. "She's going to make it."

The nurse leaned closer. "You're going to be fine, my dear. Go to sleep now, you need your rest."

***

"Who wants to go first?" Clark asked the task force members in their first update after a month of digging at the two race tracks.

Max Cumberland laid half a PayDay on the table. "Eddie and I were camped out at Hazel Park all month. We found a couple of guys trying to make a buck, but nothing worth our time. The scuttlebutt says the action is at the DRC. We think we should put all of our marbles there."

"Anyone disagree?"

"Makes sense to me," old-timer Ralston said, seemingly speaking for the group.

Clark nodded down the eight-foot walnut-veneer table at Will Robinson. "You want to lead off?"

"I'd be glad to." The black man spoke deliberately with conviction, his bald head bobbing up and down as he read from notes. "Race fixing has been going on there for the last seven years or so."

Grabbing the team's attention, his colleagues opened their pads.

"How could that be?" skinny-mini Sterling from Narcotics asked.

"Hah, everyone within blocks of Ten Mile and Dequindre is on the take."

"The police on that beat too?"

"Everyone." Will explained in precise terms. "It's a big-time, well-oiled operation run by the Mafia."

"How'd you find that out?"

"Remember Luis my top informant. He set up the surveillance house for the Freddie Salem bust?"

"Yeah, your best informant is a T-3," Clark recalled. "I had coffee with him several times last year at the Cadillac Hotel."

"Right. He contacted a friend in New York who described how the Mafia had done it." Will laughed. "Sounds like you'll be stopping in to see Luis or a friend of his on a regular basis. He has a standing order of rye toast and jelly."

"I thought it was coffee and two sweet rolls."

Will's grin broadened into a smile. "He's cutting down; orders from headquarters."

Kimberly Weston spoke. "From the conversation I heard we'll have a lot of research to do on the backside of the track."

Nancy Sterling frowned in a puzzled way. "Why so?"

"It's where the trainers, grooms and jockeys hang out." Kimberly obviously knew the track lingo.

"Sounds like there's a lot of funny stuff going on there."

"Okay." Clark squared his shoulders. "Want to divide up into teams?"

"That'd be good," Eddie said. "There's too much action going on for us to handle individually."

"Nancy and I can work together," Kimberly suggested. "It'd be best if the guys handle the backside. We'd stand out like a sore thumb if the two of us were seen wandering back there — it's a real macho environment."

Glancing at her bulging blouse, Max laughed. "You'd stand out anywhere."

She gave him her usual glare. "You're just jealous that …"

"Okay, okay, that's enough, you two," Clark interrupted. "We'll have Eddie and Max and the two women work as teams. Will and John will keep focused on Quasarano and Vitale. Earl and I will keep the other balls in the air."

***

Nicole was the talk of the group at the June poker gathering the following week. After prolonged discussion about her experience and current condition, the guys settled in around the table. Father Dom raised his hands and gave a prayer for her recuperation.

"Is she going to have a full recovery?" Carlos asked."

Earl gave him a big smile. "The doctors are positive about that. It's going to take some time … probably four, maybe six months, before she's back to normal."

Renzo jutted his jaw. "Knowing her, it'll be less than that."

"Why was she there anyway?" Carlos asked.

"The night-shift woman called Nicole in the middle of the night and she said she was sick and had to go home. The backup was on vacation, so Nicole left the boys at the neighbors and went to the store," Clark said. "I'm sure it was a setup."

Ted's dark eyes didn't blink. "I agree, for sure."

"Both of the women are being interrogated for a third time next Monday," Earl said.

Ted distressed face was accentuated by slicked-back hair that hadn't been washed in a week. "How about the bastards who did it? Do you know anything more than was in the paper?"

"Not really." Clark gave it to him straight. "Like the article noted, Nicole remembered eight or ten black guys storming the store — cursing and shouting obscenities — each wielding a baseball bat over his head, swinging at everything in sight. She crouched behind the counter to protect herself from the flying debris. A tall one pulled her up by the hair and slammed his fist into her gut. He hit her with a baseball bat two or three times, kicked her in the side, then jumped on top of her and pounded her face with his fist. That's the last thing she remembered."

Renzo crossed himself. "God, she's lucky to be alive."

Ted's mouth curled with distaste. "The paper made it sound like Billy Fletcher, Lonnie's number two man, is a prime suspect."

"That's speculation. All we know is that he's out on bond," Clark said, knowing he couldn't give his real opinion.

Ted shrugged unconsciously. "If someone got a hold of one of the other sleazebags I bet he'd point the finger at Fletcher."

***

"I smell chocolate chips, mom. Where did you hide them?"

Hearing no response, Clark peeked into the living room — her legs draped over the footstool, her nose in a novel. She continued to read.

"Mom, I know they're in here somewhere."

An eye popped over the top of the book. "Did you say something dear?"

Clark bit his tongue to keep from teasing her about her hearing. "C'mon mom, where are the cookies?"

She laid the book on her lap. "Your father and I have talked about that Young Boys Inc. organization all week. He said maybe you could shed a little light on them."

"Okay mom, tell me where the cookies are?"

She winked. "Thought you'd get the message."

"Most everything is public information."

"Good. There's a plate of chocolate chips next to *the chair*. Tell your dad to turn on the fan and snuff out the damn cigar. I'll be out as soon as I warm my tea."

"Got it." Clark turned and headed for the back porch. Opening the slider, he waved his hand through the smoke. "Put that stogie out. I'm turning on the fan."

Lewis ground the butt into the ashtray. "What's up with you?"

"Mom is coming out. She said she wants to know more about the Young Boys Inc."

"Good. I told her they were a new organization that started after I retired."

The slider opened. Balancing a cup on a matching saucer, Fran eased onto the lounger between the two. A no nonsense person, she got right to the point. "Clark, your dad tells me the Young Boys Inc. is relatively new. How could they have gained so much control in such short time?"

"That's a great question. These guys are the worst kind of criminals possible. They have street smarts and business savvy."

"I'm not getting the point."

"Plain and simple, mom. If they can't out think someone, they beat them up, or worse yet, kill them."

"That's awful."

After all of these years sitting in this chair, receiving lectures from dad and looks from mom, it's my time to do the talking. "It's just part of the story." He sucked in a heavy sigh.

Pushing back his thick hair, Clark munched on a second chocolate chip. "Best ever, mom."

She raised her hand, flipping it in a circular motion. "Get on with it. What's the rest?"

"Okay." Clark downed the rest of the cookie and wiped his lips. "About five years ago the Young Boys Inc. was formed by a group of black drug dealers around Dexter, Monterey and Linwood Avenues. Sharing a common source, they quickly reformed the entire drug business."

"What do you mean by that?" Lewis asked.

"There are four guys — each different from the other; yet, they complement each other in a strange and unusual way. Raymond 'Baby Ray' Peoples and Dwayne 'Wonderful Wayne' Davis are hustler types, movers and shakers. Milton 'Butch' Jones and Mark 'Block' Marshall are plain out thugs. The worst of all kinds. They're willing to wipe someone out at the drop of a pin."

"Nasty." Fran wrinkled her nose. "How were they able to work as a team?"

"Somehow between threats and insults, I guess." Clark cracked an odd little smile. "One who is strong in one area seems to compensate for the weakness of another. In a few short years they modeled their organization like a Fortune 500 corporation. Unlike their counterparts, they've created an organized infrastructure that is highly decentralized. They run the operation like Proctor and Gamble with divisions, departments, the whole shebang."

His Dad sat quietly in thought for a moment, and said. "Sounds a lot like the Mafia — it's hard to reach those at the top."

"You got it."

Clark watched his mother's brain working overtime. "How could they become so powerful in such a short period of time?"

"They pulled together some of the best drug masters around and packaged potent heroin brands under the catchy names we hear every day, 'Atomic Dog,' 'Starlight,' 'Rolls Royce,' and 'Hoochie Con.'"

Dad leaned against the wicker back. "So how much of the drug traffic in the city do they control?"

Clark's eyes widened with shock just thinking about it. "You won't believe this."

"C'mon, give it to me straight."

"80 percent. They'll probably clear close to a half billion dollars this year."

Fran's face fell into utter despair. "I can't believe that."

"Mom, little girls in the projects are jumping rope to the rhythmic cadence of 'Starlight,' 'Hoochie Con' and 'Rolls Royce.' They equate the names with fun."

"Oh my God." She covered her mouth. "It's an epidemic; is there no way to end it?"

"Funny you ask." Clark grinned at her. "Rumor is that Baby Ray Peoples and Block Marshall have had a falling out."

"A falling out, why?" his dad asked. "They're raking in more cash than GM."

"Why do you think?"

Lewis scrunched his shoulders.

His mother wrinkled her forehead. "Not over a woman."

"You got it. Both of them are seeing the same woman. The organization is on the brink of collapsing."

"What if it that happens?" Lewis asked.

"I hate to say it, but in some ways that'd be the worst thing that could happen," Clark speculated. "All hell could break loose. We'd have small black gangs all over the city selling drugs and battling for control. There'd be a shooting every day. All bets would be off on keeping our city safe. It'd be worse than it is now!"

CHAPTER EIGHT

Sitting at his desk in the Criminal Investigation Division on the fifth floor of police headquarters, 1300 Beaubien, He swung his swivel-rocker around to paw through a filing cabinet behind him. Clark heard a knock on the door. "C'mon in," he said, without turning around.

The door opened. He rolled back a few inches on his chair and turned halfway to see who was disturbing his peace.

Memories of the past flashed through his mind — Caroline Schaffer — the most beautiful women he'd ever known, stood before him. *A black stripper at the Sax Club, she had it all; great legs, a perfect body, and most of all she was smart as a whip. After sex we talked late into the night. The topic didn't matter; she had something intelligent to say about it. I'd have probably married her had it not been for that day when I betrayed her. How could I have been so dumb?*

Staring up at her, he asked, "Caroline, what are you doing here?"

She stood motionless for a brief moment. "I didn't think I'd ever talk to you again."

Clark interrupted her. "I guess we never know what lies ahead." *Shit, that sounded like I'm trying to open the door. I hope she didn't take it that way.* He rose and shook her hand. "How can I help you?"

Her face filled with pride. "I finished my law degree."

"Good for you — congratulations. I knew you would. Are you going to keep dancing at the club?"

"For a year or two. I have to pay off my student loans. Besides, I love to dance." She glanced at her firm cleavage. "As long as the equipment holds up, I'll keep trying to knock them out."

"You won't have to try hard," he said with a wink. "You still planning to help little kids like your grandmother did for you?"

Caroline cocked her head to the side in an easy-going manner. "That was my dream, but since I've finished my degree I'm seeing things differently."

Clark's tone rose with interest. "How so?"

"I'm seeing more of the big picture. I remember the excitement you shared when you talked about going after the Mafia. Capturing the bad guys has an entirely new meaning now. I want to be a part of that."

Thinking he'd just heard Nicole's voice, he smiled to himself. "How do you plan to start?"

Speaking with confidence, her voice sharpened, "I want to join the police department. I'm positive there's a need for a lawyer somewhere."

"You're right about that," Clark said without pause. "We need strong, honest people up and down the ladder."

Her optimism overflowed. "Where do I sign up?"

"Right here." He laughed. "I'll call Chief Hart. He'll find something for you and have the paperwork processed by the end of the day."

"Really, that fast." She glanced at him with intimate familiarity. "Too bad … I think we might have worked things out."

"I've always thought so too."

"I have to run." She turned for the door, then glanced back over her shoulder. "Thanks so much."

Clark rotated his chair and picked up the report he'd been reading, then laid it down. His mind drifted to *that day* at the restaurant where he was having lunch. Miss Hotsey Totsey, a floozy nobody, appeared flaunting herself. "One time," she said. "No one will know." *Why did I fall for that line? A twenty-two-year-old, nothing — one afternoon in her apartment and she was gone — anxious to tell everyone about our foray. Caroline found out and was gone. How could I be so stupid?*

***

Clark walked out of the McNamara Building onto Michigan Avenue and headed north, up Washington Boulevard. The west side of the street was still in the shadow of the early morning sun. A light breeze tousled his hair. Less than a year ago, he'd made this trek every other week.

Slowing his pace, he ducked into the Cadillac Hotel. The coffee shop was a favorite place for Will Robinson's top informant — a T-3 in FBI lingo — to meet. *The last time the two of us met, the agenda was Freddie Salem and the game.*

Today was a new *game.*

Clark opened the door to the small coffee shop and walked toward the small alcove wrapped around the back wall, not visible from the front door. As he strode through, he saw a familiar tan, bald head ringed with a white fringe halfway up. Nearing the booth, he spotted a tattered Detroit Tigers baseball hat sitting next to him. *I wonder who was with him.*

Arriving at the booth, Clark noticed the toast and jelly Will had mentioned. He glanced at Luis's round Puerto Rican face. "It's been a while, how have you been?"

Luis glanced at his plate. "Momma's got me on a diet. I'm trying to lose twenty-five pounds." He winked at Clark. "According to the paper you've been doing quite well."

Clark squeezed in on the other side. "Thanks to you and some of your friends." Clark glanced at the guy wearing the ball cap. *Nervous Nelly, if I ever saw one — his head bouncing around, his hand shaking; he can barely take a sip of coffee without spilling it.* Clark nodded that way. "Who's your buddy?"

"Frankie." Luis chomped into the second piece of toast and spoke with his mouth full. "Will Robinson said you wanted to know about the DRC? Frankie has been there for years. He knows every snake in the grass."

"You vouch for him?"

"Absolutely, like a brother."

Clark nodded. "Good enough for me." Clark extended his hand across the table and shook the boney hand. "Morning, I'm Clark Phillips."

"Frankie," the guy mumbled, his eyes looking down at his cup.

Clark turned to Luis. "What else do you have for me today?"

Luis slurped his coffee. "There's an IRS agent on the take. I thought you might share it with the feds. I'll give you details and be on my way so Frankie and you can talk."

"Sounds good to me." Clark opened his notebook. "Fire away."

Luis slid a piece of paper across the table. "Here's the guy's name. He works in the office on 500 Woodward."

"Internal Revenue Service's headquarters."

"Right. He lives near me up on Wyoming not far from Darby's on West Seven Mile."

"Been there, it's north of the Sax Club, right?"

"You got it." Luis downed the last of his coffee and called for a refill. "There's a nice little bar in the area with contemporary black and white décor. It's not as busy as it used to be, but it's a good place to chat without all of the commotion."

"Fine, get on with it." Clark unconsciously used his mother's hand gesture signaling him to move on.

"Sitting at the other end of the bar a couple of months ago, I watched this guy. He's spending lots of money and downing whiskey like water. Babes are hanging all over him. Next time I come in I pull up a stool next to him and we strike up a conversation — he talks a lot — the more he drinks the more he talks."

His interest peaking, Clark eased closer to the table.

"We became drinking buddies, started meeting for a drink before and after work. We go to a couple of blind pigs. Next thing I know he's spilling his guts about his gambling debts. He's in deep with the mob; it's a vicious circle."

"Sounds like the kind of guy the mob likes to own."

"Right. Last week he told me how he fixed tax returns."

"No way, why would he tell you that?"

"Damn if I know. Maybe he just needed to tell somebody, I don't know." Luis shook his head. "Anyway, I'm telling you this flat out … it's the absolute truth."

"How does he do it?"

Luis' face lit up; a slight grin appeared. "I figured you'd ask that." He eased is hand halfway across the table and wiggled his finger, in a give it to me fashion.

Getting the message, Clark pulled out an envelope and shoved it into his hand.

"Much obliged." Luis took a long sip of coffee. "This guy is in cahoots with his IRS supervisor. They prey on shady contractors. My buddy calls one in and says something like 'you have a large unpaid tax bill, you need to settle up or you're going to jail.' The contractor is nervous as hell. The IRS reps drag it out to build his insecurity. Sooner or later, the contractor says something like 'I can't let that happen. There must be a way.'"

"Bingo, he's hooked."

"How do they reel him in?" Clark asked impatiently.

"Hold on I'm getting there." Luis downed the last of his coffee and motioned to the waitress.

"The IRS guy lays it on hot and heavy — there's no other way — 'you need to pay up or go to jail.' By now the contractor is crying. The agent says, 'I can't do anything about it, but … I'll set up a meeting with my supervisor, maybe he can do something.' The guy is encouraged and meets with the supervisor a couple of weeks later."

"Why do they wait so long between sessions?"

"Ha, that's part of the strategy. They give him another line, 'the supervisor is extremely busy.' What they're doing is letting him stew for a while."

Clark raised his eyebrows. "Pretty slick I'd say."

"Slick? The guys at the IRS have it down to a science. It's like a greased pole; better yet, everything looks legit." Luis leaned over the table, and whispered, "The contractor comes in willing to do anything to save his ass. The supervisor gives him another song and dance, ending it with 'here's what I can do if you bring in twenty-five thousand dollars next week in cash, I'll write off your tax bill.'"

"I can see it now. The guy is elated and comes in the next week with the cash."

Luis gave him a smug smile. "You got it."

"How do the agents know which contractor to select?"

"Huh." Luis smiled. "The Mafia gives them the names of guys who have done 'under the table work.' He's afraid the IRS will dig into his background so he's anxious to make a deal."

Clark smiled to himself. "The contractor pays up and the IRS boys write off the debit — he's relieved; they take half and the mob gets the other half — everyone is happy!"

"That's the deal." Luis gave him a sly smile. "Then comes the sad part—the guy squanders his share and goes further in debt. He keeps digging himself deeper and deeper in debt." Luis stared at Clark. "Need anything else?"

"No, you covered it."

"Nice doing business with you." Luis stood and shook Clark's hand. "Let Will know when you need something else."

"I'll do that." Clark turned to Frankie, who was fidgeting like a cat on a hot tin roof. "Want another coffee?"

Frankie nodded his head nervously. "Could I have a bowl of oatmeal too?"

"Sure, no problem." Clark signaled the waitress and placed the order.

She refilled their mugs and was back in no time with the oatmeal. Frankie dug in like he hadn't eaten in a week.

Clark waited until he had emptied the bowl. "What can you tell me about race fixing at the DRC?"

Frankie laughed. "How many times are we going to meet?"

Clark smiled to himself, knowing Frankie really meant how much are you going to pay me? "Two fifty."

"Three hundred dollars."

"We'll start at two hundred and fifty and go from there."

The scrawny South American hesitated. "Okay, where do you want to start?"

"Let's talk about the ways to fix a race."

Frankie burst into shaky laughter. "Man, there's a hundred different ways."

Guess that was pretty dumb. Clark rephrased his thought. "Okay, let's start with the most common ways."

Frankie perked up. "I'll start with the jockeys. First of all, the DRC is not a first-class operation. Most of the jockeys are upstarts or over the hill, either way they are highly vulnerable. They're little guys, you know, a hundred and ten or fifteen pounds. You can imagine how one would react when a couple of two-hundred and fifty pound goons press him in the corner and says 'you will not come in first, second, or third.' The jockey is scared shitless."

"I can imagine." Clark paused. "Why do they want him to come in fourth or lower?"

Frankie smiled. "The Mafia plays the trifectas. That's where there are big payoffs. They can easily win ten, fifteen or twenty times the amount they bet."

Clark's brow raised in query. "So how do they determine the top three finishers?"

"They give the same treatment to all of the jockeys riding the best horses."

"So the mob knows which horses will not run in the top three."

"Right. All they have to do is bet on the various combinations of the finishing order of the other horses. It takes a small amount of dollars to cover the different options. Let's say there are twelve different possibilities — a horse could come in first, second, and third or third, second and so on."

"What if they come across a jockey who doesn't want to play ball."

"That's easy, the next morning he wakes up in the alley barely able to walk. It doesn't take long for the jockeys to fall in line."

"Wow." Clark raised his hand, motioning for him to continue. "Who's next?"

"Trainers … these guys are real pros. They know exactly how to slow a horse. It can be as simple as fitting the horse's shoes too tightly or giving the horse a belly-filling bucket of water. Those are the traditional ways. Nowadays, most of the horses are drugged. It's a little more risky because some horses react differently. Adderall and acetylpromazine, known as ACP, are the top drugs used by dopers. Adderall has a calming effect. It's the same stuff used on ADHD children. It slows the horse down."

"How do they get the drugs?"

"Ha, any drug you want, anytime, anywhere. All they have to do is step out of the stall." A bit more relaxed as he delves into familiar territory, Frankie's tone softened. "The final point I'll cover today is the backside of the track. That's where you'll have to spend most of your time."

"What's it like?"

"It's a different culture — men and women alike — hot walkers, grooms, and stable hands. They're the people who make thoroughbred racing possible and are worth their weight in gold. On the other hand, they have no ties beyond the grandstands. Most have drinking problems, are compulsive gamblers, and are battling drugs or the temptations of drugs. Often they're in and out of jail on a regular basis. Some get paid Friday morning and are broke by Friday night. They're easy prey for the mob."

"Guess I have a big learning curve." Clark hesitated, giving thought to how he might approach this situation. "I need some time to understand the culture. And, I need names. How do three weeks work for you?" Clark pulled an envelope out of his pocket and tossed it on the table.

"Fine, I'll have some names. You need to be ready … names cost more."

***

A few weeks later, Max and Kimberly, and Eddie and Nancy strolled into the DRC and picked out a table in the front row of the modern glassed-in clubhouse. The white tablecloth dining area seated eight hundred and fifty and was the envy of operators of most medium-sized tracks across the county. The white contemporary building at Schoolcraft and Middlebelt, just north of Detroit, stood like the crown jewel of Livonia.

The four were dressed like the other suburban couples out for an afternoon at the track. Playing the Kentucky Derby role, the two women sipped on mint juleps; Max had a Jack Daniels on the rocks. Eddie went to the bathroom, then grabbed a hot dog and headed to the paddock.

Picking up a program, Max explained how the odds were determined — race distances, jockey success, horse times, wins; and identifying the abbreviations and jargon. He pointed to the large tote board in the infield and explained the flashing lights of the odds and what that meant in terms of payouts.

"Can you say that again?" Nancy asked.

Max leaned back. "Say you bet two dollars on a horse with ten to one odds; if the horse wins you receive twenty dollars. If you wager five dollars at ten to one, you win fifty dollars."

"It's that simple. I thought I missed something."

"The basic process is simple." Max laughed. "The tough part is picking the winning horse."

"Which one are you betting on in the first race?" Kimberly asked, looking intently at her program.

Max pulled a bill from his wallet and held it over his head. "Five bucks on the favorite, number seven."

"It's three to one so you'll get fifteen dollars."

"*If* number seven wins," Nancy emphasized. "I'm putting two dollars on number five.

"Wow. Five to one you'll win ten dollars," Kimberly said.

"*Could* win," Max clarified. "Kimberly, want to go up with me and place your bet?"

"Sure." She stood. "I'm placing two bucks on number seven."

"Here's my two dollars," Nancy said. She repeated her bet. "I'm on number five to win."

Ten minutes later, their enthusiasm was gone; losing tickets covered the table. The three repeated the same process over the next four races — no one picked a winner — a sober mood fell over the table.

Another round of drinks freshened their spirits.

"Hey, it's about playing the game, right?" Max said, trying to provide some levity. He didn't draw a smile.

"Ten bucks gone just like that." Nancy slid an empty bowl to the side. "At least my scampi pasta was good."

Kimberly pointed. "Eddie is in the cash-out line. I wonder how much he won."

"Let's find out." Max rose and shouted. "Hey Eddie, how'd you do?"

He waved and headed their way.

Max pulled a chair out for him. "What are you drinking?"

Eddie glanced at the empty glasses lined up in front of the four. "A Coke, I'm on company time."

"A Coke? How much have you won?"

He looked at Kimberly and said matter-of-factly. "I'm ahead one hundred and ten dollars."

"A hundred and ten dollars!" Kimberly said, in an elevated tone, then sheepishly glanced around.

No one paid any attention to her.

"How'd you do that?" she whispered.

Eddie shrugged a shoulder, as if it was nothing at all. "I followed the advice of Clark's friend."

Max gave him a puzzling look. "Frankie?"

"Yeah, I called the office. Clark said to look him up."

"I'm betting on Eddie's horse in the sixth race."

Looking around, he grinned, leaned close and whispered in her ear. She glanced at the odds posted on infield board. "Eighteen to one," she blurted and covered her mouth.

Eddie gave her a big smile, then whispered, "Try number nine in the seventh."

Nancy bet two dollars on Eddie's horses in the next two races. She won $36.10 in the sixth and $42.15 in the seventh. After jumping up and down, rooting her horses to victory, she turned to Kimberly. "I'm standing in line behind Eddie for the last two races."

"I'll be right behind you."

CHAPTER NINE

Earl straightened his tie and glanced around the ballroom — glittering dignitaries and members of high society filled the room — expensive paintings displayed eloquently on the walls, heavy drapery framed the picture windows. Front and center, an elevated stage extending into a short runway stretched into the seating area.

Leaning closer to Clark, he whispered, "Do you feel out of place?"

Clark let out an exaggerated sigh. "This is really something, isn't it? I've never seen so many women's hats in my life."

"Hats?" Earl motioned Clark closer and spoke softly, "It's probably the only time some of them will be worn." He hesitated, then shot Clark a curious look. "Why did you decide to come?"

"I don't know." Clark's face seemed impassive, blank. "I kept saying 'no' to myself. Next thing I know, I called in the reservations. Oh, by the way, thanks for coming with me."

"Hey, after the way you described her I wouldn't miss this opportunity for anything." Earl glanced at the well-endowed women at the next table. "You ever see so much stuff in one place?"

Clark peeked around Earl's shoulder and laughed. "Don't even think it."

Earl gave him a small grin and picked up the program. Skimming down the list of participants, he pointed to Abby's name. "Your gal will be wearing four different outfits — sundress, evening gown, swimsuits and negligee — I can hardly wait."

"Don't say my gal. She's …"

"I know," Earl cut him off. "She's the one you banged for six months."

"It wasn't like that," Clark stated firmly.

"Okay, okay." Earl stopped, knowing it'd be best not to say anything more.

Dave Bing, former All-Star for the Detroit Pistons, stepped up to the podium. Acting as master of ceremonies, he announced, "There are three corporate sponsors that made today's event possible. I'll ask each representative to stand as the business is recognized." He paused while the audience settled in. "First, please welcome the publisher of *The Detroit News.*"

A round of hand clapping followed.

"Next, please show your appreciation to the editor of the *Detroit Free Press.*"

Applause filtered through the conference room.

"And finally, the host for today's event — please welcome the president of Saks Fifth Avenue." A standing ovation generated a second wave from him.

The curtains, stage-right opened to the roar of the audience.

Captain and Tennille bowed and warmed up with their number one hit — *Love Will Keep Us Together* — the crowd stood and swayed to the soft rock performance. *Muskrat Love* followed, and after, Tennille's vocal rendition of *Do That To Me One More Time,* mesmerized everyone. Captain, former keyboardist for the Beach Boys, didn't miss a beat. The husband and wife team had the audience dancing in the aisles when they capped off their performance with *Shop Around,* another top-ten success.

The crowd cheered wildly, calling for an encore.

The curtain closed. "More … more!" the audience chanted.

Dave Bing led the crowd, "Let's hear it one more time for Captain and Tennille."

The place went wild with excitement, stomping and cheering.

The curtains reopened to the delight of all.

Captain and Tennille took a seat on their individual benches and the two created magic with their keyboards. Following two more songs, Tennille stood. "We hope you enjoy our final selection as much we do performing it — *The Way I Want to Touch You.*

The audience sang along to the soft melody.

The two stood and bowed.

Returning to the podium, Dave Bing led the final round of cheers as the curtain closed behind them.

The curtains, stage-left opened. The audience hushed and a small combo appeared.

A buzz zoomed through the room.

Bing raised his hand, getting everyone's attention. "And now it is my privilege to introduce our own parade of gorgeous women wearing beautiful Saks Fifth Avenue attire." He nodded to the right. The first model flaunted herself halfway across the stage, stepped onto the short runway and turned to the right and left, showing off her wares.

Taking the stairs down to the main floor, she kissed Mayor Coleman Young on the cheek and leaned forward to give him a bird's eye view of her assets. He threw his arms in the air, as if to say, "I surrender."

Laughter filled the room as she carefully descended three short steps to the conference room floor.

Continuing her routine, she walked gracefully around the tables charmingly pointing to special features of the dress. Applause followed as she approached each table. Passing the last table, the band struck another beat. And so, the routine continued with each model — one by one the models paraded through the room. Dave Bing took the opportunity to describe each one's outfit and, of course, to point out her personal attributes.

The music stopped.

All eyes turned to the left side of the stage. With long, leggy strides, Abby Thompson stepped forward. Struck by her stunning beauty, Bing stumbled over his introduction.

Clark swallowed hard.

Unable to turn away, Earl stared at the most beautiful woman of all — her soft green eyes, sculptured red hair, perfectly proportioned body — dazzling in a tantalizing low-cut green sundress. She posed to the envy of all.

Flashbulbs popped.

Earl's mouth dropped open; he leaned over to Clark. "Are those real?"

Clark raised his brow and nodded. "They're as real as you and I sitting here."

"Now, I know why you came."

Floating forward to a slow beat, she ran her hands down her sides and over her hips, like a stripper might do, then sashayed down the runway.

The crowd stood, spontaneous applause and cheers followed her through the room. She responded by turning her hips from one side to the other.

Abby was a popular model and the crowd stood to roar their approval.

Clark adjusted himself.

Earl gasped, and spoke in a low tone. "I'm not sure I can take three more of her appearances."

Clark didn't respond; his mind recalled the times they'd been together and the joy they'd shared.

Earl was not disappointed — her sexy, stimulating routines continued through the presentation of evening gowns and swimsuits — the crowd's liveliness and excitement grew each time she stepped on the stage. He muttered softly, "Jesus,"

Stepping center stage, in her black high heels and filmy black negligee, her final routine left nothing to one's imagination.

Earl flopped back in his chair. "She's unreal."

Clark watched her tantalize the crowd until she stopped in front of them and gazed down at him. Their eyes connected. She slipped a business card in his hand and sashayed off. Taking her time at a table in the center of the room, she performed a mini-routine. The handsome gentleman, dressed in a blue pinstriped suit, flashed her a smile. She winked back.

Dave Bing took the microphone for the final time. The models paraded onto the stage for their final bows. Cheers filled the room. Clark stood and joined the cheering throng.

Multi-colored strobe lights circled the room and faded as the overhead lights flashed on. Slowly the audience caught a collective breath and headed for the exits.

Overwhelmed by the atmosphere, Clark and Earl took their time before joining the masses. Earl could hardly wait until they had worked their way through the milling crowd and sauntered out to the parking lot.

Halfway to Clark's Mustang, Earl pulled him aside. "I saw her hand you a card. What did she say?"

"I didn't read it."

"Why not?"

"I didn't want to be too obvious."

Question marks filled Earl's face. "Obvious? You drooled through the entire event."

Clark glanced at the card and shoved it into Earl's hand. "Here, read it for yourself."

Earl turned it over and read the back, "'Please call me, Clark. Please!' Her phone number is right here. What are you going to do?"

"Shit, I don't know."

***

THE DETROIT NEWS

June 22, 1980
Section D

Mutilated Drug Dealer Found

The mutilated body of Billy Fletcher, the number two man under suspected drug dealer, Lonnie Williams, was found today in an abandoned warehouse on the east side. Williams was indicted on eighteen federal counts last month.

Fletcher was handcuffed to a chair facing a mirror. He had been stabbed numerous times, suffering multiple wounds and slices to areas that were not life threatening. A final plunge of a knife into to his heart ended his torture.

Informants say Fletcher was the enforcer for the eastside gang. Authorities are baffled by the crime. Officials say it was not a typical gangland murder; more like a cult killing. A card with pictures of a gypsy fortune teller was found on the victim's lap. On the back a typed phrase: "The curse can't be reversed!"

The coroner stated, "I've never seen a crime scene like this. Fletcher had thirty-five to forty punctures and slices. It's like one of those torturous killings in the 1800s. From the accounts I've read about crimes of this type, it is one of the most painful, excruciating ways to die."

* * *

The poker guys greeted each other, grabbed their beer of choice and settled in for their July contest. Father Dom said a brief prayer for Nicole's continued recovery, nearly two months after her beating.

Carlos perked up. "Rosa Maria thinks she's doing much better. The women are having their July meeting at Nicole's house. They're bringing a dish for potluck, just like old times."

Earl smiled broadly. "I'm really proud of her. She's just amazing."

"One strong lady." Renzo nodded and shuffled the deck one more time. "Dealer's choice."

Receiving the first ace, Ted picked up the cards and dealt. Clark won the first hand and was off to the races, winning the next two hands. Poker lingo floated around the room for the next two hours. Clark raked in the chips time and time again.

After ten straight losing hands, Father Dom broke the ice with his usual call. "Break time."

Clark laughed. "I think we should keep playing."

"Forget it," Ted said. "I'm about ready to explode."

"Okay, if it's an emergency."

The guys hit the restroom, poked fun at each other about their playing prowess, and picked up another round of snacks. Clark was the last to return to the poker table. The guys waited patiently for him to grab another Stroh's and join them.

Unable to wait any longer, Renzo asked, "What can you tell us about that drug-land killing. Weird, uh? Do you think it was some kind of a cult?"

"It's a DEA case. Our office is not involved."

"Good then you can give us the straight scoop," Carlos added.

Earl came to Clark's defense. "Seriously guys, we receive our news from the newspaper just like you."

Recalling Ted's gypsy heritage, Father Dom turned to him. "You ever hear anything about a gypsy fortune card with the phrase 'the curse can't be reversed?'"

Ted hemmed and hawed, reluctant to talk about it. "There are lots of myths about gypsy fortune tellers. My grandfather told me about some of them. Storytelling was a family tradition."

"Any idea what that phrase could mean in this case?" Renzo questioned.

Ted rolled his shoulders. "It seems to speak for itself. A fortune teller has put a curse on him that can't be reversed — it's forever."

"C'mon, you sound like Clark," Carlos said. "What does that *mean*? For the entire gang?"

"How in hell do I know? … Probably, it depends on how you interpret it."

"Shit, does that mean there might be more killings like this?"

"Hmm, who knows?"

"C'mon, whataya think?"

Ted scratched his neck. "I'd say another murder is very likely."

Raising his brows, Earl asked, "How about the knife that was used? You know anything about that?"

"Yeah," Ted spoke with pride. "My grandfather used to put on a little show. Knife fighting is a gypsy tradition passed down from father to son in France, where he grew up. My grandfather had a folding Navaja with a five-inch blade. It's like a miniature Bowie knife, with a slightly curved blade. He kept it razor sharp."

Clark perked up. "Did he ever say how it could be used to stab someone? Was there a ritual?"

"That was part of the tradition. In the old days there were real brutal fights. Two men would slice and dice each other until eventually, one would collapse. It was an ugly death. My grandfather showed me a little sequence, just for fun."

Clark's interest grew; he dialed in. "Did he ever show you how to do it?"

"Nah, not really," Ted fibbed. "Once in a while he'd give a little show, like he was stabbing me. Slice here, poke there, slice and poke, and slice … he'd laugh and stab *there* you're dead."

***

Federal Judge Henry Limbaugh read the one hundred and eighteen counts against Barbara Nash for tax evasion, money laundering, banking fraud and racketeering, and said, "Please stand."

She rose, dressed in a perfectly fitted blue suit, not a hair out of place, looking ten years younger than the sixty-three she was. She cast an eye toward the judge and gave him a soft smile.

He didn't blink. "How do you plead?"

Impeccably dressed, William E. Bufalino, the Mafia's top legal counsel, strutted forward, like a peacock on parade. Taking his time, he opened his brief. "Honorable Judge Limbaugh, the defense moves to strike all counts, except for the forgery counts."

The room reverberated with the uproar.

"Order." The judge gaveled repeatedly. "I'll have order."

The courtroom went silent. "Mr. Bufalino, I'll have no grandstanding shenanigans in this courtroom."

The shrewd lawyer opened his arms, palms up, as if pleading innocence to the heavens.

"Move on," the judge said, curtly.

Attorney Bufalino reopened his brief and turned a page. "Regarding the tax evasion counts, the defense finds no evidence that the defendant received any financial again. The money in question went directly into Huston Nash's account. Only his signature was on the account. The defense moves to strike all tax evasion counts."

"Sustained," the judge said.

"Objection."

"Objection overruled. Next item."

Puffed-up by his first tactical success, Bufalino continued. "Regarding the money laundering counts, the defense finds no evidence that the defendant, in any way, laundered money. In earlier testimony Huston Nash testified that he and he alone, took such action. Barbara Nash did not benefit or have any financial gain. The only thing she did was to forge Huston's name — which did not involve cash. The defense moves to strike all money laundering counts."

"Sustained."

"Objection."

"Overruled. Next item."

"The law defining bank fraud is quite specific. It states that one must illegally obtain money, assets or property owned or held by another financial institution." The court master paused for emphasis.

"Again, there is no evidence that Barbara Nash accepted any assets or made any financial gain. The defense moves to strike all counts connected to bank fraud."

"Sustained."

"Objection!" the prosecutor said, knowing it was hopeless.

"Overruled. Next item."

"The defense moves to strike all racketeering counts. As secretary to the board, Mrs. Nash dutifully recorded the actions of the board. In no way is she responsible for action taken by the board."

"Sustained."

"Objection."

"Overruled. Next item."

"The defense requests a two-month postponement so the defense and prosecution can arrive at an acceptable plea bargain agreement on the forgery counts."

"Objection."

"Overruled. Two months granted."

***

Clark ordered two bowls of oatmeal and coffee.

Exactly at nine o'clock, Frankie stuck his head in the coffee shop, cased the place, and walked briskly to the hidden alcove booth, sliding in across from Clark.

Coffee and oatmeal arrived for both. "Thanks." Frankie dug in without adding sugar or cream.

Clark doctored his bowl with brown sugar and raisins. Frankie squinted, as if saying "is all that necessary."

After a few spoonsful, Clark laid his spoon on a side dish. "What do you have for me?"

Frankie continued to scoop.

Biding his time, Clark took another bite.

Frankie emptied his bowl and slurped a slug of coffee. "Got some good stuff for you," he said, muffled by his napkin.

"Good. Let's hear it."

"It's worth more than two hundred and fifty."

"We'll see after I hear what you have."

"Race fixing here started back in '75 when Anthony 'Fat Tony' Salerno, from one of New York City's Five Families, and Philly Mafia don, Angelo 'The Docile Don' Bruno, decided to move into the

Midwest. They made a deal for part of the action with Joe Zerilli, Detroit's aging godfather, and racing-fixing at Hazel Park and the DRC was underway."

"I don't need a history lesson. That's all in the FBI reports."

"Hold your horses," Frankie said, flashing back one more time. "It's important to understand the track culture and how well-oiled the system is. Five years ago Anthony 'Tony the Fixer' Ciulla, a Boston native with ties to Whitey Bulger of the Winter Hill Gang, came to town. Setting up headquarters in the Derby Bar (not to be confused with Darby's on Seven Mile) near the DRC, his presence was quickly recognized. Carrying three hundred and fifty pounds on his six-foot-four frame, every informant in town was alerted."

"What does he do, eat all day?"

"He's known for going from one bar to another." Frankie loosened up, visibly feeling more comfortable. "Tony's influence was felt overnight. His tight-knit team of Robert 'Bobby the Teacher' Owens, Salvatore 'Sally Mac' Macarano and Oscar 'Fat Jerry' Friedman, were experts at infiltrating racetracks. They knew how to get to jockeys — muscling their way around, greasing jockey's palms — doing whatever it took to get what they wanted."

Clark rose and slid out of the booth. "You'll have to come up with more than a history lesson or our relationship is over." He tossed an envelope on the table. "Here's your two hundred and fifty bucks. If you can't do better next time, forget it."

"Wait, wait … I can get current names."

"Sure, I haven't heard anything new." Clark's mouth contorted into a slight sneer. "Two weeks. I want specifics — names, places, who, what, where — not another lesson!" He turned and headed for the door.

Frankie stood. "Okay, okay, I'll have names in two weeks."

CHAPTER TEN

Nicole sat in a wheelchair on her front porch with her left leg extended in an ankle-to-hip cast, and her left forearm in a sling. Her other injuries had healed properly. A slight scar on her left cheekbone, the only visible evidence of her horrendous ordeal.

Sitting on the swing next to her, Margaret sipped on a glass of iced tea. A slightly overweight neighbor from down the street, the black woman had become Nicole's unofficial caregiver. Chatting about the three women coming for lunch, Nicole said, "You'll love them; they're my best friends."

A Ford Escort stopped out front.

Nicole pointed. "There's Wendy's new car. Let's see if you identify who they are … think you can name them?"

Margaret slowed the swing. "That one is Laverne," she said, as the tall blonde slid out of the passenger side. The back door opened and a short, round-face Mexican-American eased out. "Rosa Maria," she said softly, and pointed to the driver rounding the front of the car. "And since she was driving, of course, that one is Wendy; she's married to Renzo."

Nicole sang her praise, "Excellent, three for three."

The women waved from the curbside, hurried up the sidewalk and took turns hugging Nicole. She gestured to her neighbor friend. "I want all of you to meet Margaret, my best neighbor. She's the one who dresses me every morning."

"Not for much longer," Margaret chimed in. "The cast comes off in ten days."

"That's wonderful," Wendy said and moved to the side, while the other two took up a conversation with Margaret.

Nicole turned her wheelchair and rolled toward the door. "Come in, Margaret has the table set. You can put your dish wherever there's space."

Margaret opened the door. Nicole wheeled toward the dining room; the group right behind. "Take a chair, I'll be at the vacant spot on the end," she directed.

"Fancy," Laverne said. "A white tablecloth, water goblets, your best wine glasses. We'll have to eat at this restaurant more often."

"I should say so," Rosa Maria added.

Nicole's face glowed.

Wendy smiled. "You look great. How are you feeling?"

"Hmm, most of the day I'm fine. I start to run down around three thirty or four, so I take a nap. I have to be rested and fancied-up for wine when Earl arrives."

"Every day?" Laverne sounded surprised. "Sounds serious. You want to share anything with us?"

Deflecting the question, Nicole picked up a glass of Chianti and toasted, "Here's to the best friends ever."

"And here's to our thorn bird," Wendy added.

"Here, here!" the rest chimed in chorus.

The five enjoyed a casual lunch, chatting about their men's activities and catching up on the last three months. Laverne picked up her spoon and tapped her glass. "For some reason Nicole never answered my question." She glanced down the table at Nicole. "Anything you want to say about Earl?"

Nicole's beaming face said it all. "He is extremely thoughtful and … we're developing a relationship."

"A relationship? That's about as bland as you can make it. Let's hear about it. Has he stayed all night?"

"Laverne!" Rosa Maria exclaimed. "That's personal."

"Well, has he?"

"No," Nicole said, emphatically. "Look at me." She lifted her leg an inch with her good arm. "I wouldn't be any good anyway."

Laverne cracked a grin. "It might be interesting."

"C'mon." Nicole motioned toward her neighbor. "Margaret made tiramisu. Everyone want coffee?"

Heads nodded around the table.

Wendy picked up the plates. Rosa Maria served the dessert and Margaret filled the cups.

Laverne savored the first bite. "The Kahlua flavor is wonderful." The others nodded their agreement. "So Nicole, do you have any plans for the future?"

Nicole straightened in her chair, looking like the Nicole of old. "Yes. I have a meeting with Mayor Coleman Young at the end of the month."

The mayor, how did you arrange that?"

Nicole pointed to her head. "My brain still works. I have things to do."

Wendy questioned, "Are you making some kind of a proposal?"

"Absolutely. I want a hundred thousand dollars "seed money" grant.

"A hundred thousand dollars!" Maria frowned. "Why?"

"I'll give you an example." Nicole wheeled her chair a crank, closer to the table to emphasize her point. "There are two burnt-out buildings across the street from my main store. They're crappy. I want the city to remove the debris and flatten the lots so the cavities can be filled in with new buildings."

"Great idea." Wendy said. "You must talk with Renzo. He can give you some firm cost figures."

"That's an excellent suggestion, Wendy. I hadn't thought about drawing upon his expertise." Nicole's mood became even more optimistic. "I'd like to use the money as a matching grant. If the city will pay for the basic structure — roof, second floor and front façade — investors can do the rest."

"Do the rest?"

"Yes, complete the inside of the building and open a store."

***

"Hey mom, bake anything this week?"

"There's ginger snaps in the cookie jar."

"Perfect." Clark pulled out three, shoved one in his mouth and crunched away. "Man, these are good."

"Thank you," she called from the living room.

Heading that way, he saw her sitting in the usual place. Easing into the matching Chippendale chair next to her, he took a bite of the second cookie. "Where's dad?"

"He fell asleep out on the porch, stayed up late last night watching the Tigers lose in extra innings."

"Yeah, I went to bed early, read about it in the *Free Press* this morning.

Fran gave him a loving smile. "How are you doing?"

"Things are really hectic. My team is working hard on the race fixing case."

"Yes, you mentioned that last time." She spoke quietly. "How are other things going?"

Knowing she rarely probed into his personal life, *other than wanting him to get married,* he wondered about her intent. "Why do you ask?"

She twisted her lower lip to the side like she always does when she has an inquiring thought on her mind. "For the last few weeks you've seemed distracted — distant — like you were preoccupied about something."

Clark broke into a partial grin. "Guess you always could pick up on things like that."

"Want to talk about it?"

"Hmm, it's complex."

"So …"

"It's Abby."

"Abby? I thought the two of you split long ago when she moved back to Philadelphia."

"We did … she did. She called five or six times over the last year, said she'd made a mistake and wanted to get back together. I never called her back."

"Clark," his mother said in a harsh tone. "That wasn't appropriate."

"Hmm, maybe not. I was really upset with her when we broke up." He brushed back a stray strand of hair. "She moved back to Detroit this summer and has been trying to reach me ever since. I still haven't called her back."

"Shame on you, Clark." Fran shook her finger. "That's very inconsiderate."

"Mom, she lied to me!"

"Was another guy involved?"

"No. It was something personal, between the two of us. I can't say."

"Do you still like her?"

"I guess she's on my mind often." He confessed. "She's really something, but I still can't forget how she treated me."

"It can't have been that bad." His mother brushed back her gray-streaked hair. "People make mistakes. None of us are perfect. Maybe you should forgive her and give her another chance."

"I've thought about that, but I can't … you don't understand."

"Maybe you have to dig deeper inside yourself."

"*Mom*." Clark's frustration grew. "What if you had cheated on dad? Do you think he would have turned the other cheek and given you a second chance?"

His mother's face flushed.

Silence reigned.

Clark stared at her for the longest time. "Mom, you didn't, did you?"

Her rosy cheeks turned gray; she stammered, "I-I …" She stood and glanced at Lewis sleeping on the porch then sat back down. "It was a long time ago. I felt awful — one time, it could have been a hundred; it didn't matter — I felt like a whore."

"Mom …"

"No, let me finish. I need to say this." She sighed. "After crying for a month, I finally told your father. He was crushed; he didn't curse or shout. He just sat there and stared; his stare cut me to the bone." Fran sniffed, pulled out a kerchief, and blew her nose. "We didn't talk for a couple of weeks. I prayed every night for forgiveness. He sat in his wicker chair and stared into the night. Finally, one night after dinner, he asked, 'What do you want to do?' It was the last thing I expected. Tears ran down my cheek. I choked up and somehow squeezed out the words, 'I want to be with you the rest of my life.'"

"What did he say? How did he react?" Clark asked hurriedly.

"It wasn't his actions, it was his words and how he said them."

"Mom, what did he say?"

She paused and formed a soft smile. "'Could I have a piece of warm apple pie?'"

"That's it?"

"Yes. They were the sweetest words I ever heard."

***

Stopping in the middle of the Ghostbar doorway, Earl admired the slick mahogany bar, mirrored backbar and black-leather stools. "Wow. This is quite an upgrade from the T.J.'s."

Clark motioned him in. Earl slid into the club chair across from him and rubbed his hands along the black leather. "You receive a pay increase?" he jested.

"Nah, I just wanted a quiet place where we could talk."

"This better be important." Earl glanced at his watch. "I could be having wine and cheese with Nicole right now."

"Sounds like things are really going well."

"She's the best. It couldn't be better."

"Good for you." Clark stirred his gin with the last olive remaining on the toothpick. "I really appreciate you stopping by."

"Well …" Earl motioned for him to keep on speaking. "It's Abby, isn't it?"

"Yeah," Clark said. "I talked to my mom about her."

"You told your mother everything?" "Earl asked, his tone elevated.

"Not about that." Clark waved his hand. "We talked in general terms, none of the Mafia-related stuff."

Earl gave him a blank look. "Did you come to a conclusion?"

"Not really." Clark twisted his lips into a wry smile. "She reminded me that people make mistakes and …"

Earl cut him off. "Funny, I had the same thought the other night." He paused; his face lit up. "You know, your track record with women isn't all that good. I bet there are lots of women who wish they had a second chance with you."

"At least I wasn't whoring around."

"Hmm, that's your opinion." Earl raised a brow. "Better to say you weren't getting paid."

"Touché." Clark raised his glass and clinked Earl's. "I'll drink to that."

"So are you going to ask her out?"

"Shit, I don't know. That's why I'm talking with you."

"Man, I keep seeing her parading up and down that runway and … the way she kept glancing at you. My bottom half says go for it; my brain says 'beware.'"

"You're a lot of help."

"Crap, you asked me. I told you what I thought."

"Want another vodka and tonic?"

"You having another?"

Clark nodded and twirled his hand in the air, getting the barmaid's attention.

The two sat in silence. Earl bided his time, waiting for Clark to work through his thoughts.

The barmaid slowly unloaded the drinks from the tray, making sure Earl got an eyeful.

"I'm going to do it," Clark stated as the server walked away.

"The barmaid?" Earl said in surprise.

"Hell no. How'd you come up with an idea like that?"

"Shit man, she put her knockers on the tray and gave me the sign. What am I supposed to be thinking about?"

Clark sighed. "Have a drink."

Earl backed off. "Okay, so you are going to do it. I guess that means asking Abby out for a date."

"Yep, I'm going to forgive her."

Trying to determine Clark's reasoning, Earl asked, "Which part are you going to forgive? The fact she was a call girl? The fact the Mafia paid her? Or, the fact she lied to you?"

Clark picked up his glass and took a long sip.

Earl sat motionless.

Clark didn't blink.

"Okay, let's analyze from a different angle." Earl said. "Is the fact she lied to you the most troubling issue?"

"Well, no. At least she finally told me the truth. Obviously, that was bothering her too. I guess she earned a point for that."

"Is the fact she was a call girl most troubling?"

"Hmm, at first I thought about that a lot. It's not like she was a whore picking up stray guys at a bar."

"So you're upset because she duped you. Again, is that the most troubling fact?"

"Yeah, I guess. It goes against everything I ever thought — I gave her classified information. I don't understand why I told her those things, but I did."

Earl cocked his head to left, and back. "Do you know what you've just said?"

"Yeah, I don't understand …"

Earl cut him off. "No. That's not the point. You used the word 'I' six times."

"Big deal."

"That says to me you're more concerned about your feelings than you are about the way you feel about her. Does that make sense?"

Clark picked up his glass, shook it and drained the last of the gin. "Kind of, I guess … I have to sleep on it."

***

The mayor's secretary motioned Nicole and Earl toward leather chairs in the reception area. "He'll be out shortly, Mrs. Weatherspoon."

"Thank you."

Earl leaned closer to Nicole. "This is the furthest you've walked since you were released. Are you going to be okay?"

She dabbed the moisture above her lip with a tissue and took in a deep breath. "I'll be fine."

The door opened. An impeccably dressed, gray-haired black man strode forward and extended his hand. "Mrs. Weatherspoon it is indeed an honor to meet one of the bravest women in our great city." Examining her lovely face, he hesitated. "And may I add one of the most beautiful ones."

"Nice to meet you Mayor Young," she said, clasping his hand firmly, in a business-like fashion.

"Please, come in and have a seat." The mayor pointed to the small grouping of two burgundy leather-clad chairs with an end table between them.

Nicole eased into the one to his right and sat upright, with a view of the Detroit riverfront. Turning his chair to face her, he straightened his tie. "I've heard so much about your many successes. It is indeed a pleasure to finally meet you. I hope your recovery is progressing well."

"Yes, thank you very much. My doctor has cleared me to go back to work on a limited schedule."

"Good for you," he said; his tone showed genuine interest. "Tell me about this economic development project you have in mind."

"It's about revitalizing the neighborhoods of the city — it's about the people — the forgotten ones. Those living with the aftermath. They're the ones who make the city move."

"The forgotten ones! Why do you say that?"

"Not to take offense, Mr. Mayor, you've made tremendous strides in improving the downtown area — the Joe Lewis Arena,

Renaissance Center, Riverfront Condominiums and the Millender Center Apartments — each one makes a wonderful statement about the revitalization of our city. I applaud your efforts. You've made a leadership difference."

"Thank you ..."

She cut him off, taking charge of the meeting. "The neighborhoods are dying; there's no sense of community. They are crime infested and drug-ridden with a gangland killing every day. People in our inner city have no hope. I'm not willing to watch my community die."

"I'm glad to hear that. We need more people with your resolve."

"I appreciate that, Mr. Mayor. As you know, the people in the eight communities around my stores have banded together. Our neighborhood watch programs have created crime-free zones. City Council has added new curbs and sidewalks, new streets and lamp posts. Still, there is more to be done."

Her vibrancy and enthusiasm peaked his interest. "How can I help?"

"Near my main store there are two burned-out buildings. We have to clean up these unsightly areas and breathe new life into them. It's important to fill in the cavities and make the communities whole again."

"I'm intrigued." Mayor Young leaned back in his chair. "How do you propose *we* do that?"

"I'd like for you to provide "seed money" grants to stimulate growth and encourage local entrepreneurs to rebuild our neighborhoods." She showed off her beautiful smile. "And for you, Mr. Mayor, it's about votes!"

"Votes?" He cocked his head, obviously intrigued.

"There are thousands of votes in the neighborhoods."

Like a ringing bell, she had his attention. He slid forward in his chair. "I see your point."

Knowing she had struck a chord, she plowed forward. "It's up to you, Mr. Mayor. City wrecking crews could demolish the dilapidated buildings and plant grass in the vacant areas, until they were redeveloped. Your office could provide "seed money" to help construct new buildings — the core structures, roofs, second floor and front façade. That will cost roughly fifty thousand dollars a building."

"What happens after that?"

"We'll encourage local people to reinvest in the community. We'll have them sign a contract that states if they finish the inside of the building and successfully operate a business for five years, the building will be turned over to them — free and clear."

Mayor Young smiled. "Sounds more like Seed, Feed, and Deed. SFD, I like that."

"If the title works for you; it works for me."

"I like your style." The mayor rose and extended his hand. "Okay, I'll fund two buildings." He nodded in contemplation. "If you have those stores operating within in a year, I'll do two more."

"And then?" she pressed him for more.

He smiled, getting the message. "I'll do two more around another one of your locations."

CHAPTER ELEVEN

Sliding into the booth across from Frankie, Clark's jaw dropped. "Hey, what's going on?"

In place of his usual bowl of cereal, the skinny informant continued to work on a platter of eggs, sausage, pancakes, hash browns, and toast. Shoveling in the remains of a pancake, syrup oozing from his mouth, Frankie gave Clark a pleased glance. "I have plenty of names …" He paused, swallowing half a mouthful. "Figured they'd be worth a little more."

"We'll see." Clark ordered a couple slices of white toast and peanut butter to go along with his coffee.

Frankie shoved his empty plate aside. "I have it all laid out; all you have to do is take a few notes."

"Good. Let's get started."

Frankie picked up the booklet lying on the table next to his plate and spread it open in front of Clark. "This is the DRC employee directory. There are roughly five hundred employees listed with home addresses, phone numbers and photos for some."

Clark flipped through several pages and stopped. "Some of the individuals have notations by their names. What's that all about?"

"One hundred and thirty-nine of them to be exact."

Surprise filled Clark's face.

"Those are the ones involved in race fixing. By the time your team is finished with the list, the number will probably double."

"It seems like you used some kind of a code."

"Right. I listed the kind of work each person does. Several people have jobs that are pretty standard, you know — jockey, trainer, groomer, and so forth — there's a note by their names. I've described several others whose jobs aren't so obvious and made up short descriptions for each one."

"Hold on. I need to write this down." Clark opened a small notebook and pulled out a pen."

Frankie reached across the table and pointed to the first notation. "There's a half dozen groupings. They're not official just what the person is called."

"All right, go ahead."

"Bettors — they're lowly guys hired by the mob to place bets. Rarely would anyone in the mob ever place a bet. They're too smart to be directly involved in anything that might be construed as illegal. Next, are the runners — they are nobodies hired by the mob to cash in winning tickets and return the winnings to their boss."

"Huh, sounds like what I deal with."

"It's no different at the track." Frankie waved his mug toward the waitress and received a nod. "There are the dopers, these are trainers involved in drugging the horses. Drug couriers are the guys who transfer drugs from a local source to the trainers. Next are the race watchers, they stand with one hand on the pay-phone receiver and the other on a pair of binoculars aimed at the starting gate. They watch to see if a horse stumbles, breaks poorly or got off to a great start, so a person at a remote location can place a bet."

"Hold it, I don't understand how that works."

Frankie puffed up with pride in his knowledge, "There's a three- to five-second delay in the transmission of the race to a remote location. Time for his buddy there to place the bet."

"Pretty slick, I'd say."

Frankie gave him a sly grin. "Last are the talkers. Sorry, I couldn't come up with something better. These guys love to talk; only half of what they say is probably true, but they're a good source of information." Frankie downed the last of his coffee. "Have questions about these?"

Clark rubbed his jaw. "I don't think so," he said hesitantly, then glanced up from his notepad. "You have anything else?"

"Not today. That ought to be enough to keep your boys busy. Next time I'll give you information on the mobsters at the next level. Fair enough?"

Clark nodded and tossed two envelopes in front of him.

Frankie ran his fingers across each one and opened the puffier one. Pulling out ten one hundred bills, he grinned. "Fair enough." He glanced at the other one.

"Open it up. It's the one you would have received if you didn't produce."

Frankie took his time opening it and peeking inside. "There's nothing in it."

"Right."

***

THE DETROIT NEWS
August 19, 1980

SOCIALITE GIVEN REDUCED SENTENCE IN PLEA BARGAIN

Ruling in federal court today, the Honorable Henry Limbaugh accepted the plea bargain for Barbara Nash as agreed upon by the defendant's legal counsel William E. Bufalino and the federal prosecutor. Mrs. Nash will serve eighteen months in a minimum security correctional facility and then placed on probation for five years.

Clark tossed the paper on the conference table.

"I told you Bufalino would pull out all of the stops," Eddie said, showing his dismay.

"You nailed it," Max added. "She'll be living at one of those fancy federal country clubs."

"And will probably receive time off for good behavior." John Ralston shook his head. "Bufalino is a magician."

"How many years do you think Freddie Salem will receive?" Max asked.

"Huh." Eddie shook his head. "Based on the Nash case I'd say three to five years at most."

"Three to five!" Max paused. "He probably has two or three million dollars socked away. He must figure it was worth it."

"That's why Bufalino makes the big bucks.

"I guess."

"Talking about Bufalino, how's your digging into Jimmy Quasarano and Peter Vitale going," Clark asked.

Will and John nodded to each other. "Go ahead, Will, tell them about Jimmy Q."

Will cleared his throat. "Jimmy Q is the highest ranking Detroit Mafia official ever indicted. He tripped himself up on a little two hundred and seventy-thousand-dollar extortion deal."

"Little, that's not chicken feed," Nancy Sterling said.

Will belly-laughed. "It is for Jimmy Q. He's been raking in millions from drug trafficking for years."

As was his habit, Clark spoke directly. "Just so everyone is on the same page, give us a quick update on him."

"It's insane." Will smiled sardonically. "Jimmy Q has been in the middle of most everything; he's been arrested for disorderly conduct, armed robbery, shootings, wiretapping, gambling, racketeering and conspiring in heroin operations. His name is associated with two dozen gangland homicides, and he's still free."

"There's not much left," Max quipped.

"One of his best moves was to marry the daughter of Sicilian Mafia boss Vito Vitale. It gave him a direct source of heroin. Like so many other mob leaders, he reinvested his profits in land purchases and a series of legitimate companies, like the Motor City Barber and Supply, County Growers, Inc. and Concrete Paving Corporation."

"He sounds more like a business conglomerate," Eddie suggested.

"You're right on." Max nodded. "He received his most unwanted attention from his joint venture with Peter and Paul Vitale at the Central Sanitation Service, a major waste-disposal company."

Kimberly perked up. "That's the place where some people speculate Jimmy Hoffa's body was incinerated."

"You got it." Will lifted his head from his notes to look at her. "The feds searched the place once for evidence tied to Hoffa and found nothing. The FBI received new information and got a second search warrant. Interestingly, the place burned down the day before the agents were to step inside."

"Doesn't sound unusual to me," Eddie bemoaned. "Sounds like business as usual for the Mafia."

Clark turned to John Ralston. "Tell us about Peter Vitale."

"Peter V. is connected to every important mobster in town — Frank Coppola, Angelo Meli, Papa John Priziola, Peter Corrado — and married to Salvatore 'Sam' Zerilli's daughter."

"He's a heavyweight in Greektown, isn't he?" Eddie asked.

Smiling, John cleared his throat. "His brother Paul is the vice boss for Greektown. Peter manages the Grecian Gardens, which gives him direct access to gamblers. He's the head of the Mafia's gambling operation."

Will raised his hand. "If that finishes the updates, I'd like to change the subject."

Receiving blank expressions from the others, Clark nodded. "Fine, go ahead."

"I have a funny feeling about the druggie mutilation."

"Why so?" Max asked.

"Usually, there's speculation and rumors flying all over town. I've checked with several of my sources. There's nothing out there, not even a sniff."

"I was about ready to say the same thing," Max interjected. "No one knows anything; no one is talking."

"That's strange," Kimberly popped up. "Has Clifford said anything about the murder?"

"As a matter of fact, he did. At our meeting last Friday, he said the FBI's head of the Criminal Investigation Division in Washington, D.C. called and was sending two special agents. Apparently, that's standard operating procedure when something strange like this occurs."

"That's good to know."

Clark glanced at her. "Since you're wondering about that case, I'll fill you in on my recent meeting with the DRC informant."

Kimberly chuckled. "Sounds like more work is coming."

Clark handed out copies of the DRC staff directory along with his notes. "One hundred and thirty-nine suspects. Divide them up and build your cases."

Nancy Sterling made a face, frowning. "How in the world did you come up with these names; and categorized too?"

Clark snickered. "I try to contribute a little something special every now and then."

***

Earl moseyed down the fifth floor hallway of 1300 Beaubien and tapped on the doorframe of Clark's office — his head hung low; his broad smile missing. "Got a minute?"

"Of course." Clark pivoted his chair to face Earl and glanced up. "What the hell is wrong? You look like you lost your last friend." Clark pointed to the side chair. "Have a seat." Earl closed the door and sat down.

"What's going on?"

"I've been struggling all week about Nicole." Clark's interest peaked. "I'm taking her to dinner next Saturday night and can't decide… you know it has to be just right for her."

"That's *it*?" Clark acted bewildered. "Hell, you've been to T.J.'s and a half dozen other places since she got out of the hospital so what's the problem?"

"It's not that. I want Saturday night to be special, not too fancy, just a place that will be memorable. You know, in case we want to come back and celebrate someday."

"You got something *special* in mind?"

"No, I just want the night to be meaningful. "Have a suggestion?"

Clark paused; his mind sorting. "Okay, here's the plan." He pulled open the center drawer and rummaged through the papers. "Here's the card for the manager of Cliff Bell's … he's a good friend. Go down there and tell him I sent you."

Earl gave him an inquisitive look.

"Give him twenty bucks and tell him you want a romantic booth and you want the waitress to place a rose in a bud vase in front of Nicole when the drinks are served." Clark hesitated. "What's Nicole's favorite color?"

"Yellow."

"Perfect, have them get a yellow rose."

The phone rang. "Just a minute," he said to Earl. Clark picked up the receiver. "Clark Phillips." He turned to Earl and mouthed, "It's Abby."

Earl gave Clark a thumbs up and winked. "Go for it!" he whispered.

Clark nodded for a minute or two, then held the phone between the two of them so Earl could hear. Abby sang his praise and pleaded. "So will you meet me for lunch at Marcus's tomorrow?"

Letting out a deep sigh, Clark asked, "Could I have a piece of warm apple pie?"

"Clark … Clark, is that you?"

He pulled the phone closer to his mouth. "Yes. Could I have a piece of warm apple pie?"

Abby stumbled, "Ah … yes, of course, I'll bake one tonight."

"Nah, I was just joking. Yeah, I'll meet you there," Clark said and hung up.

Earl gave Clark a bizarre glance. "What the hell was that about?"

"It's something I heard one time. I'll tell you someday. Now, get your butt down to Cliff Bell's."

***

Abby arrived at the East McNichols Road restaurant fifteen minutes early and spotted two vacant red vinyl stools. Sitting down on the end one, she glanced around — no tables, no booths. Nothing had changed since it was established in 1929. Recalling the first time she'd been there with Clark, she smiled to herself. *Plain and simple with a series of horseshoe-like counters weaving down the middle of the place. And best of all, steak burgers served on hot dog buns. How cute!*

Dressed-down in a long-sleeved green plaid shirt paired with old jeans and little makeup, she fit right in. Wanting to convey her feelings in the best possible way, she'd practiced her lines umpteen times. *He must think I'm the worst person in the world. I want to convey the torment I've gone through and how I've agonized over my actions. If I can only get him to realize I'm just a regular kid from South Philly — an honor student, a state highschool track champion, a cheerleader — who worked hard to achieve her goals. Sure, I took advantage of my great body. Who would have turned down that kind of money? The Detroit assignment was simply icing on the cake — twenty-five grand a month, a new corvette, a plush riverfront apartment and all expenses paid — hell, who could have asked for more?*

"Hah," she said under her breath. *I've been with sport's stars, celebrities, some of the most famous men in the world; how did I know I'd fall in love with a Detroit police detective?*

Clark opened the door and stepped in. Wearing a red crew-neck sweater and jeans, his hair ruffled by the early fall breeze, he too looked the part. He spotted Abby — her soft green eyes sparkled as usual.

Easing onto the stool next to her, an awkward feeling came over him. Sitting next to her was not like he had planned — his mind went blank.

Each one seemed pensive; afraid to make a false step; afraid to open the conversation.

Abby broke the ice, "How have you been?"

Unsure of his feelings, he rolled his shoulders. "Same ol', same ol'."

"From the stories I've read you've been quite busy nabbing the bad guys."

Ignoring her praise, Clark recalled how she'd set him up before; he took a deep breath, wondering how he'd ever put her betrayal aside. At the same time, he had feelings for her and didn't want to offend her.

An older waitress appeared in front of him and placed a large piece of warm apple pie in front of Clark. "Welcome home."

He didn't know how to respond. *She's dashed my negative thoughts; still, I don't want to give her the wrong impression. I ...* He settled for a polite thanks to the waitress and turned toward Abby. "Thanks, that was a very creative gesture."

"It's more than creative," she purred, "it came from my heart."

Clark picked up a fork and sliced off a small piece. Taking a bite, he savored the flavor. "This is really good. Would you like a bite?"

"No, thank you," she said softly, giving him a curious look. "Where did you ever come up with that homespun phrase?"

A grin parted Clark's lips. "It's something my dad once said ..." He paused. She waited for him to say more. "It was like he was saying 'okay, things happen. I'm willing to move on — it's time to forgive and to forget.'"

"Are you willing to do that?" she asked, her tone anxious, sincere.

"Hmm, sometimes part of me says 'yes,' but I have to admit I'm confused, other times I'm not so sure."

Abby seemed sympathetic, earnestly listening to him. "I know it's a lot to ask, but I'd like for you to try." She placed her hand on top of his. "I'll help in any way I can. Would you try?" Clark sat and stared. Sensing his discomfort, she patted his hand. "Why don't we order?" She pointed to the specials. "I'm having a burger with chili, cheese and onions, and order of fries."

CHAPTER TWELVE

Clark drizzled a stream of maple syrup over a mound of whipped cream and blueberries. Glancing up from the Belgium waffle, he winked at Frankie. "Right on time. I just ordered the Michigan Farmer's Special for you."

Sliding into the booth, a slow grin grew on Frankie's face. "Trying to butter me up, huh?"

"I took a lesson from you." Clark laughed. "Use every angle I can."

Frankie chuckled. "You're all right."

The waitress slid a platter of eggs, sausage, hash browns and toast in front of Frankie and then unloaded a second plate of pancakes.

"What's that for?"

Clark chuckled. "Figure you'd earned it." The two talked about inconsequential things. The waitress refilled their mugs. Finishing first, Clark took a long sip of coffee and pushed his plate away.

"Do you have the information you mentioned last time?"

Frankie shoved in the last bite, not skipping a beat, and pointed to his puffed cheeks.

Knowing Frankie had food on his mind, Clark took another long sip of coffee.

A few minutes passed in silence.

Frankie wiped his face with his napkin. "I'm finished with lieutenants Friedman and Owen, and have a couple more sources to follow-up on Macarano. Okay, if I start with Friedman?"

"Fine with me." Clark opened his black notebook and motioned for him to go ahead.

Frankie cleared his throat and with elongated syllables imitated a prizefight announcer, "'Fat Jerry'… Friedman … from the City of Philadelphia checks in at the Pontchartrain Hotel on Friday nights." Glancing at Clark with a smile, he asked, "How'd that sound?"

Clark frowned, feigning disgust. "Better stick with the race track."

"Damn, my girlfriend said the same thing." Frankie picked up his mug and downed the dregs. "Okay, here's the routine. A cabbie pulls up Friday afternoon to the Pontchartrain and removes a big suitcase from the trunk. The bellman grabs it and motions to Friedman. Carrying a small handbag, Friedman follows the man inside."

"Any idea about the contents?"

Frankie spoke confidently. "A friend of mine from Philly says Friedman has a contact with a pharmaceutical guy who works in a drug manufacturing company in Jersey. I assume it's full of drugs."

"Sounds like it."

"You guys need to be in the lobby early Saturday morning. You can't miss him, at two hundred and ninety pounds, with the suitcase in tow. The cab will take him to the Derby Bar across the street from the DRC." Frankie paused. "The FBI has had the place under surveillance for years; I assume you don't want anything more about that place."

"Right. The FBI has everything we need to know about the mob's headquarters. Anything else I should know about 'Fat Jerry?'"

Frankie smiled, as if hoping Clark would ask. "He's connected with the underworld out east — big time — good friends with Anthony 'Fat Tony' Salerno, the boss of New York's Genovese crime family. He also chums around with Pasquale 'Pat the Cat' Spirito, a key guy in the Philly Mob."

"Sounds like a national cartel."

Frankie's eyes darted up to Clark's. "The syndicate families of New York, Boston, Detroit, Chicago and Philly are far more connected than you'd expect."

Sticking to his agenda, Clark moved on. "Is that it on Friedman?"

"Not quite," Frankie stated emphatically. "On Saturday afternoon, he's loaded with cash. That's when he makes the big wagers on the fixed races for the crime families back east."

"You mean he actually walks up and buys the tickets?"

"You bet. He's as arrogant as hell. Guess he wouldn't trust anyone else with the kind of money he's handling." Frankie paused to catch a breath. "You have any questions before I go onto Owen?"

Clark flipped a page. "No, go ahead."

"Robert 'Bobby the Teacher' Owen," he stated in that exaggerated tone; then glanced over at the frown growing on Clark's face. He stopped trying to be funny. "Sometimes I think Bobby is the nicest guy I ever met; he chitchats, laughs and is funny as hell. Next thing, I hear about his other side — a kickass, mean SOB."

"A Jekyll and Hyde, huh?"

"You got it. When he walks into a horse stall people back away. He's either muscling someone around or greasing his palm. No question. He's the top dog at the DRC and oversees all race-fixing activity for the Mafia."

 "Sounds like a real snake in the grass."

Frankie smiled coolly. "He's smarter than hell too, and really good with numbers. I stood behind him once in the wager-line. He was smooth, I tell you; as smooth as one could be. He calmly placed his bets. Knowing the three top horses in the race had been fixed, he boxed his trifecta bets."

"Boxed?" Clark questioned.

"In a trifecta bet you have to pick the order of the top three finishers in a race — win, place and show. He's rigged the race — paid off the jockeys or drugged the top horses so he knows they'll run out of the money. Then it's easy; he bets the other combinations in a box bet — no matter the outcome of the race, he has the winning combination for first, second and third."

"So he wins big money."

"*Big* money … you better believe it. I made a mental note one afternoon of his bets. After the end of the racing day, I figured his winnings were over eighty grand."

***

THE DETROIT NEWS

September 7, 1980

GAMBLING GURU FREDDY SALEM INDICTED

Freddie "The Saint" Salem was indicted today on a dozen counts of illegal gambling, tax evasion, and a long list of other charges. Bail was set at $500,000.

Known as a smooth operation, Salem ran a nice game for high rollers from across the county. For years the location of "The Game" on Euclid Street had eluded police and federal officials. Through the joint effort of Detroit's Special Crimes Task Force headed by Detective Clark Phillips and the FBI'S Strike Force, the north side operation was busted on April 19, 1980.

***

Standing in front of the ten-foot walnut door, Jake Nicolette's personal bodyguard gave the all clear sign. He watched as the drivers of the four new Buick Electras parked in the circular driveway below, jumped out and hurried around their cars to open the doors. One by one, the Mafia's number two, three, four and five men slid out of the back seats and strolled up to the portico.

The massive door opened wide casting a stream of the late afternoon light down the hallway. Receiving a nod from the gatekeeper, the four walked down the highly-polished terrazzo floor. Passing several Romanesque paintings, a life-size sculpture of Mark Anthony, a statue of Emperor Augustine and a bust of Julius Cesar, each man paid homage with pride.

At the end of the hallway off to the left, Jake Nicolette waited.

Tony Minelli was the first to be embraced and kissed on the cheek. Now in his eighties, Tony had been a long-time friend and Jake's most trusted confidant. "Glad you could come on such short notice," Jake said. "Annabella has outdone herself once again. Fill up a plate and fix yourself a drink."

Following suit, Angelo Travaglini, Joe DiGregorio and his prize pupil, Blackie Giardini, paid their respects and loaded their plates. Jake added ice and a splash of Jack Daniels to his glass and eased into the large black leather chair at the end of the table. Taking a sip, he made his way through a medley of salmon, smoked oysters, and kipper and shrimp that Annabella had prepared.

While loading his plate, Angelo gushed, "She's a wonderful cook that Annabella; her French heritage shows."

Jake smiled to himself. *It's not unusual for Annabella to receive such accolades; her beauty and cooking skills are matched only by her brains. Truth be known, I often ask for her advice.* He nodded to himself taking the compliment in stride. "Who could expect more; after all, she was named after Annabella, the most famous French entertainer of all."

The sixty-eight-year-old Joe DiGregorio's face glowed. "I've seen all of her movies. No one better."

The group finished off all the appetizers. Jake glanced at his colleagues and said in his low-key manner, "Freshen up your drinks, this may take a long time."

The underlings filled their glasses with ice and a second round.

Waiting at the end of the eight-foot table for the others to return, Jake turned to his adviser. He asked with a touch of compassion, "How's Freddie Salem doing?

Consigliere Minelli responded, "I chatted with him last week. He knows the routine, a couple of years in the pen and he'll be back in business again."

"Good." Jake's demeanor turned cold; his mind focused on the challenges ahead. As his crew filtered back in he said, "I have serious trepidations about the information I'm receiving from the DRC. Beyond Ciulla's yapping to the feds, you hear anything?"

Underboss Angelo's hand flew up barely before the words were out of his mouth. "Clark Phillips' people are all over the DRC. They're pressuring everyone."

"I've heard the same," Street Boss DiGregorio acknowledged.

"It's a big ticket for us." Jake glanced at the Consigliere and wondered aloud, "Any suggestions, Tony?"

Running his fingers up his plentiful sideburns, the wise old man stroked a few remaining gray hairs on the side of his head. "It's important to know when to hold 'em and when to fold 'em."

Catching the Boss's attention, Jake listened intently. "My exact sentiments. Anyone have a different thought?"

No one said a word.

"Angelo, put the wheels in motion. Cut every link with the DRC. Don't leave a stone unturned. Make it seem like the local guys are doing everything on their own."

"Got it." The powerfully-built Angelo said. "By the end of the week we'll have muzzled all of them."

"Good," Jake said; his voice strong yet deceptively soft. "Now onto the other problem — Clark Phillips — anyone have any thoughts?"

"We ought to rub him out," DiGregorio suggested.

The Consigliere bristled. "Jesus Christ Joe, we can't do that. William Webster and the entire Washington contingent from FBI headquarters would be down on our ass."

"Sometimes it's better to take action rather than pussyfoot around," the aging DiGregorio said.

Jake raised his hand. "Tony is right. That's too risky."

Drawing out a thought, Angelo paused. "How about leaning on Phillips' buddies like we did a couple years ago? That worked pretty well."

"Nothing to lose," Tony said. "I prefer the indirect approach anyway."

"Makes sense. Have any ideas on how we might move forward?"

The senior men stared at each other.

Blackie eased up to the edge of the table. "I think we ought to double down."

Four heads turned toward Blackie.

"Double down?" Jake raised his hand for silence from the others. "What do you have in mind?"

Unaccustomed to being center-stage in front of the leadership group, Blackie took his time collecting his thoughts. "I think we should turn up the heat on his buddies like Angelo said. Equally important, we have to crank up our own initiative."

Catching his colleagues off guard, no one said a word — quizzical expressions shot around the table.

"I like the sound of that," Jake said, his confidence in Blackie showing. "Let's hear more."

"As I mentioned, there's no question we have to put the pressure on his buddies, but we have to do more," Blackie said, speaking the obvious.

"Do more?" the Consigliere asked.

"We need Clark's friends to help us redefine our operation."

DiGregorio seemed baffled. "Could you give us an example or two?"

Blackie removed his sunglasses, unconsciously twirled them a moment and placed them on the table. "Here's my take on the situation. Phillips and his crew busted 'Freddie's game.' They nailed Lonnie Williams' eastside drug gang. And they're about to shut down the remaining piece of our racing game."

Angelo waved his hand in the air dismissively. "We know that."

Blackie nodded with a self-confident smile. "The black gangs have taken the streets. Drugs are flowing rampant. The Arab Mafia is cutting into our sole supply of drugs. We can't be anal; we have to move beyond the past. Pass off the race gambling, to casinos."

"Shit," Jake said in an usual outburst. "We got stung by the casino deals in Vegas."

Still smug, Blackie took his time drawing out his idea slowly, for maximum effect. "Gambling is the wave of the future. Today there are casinos in Vegas and Atlantic City. Tomorrow, there'll be casinos in most of the warm and plush places around the county. The little guys on the streets of Detroit will be left out, right?"

Heads nodded.

"So here's my plan." Blackie looked at them intently making sure his superiors were on board. "We need to transform some of our blind pigs into 'mini casinos' so Joe Six Pack can have a ball."

Groans rolled around the table.

Jake tapped the hardwood surface. "You've peaked my interest … proceed."

"Let's say for example, we upscale ten of our best locations and make them into full-service casinos with chandeliers, gaming tables, and carpet on the walls."

"Full service?" the Consigliere asked.

"The whole shebang — crap tables, black jack, roulette — classy prostitutes upstairs. You name it, we got it."

"I like that." Angelo tossed back his long black hair. "We could have Phillips' buddy do the blind pig remodeling, and Ted-what's-his-name, take care of housing the prostitutes."

Blackie smiled. "You're right on it."

"Whoa, wait a minute," the Consigliere called. "You're moving way too fast. I want to hear more details."

Blackie hesitated, knowing he had the group eating out of his hand. "First, we've all agreed we can't replace Freddie Salem — his name recognition and reputation are beyond reproach — there's no way we'll be able to attract high rollers from Chicago and New York — they'll be going to the big name places."

"Absolutely," Jake reinforced the point. "I'm already getting calls. The big hitters are headed for Atlantic City and Vegas."

Blackie nodded to him, acknowledging their agreement. "We need to create our own niche — a place for the guys who can't afford to go to Vegas."

"Why not?" Angelo smirked. "If we don't take the lead they'll be going to St. Louis, Cincinnati, New Orleans, and who knows where else. We have to give the local guy a place to go without leaving town."

"It could be a bonanza for us," DiGregorio said, getting on board.

"I like the concept," the Consigliere said.

"We take our most secure blind pigs and have Phillips' buddy Renzo Ricciuti do the work. He'll do it cheap and we have him by the balls."

Tony Minelli, the Consigliere nodded. "Have you given any thought to how we keep all of this quiet?"

"Yes, I have," Blackie said, knowing he was on a roll. "I figure the guys aren't going to say anything to their wives or their friends, unless they bring another guy along next time. For the cops," he continued without a pause, "we up their ante; give them a fifty or hundred buck gaming-chit, or if they want a little pussy, they have a free pass upstairs. Either way, a couple of pictures of them in the place will make us as secure as hell."

"It sounds better all the time," Jake added.

"There's more." Blackie gloated. "You know that old apartment building we bought on Gratiot a few years ago?"

"Yeah, it has twenty, twenty-five apartments," the Street Boss said. "A rat hole, if you ask me."

"Right. We'll have Ricciuti spruce it up, install some carpet, repair the plaster, and add a coat of paint. Best of all, we'll tell Ted to run it free for us."

"Free." Consigliere Minelli frowned. "Why would he do that?"

"Because we're going to provide no-hassle protection for his apartment buildings."

"I like that." Angelo beamed. "It's a terrific plan."

Blackie raised his hand. "Wait a minute, there's one more piece."

Surprise registered on the faces around the table.

"Okay," Jake said. "Let's hear it."

"We'll need more cars for the prostitutes to move around. So we call Mr. Montes, Clark's used-car buddy, and tell him to double our supply of cars." Blackie paused before dropping the last bomb. "In return, we'll tell him to launder money for us through his sales."

Two hands went up.

"Hold on," Blackie said, basking in glory. "Used car places are perfect to launder money. No one has a clue of what's going on; used-car salesmen are the greatest *legal* conmen on earth. Let's say, for example, a salesman says 'I'll give you five thousand for your car.' Hell, maybe it's worth three or four. We record two thousand instead of five. There is no way to trace anything. Whatever Mr. Montes records in the books is final."

Jake's ears perked up. "We could launder two, three, or maybe four grand per car."

Minelli's face revealed his enthusiasm. "I like it."

Knowing he'd nailed the concept, Blackie spoke unassumingly. "It's a win-win situation."

Jake smiled, pridefully. "Blackie, you've earned your stripes. Joe's been wanting to retire to Florida for some time." He rose, walked over to Blackie, and gave him a man-size embrace. "It's time. Welcome aboard Street Boss Blackie Giardini."

CHAPTER THIRTEEN

A middle-aged waitress eased in behind Nicole, two Old Fashioned glasses and a crystal bud vase on her tray.

Earl gave her a subtle nod.

Stepping forward with a graceful flair, she placed a yellow rose in front of her.

Taken by the moment, Nicole sat speechless: her eyes teared. Searching for the right words, she choked up. "It-it's perfect … you're so thoughtful. I'll remember tonight forever."

Knowing he'd hit a homerun, Earl's face beamed. "I can't tell you how long it's been since I felt this way."

She reached across the glossy tabletop and placed her hand on top of his. Their eyes connected like never before — words need not be spoken. "It seems like an eternity for me, too."

Still shaking her head in wonderment, she thought aloud, "How did you ever come up with such a wonderful idea?"

"I wish I could say it was my own, but I can't. Clark made the suggestion."

"He's such a great guy; he's always thinking of others."

Agreeing with her, Earl went on to tell her how his conversation with Clark had evolved.

"How it happened is not the point." She sniffled. "What's important is that you wanted to make tonight special."

Earl picked up his vodka and tonic and held it high. "Here's to you and the best evening ever."

Clinking his glass, her soft smile blossomed. "And here's to the two of us."

Half embarrassed and half excited, Earl glimpsed at the restaurant's luxurious mahogany paneling and brass décor. "This place has a terrific history," he mused.

"Did you learn that from Clark, too?" she jested.

"No." Earl gave her a prideful look. "The manager filled me in while I was waiting."

She tossed him a reassuring glance. "Well, let's hear it."

"Back in the Prohibition era, Cliff Bell had a string of speakeasies in downtown Detroit," Earl puffed up like *the man in the know*. As times changed, he opened saloons, burlesque places, and restaurants. He brought big-time entertainment from New York, and in 1935 built Cliff Bells, his signature club, right here on 2030 Park Avenue."

Nicole hummed an old-time melody. "I can hear Duke Ellington playing *Mood Indigo*, Bing Crosby crooning *Star Dust*, and the other stars singing the hits of the day — *Stormy Weather* and *Don't Fence Me In*."

Earl sat in amazement. "How'd you know all of those?"

Her smile broadened. "My grandmother used to sing them to me."

Feeling comfortable, Earl got more serious. "This place is really neat, especially when you're sitting across from me."

"Aren't you sweet," she replied softly. "And thanks again, for taking me to the mayor's office. I would not have been able to manage on my own."

"I was just the driver. You're the one who came home with a bag of money."

"It felt good; I really feel like I'm getting back into the swing of things."

"Swing of things!" Earl shook his head in amazement. "The mayor agreed in less than a half hour."

She smiled wryly. "I knew I had him hooked when I mentioned *votes*; his whole demeanor changed after that," her words trailed off.

Watching her glow fade, Earl knew something was on her mind. "Something bothering you?"

She spoke hesitantly. "I have to jump-start the store building process."

"Nicole, you can't produce miracles overnight."

Impassively polite, she said. "I have to come up with another hundred and thirty thousand dollars."

Earl seemed perplexed. "Am I missing something?"

"The mayor's money was only the first step. People are not going to appear overnight just because there is a shell of a building."

"Okay," he said, knowing she had a plan in her head. "Why do you need an additional hundred and thirty thousand?"

"To get people's attention. I could use it as an incentive to encourage former residents to return to the city. They could match it with their own money and sweat equity, to redevelop."

Her words gave him pause; yet, he knew better than to question too much. "That sounds laudable, Nicole, but the people left because the city was dying. They've established new lives in suburbia."

"That's the point, Earl. That's why I need an incentive — something that will grab their attention and rekindle their hope. They need to be excited about their dreams and become part of the city's rebirth."

"I'm sorry. I'm not up to speed."

"According to Renzo, it'll cost one hundred and thirty thousand to finish the inside of each building. I'd like to make it a fifty/fifty proposition for those willing to move back."

"Why that much?"

"Half on us and half on them." Nicole shifted into high gear. "It makes a statement that — *we want you!* It'll create a positive feeling between them and they'll bring a can-do attitude with them."

"Many of them are seniors now, maybe retired."

"Fine. We'll make the same offer to their kids so the family can continue its tradition."

Earl shook his head, knowing there was no way to dissuade her. "Okay, how can I help?"

She looked at him with an expression of gratitude. "Put on your thinking cap. We can tell them the mayor will do a hundred thousand dollars' worth of work; we'll give sixty-five thousand if they match it with their own sixty-five thousand. That's a three-to-one return—they have to buy in."

Earl gave her double thumbs up. "When you put it that way I get it. Yes, I'm on board."

"I need a slogan, something to rally around."

Earl thought. "How about ... together we can rebuild our community."

"Hmm, it's okay, but we need something short and catchy."

Earl rubbed his hand over his bald head a couple of times; his eyes lit up. "I have it."

Anticipation jumped from her mouth. "Okay, let's hear it."

"Return. Rebuild. Rebirth."

"Oh Earl, that's perfect." She laughed with relief. "Three R's. We can make bumper stickers!"

"Would you like to order now?" the waitress asked.

Nicole quieted, embarrassed. "Yes, I'm sorry. I got carried away."

"Could we have another minute, please?" Earl said politely.

Nicole picked up the menu, read the entries, and idly glanced over the top. She noticed a man sitting at the bar.

He grinned and turned away.

Feeling uncomfortable, she looked at him again, then leaned across the table. "Earl, don't look now, but there's a man at the bar who keeps staring at me. He's kind of creepy."

Taking his time, Earl eased back and casually glanced in that direction — his eyes rested on the ones staring back at him. "Wait here," he said. "I'll see what's going on with him."

Earl slid casually out of the booth and walked over to the fellow—a thin-faced man with long, greasy hair. The guy turned toward the bar and took a sip of beer.

Earl tapped him on the shoulder. "Excuse me."

He turned halfway on the barstool.

"My friend noticed you were staring at her. Can I help you?"

Seeming unsettled, the man stammered, "I-I … I'm sorry. I didn't mean to stare. Please give her my apologies." He rubbed his stubble. "Last night my wife and I had dinner here and we sat in that booth. She thinks her wedding ring may be have slipped off and fallen on the floor. I wanted to say something, but the two of you were involved in a conversation. I didn't want to interrupt."

"That was very thoughtful." Earl called to a passing waitress. "Miss."

She turned his way.

"Would it be okay if we move down two booths so this gentleman can have ours?"

She glanced at the empty booth. "Sure. I'll tell your waitress."

He winked at her. "Thank you."

The stranger slid off the stool and extended his hand. "Thanks, I appreciate that."

"No problem." Earl shook his hand, walked back to the booth, and picked up their drinks.

"What was that all about?"

"I'll tell you in a minute. We're moving down two booths."

Nicole slowly picked up her purse, the vase, and followed him. Sliding into the booth, she waited anxiously for him to sit down. "What's going on?"

Earl explained the details of his conversation with the guy and tried to get back in the mood.

"That was very nice of you." Nicole stuck her head in the menu, then motioned for Earl to lean forward. "Earl," she whispered. "He doesn't seem like the married type. He hasn't shaved in three or four days. I don't think he would have brought his wife in here dressed like that."

"I agree. He's wearing old beat-up shoes too. A guy wouldn't wear them to a place like this."

"Hmm." Nicole laid down the menu. "Something funny is going on."

"Maybe so," he said, trying to shake off the disruption. "Want to share the jumbo lump crab cakes appetizer?"

"That'll be fine," she said disinterestedly.

Earl pushed his menu aside. "Okay, what is it?"

"I hear pounding. Do you hear it?"

"Kind of." Earl leaned to the side and peeked down the aisle. "The guy is under the table. I can see his feet hanging out. He's probably feeling for the ring."

"It sounds more like he's pounding on something."

Earl eased back. "Shh, he's coming this way."

The man stopped in front of Earl. "Thanks, I found it," he mumbled and walked out.

"Strange." Nicole went back to the menu. "Yes, let's start with the crab cakes."

Earl placed their orders and asked the waitress to bring a moderately priced bottle of Chianti. Placing his elbows on the table, he folded his hands to steady his chin.

His silence drew a bewildered comment from her. "Now you're the one who is somewhere else. Are you thinking about the man?"

Earl nodded, still in deep thought. "There was a robbery down the street four or five years ago."

"So." Nicole was confused. "Why did that pop into your mind?"

"I remember Clark telling me that one of the robbers was found in Cliff Bells having lunch."

"Right here?"

"Yes, I know because this is one of Clark's favorite places. They caught the other guy with half of the loot. The rest, some eighty grand was never found."

Nicole's eyes lit up. "Do you think he's the one?"

"It's possible, he could have just gotten out of jail." Earl ran his hand over his shiny head. "I'm thinking …" He raised his hand and motioned to their waitress.

She hurried over. "Is there something else I can get you, sir?"

Earl pursed his lips, "I have a couple of questions."

"Sure," she said hesitantly.

"Have you worked here long?"

"Yes," she said with apprehension. "Ten years, going on eleven."

"Was Cliff Bells closed for remodeling a few years ago?"

"Three years ago. They upgraded the kitchen and added some additional seating."

"Additional seating, where?"

"Four tables over there." She pointed across the room. "And the two booths behind your lady friend."

Bells rang in Earl's head. "So this used to be the last booth?"

"Correct."

"Thank you," he nodded.

Nicole leaned over the table, and whispered, "Why did you ask that?"

"Hold on." He glanced around the restaurant, his juices flowing. "If you were a bank robber and came into Cliff Bells, which side of this booth would you sit on?"

She thought for a moment. "I'd sit on the side where you are, so if a policeman came in he'd see the back of my head."

"Exactly." Earl bent over toward the wall and ran his hand under the leather padding. Pushing hard, a panel popped loose. He reached inside and felt around. A startled expression raced across his face.

Nicole appeared concerned. "Are you all right?"

Earl's mind whirled.

"Are you okay?" she asked again.

He took a deep breath and sighed. "I think I found the loot."

"The missing loot?"

"Yes, from the bank robbery. I'm sitting on it."

Casting him a questioning look, she asked, "Are you positive?"

Earl pulled his hand from underneath the bench seat and extended it under the table toward her. "Here, take a peek."

Nicole reached under the table and wrapped her hand around his; he slid a crumpled piece of paper into her hand. Leaning back in the booth, she peeked under the edge of the table. "Oh my," she said, peering at a hundred-dollar bill.

The two stared at each other — flabbergasted.

The waitress appeared, poured the wine and served the salads — their thoughts remained on the loot. Earl picked up his glass and dutifully toasted her. "Here's to a very special woman."

"Thank you," she said. "What are you going to do?"

"Normally, it'd be a no brainer. I'd package it up and take it down to the station."

Nicole wrinkled her forehead. "Why did you say normally?"

"It's a hang-up I have. The officers in the charge of stolen property are the worst ones on the force — they're all corrupt as hell. The money will never see the light of day; they'll put it in their pockets and it'll be gone. Poof, just like that!"

"Even so Earl, that's their problem. You don't have a choice."

He raised his brow. "It'd be a nice way to jump-start your project."

"Earl! Don't even think that."

"I know." He twisted his lips into a half-grin. "First things first, we have to see how much is here. Would you take your purse to the car and dump out everything so we can put the money in it?"

***

Sitting in the corner booth of Blackie's favorite hangout, Joey slapped his leg and with a big smile, raised a beer. "Here's to the new Street Boss."

Blackie tipped a glass to his confidant. "You made it possible. Here's to our team."

"Thanks, boss, I appreciate that. But, coming up with that mini-casino idea and leaning on Phillips' buddies to pull it off … that was s stroke of genius."

Blackie glanced around the small neighborhood bar — nothing had changed in a decade — but today it was different. *Vicky Cromwell is gone. I feel empty!*

He adjusted his sunglasses. "I surprised myself," he admitted. "I've thought about the mini-casino idea for some time, but the longer I talked the more the pieces seemed to fall in place."

"However you did it; you pulled off the coup of the year."

Blackie gloated briefly, then moved on to the business at hand. "Who's next?"

"Renzo Ricciuti, the construction man will be coming in at ten." Joey glanced at his watch. "In five minutes, boss. You want me to set up a meeting with Carlos Montes and Ted Moomau?"

Blackie brushed a stray hair off his forehead. "Let's do Montes next week and Moomau the following one."

"Got it." Joey made a note and glimpsed up at Blackie, looking sad — pensive. "You okay, boss?"

Joey wrinkled his nose. "I never thought I'd feel this way. I really miss Vicky."

"You want me to bring her back?"

"Nah, it's her life. She has to pursue her dream." Blackie hesitated. "I have to move on too. Find me someone else."

"You want me to check around the regular places?"

Nodding absently, Blackie drifted in thought about Vicky. "Yeah, but I don't want some kind of a floozy. Find someone with depth, someone I can confide in."

Joey raised a dark eyebrow. "Jesus boss, I'm not a miracle worker."

The front door opened. A short, black curly-haired man walked in. Placing his hand over his eyes, he squinted.

"Over here, Mr. Ricciuti," a deep, raspy voice called.

CHAPTER FOURTEEN

Sitting at the poker table, Renzo answered Carlos, "Yeah. I'm doing some jobs for the Mafia."

"You're what?" Ted interrupted.

"Shit Ted, don't go off the deep end." Renzo picked up the cards and shuffled the deck. "I didn't have a choice. It was either that or they'd shut me down."

"That's bullshit! I'd never let them shut me down."

"Now, now." Father Dom raised his hand. "I'd like to say a short prayer about the well being of all of us." Ending his remarks, the Father continued without pause. "I'd like to know more about the remodeling you're doing, Renzo."

"We're doubling the size of an old blind pig, sprucing up the place, and making it appear brand new — adding drywall, carpeting and disco lighting. My finish carpenter is building a bookcase that pivots between the regular bar and the backroom. It's tucked away in a small alcove so no one can see it. I assume there'll be a thug guarding the backroom."

"Carlos raised his dark eyebrows. "Sounds like something out of a movie."

"Could be." Renzo's mouth twisted into a quirky smile. "The backroom takes up half of the building next door. There's plenty of space for craps and blackjack tables."

"I suppose you're going to put in slots too," Ted said sarcastically.

"No. I asked the same question. Slots take up a lot of room and are too noisy. Most important, slots attract a different kind of crowd. The mob wants to focus on real gamblers. They know once they've hooked the guy down the street, he'll be on the line for a long time."

"Huh." Ted grunted. "You sound like you're one of them."

Renzo bit his tongue.

Father Dom gave Ted a quieting glance. "Doing anything else, Renzo?"

"Yeah, off to one side we're building a small area where they'll place a couple of sofas and lounging chairs. That's where the prostitutes will work. I'm adding a stairwell there too, so they'll have direct access to the three bedrooms on the second floor." He turned briefly toward Father Dom. "Cover your ears," he jested. "The customers will be able to pick the style of room they want — New Orleans brothel, country and western, or downtown Manhattan suite — they're all upscale, real classy places."

Carlos saw dollar signs. "How much is this project costing?"

"A bundle." Renzo contorted his lips. "I'll probably lose two or three grand."

Carlos grimaced.

Ted shifted uncomfortably; his face reddened.

Father Dom jumped in. "My son, how can you afford to lose money on a job?"

"It keeps my crews busy. I can't afford to lose them."

"That's a phony rationalization," Ted shouted.

"C'mon, Ted." Clark interjected. "Renzo has the floor."

Renzo waited for Clark's nod. "Like I've said many times. My business is based on delivering a quality job, on time, at an affordable price. The Mafia assures me that there'll be no problems or delays. I'm stuck between a rock and a hard place."

"I understand that." Carlos said, knowing he was next in line.

"Anyway, in eight or nine months all of this will be over and I'll be able get back to my normal routine."

"That long?" Father Dom questioned. "How many blind pigs are you remodeling for the mob?

"Ten." Wrinkling his nose, Renzo paused. "The real problem is the asshole who owns the place where I'm working now. He's a real slob, must weigh two hundred and sixty pounds. All he does is strut around and brag about the free pussy he gets from the Mafia."

"What's his name?" Ted inquired.

"Sammy Narduzzi; he's a real pain in the butt."

"You have a lot more tolerance than I would." Ted said.

"I guess mine will be tested next week." Carlos admitted. "I have a meeting with your friend, Blackie Giardini."

"He's not my *friend*," Renzo reacted. "But, I have to admit he's a fairly decent guy, not like his right-hand man — Joey Naples — he's the pushy one."

The priest gazed across the table at Clark. "Can't you do something about this?"

"Maybe, down the road," Clark said, unenthusiastically.

"Down the road?" Ted shouted. "What does that mean?"

Clark spoke calmly, "Renzo and I have talked. This is the mob's first step like before, when they applied pressure on all of you."

"I don't like that," an angry, red-faced Ted said.

"Cool your jets, Ted." Carlos tapped him on the forearm. "Clark knows more about dealing with the Mafia than we do."

Reining in his frustration, Ted ran a hand over his jaw. "So what's the plan?"

"I have to wait and see." Clark grabbed a beer. "I'm sure they'll come knocking on all of your doors."

"For what?" Ted asked.

"Who knows?" Clark said, lightheartedly. "We have to wait till they reveal their hand. In the meantime, it's like always, play it cool."

***

Carlos walked into the dimly lit bar the following week. Easing onto a chair, he stared at the silver-haired man. "Are you Blackie Giardini?"

The man dressed in black with large black sunglasses nodded. "You Carlos Montes, the guy with the 'Buy American' signs plastered all over the inner city?"

"Yes, sir."

"Great idea." Blackie said, his compliment sincere. "Being a businessman like yourself, I'll cut to the chase."

Carlos straightened, waiting for a punch in the gut.

"We're doubling your monthly allocation."

"Eight cars — I can't afford that," Carlos said; his tone sharper than planned.

Joey slammed his hand on the table. "You can't afford not to."

Recalling Clark's advice, Carlos backed off. "And what do I get for that?"

Blackie took off his glasses, twirled them once in the air. "An opportunity."

Puzzled, Carlos frowned. "An opportunity for what?"

"To help us out." Blackie slipped his glasses back on. "The feds are clamping down on our options to launder money …"

"Oh no." Carlos cut him off. "I'm not doing that. I could be arrested and go to jail."

"It's no big deal. You fudge the numbers on each car and we come away with an extra grand. It doesn't affect you, and we win."

"Doesn't *affect* me?" Carlos flicked his forefinger at Blackie. "I have to keep two sets of books. The feds find out, you go scot-free and I go to jail. No way!"

"No way for Jose," Joey taunted. "The only way for Carlos."

"Funny, funny."

"We're not joking." Blackie interceded. He motioned to the guy standing behind him. "Joey, tell him how he's going to do it."

***

Ted strolled into the den of iniquity — the air dramatically different. Clark had told him to cool it, but Ted was pissed-off from the get-go — there was no way he would be bullied or accept a compromise.

Blackie slipped off his sunglasses. "Last year we proposed a way for you to help yourself and assist Clark Phillips."

Ted's body stiffened; his stare at Blackie intensified. "My answer is still 'no.' I have a waiting list more than a year long. I am not going to house your prostitutes."

Sensing Ted's combative tone, Blackie softened his voice. "We respect your high standards. That's why I've come up with an alternative plan."

"Alternative plan?" Ted asked, sharply. "Like what?"

Blackie turned to Joey. "Tell him what we have in mind."

"A pleasure." Joey gave Blackie a prideful glance. "We have a twenty-unit apartment building not too far from one of your places. We need someone to manage it. We figured it'd be right up your alley."

"Manage?" Caught off guard, Ted shook his head. "What does that mean?"

"Manage — like I said," Joey said harshly. "Take care of the place, repair and fix things. You know, see that everything is in proper working order. We've set an apartment aside for a woman to deal with their personal issues."

"Shit, a den mother won't help me." Ted said, angrily. "What do *I* get out of it?"

Joey grinned. "All the pussy you want."

Ted bristled. "I don't want your goddamn whores. You can go screw them yourself."

Joey's face reddened. "What more could you ask for? Your staff does the work and you get a little on the side."

"Hell, I'd have to add staff, pay for supplies and materials. You're crazier than hell."

"Hey, look at it this way. You don't have to pay for protection and all of your residents in your apartment buildings will be safe."

"Good idea?" Ted stiffened. "It'll be a goddamn zoo. No, I'm not going to do it."

"Mr. Moomau, I've put it as nicely as I could." Joey spoke his next words with biting emphasis. "You don't seem to get it. I'm not *asking* you."

Shaking his head, Ted ran his fingers over his red-hot face.

"Mr. Moomau, I had hoped we would agree amiably without us having a couple of the boys pay a visit to your doctor friend."

Ted jumped up and pointed a finger. "If anyone lays a hand on her, you'll be a dead son-of-a-bitch."

Joey leaned over the table, their noses inches apart.

Blackie scrambled to his feet and lunged between the two. "Okay, that's it." He handed Ted an envelope. "Here's a set of keys and the address. The remolding will be done next Monday. You start in two weeks. That'll give you a couple of weeks to get things shipshape. The women will move in on the first of the month."

Staring at Joey, Ted snatched the envelope and stormed out.

***

Frankie shoved in the last piece of pancake and washed it down with the last of his coffee. "There's not much more I can say about Anthony 'Tony the Fixer' Ciulla. He was the best horse-racing fixer of all times."

Clark grabbed a napkin from the table and wiped his mouth. "I've read the local FBI files on Ciulla, his meetings at the Derby Bar, and how he divvied up the loot. His file has expanded tenfold since he spilled the beans to the feds back in '76."

"He didn't have a choice. The feds had him dead to rights so he decided to cover his ass." Brimming with a smile, Frankie's head bobbed. "Not a bad deal if you ask me. The feds put forty guys in jail and Tony goes free with his millions tucked away. He's in a witness-protection program somewhere with his wife. It sounds a lot better to me than rotting away in prison."

"I've read about all of that," Clark said, finishing the last of his coffee. "How'd he get into the racket in the first place? And, why did he end up in Detroit?"

"Huh." Frankie hailed the waitress for another coffee. "How much time do you have?"

"Skip the details." Clark gave him a hand gesture to move along. "Just give me the facts."

"Okay." Frankie slurped his coffee. "Damn, that's hot." He took a sip of water. "Tony grew up around the racetrack. His dad was an avid horseplayer. He used to pass hot dogs to his kid through the wire fence around the track."

Clark's questioning frown reminded Frankie, no details.

"Back then kids weren't allowed in the track."

"Got it." Clark nodded.

"Tony started hanging around with some older acquaintances who were fixing races at the county fair. And the rest is history."

"How does a kid from out east, end up in Detroit?"

"Hah." Frankie laughed. "Ciulla was on a fast track. He formed his own race-fixing team and moved on to Suffolk Downs in East Boston, and then Rockingham in New Hampshire, Lincoln Downs and Narragansett in Rhode Island. By the time he was twenty-six, the Thoroughbred Racing Protective Bureau had barred him from fifty-five tracks."

"He must have been a real mover and shaker."

"Yeah, and at six-foot-four and three hundred and forty pounds, when he moved you knew it."

"Sounds like he a downed a lot of hot dogs," Clark jested.

"I guess. After that, he moved to the Maryland tracks — Bowie, Laurel, Pimlico and Timonium. Size or location didn't matter — Delaware Park, Liberty Bell, Keystone and Penn National. He even bragged about taking his family on a trip into the mountains and stopping by Pocono Downs. 'It was like shooting fish in a barrel,' he told the feds."

"So why Detroit?"

"I'm not sure. Maybe he wore out his welcome everywhere else. Regardless of why, he had the nod from the Detroit Boss and support from the Philly Boss and the Genovese Family in New York. Next thing I know he's in Detroit and race-fixing was on — big time!"

***

"That's how it all started," Clark said, following his briefing to the task force.

Kimberly's mouth hung open, intent on his story.

"Interesting," Eddie said, his face registering surprise. "I knew there was an informal alliance between the big-city Mafias, but I never imagined their actions were coordinated to that extent."

Nancy Sterling raised a brow. "It's kind of scary, isn't it?"

"You're telling me," Will Robinson said. "All my life I've been trying to connect one street crook with another, I guess that was small potatoes."

"It may have seemed like small potatoes, but it wasn't," Clark reassured him. "Each step forward is a positive action."

"Hey," Max said. "I've been meeting with one of the local representatives of the TRPB ..."

"Excuse me?" Kimberly interrupted.

"Sorry, the Thoroughbred Racing Protective Bureau. They're the national investigative agency run by the Thoroughbred Racing Associations of North America. They're charged with the task to expose and investigate all activity that might be judged prejudicial to horse racing."

"That's a mouthful," John Ralston quipped. "What kind of success have they had?"

"Mixed at best." Max shook his head. "It's a self-policing agency that sounds better on paper than it really is. It was formed thirty-five years ago. Spencer Drayton, Sr., a former administrative assistant to J. Edgar Hoover, was the first head and modeled it after the FBI. He brought several of his colleagues with him."

"So who are they really?" Ralston asked.

"Well," Max paused before he finished. "It looks like window-dressing if you ask me. They all have fancy titles and job descriptions, but no power to levy penalties."

"I think you're right," Clark agreed.

"Obviously, the TRPB representative was pleased to learn about our interest. They're overwhelmed, understaffed, and feel helpless," Max said. "The best part is the files of information they have."

"Great." Clark glanced around the table. "Anyone else have something to report?"

Kimberly raised her hand. "I do."

Clark nodded her way.

"I've completed my review of the interstate gambling law you requested."

"Go ahead."

"It's fairly simple. For the feds to prosecute under the law they must provide evidence that five or more people have gotten together to alter the outcome of a sporting event. And, most important, their action must have crossed state lines."

"State lines … how do we prove that?" Ralston asked.

"It's easier than you think." Max nodded. "Reporting on a simulcast race in another state is a good example. Making a call to Vegas for the odds is another. It's the kind of stuff these guys do on a daily basis."

CHAPTER FIFTEEN

Clark glimpsed up at the clock in T.J.'s — 11:45 — and nodded to the hostess. Strolling toward *the booth*, he took in the eclectic collection of objects displayed in their normal locations; yet, somehow something felt different.

A tall, slender waitress sat a bottle of Stroh's in front of him and winked. "Anyone joining you today?"

"A friend. You can bring us a couple waters."

She nodded and disappeared.

Clark smoothed his crop of sandy-brown hair. *Why in the hell did I agree to meet her for lunch? How stupid can I be? I should have said 'no' and that would have been the end of it. Why I did I go to the style show and agree to meet her at Marcus? Goddamn warm apple pie, what's wrong with me?* Negative thoughts flitted through his mind; still, he waited with anticipation for her to walk in.

Her silhouette appeared in the doorway.

A charge shot through him; he waved.

Without hesitation, she glided across the old oak floor and extended her hand. "I hope I'm not late," Abby hummed.

He pointed to the clock overhead — two hands straight up. "Right on time."

Easing in across from him, her lovely face seemed lovelier than ever. Her short silky red hair shaped her head; an emerald green blouse accented her deep green eyes. Recalling earlier times, he hesitated; thoughts of the good times were quickly replaced by those of the pits. Unable to come up with something more profound, he asked, "How have you been?"

"I've been fine, working hard on my new job."

He gave her a blank stare, an ugly thought of her phony job with GM flashed.

"I'm a computer programmer for Saks Fifth Avenue."

Unable to stop from asking, he smirked. "I suppose this is a *real* job." He bit his tongue. "I shouldn't have said that. I'm sorry, it just came out."

"You have every right to do so." She laughed outright. "As a matter of fact, I'm glad you did. I want you to say how you feel. It's better to clear the air."

Feeling uncomfortable, her words weren't reassuring.

"I know I hurt you deeply. I feel badly," Abby said, her remorse evident. "I want to listen to you and help make things better."

Clark turned his head away, glanced at the stoplights in the entranceway — red, green, and yellow, all shining brightly — his mind signaling the same confusion. "Sometimes I feel like giving it a try; then it's the last thing I want to do."

Giving him a sincere look, she spoke sympathetically. "I understand. Maybe it would help if I told you the rest of the story, so you'd learn who I really am."

"Who you are?" He mocked with a scowl of disdain. "I know *what* you are."

Her smiling face turned sorrowful. "I'm not like that at all!"

"Okay, I'll say it nicely. You're a call girl."

"It isn't like I *planned* to be that way."

"Thanks a lot. Is that supposed to make me feel better?" His voice was heavy with condescension, then paused. "Okay." He said finally. "How did it start?"

"Do you really want to know?"

"Of course," he said, his tone slightly elevated. "That's what I asked you, didn't I?"

She stared for the longest moment. "If you want me to leave I will."

"No, we're here ..." Clark nodded for her to continue, "go ahead, tell me."

Feeling it was hopeless to go on, she bit her lip and started anyway. "I was a computer programmer at Bloomingdale's in Philadelphia and did some modeling for them on the side. One day a corporate vice president asked me if I would be his escort to an important meeting."

"Escort, you mean ..."

"No, not that kind. I simply had to go with him. He said he'd pick me up in the lobby of my apartment building and drop me off at the end of the night; nothing would happen. I was fine with that. Two months later there was another event and then another. He paid my way to New York, Atlanta and L. A., and started giving me a thousand dollars on the way home."

"Just for being with him at the event?"

"Yes, honest to God. I didn't want to take it. He insisted; said the company expected him to turn in that amount on his expense report. No questions would be asked." She paused. "Next thing I know his secretary calls and tells me he had a massive heart attack and died."

"So that was it?"

"No, I dated another guy for six months. I really liked him. He asked me to spend the weekend at Martha's Vineyard. Of course, I said yes. Afterward, he insisted I accept an envelope. I didn't know it had two thousand dollars in it until he was out the door. A few weeks later one of his handsome friends asked me to go to Aruba. I said 'no, no.' He laid ten thousand dollars on the table. Next, a famous athlete offered me twenty-five thousand to go on a weeklong yacht trip with him." She paused, nearly in tears. "It happened so fast I didn't know what happened."

Clark stared without a word. "How'd you become connected with the mob?

"One of the guys I met was a higher up in the Philadelphia Mob — an assistant to Mafia Don Angelo Bruno. He's the one who talked to me about coming to Detroit. You know the rest."

"So where do you work now?"

"I'm a computer programmer and model at Saks."

"C'mon, you can do better than that." He paused, his thoughts muddled. "Last time it was GM, and this one is *supposed* to be real." He hesitated. "I'm sorry, I just have a hard time thinking this one is legit."

"I don't expect you to believe me, but it's true."

His mind wandered. *Sure and pump all the information out of me you can.* "Other than modeling, why was Saks Fifth Avenue interested in hiring you?"

Abby perked up. "I graduated cum laude with a major in computer science from Penn. When I worked at Bloomindale's in Philly, we introduced a series of cutting-edge fashion designers like Ralph Lauren, Perry Ellis and Norma Kamali. It was a big deal in the upscale-retail market. I showed her how to access the computer program we used. The HR woman at Saks offered me a job on the spot.”

Clark stared as if none that was of any consequence. “Have you picked out a burger?” he looked down at the menu.

“The Tex Mex Lentil Burger sounds intriguing.”

“I’ve never had that. Let’s have one and share the fries.”

She nodded.

Clark motioned to the waitress and placed their order.

“So what’s the rest of the story about Clark Phillips,” Abby asked, in hopes he might loosen up.

“Hell, you know everything. At least I’ve been truthful.”

Ignoring his condescending tone, she remained silent for the longest time. “C’mon, Clark, I want to know more about you than your rendition of an inner-city kid, a jock and graduating with honors from U of D.”

She waited for a response. Nothing forthcoming, she tried another track. “Tell me about your parents, what are they like? Did they like that you became a policeman?”

Clark motioned for the waitress to refill his soda, then took a long sip. “My mom, Fran, taught history in high school for thirty-five years. She was a real buff on the Louisiana Purchase; still teaches a course on that at Wayne State. My dad’s name is Lewis. That’s how she came up with Clark for me.”

“How cute. Lewis and Clark, I like that.”

“Mom is a real dynamo; she’s involved in all kinds of activities — church, library, neighborhood watch, book club, cooking club — you name it, she’s held a leadership role in it.”

The waitress placed their luncheon plates on the table. Clark grabbed his burger and took a bite. “Hey, this is really good.” He chewed slowly, finished his bite and said, “My dad walked the beat. Two or three times a week his best friend John Ralston would stop by and the two of them would commiserate about the corruption in the Detroit police force. I listened to all of their stories. Guess I knew all along I would be a policeman.”

He stabbed a fry and nibbled on it. “My uncle worked at the Cadillac plant up the street on Scotten Avenue, not far from where I went to high school. I worked there a couple of summers. It didn’t take long for me to realize I didn’t want to do *that* the rest of my life.”

Stuffing a couple of fries in his mouth, Clark paused. "How about your folks?"

"My mother," Abby twisted her lips into a quirky smile, "she's just the opposite of your mom — kind of stuffy, always prim and proper — always on stage." A small grin crossed her face. "Dad was a lot like your family. He worked day and night; started out as a tailor in a local Jewish men's store. It wasn't long before he was a part owner and then opened his own store. He was my beacon." Her face glowed. "At every turn in my life he was there, pushing me to do more. I was in the honor society, won the state's four-hundred-meter championship and was offered an athletic scholarship."

Clark chimed in, "That's amazing."

"I turned it down and accepted an academic scholarship to the University of Pennsylvania."

"Wow, you did a lot," Clark said, pushing his empty plate away.

"Sounds like our backgrounds were pretty similar." She stopped and remained silent, as if collecting her thoughts.

Clark stared across the restaurant, not sure of what to say.

She reached over and placed her hand on top of his. "I don't want to be overly pushy, but I'd like to see you again. Would you like to have dinner sometime? I could meet wherever."

He mulled it over. *Sounds nice. Shit, I'm no fool about her anymore. I can't trust her. She's ... oh well, what the hell.* "Sure, how about two weeks from Friday at Cliff Bells? I'll make reservations for seven, is that okay?"

"Sounds perfect."

***

Earl and Clark walked into T.J.'s for their weekly luncheon and headed for *the booth.* As usual, two bottles of Stroh's appeared out of nowhere. The two quickly placed their standing orders. Earl tossed the front page of the September 22nd edition of the *Detroit Free Press* on the table. "Whataya think about that?"

Clark glanced at the headlines: **DRUG LORD'S BODY FOUND MUTILATED!** "Yeah, I read it this morning. Well, Lonnie Williams won't be going to trial."

"You got that right." Earl chuckled. "You think his murder was part of the black gang's power struggle?"

"Hmm, I don't think so." Clark shook his head. "His body was mutilated exactly like Billy Fletcher's."

"Taking out number one and two leaves the east side gang highly venerable. A copycat killing would send a strong message."

"Could be, but …" Clark took his time connecting the dots. "The preliminary report from the coroner is too exacting. Being handcuffed to a chair facing a mirror and the gypsy fortune teller card with the phrase 'the curse can't be reversed' could be copied, but Lonnie was stabbed in the exact same locations as Fletcher was three months ago. No way would another person know that. It had to be the same person."

"Do you think it's a serial killer?"

"Either that or some kind of a cult killer, or somebody with a vendetta."

"Maybe all of 'em."

"Whatever. I don't like it."

Collecting his thoughts, Earl paused. "Mind if I change the subject?"

Clark nodded. "Your agenda."

"A few years ago I heard a lot about Chief Hart's house cleaning program, but nothing recently. Anything new happening?"

"He's playing it cool, doing everything in a low key manner so the union doesn't get all wrapped up in the firings. He's removed a hundred bad cops from the street and is on pace to achieve the mayor's composition goal of having a fifty/fifty — black and white force."

"Wouldn't that be something? When the mayor took office in '74 only 10 percent of the force was black. Any changes downtown?"

"Hah." Clark shook his head, revealing his frustration. "1300 Beaubien hasn't changed a bit. Headquarters is as corrupt as ever."

"How about the unit in charge of stolen and recovered property?"

"They're the worst." Clark laughed. "Whenever I talk to them, they give me the runaround. I've checked lockers where drugs and sizeable amounts of money should be — not a speck of dust or a red cent. If I had my druthers, I'd avoid turning *any* confiscated property over to them."

Getting to his agenda, Earl faked confusion. "How would you handle it?"

"I'd come up with something. I don't know. Maybe I'd work behind the scenes and suggest the person involved make an anonymous contribution to a non-profit group. If they'd do anything constructive, it'd be better that benefiting those bastards."

"How can you say that?" Earl inquired. "That's not legal."

"I know, but putting money in their pockets is not legal either."

"Good point." Earl sighed. "Either way, it'd be a tough decision."

"Right." Clark wiped his mouth. "How about some free advice from you?"

Earl replied with a hand flip. "Sure, the floor is yours."

Clark hemmed and hawed. "I've had a couple of lunches with Abby and am thinking maybe it might be …"

"Shit," Earl cut him off. "I could've told you that when I saw her walk down the runway."

"No Earl, it's more than her body. She's been truthful about herself for a change, laid it all out for me."

"How do you know she's been truthful this time?"

"I can tell Earl, she's sincere."

"You felt that way last year."

"Yeah, I know but …"

Earl interrupted, "Take your time. Slow down, Clark. There's no reason to rush back to her." Earl ran his hand over his shaved head. "And, most important, don't get yourself in a position where you're alone with her. You know how a woman can be."

"Are you trying to tell me something about Nicole?"

"No, although I wouldn't mind that. I'm talking about women in general. Besides your record with them — especially Abby — is not all that great."

"Don't worry. I'm not rushing into anything."

"Maybe not …" Earl said hesitantly, "but you're acting more and more like a dog in heat. You need to cool your jets."

***

J.J. blew out the two candles on his birthday cake.

J.D. jumped for joy. "I want the piece with the two flowers on it!"

Nicole gave him *the eye*. "It's J.J.'s birthday. You cut; he picks."

J.D.'s lower lip protruded.

"Stop that, right now," she directed. "*I'll* cut the cake."

J.D. came to attention.

Earl tapped him on the head and winked. "Good boy."

The boy's lips formed a bright smile.

Nicole cut the chocolate cake and the four celebrated for the first time, as a group.

Sometime after the two boys had fallen asleep, Nicole and Earl had a rare moment of peace and tranquility. Leaning back on the sofa, she released a long sigh. "What a day, huh?" Stretching her hands over her head, she asked, "Would you fix us a drink?"

"Yes, of course," Earl said, a hint of his excitement showing. He stood and headed for the kitchen. "Anything in particular?"

"Your pleasure." she purred.

That wouldn't be something to drink. Raising his eyebrows, he asked, "How about Grand Marnier?

"Perfect." She kicked off her high heels and wiggled her toes.

Returning from the kitchen, Earl glanced her way. She was sexier than ever, especially with her legs spread slightly in an unintentional way.

"Here's your drink, dear."

She sat up abruptly. "Thank you, Earl, you're a sweetie."

He clinked her glass. "Here's to the most terrific woman in the world."

She glanced at him; a broad smile parting her vibrant red lips.

Joining her at the end of the sofa, Earl tried to think of something appropriate to say. *Shit, I never missed a free throw at the end of a basketball game. But I can't come up with a simple, witty line.*

Flashing him a sensual smile, she downed the Grand Marnier and raised her glass. "I'll have another, please."

She stood and flitted down the hallway.

Earl refilled their glasses and sat them on the coffee table. Easing onto the sofa, he leaned back. *She is the most beautiful woman I've ever known. If ever I could make her my own, I'd do anything.*

Nicole appeared — like a miracle out of nowhere — dressed in a short black negligee. Showing off herself in a way she'd rarely done, moving to the beat of the soft-jazz station, she ran her hands across her breasts and down her sides, sensually caressing her body.

Taking it all in, Earl's mind reeling, his desires spiked.

Stopping directly in front him, she pivoted her hips from side to side, then gently touched his fingertips — her electricity pulling him — his desires moving him to the bedroom.

CHAPTER SIXTEEN

The women gathered at the Roman Village on the first Wednesday of October. Nicole arrived last. Owner Anthony Rugiero opened the door and extended his hand. "You must be Nicole Weatherspoon."

Taken by surprise, she took a step back. "Yes, I am."

"It's a pleasure to meet you," he said enthusiastically. "I've heard so many good things about your accomplishments, I just wanted to say hi." He handed her a bottle of wine. "This is my favorite Chianti. I hope you'll enjoy it some night on a special occasion."

"How nice, you didn't have to do that. I'll share it with my friends today."

"No need." He pointed toward their table by the mural-embellished wall. "There are two bottles on the table for lunch. This one is especially for you."

She smiled graciously. "Thank you, thank you so much." Towering a foot above him, she leaned over and kissed him on the forehead.

"I won't wash there the rest of the week," he jested.

"Get out of here," Nicole teased and pushed him gently on the chest. She turned toward their table.

Standing with their glasses raised high, Laverne had already poured the wine. "Here's to our own Detroit thorn bird."

"Here, here!" Wendy and Rosa Maria chimed in.

Overwhelmed, Nicole asked, "What's this all about?"

"You're a dynamo in the neighborhoods around your stores and …" glancing at the group, Wendy hesitated, "we were hoping you'll tell us more about the latest developments."

Nicole eased slowly onto her chair. "I haven't done anything new lately."

"Don't be coy with us." Wendy winked at the others.

Nicole shook her head, unable to fathom the point.

"C'mon, tell us about Earl," Rosa Maria volunteered.

Nicole shrugged her shoulders. "There's not much to say."

"Not much to say?" Laverne chuckled. "I bet you can say a lot. Is he good in bed? Does he have a big one? We want to know *everything*."

Taken aback, Nicole was slow to respond.

"C'mon, it's just us girls," Laverne pressed.

Nicole paused for the longest time. "Okay, but one question at a time and I'm not getting into anything personal."

"Boo!" Wendy blasted through her cupped her hands. "Well then, we might as well order."

"Yes. I'm starved," Laverne announced.

The foursome had salads, pasta and Italian bread. Between each bite, questions flew. By the time they'd finished lunch, Nicole had barely taken a bite.

Deflecting the last intimate questions, she raised her hands, palms up in front of her. "Enough, I'm finishing my lunch while you're talking about those creepy murders."

Wendy jumped in. "Renzo and I think it's part of a black gang war, maybe a power play by one of them."

"Yeah, that's what Carlos and I are thinking."

Laverne stroked her long blonde hair. "I think there's a nut out there. The killings are too much alike. It sounds like some kind of a cult. Maybe it's someone performing a ritual."

Nicole moved closer to the table. "I'm on Laverne's side. Earl doesn't think it's gang activity. Most of them don't plan ahead that much. It's someone far more calculating."

***

"You're in a little early this morning, aren't you?"

"Maybe so," Joey said excitedly.

Picking up on his tone, Blackie questioned, "Something going on?"

Joey smirked, trying to hold back as long as he could.

"C'mon, what is it?"

Unable to resist, Joey erupted, "I found the perfect woman for you."

Blackie perked up; his interests elevated for the first time in weeks. "Tell me about her."

"She's a black, has great legs and a body that won't quit."

"Can she talk?" Blackie quipped.

"She can do more than that. From the things I've heard she's smart as a whip," Joey said sincerely. "And here's the best news, she got pissed off and dumped Clark Phillips."

A broad smile revealed Blackie's perfectly white teeth. "You gotta be shittin' me."

"No, I'm not. I talked with her at the Sax Club where she dances."

"Do you have a picture of her?"

Shaking his head, Joey gloated. "I have something better than that."

"Better?"

Joey peered at his watch. "She should be walking in anytime."

Seeing a stream of light cascade from the open front door, Blackie straightened his tie and watched the hottest woman he'd ever seen strutting in; he couldn't keep from staring at her tight miniskirt, her Tina Turner legs.

"So Boss, whataya think?" Joey whispered, his eyes taking her in too.

"Holy shit," Blackie mumbled to his confident; his eyes glued on her hips, he whispered, "You sure she talks?"

Stepping into the room on elevated platform high heels, she towered over the two men. Blackie stood and extended his hand. "I'm Blackie Giardini and this is my associate Joey Naples."

She smiled at him and nodded to Joey. "Caroline Schaffer."

"Please, have a chair," Blackie said, pointing to the end of the booth.

She sat down and cast a sideways look at Blackie. "Your assistant said we might have something worth talking about. I'm listening."

Taken by her direct, aggressive nature, Blackie hesitated.

She wasted no time. "I'm not here on a lark. If this is no more than a peep-show I'm out of here."

"No, no," Blackie stammered, sounding more like a teenage boy.

"Well …" She waited through a moment of silence, then stood and turned for the door.

"Wait, wait." Blackie waved his hands frantically. "Please sit down. Could I get you a cup of coffee?"

Easing back into the chair, she said, "No, thank you."

Collecting his thoughts, Blackie took his time — but not too much. "You're an extremely attractive woman. I'd like to offer you a position in our organization."

Her lower lip took a downward turn; she asked, "A position?"

"Well, it's really not *work* … all you have to do is be my friend."

She gave him a disgusting look. "Your friend!"

"You know, a companion."

"You want me to be your mistress." Caroline threw him a disgusting look. "Screw you. I don't do that. You can get all you want on 12th Street." She bolted from the chair and stepped off the booth's platform.

"Stop. I have another opportunity."

"Another opportunity," she said sarcastically. "You think being your mistress is an opportunity?"

"No. I didn't mean it that way." Blackie pleaded. "I like your spunk. You'll be perfect for what I have in mind."

"I'm sorry, Mr. Blackie. Spunk or no spunk I'm not interested." She turned to leave.

Blackie took off his glasses and twirled them unconsciously. "I'll double your salary, whatever it is."

Getting her attention, Caroline stopped, raised her brow and turned halfway around, not realizing she was showing off her voluptuous profile. Unable to take his eyes off her, Blackie slipped on his sunglasses. "Please hear me out."

"You don't know how much I make."

"It doesn't matter. I'll pay you whatever it takes."

"Ha, I've heard that before. And what comes next?"

"Nothing, there's no next time. It isn't like that."

Glancing at him, she paused as her demeanor softened only a little; her mind still questioned his intent.

"Give me ten minutes." Blackie motioned for her to sit down. "If you don't like what I have to say you can be on your way."

She glanced at her watch and eased onto the chair. "The clock is running."

"We need a woman of your stature to help a group of women in our organization."

"Young women?"

"They're kids, caught up in the system with no one to help them."

Visions of Caroline's grandmother picking her up off the street flashed in her mind; unconsciously, she gave him more attention than she'd intended.

"We want to give them a second chance. Obviously, we don't have the expertise. I need someone like you who'll guide them — step-by-step — help them become responsible young women, and down the road be in a position to manage their own lives." He paused. "So, how about it?"

Caroline took her time, reflecting. *I had talked with Clark before the meeting, but never in my wildest thoughts had I anticipated he'd ask me to do anything other than spread my legs.* Shaking her head, she wondered about his intent. "I don't have a clue what you are talking about."

"These young women work at our places …"

"Prostitutes," she interrupted.

"Yes, we have an apartment building full of them. We have to help them learn about our culture."

Not grasping his meaning, Caroline tossed him a questioning glance. "I don't get it."

"They were okay in the past, but we're upgrading our clientele. The women must be able to hold a normal conversation with a guy and act a little classier. Otherwise, we'll lose their business."

"So your interest is not really in the welfare of the women. It's all about the money."

"Yes, we have our selfish priorities. But no, I have to admit, these are decent young women from Mexico and they deserve a second chance."

"How many are there?

"Thirty-five, maybe forty." He hesitated. "Do you speak Spanish?"

"Yes."

"Perfect. I'll triple your salary."

"Hold on." She raised her hand. "Let me get this clear. You want me to teach roughly forty prostitutes with limited English skills, how to dress, eat, act and behave properly, so they can satisfy your customers."

"Yeah, but you'll be doing something that will help them the rest of their lives. Will you do it?"

"You're crazier than hell. I'm not going to be a den mother. I decided long ago I didn't want any kids. I'm sure in hell not going to raise forty whores. You have to hire a live-in social worker and a charm-school teacher."

Blackie ran his fingers through his long silver hair. "If I provide an apartment for a social worker and give her a budget to hire an assistant, would you teach them the social graces?"

"Mr. Blackie," Caroline said, pointing her index finger at him. "No matter how much I might be inclined to do so, the answer is still 'no.' I'm a college graduate with a big-time student loan debt. I can't give up my full-time job to pursue your scheme."

Blackie flopped back against the booth. "Dancing at the Sax Club five nights a week, how much do you make?"

She hesitated. "A hundred and fifty dollars a night plus tips."

"That's seven hundred and fifty dollars, plus, plus, a week." His face looked like a calculator. "I'll pay you five hundred dollars *a day* and another five hundred for a day on the weekend. That's three thousand dollars, four times more than you're making now. You can pay off your student loan debt in no time. So, whataya say about that?"

Unknowingly, Blackie had nailed her long-time goal. She recalled being homeless as a kid, remembered how the pimps had treated her and the tricks she'd turned before she was twelve — her early life had been a nightmare. Seemingly for no reason at all, she jumped up and extended her hand. "Deal."

***

Walking into Clifford McGill's office, Clark came face to face with two new blue suits. Clifford did the honors. "Clark, I want you to meet the two men from Washington, D.C. I mentioned over the phone. They'll be heading up the FBI investigation on the murders of Lonnie Williams and Billy Fletcher."

"Does the FBI always respond in such short order?"

Clifford loosened his tie. "Not on typical homicides, but when things are strange like these murders, it's standard operating procedure."

Clark extended his hand to the man on Clifford's left. "Hi, I'm Clark Phillips, glad to meet you."

The slightly built, accountant-type man, wearing "Mr. Peeper's" style glasses gave him a partial grin. "Pat Fitzpatrick, from Montclair, New Jersey; married with three children, thirty-two years in the agency," he stated matter-of-factly.

"Clark Phillips, single, Detroit PD, fourteen years," he responded in cadence. "Guess you know which side of the street Don Angelo Bruno parks his car."

"You're right." Pat winked. "I spent seventeen years investigating the Philadelphia Mob. Tell me the street and I'll tell you where he parks."

Clark turned to the other agent, a trim, dark haired, six-footer. "I'm Dick Woodson from Valparaiso, Indiana; single, been with the agency ten years. My entire career has been in Chicago, most of the time dealing with the Chicago Outfit."

"Do you have any connection with Detroit?"

"Yes, *do* I?" he chuckled. "Whenever one of our guys call from Detroit Metro and says Anthony LaPiana, Jr. is checking in, I'm on my way to O'Hare."

"LaPiana?" Clark raised his brow, "I know the name, but that's about it."

"'Chicago Tony,' as everyone back home calls him — as loose as loose can be when he's in Chicago — a big show off and freewheeling spender. Guess he thinks no one is watching. He takes us to all kinds of unknown meeting places. I usually have an extra agent with me when he's in town just to make sure we can keep track of his moves."

Clifford motioned for the three to join him at the small round table in front of the picture window. "Anyone want a soda?"

"Yeah, I'll have one," Dick said.

Catching their nods, he pointed to the row of Coke and Sprite cans on the table. "Help yourselves."

Each one grabbed a can and popped the top. Clifford took the remaining Sprite.

"I know you've read all of the reports, but Clark and I are going to walk you through the Fletcher and Williams' cases so we're all on the same page."

"Sounds good," Dick said.

Pat nodded his agreement.

Forty-five minutes later, Clifford turned to the new agents. "Need anything else?"

Pat gave him an Irish smile. "You covered it all." He cupped his hands over his face for a moment, then placed them palms down on the table. "Is there a possibility one of the other black gangs would bring someone in to do the job?"

Tapping his fingers on the table, Clark thought aloud. "Anything is possible, but I don't think so. Our black gangs are all over the board; they don't act with much planning."

"Anyone else?" Dick asked.

Having second thoughts, Clark raised his hand. "Now that you mention it, the YBI has that kind of organizational capacity."

"Excuse me?"

"The Young Boys Inc. — they're the big kahuna of the black gangs. Lonnie Williams was a lieutenant with them. Someone might move up in the organization, but other than that there wouldn't be much in it."

"Not unless they were interested in cutting out a middleman totally and taking all of the profits," Dick suggested.

Clark nodded his agreement. "Good point."

"Who knows, it could be internal strife or someone sleeping with another guy's woman."

"Now there's a possibility," Clark said, recalling the falling out between YBI leaders Ray Peoples and Block Marshall, who'd both been involved with the same woman.

Pat raised his hand. "Who are their drug suppliers?"

"Interesting question." Clifford eased up to the table. "We busted their chain last year. We need to do some digging on their current sources."

"Do you think they're getting heroin and cocaine from the Mafia?" Pat asked.

"Not the YBI; they go direct for their drugs. Although ..." Clifford rubbed his upper lip. "The Italian Mafia controls about 80 percent of the other drug traffic. The Arab Mafia is squeezing in too. There could be something going on there."

"Have you heard anything from your informants?"

Clark shook his head. "Not a peep. The city has clammed up."

CHAPTER SEVENTEEN

Nicole pulled herself upright in bed, stuffed a pillow behind her and leaned back against the headboard. Peering at him in the dim light of a flickering candle, she ran her fingers across Earl's square shoulders, a soft smile of affection playing on her lips. Admiring his broad back, she pulled the sheets gently up to his neck. Fond memories of Alsye flitted across her thoughts. Now, Earl was the most meaningful part of her life.

Glancing up at the fan that turned lazily overhead, her mind swirled with jumbled questions — a hundred miles an hour every waking moment. *How do I increase the marketing of our stores? I need to strengthen the operation of the neighborhood watch programs. I have to redevelop the area around my stores. How will I come up with the matching funds for the renovation projects? How should we deal with loot from the robbery? We have to turn the money in. It doesn't matter how bad the cops are, they're still the police. The officers dealing with stolen property can't be that crooked.* Her mind paused. *Earl hasn't said a word since he found the money. I wonder if he's had second thoughts. Has he talked to Clark? We have to talk.*

She reached to the side, pulled the sheet down to his waist and rubbed Earl's back. He didn't move; his body drained from their extended sex. She pushed gently on his side. "Earl, can we talk?"

His muscular body lay like a sack of potatoes, without a stir.

She placed her hand on his shoulder and pushed more vigorously. Her voice rose. "Earl, we have to talk."

He rustled and turned his head. "Is it time to get up?"

"No. It's three o'clock. We need to talk."

"Can it wait till morning?"

"No." She pressed against his shoulder. "We have to talk now, it's important."

Knowing he had no other choice, he rolled over and rubbed his eyes. Taking his time, he doubled his pillow and propped himself up. "Okay, I'm ready."

"I want to talk about the money."

"The money?" he questioned.

"The money you found from the robbery."

"Got it, the eighty-two thousand tucked away in your closet."

"Are the cops in the stolen property department really that bad? Have you talked to Clark? What does he think?"

"One question at a time, Nicole." Collecting his thoughts, Earl took a deep breath.

"I think we should turn it in. How about you?"

Earl rubbed his face while he worked up a reply. "That's not easy to answer. I still have mixed feelings. I know what's proper, but…"

She interrupted. "Have you talked to Clark?"

Earl lifted his head. "He feels strongly about the cops in the stolen property department, and insists they will take the money and run."

"How could they do that?"

"These guys have been picking the public's pockets for years. They know every trick of the trade."

"Did Clark give you any ideas of how he'd deal with a situation like this?" she asked impulsively.

"He said it goes against everything he believes, but unofficially, he'd advise a person to give the money to charity. That way the person who found it would know it would do some good."

"Hmm, I don't know … that's just not right."

"That's the issue; we're stuck in the middle." He stretched his arms over his head. "Still, it's something to consider."

"Did Clark give you any other suggestions?"

"Not really." Earl stroked his shiny head. "I've been doing a little digging on my own. If you were to keep it, you might think about setting up a foundation."

"I don't know much about that. How do they work?"

"It'd be pretty much like the United Way, except in our case funds would be restricted to whatever mission you define."

Nicole gave him an inquisitive look. "A defined mission, like what?"

"Well." Earl thought for a moment. "The United Way's mission is to support other agencies. You could have a foundation with a mission to support people and projects committed to improving inner-city neighborhoods."

"Hmm, I like that," she said, her mind cranking into another gear. "Would the eighty-two thousand be enough to start one?"

"I suppose, I haven't gotten that far."

"How would we start a foundation?"

Earl gave her an encouraging grin. "You'd have to obtain legal help."

"Once we do that, how long would it take?"

"Slow down, Nicole. You're way beyond my pay grade."

"What do you know about funding a foundation?"

"Not much." He rubbed his head. "I do know you have to be careful about transferring money from one bank account to another."

"Why so?"

"The feds monitor all financial transactions of ten thousand dollars and above."

"Why do they do that?"

"It's the law. Whenever there's a bank deposit or withdrawal it automatically sends a red flag to the feds. It's a way for the government to limit money laundering." He broke into a partial grin. "You'd be surprised how many penny-ante crooks have been tripped up by the law."

"Hmm." She glanced at the fan blades, her mind twirling faster, and leaned over to kiss him on the top of his head. "You can go back to sleep. I have to write all of this down."

***

Meeting for the second time in October, Clark paced in front of the south window of the McNamara Building. Waiting for the task force members to arrive for the special meeting, he thought about the call he'd received last night from Chief Hart. The murders of Fletcher and Williams had his attention. Public pressure had mounted astronomically; the media was on his case. Trying to salvage the situation, he had convinced the FBI to form a joint team to address the situation.

Members of his team filed in, some unshaven, others obviously without taking a shower. Nancy Sterling rushed in, her hair still damp. "Sorry I'm late. I just stepped out of the shower when you called.

"No problem. We're just getting assembled." Clark closed the door and eased into the swiveled-rocker at the head of the table. "Okay," he said, getting right to the point. "At ten o'clock this morning Chief Hart and Clifford McGill will host a joint press conference to announce the formation of a special group to investigate the murders of Lonnie Williams and Billy Fletcher. Two agents from Washington D.C. will be introduced by Clifford. Chief Hart will name another Detroit police officer and our own Kimberly, to this new group."

Max jumped up. "All right. Let's hear it for Kimberly," he said, leading the group's applause.

She blushed as usual, then pointed to her number one agitator. "Thank you."

"In addition, they have asked me to head up the group," Clark said modestly.

"Don't they think you have enough to do?" Earl lamented.

"It isn't that." Clark paused, gazing down the length of the table. "They want to keep continuity in our efforts rather than have disconnected efforts underway." He turned to Earl. "Besides, I told them my assistant could pick up part of my load."

Earl frowned. "Lucky me."

Max laughed. "Hey, somebody around here has to do the work."

"So what part of your workload am I going to pick up?" Earl asked with interest.

"Routine office things to start with, and the meeting with the guys. I have a gut-level feeling the Mafia is going to ramp things up with them."

"Anyone have another question?" He glanced at each person around the table.

"What are they going to call the group?" Ralston asked.

"That hadn't been determined when the Chief called. I guess we'll find that out in a couple of hours. Anything else?"

No one said a word.

"Good. As long as were assembled, I'd like for Kimberly to give her final report on the DRC, Kimberly."

She winked at Clark. "After all of that, I guess my report won't sound very exciting, anyway here goes." She picked up a stapled copy from the stack in front of her. "I have a detailed report for each of you so I'll keep it brief."

Max piped up, "That'll be a first."

She didn't dismiss the chance. "It'd be like you missing a meal," she zinged back.

He leaned back in his chair. "Truce!"

"We've arrested ninety-two DRC staff members. Another eighteen warrants are in the works and sixty-three cases are in progress." Stopping abruptly, she shot a dagger at Max. "Is that short enough?"

He zipped his lips with his thumb and index finger.

John Ralston raised a hand. "Any chance of getting someone higher up the ladder?"

She hesitated.

Eddie kicked the table leg, taking her silence for a no. "Damn. The Mafia duped us again. They tossed us a bunch of crumbs — not one kingpin, not even a capo. They've outdone us again."

Ralston eyed him seriously. "You're right. No one at the top, but at least we've cleaned away most of the scum-bums."

"Hey, look at it this way," Clark noted, "at least people in town can go to the races and have a fair chance of winning." He nodded to Kimberly. "Thanks. Another job well done."

***

Sitting in the same chair, four hours later, Clark turned to the dark haired, burly cop to his right. "Pag, would you give us a brief summary of your background?"

"Sure." He gave Clark a slight nod. "I'm Joseph Pagnozzi, but I prefer Pag. I'm married with two kids and four grandchildren. I graduated from Detroit Denby High School. As a kid, I knew most of the guys who are now on the Mafia organizational chart. In fact, I talk with a couple of them once in a while at one of our old hangouts."

"Really." Clark shot him a surprised look. "You mean …"

Pag cut him off. "Hey, we were kids. We played ball together. We're still friends. That may sound strange, but we have a special affinity for each other. It's nothing for us to talk about the good ole' days and have a beer."

"You talked to anyone recently?" Clark asked, trying not to sound too intent.

"Interesting you ask. That was going to be my next point. I talked to Blackie Giardini last night."

"*The* Blackie Giardini?"

"Yeah, Blackie was the catcher on my Little League team. I played short."

"Did he say anything about you being appointed to our group?"

"Hell yes." Pag chuckled. "He knew about it, probably before you were asked."

"That sounds just like 1300 Beaubien." Clark collected his thoughts. "Do you talk to Blackie often?"

"Not really, maybe twice a year at our old neighborhood bar where he holds court."

Clark cocked his head to the side. "The place just off East Warren?"

"Yeah, you been there?"

"No. Some of my friends have. I heard it's pretty intimidating."

"Hey, it's to be expected. You're on his turf." Pag mused. "He has an elevated booth and he is obviously in charge."

"Guess you know him pretty well."

"Yeah." Pag's expression was oddly compassionate. "Growing up, he was like a brother, and then we went our separate ways. We don't talk much about work."

"Each of you knowing you're on the other side of the fence, is it a difficult situation for you?

"Nah." Pag's eyes brightened. "But last night was different. He let me know right from the get-go the Mafia was equally concerned about the killings."

"Really?"

"Yes. He usually says nothing or is very low key with his work-related comments, but this time he kept coming back to the same point, over and over again."

"What did you glean from all of that?"

"When the guys above him are concerned, Blackie is worried." Pag took his time. "I'm confident the Mafia was not involved in the killings. Secondly, they have an inkling someone in the mob could be hit next."

Befuddled by Pag's observations, Clark asked. "Did he say that?"

"No, but his tone made it clear. The Mafia higher-ups don't know what to expect."

"You mean the FBI and mob are actually on the same page?"

Pag grinned and shook his head. "Crazy as it may seem, I think so."

"Huh, let's finish up the introductions and take a ten-minute break."

***

Reassembling around the conference table, Clark clicked off the heads — Kimberly and Pag to the right; the two FBI agents, Fitzpatrick and Woodson, to the left.

Clark opened his notebook. "I'd like to hear everyone's initial thoughts."

Dick Woodson raised his hand. "I'd like to hear more about the YBI and the other black gangs in town."

"I agree," Fitzpatrick said. "Internal gang warfare is the first priority for me too."

"Okay." Clark jotted a note. "I'll have Will Robinson from our Special Crimes Task Force come to our next meeting. He'll give us a short course on the black gangs in Detroit."

"I like that," Woodson said. Fitzpatrick agreed.

"Pag, what do you think?"

The veteran officer raised his dark, bushy eyebrows. "I'm interested in the drug-business angle. That's big money with lots of people controlling the flow of heroin and cocaine. In Philly there's a real drug battle going on between the Arab Mafia and the Italian Mafia."

"You can throw in the Chaldean Mafia," Woodson said. "They've developed a network to move drugs from Phoenix and San Diego to the Midwest. They have a very violent track record in Chicago — body dismemberment and beheadings are nothing for them — they could be here, too."

"While limited to Greektown, you can't eliminate the Greek Mafia, either" Pag said, taking a short breath. "And don't forget the Black Mafia. They're another force not to be recanted."

"Kimberly, what's your take on the murders?" Clark asked.

"Hmm, I'm not sure." She wrinkled her nose. "I'm still thinking it's some kind of a cult. Everything is so precise. It's like the person has done this a hundred times."

"Maybe it's a copycat," someone said.

"I thought about that, but someone would have to study all of the details and execute them to that level. Hmm, I don't think so."

"Why would someone do it now and why those two?" Woodson asked.

"Their names and pictures have been plastered all over. Maybe it's a warning." Kimberly pushed her blonde hair aside, adding, "It's been a media circus around here."

"She's right about that," Pag said.

"Maybe someone wanted to do us a public service," Kimberly said, tongue in cheek.

Woodson gave her a little laugh. "Public service, getting even, that's an interesting thought."

CHAPTER EIGHTEEN

Clark took his time slicing the last piece of his New York strip, slid it around in the juice on his plate, and took a bite. Savoring the flavor, he chewed slowly, his senses reveling in the romantic ambience of Cliff Bells. He couldn't recall ever feeling so relaxed.

Placing her hand on top of his, Abby squeezed gently. "Was your steak as tender as the one I had last week?"

Scanning her lovely face, his eyes drifted to her low-cut sweater. His heart twitterpated.

"The steak was excellent," he said, recalling the one she'd prepared, followed by all night lovemaking. "Not as good as the one you prepared that night, " his words trailed off. *Goddamn, why did I say that?*

"Thank you," she purred. "You're so sweet." She caressed his hand, running her index finger slowly up, down, and around his fingers. "I remember that night too."

Glancing at her soft smile, he thought: *She looks as good as she did that night. I can't recall how many times we did it; we replayed every game in the 1968 World Series between the Tigers and the St. Louis Cardinals. She knew every play from Bob Gibson's record setting seventeen strikeouts in the first game, to the fly ball Curt Flood misjudged in game seven, giving the Tigers a series win.*

She squeezed his hand. "You okay?"

Clark's brain rushed back to reality. "Would you like an after dinner drink?" he said without thinking.

She took her time responding, searching his eyes for a clue to his thoughts. "I was thinking we might have an aperitif at my place."

"I-I-I."

She pressed her index finger softly onto his lips. "You don't have to. It was just something I've been thinking about."

Thinking about? Christ, that's all *I've been thinking about.* His mind flipped back to Earl's warning, "Don't be alone with her again."

Gazing at the lush, dark wood backbar for the longest time, Clark's eyes were unreadable. *Earl was right. One slip at her place and I'd be a goner.* He glanced back at her beaming face. *Hell, why not, nothing has to happen. I can handle the situation.*

"If you don't want to that's okay," she said again, more sensually than before. "I just thought maybe a relaxing drink might be a nice way to cap off a wonderful evening. You could follow me to my place. It isn't far."

Clark's heart raced; he swallowed hard. "Okay, one drink."

***

Driving slowly across town the next morning, Clark retraced their night at her place. It had started out like she said — "One drink."

She'd placed a tray of cordials on the coffee table. *We sat on the sofa sipping and talking about nothing — it didn't matter — I was used to drinking Tanqueray straight up. The amount of booze in those little glasses has never had an effect. I felt relaxed; I was in control. We talked about the good times — going to Tiger games, the theatre, and dining out — she talked through the weekend on Mackinaw Island and explained how that magical trip had changed her life, falling in love with me. I felt like we'd never been apart.*

Glancing around at a four-way intersection, he tried to determine where he was. A honk from the car behind started him rolling through the green light; his brain shifted back to her.

A few blocks later, Clark slammed on his brakes at a red light as an eighteen-wheeler flew by, rocking his car; his life passed before him. Hearing a honk from behind, Clark glanced up at the green light and waved to the rear-view mirror. By the time he turned onto the Southfield Parkway, his mind was back in bed with her.

Turning into his parking space, he wondered — *it's wonderful when I'm with her — everything seems so right. Hell, I thought that before and look where I ended up.*

***

Arriving early for November poker, Renzo, Carlos and Ted plopped down at the booth in the far corner of the Sax Club. Ted ordered two pitchers of beer. The guys talked about the upcoming Thanksgiving Day game between the Chicago Bears and the Lions.

Walking in shortly after, Clark and Earl picked up on Renzo's "hi" sign and headed their way. The murders of Fletcher and Williams were back on the everyone's mind. Before the two could pick up their beers, the three guys fired questions in rapid succession: "Do you think Fletcher and Williams were victims of a black gang war? This is weird; do you think there is some kind of a nut loose in town? Is the Mafia involved?"

"Hold on." Clark raised his hands to halt their jumbled words. "We don't know much more than you guys, so let's take your questions one at a time."

Ted popped off first and the other guys followed suit. Clark repeated the facts reported in the paper. Earl expanded on a point or two without divulging anything new.

"C'mon, we've had enough. Give us the *real* scoop," Ted complained.

Trying to calm the group, Clark took his time, speaking in precise terms. "This is a strange case. The stories in the paper reveal everything we know. The feds are in town. We're all trying to figure out what is going on."

Following a moment of brooding, Carlos changed the subject. "It sounds like double duty for you, Clark. Isn't there anyone else who can do the job?"

"I know it looks that way," he admitted. "But, Chief Hart wanted to maintain continuity. He feels there is a possible connection. I'll be working with the feds on both fronts. Earl will be picking up part of my load. I'm assigning him the task of working with you guys."

"That'll be a relief," Renzo cracked. "So we won't see you as much."

"Yeah," Ted agreed. "Sounds great to me."

Clark raised both hands at their mocking. "Okay, okay, I can tell you're going to miss me."

"Miss who?" Renzo laughed.

"Right. I got it." After a quick, amused glance at him, Clark said, "Enough of the bullshit, I'd like to hear about the incidents each of you called me about, so Earl can get up to speed. Renzo, want to start?"

He filled the empty glasses; his hand shaking slightly, rushing his words. "I was scared shitless. There were three thugs pushing me around in my office. I didn't know *what* they were going to do."

"Slow down," Earl advised. "Take a drink."

Renzo grabbed his glass and took a slug. "The next day a couple of thugs were at my job sites; they kicked in drywall, ripped out electrical wiring, and broke a couple of toilets. My foreman tried to reason with them. A goon jumped him from behind and another guy gave him a couple of uppercuts. They told him 'he was moving too slow' and wanted him to complete a second blind pig this month. Shit, if I did that, I wouldn't be able to complete any other jobs."

"I hate to hear that, but it's a good lesson for all of us," Clark said in a calm voice. "When the goons come around you have to play it cool; these guys only know one way to solve a problem." He gave Renzo a compassionate look and turned to Carlos. "Tell us about your experience."

Carlos wiped the moisture from his upper lip and spoke rapidly, his voice quavering, "In addition to increasing the number of cars I mentioned before, they've walked me through the procedure I had to follow in the money-laundering scheme. I can't handle that, Clark. I could go to prison."

"Relax Carlos you're not going to jail. Just tell us their plan."

Trying to describe the event, Carlos stammered, repeated, and jumped around. Clark listened patiently.

"That's it?" Clark questioned.

"That's it? I was lucky. Damn, they could have busted up my place. Money laundering, I could go to jail."

"Let's slow down." Clark raised his hands for emphasis. "That's the same thing they did to another auto dealer a few years ago. Everything will be documented; you're protected. You're *not* going to jail."

Carlos grimaced. "These guys are scary."

Clark glanced at Ted, noticing the dark rings circling his eyes. "You seem to be very tired, are you okay?"

"I had a bunch of guys over last night. We played cards till daybreak."

"I hope you won a few bucks."

Ted laughed. "I did better than that. I won enough to pay a month's payment for one of my buildings."

"Good for you." Clark shifted back to the main point. "How'd your Mafia visit go, Ted?"

"I had a couple of guys stop by, too." He tossed back his long black hair. "I got into a shoving-match. One of their goons took a swing at me."

Concerned, Clark said, "Did he hit you?"

"Nah, I stepped back. His buddy pulled him away."

"Anything else?"

"Yeah." Ted wrinkled his nose. "After that, two of my tenants were harassed. From their descriptions, it sounded like the same two goons."

Clark eased closer to the table, feeling like a counselor, adviser and mediator. "Guys, based on our experiences during the Kingston case, this is only the beginning. More than ever you have to play their game, be patient, and for God's sake, don't lose your cool." Clark glared across the table. "Ted, no more shoving some punk just because you're pissed off. You have to play along for the time being, okay?"

"Yeah, I got it," he said begrudgingly.

***

Caroline stretched back in the old, rickety, straight back chair and looked around the makeshift office. *I can't believe I agreed to do this. Had it not been for Clark I would have never played along with Blackie. This office is the pits — a desk, chair, and a straight back chair across from me — nothing on the walls. And these poor young women, I can't believe the way they're treated. They work six nights a week and have no time for a life of their own. Oh well, one more to interview and I'll be ready to develop a plan to help them become young ladies.*

The office door opened.

Snapping back to her job, Caroline glanced at the glowing face in the doorway. Unable to ignore her distinctive smile, Caroline smiled back and motioned for the petite Mexican-American to come in. The young woman stepped forward and stood erect; her perfect posture overwhelmed only by her look of excitement.

Caroline spoke in Spanish, "Tu hablas ingles?" (You speak English?)

"Yes. I practice every day," the young girl said in perfect English. "It's a custom I must learn — 'when in America do as Americans do.'"

"Very good." A grin parted Caroline's full lips. "Tell me about yourself — your name and where are you from."

She nodded. "My name is Consuelo Morales."

"Your English is very good. Do you know the meaning of Consuelo?"

"Yes." She raised her head proudly. "One who brings consolation."

Caroline inspected her lovely face one more time. "Your eyes are beautiful. Where are you from?"

"Thank you." Consuelo blushed. "La Gloria, Mexico. It's a small town off Road 85 between Guadalupe and Laredo, Texas. Do you know where that is?"

"Yes. You're the fourth woman from there. I looked it up on the atlas. Are there other women in Detroit from La Gloria?

The woman nodded in agreement and zipped her lip with her thumb and forefinger.

Giving her a befuddled stare, Caroline frowned. "What does that mean?"

She whispered as if someone might hear. "There is one other. We're not allowed to talk about her."

"It is okay to talk to me. It's part of my job. I'm here to help you become a better person."

The eighteen-year-old gave her a mystified expression.

Caroline hoped her reassuring smile helped. "Please sit down and tell me your friend's name and where she lives."

Consuelo spoke softly. "Her name is Feliciana Rivera. I don't know where she lives; she is a student at Macomb Community College. She receives special treatment."

"Special treatment?"

"She has her own apartment and a part-time job. She doesn't have to do the things we do; do you understand?"

"Yes. Why does she get special privileges?"

"I don't know. We all came here on the same bus. After a week or so, *the man* took her away. I've not seen her in almost two years."

"*The man* ... is he the one who stops by regularly?"

"Yes, the one with long, curly hair. He picks out the woman he wants for the day."

Caroline bristled, her mouth curled with distaste. "He has sex with them?"

"Yes, all the time."

"Have you had sex with him?"

"Yes." She hung her head. "He makes me do strange things."

"Are there other men who come by?"

"No. He's the only one."

***

Caroline flung open the door to the neighborhood bar and stormed toward Blackie and Joey. Bolting onto the platform, she threw down a bundle of keys, and shouted, "I quit!"

Shocked by her appearance and angry tone, Blackie hesitated and said calmly, "Hold on, sit down and relax. Joey will pour you a beer."

"I don't want a goddamn beer," she said, easing reluctantly onto the chair at the end of the booth. "I want my final check. I'm out of here."

"Your final check?" Blackie said. "Slow down, I don't have a clue what you're …"

She cut him off, "I'll tell you what's going on. Your head of prostitution stops by every day and screws whichever girl he wants. That's bullshit!"

"My head of prostitution …"

She interrupted, "You know who I mean; the Mafia's higher-up guy of prostitution."

"Patrick Gatt?"

"Yes, Patrick 'Pat the Pimp' Gatt as he likes to be called. How can I teach my women how to have a speck of decency when your asshole flunky comes strutting in, flaunting his gold chain on his disgusting hairy chest, and taking the one he wants for the afternoon?"

"Wait now, I don't know anything about this. There must be a way we can work this out."

"You can work it out by getting his ass out of my building." She jumped up, grabbed the keys and headed out. Grabbing the door knob, she hollered over her shoulder, "You have two days."

***

"I understand you're asking for me," a calm voice said.

Caroline peered up from her desk and took a double take at the dude, his hair curled around his head. Her mouth twisted into a sneer. "Yes, Mr. Patrick Gatt, I am."

He pulled the straight back chair in front of the desk.

"Don't sit down. You won't be staying that long."

"Wait a minute," the cocky guy said. "Who do you think you are?"

"I'm Caroline Schaffer and I'm in charge of this building and the women who live here."

"They're prostitutes; they work for me."

"Maybe so, but just because you're the head of prostitution doesn't give you the right to screw anyone, anytime you want. These women are *not* your private stock. I have full responsibility for everyone in this building and I want you to leave right now. Do you understand?"

He stepped forward and slammed his hand on the desk. "I understand no goddamn black stripper is going to tell me what to do."

Caroline rose, a storm brewing on her lovely face. She rushed around the desk coming face to face with the SOB. "*This* goddamn black stripper is telling you to get your ass off of these premises. If you don't, I'll call the police and have you arrested for trespassing." She took a short breath and picked up the phone. "And if I hear about you being in this building again, I'll have you arrested for trespassing *and* solicitation. Do you understand that?"

Gatt sneered at her for the longest moment, took a couple of steps backward, then turned and headed toward the door. He stopped.

"Don't turn around," she snapped. "Get your ass out of here or I'm dialing the police!"

CHAPTER NINETEEN

Caroline drove her blue '79 Pontiac Firebird east on Twelve Mile Road, turned south on Hayes and pulled into the icy parking lot. Following campus directions, she walked carefully on the snow-packed sidewalk past the entrance to Macomb Community College and headed for the snack bar.

She spotted a table for four near the window, picked up a large coffee, and draped her winter coat over a chair at the table. Taking a sip, she gazed abstractedly at the naked trees and frozen grass. She watched a tall woman walk gingerly across the icy quad, struggling like a newborn fawn to remain upright.

Stepping into the snack bar, the woman purchased a hot chocolate and hurried past the half-full tables. "I assume you're Caroline Schaffer," she said to Caroline's nod. "Sorry I'm late." She placed her paper cup on the table, then twisted and squirmed, trying to free herself from her heavy parka. "I'm not used to this winter weather."

Caroline stood and helped pull her arms out of the sleeves. "I've lived here all my life and I still struggle on days like this," she said. "Good morning, yes, I'm Caroline."

Rubbing her hands together, the Mexican woman said, "My hands are freezing, I hope you don't mind," she grasped Caroline's hand. "I'm glad to meet you. I'm Feliciana Rivera."

She's not like I thought she'd be at all — quite slender and taller than I had expected — her black waist-length hair is attractive in a single braid. Caroline gave her a welcoming smile. "Thanks for meeting with me."

"It's my privilege." Feliciana's face brightened. "I haven't talked with anyone who knew my classmates from La Gloria. How are they?"

"They're fine," Caroline fibbed. "And working hard."

"Do you know when they'll be going home?"

A strange question, Caroline thought, trying to sort out a possible meaning. "I've not talked to them about that. Do you have plans?"

"Yes," she bubbled like a kid opening Christmas presents. "After I complete my associate degree this spring, I'll fly to Laredo. Father Gonzalez from the Catholic Church in La Gloria will pick me up and take me to my parent's home. I will be there all summer. I'm so excited. The priest has made arrangements for me to speak with several girls and their parents about coming to the U.S."

Caroline's mind scrambled, trying to clarify her comments. "I'm not clear about the arrangements you're talking about."

"It's a fantastic opportunity. I'm so excited to tell others about my experiences so they will want to come. Next year I will go to Wayne State University to finish my degree. I'll be the first one in my family to do that, and all because of the Catholic Church. I would have never been able to obtain a college degree had it not been for Father Gonzalez. He's such a wonderful man."

Not wanting her questions to sound overly probing, Caroline shifted her questions. "How did you learn about the program?"

Feliciana blushed. "I'm so sorry, I didn't answer your earlier question. I'm so excited about the program." She paused, collecting her thoughts. "About three years ago, there was a notice in the church bulletin. It sounded too good to be true, but lots of my girlfriends and our parents went to the meeting. Father Gonzalez explained that several churches in Mexico had formed a partnership with the Catholic Archdiocese of Detroit."

"You're positive it was the Catholic Archdiocese of Detroit?"

"Oh yes. It was printed on top of the application form."

"How you were selected?"

"There were many of us, maybe fifteen. Father Gonzalez talked to our parents, and we went through interviews and had a fun time."

Caroline's legal mind grabbed *the phrase*. "Fun time?"

Feliciana looked down. A shy, embarrassed expression shrouded her face. "It was like a style show; we paraded around in fancy dresses."

"Why did you do that?'

"Father said it was important for us to walk and act proper in America. He didn't want people to laugh at us."

"Did you have to do anything else?"

176

Feliciana pursed her lips. "You won't tell my parents or anyone, will you?"

"No, of course not," Caroline stretched the truth. "I'm only trying to understand the procedure."

"Well, we didn't have to perform or do anything like that. He just asked us to show off a little, you know, like we were teasing a boyfriend."

"What did you do?"

"As you can see, I don't have much up top, so pulled my skirt up my leg, you know, kind of in a sexy way."

"And the other girls?"

Feliciana's eyes brightened. "Some of them leaned seductively forward, showing off their cleavage, others pulled their tops to the side, revealing a portion of their breasts. Everyone laughed. We had lots of fun."

Caroline pursued like a terrier. "You mentioned earlier some arrangements had been made for you for the summer. Would you tell me about them?"

"Yes, part of my responsibility is to go back and talk to girls in a nearby town about the program, so maybe they will come to Detroit. That's the best part, standing in front of them, holding up my associate degree, and telling them about the wonderful opportunity of studying in the U.S."

Caroline sat in disbelief, realizing she had stumbled onto a Catholic Church/Mafia international prostitution scheme. "Has the church helped you in other ways?"

"Yes. They found me a part-time job at the bowling alley across the street from my apartment. The church pays my rent."

"What else can you tell me?"

"Things are working out really well. I have money in the bank and have met a nice young man. It couldn't be better."

"Good for you. Is there a person from the church here who helps you?"

"Yes. He calls me every couple of weeks to make sure I'm doing all right."

"Do you know his name?"

"James."

"James," Caroline repeated. "Do you know his last name?"

"No. When there is an emergency or I need to talk to him I go down to the apartment manager and he calls him."

"That must make you feel good, knowing someone is looking out for you."

"It does. When I moved up here I wouldn't have been able to make it without him."

Giving Feliciana a polite smile, Caroline's mind worked overtime. "I think it'd be best not to tell him about our visit. There's no need to get anyone in trouble."

"Yes. I understand."

***

Nicole raised a glass of wine to the somber faces of the other three women. "C'mon, we'll be able to work our way through all of this. I'm sure of it."

"I hope so." Wendy managed a tight grin. "I'm afraid something will happen to Carlos. I can't imagine going through the things you did when they killed Alsye."

Nicole bit her bottom lip, not wanting to reveal her true feelings. She raised her glass even higher, forcing the others to follow suit. "Here's to the future. The best is yet to come."

"I'll drink to that," Lavern stated.

Rosa Maria gazed at Nicole. "How do you stay so positive?"

Nicole acted cool and collected. "That's the kind of behavior we all have to demonstrate. We have to be strong. That's the best thing we can do for our men."

Laverne nodded with an odd little smile. "Good point. I never thought about it that way. Ted is going through hell. I have to lend a helping hand."

"Right." Nicole's voice remained perfectly calm. "Together, we'll all be stronger."

"Yes, I agree," Wendy said. "Let's talk about the Christmas Party, it's only three weeks away."

"I can't believe the year is almost gone." Laverne took a long sip of her Chianti. "I think we should do the same thing we did last year, here at the Roman Village."

"Yes." Rosa Maria stated; her voice stronger than before. "The food was great and everyone enjoyed listening to the four old guys play traditional Italian songs."

"Renzo had a ball." Wendy gave her a thumbs up. "He talked about it for weeks."

"Done, I'll take care of it," Nicole said. "I assume we should invite Father Dom."

"Yes, he's a real hoot after he's had a couple of drinks."

"How about Sharon?" Wendy asked. "I assume she'll be home for the holidays."

"Hmm, I'm not positive. I'll ask Earl to check with Clark."

***

T.J.'s was packed Friday night when Clark walked in with Abby. The receptionist admired Abby's perfect shape, winked at Clark, and led them to *the booth.*

Abby hesitated, her mind trying to take in the eclectic décor. She slid in on Clark's side of the booth. "Have you been coming here for a long time?"

He acted as if he knew her question was coming. "Most of my life I'd expect."

"Every time I come in, I see something new," Abby said. "Has the same basic décor always been here?"

"Just about. They've added a few items here and there, but essentially it's the same."

"I love it. There's nothing like this in Philly."

Clark ordered a pitcher of beer and leaned back. *I can't wait to see Earl's and Nicole's expressions when they see Abby. I hope Nicole likes her.*

The waitress sat a pitcher and four glasses on the table.

"Thanks." Clark poured two half-full and picked up his. "Here's to a fun evening with my best friends."

Abby clinked his glass. "You talked about Nicole and Earl so much I can hardly wait to meet them."

"They're a great pair. Both of them went through horrible experiences the first time around. I hope the best is yet to come for them."

Abby gave him a compassionate look. "It has to be hard for the two of them … forgetting is difficult for all of us." Abby paused. "If we don't, we'll never see the future."

Clark nodded to himself. *She may be more prophetic than she realizes. Remembering the good times is easy — the walks in the park,*

"Hey Clark." Earl waved from the front door and guided Nicole toward *the booth.*

Clark squeezed Abby's thigh. "Here they come."

"My gosh, she's beautiful," Abby whispered.

Standing in front of the booth like a proud peacock, Earl introduced Nicole to Abby.

The two women eyed each other, both relishing in the beauty of the other. Nicole reached her hand across the table. "I've heard so much about you. I'm pleased to meet you."

Abby's eye's sparkled. They clasped hands in greeting. "The pleasure is mine. As Clark says, 'you're the first and foremost thorn bird of Detroit.' It's an honor."

Nicole waved a hand nonchalantly. "I'm only doing things that have to be done." She laughed. "After all, someone has to do it."

"You're right about that." Abby's friendly smile widened. "We're going to hit it off just fine."

"I think so too."

The four ordered appetizers, exclaiming over the sumptuous menu.

A slight, amiable man approached, easing into the booth next to Earl. Jimmy Fender called to the waitress, "A round for the table."

"Abby, I'd like you to meet the best piano player in the world," Clark said.

The quiet, shy, nerdy-looking guy snuck a peek at her.

"I'm serious, Jimmy. How many national tours have you turned down?"

His wiry hair flew side to side.

"C'mon Jimmy, how many?" Clark pressed.

He held up three fingers. "But Clark, you know that's not important. I'd rather be having a beer with my best friends."

"You're my kind of guy." Abby winked at him. "Clark tells me you can play most anything; do you have a favorite song and artist?"

"That's hard to say."

She flashed her sexy smile that would wilt any man. "C'mon, is it Jimmy Rogers, Stevie Wonder, or maybe Smokey Robinson?"

180

Staring at her, Jimmy opened up hesitantly. "Actually, it's Beethoven; and I love 'Werewolves of London' by Warren Zevon."

"Wow, that's quite a range."

He broke into a partial grin. "Guess, you're right. I enjoy playing most anything. I grew up with many of the Motown stars playing in local jazz and rhythm and blues places."

Nicole's interest peaked. "How did you ever create such an interest in the piano?

Surprised by her interest, Jimmy managed a smile. "When I was young things were really good in Detroit. Guys were making big money in the plants. Families were buying new cars, refrigerators, televisions, stereos — everything. Motown was hot. It was an unbelievable time."

Earl chimed in, "Yeah, Motown's 'Hitsville's' office located on 2648 West Grand Boulevard. They were cranking out top tunes like crazy — the Supremes, The Four Tops, Diana Ross, the Jackson 5, Marvin Gaye, and Stevie Wonder — over a hundred top ten records in no time."

Jimmy smiled at Earl and jumped back in, "Dad bought mother a piano. She loved it. I sat by her side every day. Pretty soon we're playing duets. Next thing I know I'm running home from school to play along with the radio, then I made a record and was on the radio station. My career exploded."

Abby gave him a curious look. "You mentioned earlier you didn't want to go on tour. Why not?"

His grin grew into a pleasant smile. "I'm a Detroit kid. I love it here and I love playing the joints 'round town' — performing for *real people*. Life on tour is not for me — traveling most of the week, getting laid, hitting the bottle, using drugs — that's not for me. I'm a regular guy who loves to play the piano."

The manager tapped him on the shoulder. "It's almost time, Jimmy."

He glanced at Abby and Nicole. "Nice chatting with the two of you. We'll have to do it again." He rose and turned to the piano.

Earl glanced at Clark. "Who was that masked man?"

"Darned if I know," Clark said. "I've never heard him talk that much in a week."

"The two of you have been putting us on. He isn't a shy guy." Nicole said, giving Earl a puzzled look.

"He was totally different tonight."

"Yes," Abby said firmly. "He's a super guy."

Clark shook his head and turned to Nicole. "Anything new with you?"

"As a matter of fact, there is."

Clark and Abby glanced at each other, not sure what to expect.

"I'm forming a foundation and going to call it the Thorn Bird Way. I'm raising money to support people and organizations trying to improve their local neighborhoods."

"That's a wonderful idea." Abby put her hands together in silent applause. "How did you come up with that kind of concept?"

"Earl and I were talking one night …"

Earl tossed in his two cents' worth. "Nicole was talking; I was trying to sleep."

Abby and Clark laughed; he poked her in the side. "I can see it now."

Nicole gave him *the eye,* mockingly. "Actually, Earl had the idea. I simply filled in the blanks. Our leaders can bring back downtown, but it's the people who have to clean up the neighborhoods."

"You're right about that." Clark gave her a thumbs up. "Good for you."

Sounding like she had practiced the line, Nicole stated, "Detroit can't come back until the people bring it back."

CHAPTER TWENTY

THE DETROIT NEWS
December 22, 1980

EAST SIDE BAR OWNER
FOUND DEAD
— BODY MUTILATED —

The mutilated body of Sam Narduzzi, owner of "The Last Stop" on East Warren, was found early this morning after his wife reported he had not arrived home at his normal time. The lock of the door to his back room had been tampered with. Informants indicate Narduzzi often hosted mob-associated, gambling sessions well into the early morning.

Officials indicated the crime scene was identical to the June 22 and September 22 murders of Young Boys Inc. members, Lonnie Williams and Billy Fletcher. A card with a gypsy fortune teller was found on Narduzzi's lap; on the back a typed phrase read: "The curse can't be reversed!"

As with the previous murders, Narduzzi was handcuffed to a chair facing a full-length mirror and stabbed numerous times, suffering several punctures and slices in non-life threatening areas, before the final blow.

"This changes the whole game," Woodson, the clean cut agent from Valparaiso, said.

"You're telling me." Pag yawned. "I had a call from Blackie at six o'clock this morning."

"Giardini?" Woodson asked.

"Yeah, he said to tell Clark at your meeting this morning that 'the Mafia will do anything' they can to help find the killer."

Still rubbing the sand from his eyes, Clark's brain suddenly came alive. "How'd he know we were having a seven thirty meeting?"

Finding humor in Clark's question, Pag grinned. "He didn't. He's sneaky that way, baiting me to respond."

"Fitzpatrick, what's your take on this?" Clark asked the expert on the Philly mob.

"The way Pag described his relationship with Blackie I think the Mafia is as nervous as hell. The likelihood of Blackie setting up a smokescreen is out of the question. That takes us back to the black gangs and the other drug cartels."

Kimberly sat her cup on the table and eased into her chair. "Don't forget the cult or weirdo angle."

"Okay …" Fitzpatrick said, as if believing that was a remote possibility. Her look gave him pause. "I suppose it could be a combination of any of these options."

Kimberly's smile widened. "Someone in cahoots with a cult, maybe a cult is out to do their own thing."

Woodson frowned. "What does that mean?"

Kimberly scrunched her face in thought. "I don't know; I was thinking out loud."

"Hmm, interesting."

Clark waited, letting the silence lengthen as they each contemplated the probabilities. "Other than the possibility of Narduzzi selling drugs, do you see any connection between the murders?"

"Nothing pops up." Fitzpatrick shook his head. "Two black gang members, a mob associate operating a newly renovated blind pig. Shit, I don't see any connection." He paused, trying to come up with an alternative. "Just because we don't see a connection today doesn't mean there isn't one."

"Good point." Pag tossed out an inquisitive look. "Where to now?"

Clark put on his team leader hat. "The first order of business is to have Will in again so we know what he's hearing on the streets about the black gangs."

"Yes, we have to do that …" Kimberly paused, rubbing her temple. "I'm troubled, too, by the repetitive nature of twenty-two — June 22, September 22, and December 22 — all exactly three months apart. It can't be coincidence. I'm locking my doors on March 22."

"You're overreacting," Pag jabbed.

"Truce," Clark proclaimed.

"Hey, wait a minute," Woodson said. "There may be something to the twenty-second. Maybe it's the person's birthday."

Pag downed the rest of his coffee. "Could be someone's favorite number."

Kimberly gave the guys a curious look. "Anyone know anything about numerology?"

Her glance caught blank stares around the table. "I'm taking a lesson on it," she offered.

***

Later that same morning Mafia leaders huddled around the long walnut table in Jake Nicolette's home. "I don't like this one bit," he said.

The Consigliere rubbed the furry fringe around his bald head. "Anyone know if Narduzzi was dealing drugs through the YBI?"

Newly appointed Street Boss Giardini's brow creased as he spoke, "We've told the guys a hundred times not to deal with them." He slowed. "Anything is possible, but Sam … he'd be the last one to do that."

"I heard Sam was a hothead," Angelo said. "Maybe he got sideways with someone."

"Could be. Hell, it could be the beer man, the kid who delivers pizza, or a prostitute. Who the hell knows," Blackie said, the crease in his brow deepening in frustration. They all muttered in agreement.

"Hold on guys." Jake raised his hand, motioning for calm. "This is a strange case; and a mutilation just like the others. Not something done by your average whacko."

"Jake is right." Consigliere Minelli took his time weighing the issue. "This is not a spontaneous fit of rage. It was a planned hit to send a message."

"A message?" Angelo gave him a bewildered look. "To whom?"

The wise old man unconsciously stroked his fuzzy fringe. "That's why it's so troubling," the Consigliere said. "It could be any one of us, or all of us."

Angelo scowled and said worriedly, "Any or all, what the hell does that mean?"

"It means it could be an outsider who has a bone to pick with any one of us; or just has a grudge against all of us."

"Like a cop."

"Could be." The Consigliere nodded. "Any and all of the above — black gangs, the mob or anyone associated with one of them — who knows?"

"Why do you say that?" Jake asked.

"Who else would send the same message to black gangs and us?"

"Good point." Jake nodded his agreement.

"Without any real clues, it sounds like we're back to square one," Angelo said. "It could be a banker, beer man or barber … a nut." He finished with a half-hearted smile.

Jake cast him a disconcerting eye. "Angelo, this is not something to joke about. If it is a nut, any one of us could be on the list."

"Who has the balls to do something like that?"

"Enough, Angelo," the Consigliere said. "You're sounding as paranoid as Jimmy Hoffa. We have to explore all of the options, regardless of how illogical or remote they may seem."

Angelo sighed. "I guess you are right; but who'd have something to gain by knocking off these guys?"

Jake raised his hand. "Blackie, when you talked to Pag this morning, did he give you any insights?"

Blackie shook his head "He played it straight up; he didn't even acknowledge there was a meeting this morning."

***

Clark cracked open the sliding door. "Dad, why are you out here? It's freezing."

"Figured I'd have one more Corona this year."

"Snuff that damn thing out. I'll meet you in the den."

It was no more than an eight-by-eight-foot space tucked under the stairs to the second floor. Reaching the archway, he laughed to himself. *The room hasn't changed since I was a kid — an old TV wedged under the stairs, a side-chair and his dad's favorite blackened-arm leather chair.*

Clark waited on a chair in the small cubicle.

Lewis appeared moments later, easing into his old leather chair.

"Guess we made it through another year," Clark said.

"And a good one it was for you."

Clark grinned. "Another one like this and we'll put a real dent in mob activity."

"That's better than the city is doing." Lewis picked up a newspaper. "Did you read that recent article on the city's population decline?"

"Yeah, the last decade was down 23 percent. A year or so after the riots, I figured things would level off. Shit, there's been no change in the downward slope."

"Worse yet, the article says the amount of federal aid will be cut because of the decline. That doesn't make sense to me. It seems like we should be receiving more if we need more."

"Hey, don't talk to me about federal formulas, I can't make sense of any of them."

"Talk about making sense … you talked to your mother about that woman you're seeing?"

"Ah no, why?"

"She's got a burr under her saddle about something. You better tell her what's going on."

***

Riding in the elevator, Clark watched the floors flash by. He wondered why Sharon had invited him to her place in the afternoon of the Christmas party. *I've never heard her like that before. She was so excited, like the party had already started. I have to tell her I've met someone else. Shit, I don't want to hurt her.*

The elevator door opened and he strolled down the hallway. Pulling out the key to her apartment, he heard loud music. *Sounds like she's on a real high.* He glimpsed at his watch, two o'clock. *What does she want to talk about?*

Clark opened the door. Marvin Gaye's "I Heard It through the Grapevine" blasted. *Shit, I bet she knows about Abby.*

"Sharon," he called.

"I'm in the kitchen … c'mon in."

Tossing his jacket on a chair Clark followed the music. Turning into the doorway, he saw her half-clad body. "Sharon, where are your pants?"

"I took them off. I'm celebrating," she slurred, turning to face him. Wearing black panties and bra with one of his white dress shirts, she handed him a glass. "Here's your Tanqueray and olives."

"Can you turn the music down?"

She took a sip of Jack Daniels. "Why? It's my favorite song."

"Okay." Clark sighed, *that's a relief. I thought she was sending me a message.* "How long have you been drinking?"

She pointed at the half-full whiskey bottle. "Since the top of the bottle."

"I'm putting it away." He picked up the bottle of Jack Daniels. "You're drunk."

"You're right." She flipped off the shirt and slinked toward him, flaunting her modest breasts. "Are you ready to celebrate with me?" She stumbled and fell against him.

Clark caught her and held tight, keeping her from falling to the floor.

Glancing up, she slurred, "Want to do it one last time?"

"One last time?" Clark frowned, trying to decipher its meaning. Struggling to hold her upright, he put his arm around her waist and guided her onto the sofa.

"We're not doing it one last time; you're drunk."

"I got the appointment to go to England. I told you I sent my research there. I got it. Three years. Here, fill my glass and I'll tell you more."

"I'm not filling your glass. I'm making a pot of coffee."

"You do what you want. I'm going to sleep." Her eyes closed and her chin fell on her chest.

Twisting her to the side, he pulled on her arms, stretching her out onto the sofa and tucked an Afghan around her limp body. *Merry Christmas, she's drunk five hours before the party.*

***

Four hours later, Sharon lifted her head. "What time is it?" she mumbled.

"Six thirty."

Her arms stirred; she kicked at the Afghan. "I have to get dressed."

Sitting next to her, Clark gently laid his hand on her forehead. "You're not in any shape to go anywhere. Here, drink this," he said, handing her a cup of coffee. "It'll take most of the evening to sober you up."

She grunted, barely able to hold up her head.

Following a second cup of coffee, she sat straighter on the sofa. Clark propped a couple of pillows behind her back and sat in the chair across from her. "You usually have just two glasses of wine. Why did you get soused?"

"I'm sorry Clark," she said, apologetically. "I didn't mean to mess up the night."

"Don't worry about it. I called Nicole and gave her our regrets. I told her you were under the weather."

"Thanks, you're a sweetie."

"Why did you go on a personal binge?" he asked again, with concern.

"I don't know." She shook her head. "I kept rereading my appointment, sipping on a Jack Daniels and jumping up and down, shouting, then I had another. Guess I got carried away."

"You kept talking about celebrating and an appointment letter. Can I see it?"

"Oh, sorry I forgot." She pointed toward the kitchen. "The letter is on the counter. You can read it for yourself."

Following her directions, he walked to the counter, picked up the letter and sipped his Tanqueray while he read. "Wow, this is great." He hustled back waving the letter, flashing its engraved letterhead —

University of Leicester — it printed like a prized jewel. This is wonderful, tell me about the three-year appointment."

"Remember when we met on the yacht? You asked me about the type of research I was doing?"

"Yes, you said it had the potential to change future criminal investigations. It'll be like connecting the dots."

"Right, it's cutting-edge research on DNA." Sharon sat up straight, warming to her subject. "Professor Alec Jeffreys at Leicester is way ahead of everyone." Her enthusiasm exploded. "He's broken the genetic code."

"Tell me more."

"He's able to connect hair follicles on a person's hair brush with other items found at the crime scene."

"That will change the way crime-scene people work."

"*Hello*," she jested. "That's why I'm so excited. I'm fired up; I can't stop talking about it!"

"Hey, that's a better high than downing Jack Daniels," he joked.

"You're right." Laying her head back on the pillow, her adrenaline expiring, a throbbing headache taking over. "Guess you know the meaning for us?"

"Yeah." Clark nodded. "You'll be dating those Englishmen for the next three years."

She wrinkled her nose.

Knowing he had to tell her, Clark straightened his shoulders. "I don't want to rain on your parade, but there is something I have to say."

Picking up on his tone, Sharon stared at him. "You've met someone else, haven't you?"

"Ah yes, how'd you ..."

She cut him off. "I thought so. You haven't been calling on a regular basis, and yesterday I thought Laverne was going to say something at lunch, but she stopped abruptly. I got a funny feeling in my gut."

"I planned to tell you tonight."

"Huh, maybe the Jack Daniels idea wasn't such a bad idea after all."

CHAPTER TWENTY-ONE

Clifford McGill tipped the cab driver and led the way to the J. Edgar Hoover Building. Turning toward him, Clark asked, "Do you come to Washington, D.C. often?"

"Not much anymore. I used to come on a regular basis. Since I moved to Detroit I have plenty to keep me busy."

"Don't we all?" Clark nodded and followed him inside.

The two men signed in and within minutes were on the elevator to the fifth floor. Stepping into the hallway, Clifford picked up the pace. Clark hustled to keep up.

Several strides ahead, Clifford slowed and slipped into a nondescript conference room. Catching up with him, Clark peeked inside — a photo of President Carter hung on the wall beside a lonely American flag positioned in the corner. *More sterile than I expected for the nation's FBI headquarters.*

Looking at his watch, Clifford noted, "We're a few minutes early. Grab yourself a soda." He pointed to a row of cans on the small table near the picture window. "I'm hitting the head."

Clark picked up a soda and eased into a black swivel-rocker across from the manila file Clifford had placed on the conference table.

Before long Clifford returned and introductions were underway — Clifford and Clark; Woodson and Fitzpatrick, the two agents he'd already met; Jack Grimes an older FBI agent; the executive assistant director representing the FBI, Director William Webster; and at the end of the table, the Head of the FBI Criminal Investigation Division.

The executive assistant director stood and opened with his remarks, "On behalf of Mr. Webster, I'd like to thank each of you for interrupting your busy schedules. This is a critically important issue to all of us. The Director is personally concerned with the recent murders in Detroit and sends his regards. He is testifying on the hill today and will not be able to join us." The young assistant nodded to the man at the end of the table.

"Thank you," the blue-suited division head said. "We are gravely concerned by the reports we've received from Detroit. The city has had a long history of violence, but nothing as brutal as these recent mutilations. They have us all on alert."

"For good reason, sir," Clifford interjected. "The entire city of Detroit is on pins and needles."

"I can imagine," the head responded, opening the file in front of him and pulling out a sheet of paper. "Last week I sent out this memo to our agents, nationwide, asking them to search their files for any murder that might, in any way, resemble these killings."

Woodson eased forward. "Have you heard anything, yet?"

"I've had a few responses, but quite frankly nothing substantial. That's why I asked Jack Grimes to join us today. He's a retired Seattle FBI agent and now a consultant for us." The silver-haired man nodded to the right. "Jack, would you share the information we discussed earlier?"

"Yes sir, it'd be a pleasure." The lanky, square-jawed agent straightened in his chair. "For thirty-eight years I've followed a series of murders that occurred in Seattle during WWII, starting in 1942."

Running his fingers through his hair, he had Clark's attention. "That's the year I was born."

Grimes nodded. "It's been a lifelong project. You'll be interested to know your crime scene reports are amazingly similar to the cases I've researched."

Clark shifted uneasily in his chair. "The location of the punctures and slashes, too?"

"Yes," the retired agent said in a frank and honest way. "I'll bet the photos of the wounds taken in the '40s are within a half inch of those you've seen."

"That's crazy." Clark hesitated, unable to believe his words. "Thirty-five, forty wounds, and they're all alike."

He gave Clark a sadly disappointing nod.

"That's slightly over thirty-eight years ago." Clifford hesitated slightly. "Do you really believe the same person could have committed the crimes in 1942 and now?"

Grimes rubbed his jaw. "If it isn't the same person, he followed the same playbook."

192

"You said he," Clifford noted. "Are you positive it's a male?"

"Yes, I am." Grimes took his time first describing the cases, then comparing the crime scenes in the two cities. "The angle of the wounds indicate the person was around six feet, maybe six-one. The force of the fatal blows came from an individual with considerable strength. Most gypsy women are short, between five feet one and five-six. Lastly, in the gypsy culture, it's the man who is skilled with a knife." He paused briefly. "I'd say it's highly likely the killer is a man … 99 percent."

The men at the table sat in stunned silence. Clark looked at Clifford. Woodson turned his head to Fitzpatrick. Fitzpatrick raised his hand. "How did you conclude it was a gypsy?"

"I'll come back to that in a minute." Grimes shuffled his notes. "I can tell you one thing, in thirty-eight years I've followed thousands of leads, each one ended up as a dead end."

Woodson looked at Grimes with an expression of surprise. "Thirty-eight years, could you give a brief summary of your findings?"

The gray-haired Grimes nodded. "The first murder occurred in March 1942 and the last one of the seven, in September of 1943."

"Seven killings," Fitzpatrick blurted.

"Seven murders with exactly the same description and M.O., and only one common thread." He paused.

Anticipation filled the room.

"Each victim had a connection to organized crime."

Clark gave him a wry grin. "The same is true with us."

"So I noted." Grimes drained the last of his soda. "I suppose you're trying to connect the murders with the gangs or the mob."

"Absolutely." Fitzpatrick asked. "Why not?"

"Because I can tell you right now you're wasting time," Grimes spouted.

"Wasting time! It's the most logical thing to do."

"Protocol or not, I can tell you from my experience you're wasting your time."

"Why do you say that?" Woodson asked.

"I did the same thing for the first five years. By the time I decided to take a different approach the trail was cold. I'd suggest you explore every non-traditional approach you can."

Fitzpatrick turned to Clark, and said softly, "Sounds like Kimberly may be on the right track."

"Sorry?" Grimes said.

"Nothing." Clark waved him off. "It's an in-house joke."

"Anything else?" Woodson asked Grimes.

"One thing," he said deliberately, slowly. "If there is one more killing of this type the media will go bananas."

"Could you explain?" Clark asked.

"Four seems to be the media's breaking point. There'll be story after story, repeating the same thing, showing the same photos — the public will go berserk. Your police chief will be hammered." He paused, taking a deep breath. "The best advice I can provide is to stay on the straight and narrow. The media has no interest in finding the killer. Their goal is to sell newspapers. Keep your details to the press as limited as possible."

"That's a sad commentary," Clifford bemoaned.

"Sorry, that's how I feel." Grimes shrugged unconsciously. "Our media picked up on the gypsy fortune teller calling card and dubbed him the 'Gypsy Gestapo.'"

Clark took a double take. 'Gypsy Gestapo?' That's a paradox; the Nazis killed over a half-million gypsies during the Holocaust."

"You're right." The retired agent nodded, impressed with Clark's knowledge. "Gypsies, like Jews, were on the Gestapo's 'vermin' list, those harmful to the goals of the Reich."

Clark looked at him with a puzzled frown.

"Remember, Clark, this was 1942 during WW II. Suspicion was high and fear mongering rampant. People didn't trust anyone. Add to the general perception of fortune tellers and it didn't bode well for them."

"So the name stuck," Fitzpatrick stated.

"Right." With a little laugh, Grimes checked his notes. "Someone asked earlier if I really thought the killings were done by a gypsy?" He glanced around.

"Yes, I did." Fitzpatrick raised his hand.

"While nothing is absolute. I'm as positive as I can be."

"How did you draw that conclusion?" Woodson asked.

"Through a couple of points and one I'd like to reemphasize. First and most obvious, is the fortune teller calling card and the phrase typed on it. It could have been copied. Gypsies tell me that the person would have to be extremely knowledgeable about their culture. Second, is the victim's wounds. The use of the Navaja knife is another tipoff. The Navaja is rarely used by other than gypsies. And last, again, I'm back to the basic nature of gypsies. I've never ended with so many dead ends. They're masters at deception. There just has to be a gypsy connection."

Baffled, Clark raised his hand. "Gypsies are known as con artists, ruffians and thieves. They've rarely been known as murderers. And I can't recall any case of a gypsy serial killer."

"In general you're correct. They are commonly associated with various scams — fortunetelling, bogus home repair, distraction thievery, home invasion, or insurance fraud."

Clark raised his hand. "As I recall, gypsies usually work in pairs, is that true?"

The expert winked at him. "Yes, sometimes they involve the entire family." He paused. "Did you major in history?"

"No." Clark grinned. "My mother was a history teacher. I learned a lot around the kitchen table."

"Sounds like it … you have excellent insights, too."

Clifford leaned back with a thoughtful expression. "Do you think we're after two people?"

"Based upon gypsy tendencies, that's entirely possible."

Clark looked perplexed. "Earlier you said gypsies were non-violent 'for the most part.'"

"Perceptive, too, aren't you?" Grimes rubbed his chin. "There's one small group known as the Romani. They are of Romanian descent and often referred to as killer gypsies. I've tracked forty or fifty murders in the U.S. since 1900 that may be attributable to them."

"Have you picked up any leads from those cases?" Clifford asked.

"Huh," Grimes grunted. "Not one." He flipped his palms up, in a questioning manner. "Here's my take on gypsies. They're modern-day nomads. They move frequently from location to location. They're experts in giving false identification. They commonly use January 1 as their birth date. Many have adopted the same names, like Anderson or Marks. And, most important for us to remember, they are masters of disguise. Most have not been photographed or fingerprinted. Their culture emphasizes separation from mainstream society which they consider corrupt …"

Fitzpatrick interrupted. "They see *us* as corrupt; they're the ones who are robbers and thieves."

"That depends upon how you were raised. For them, thievery is a way of life." Grimes noted. "They live in tight-knit communities. Many of their children do not go to school or associate with those who do. Their kids are raised with a belief that stealing is okay."

"Wait a minute." Fitzpatrick frowned. "I was with you up to this point, but thievery is okay? That's a real stretch."

Grimes grinned. "That's the same thought I had when I dug up the research. Gypsies choose a life of thievery; it's as natural to them as eating and sleeping."

Fitzpatrick gave him a bewildered look. "C'mon, you're putting us on, aren't you?"

"No, I'm not." He slipped a sheet of paper out from his folder. "Here, I'll read the essence of a piece of research I found. The belief can be traced back to the crucifixion:

"Four nails were made for the crucifixion; one for each hand of Jesus, one for his feet, and a gold one for his heart. Late at night a gypsy boy stole the golden nail. The next morning God appeared and praised the child for his act of thievery. He had saved Jesus from having the nail plunged into his heart. In payment for the boy's deed, God gave gypsies the right to steal with no moral consequences ... forever and ever."

Glazed eyes stared around the room in disbelief.

***

Father Dom folded his bible and looked up at the black woman standing in his office doorway. Casting her a soft smile, he motioned her in. "Ms. Schaffer, I presume, so nice to meet you." He stood and greeted her. "Would you like a cup of tea?"

"That would be nice."

The white-haired priest closed the door behind her and ambled across the room to the corner table. Picking up a small pot, he stated, "Specially steeped for you," in a jovial manner and handed her a full cup and saucer.

Sliding back behind his large oak desk, he took out a pad and pen. "I understand you have something you'd like to share in confidence."

"You might put it that way." She took a short sip of the hot brown liquid. "I guess that's not new for you."

He released an exaggerated sigh. "I've heard 'in confidence' a few times."

Caroline eased to the edge of her chair. "Father, the information I'm about to share may seem a little far fetched at first, but I want you to hear me out."

"Yes, of course." He gave her a gentle, inquisitive smile. "Go ahead, my child. What is it?"

"I've uncovered a prostitution ring jointly operated by the Mafia and the archdiocese."

"No, that's not possible," he said briskly.

"I warned you."

He zipped his lip.

Taking a deep, calming breath, Caroline began to describe her role in the apartment building and how she'd collected the information from Consuelo and Feliciana.

Father Dom shook his head. "As a lawyer you know that isn't much to go on."

"Maybe not from a legal perspective, but my gut-level instincts say something is going on in the archdioceses." She hesitated. "I'd be most willing to help find out what's going on if you want."

"I appreciate the offer." He forced out a sympathetic grin. "The church handles matters of this type within our own ranks."

Caroline pressed forward. "I …"

"Let's not go there," he said, his voice trailing off. "I'll see if my research bears out your conclusion."

"I have evidence." She looked confounded. "Why, do you think I'd come to you without proof?"

"Don't misunderstand me. If there's a wrongdoing, I'll get to the bottom of it." He laughed, a little. "The crux of your findings is that a woman saw a letterhead with the Catholic Archdiocese of Detroit on it?"

"Yes."

"That could have been a fake. For argument's sake, let's assume it came from someone inside the archdiocese."

Caroline remained focused on him.

"We have two hundred and twenty-five parishes, over three hundred and fifty schools, nearly two hundred people employed in this building, and over two hundred thousand students enrolled. The potential numbers within our own ranks is astronomical."

Caroline leaned forward. "It came from Father Gonzalez in Los Herreras, Mexico. That makes it sound real; maybe someone in the upper echelon."

"That's a possibility."

"There's a local contact named James.

He nodded. "I'll start snooping around to see how many James's I can find."

***

Picking up on Clark's tradition, Earl slid into the far booth at the Sax Club, ordered a pitcher of beer and waited for his amigos. It didn't take long before Renzo, Carlos and Ted trucked in.

Barely into the booth, an overly hyper Renzo spoke. "You wouldn't believe it, Earl. The bastards were all over my office, busting up the furniture, tipping over file cabinets, kicking holes in the walls. By the time they left my secretary and I were huddled in a corner — the place is in shambles."

"Hey, you're not the Lone Ranger." Carlos said, his voice filled with fright. "By the time they left my place, I had four automobiles ablaze."

Earl glanced Ted's way. "How about you?"

He didn't move; simply stared back.

"Well?"

"Guess I got off easy. A couple of my tenants were shoved around, no one was hurt. It didn't matter — two single women moved out and another couple is trying to find a new place. If they hit me one more time, I'll start losing residents by the dozens."

"How are we supposed to handle this?" Renzo asked out of frustration.

Earl hemmed and hawed, trying to come up with Clark's words.

Renzo gave him a friendly slap on the back. "You don't have to do the same thing Clark would. The four of us have to figure this out."

Relief broke over Earl's face as a smile grew ear to ear. "Thanks Renzo, I needed that."

"Good. Now, let's get on with it."

"They've upped the ante," Earl said, his brain already in gear. "We're at a crossroads; we either live with their harassment or we come up with some form of action."

"That sounds nice, Earl," a reluctant Carlos said hesitantly. "But we can't take them on. They'll destroy our businesses; worse yet, maybe kill one of us."

"The bastards aren't going to stop me," Ted blurted out harshly.

"Relax Ted," Earl said with a calming voice. "We have to think this through rationally. A knee-jerk reaction is the worst thing we could do."

"You're right." Carlos nodded. "If we don't work together, they'll pick us off one by one."

Renzo gave Earl an inquisitive look. "You're sounding more like Nicole all the time."

Carlos perked up. "Maybe we ought to ask her to join our group."

"Yeah, why not? She might have some ideas on the best way to handle them. That okay with you, Earl?"

"Fine with me," Earl said with pride in Nicole. "I'll set up a lunch meeting at T.J.'s for the five of us."

***

Detroit Free Press
January 1981

MAFIA KINGPIN QUASARANO CONVICTED

Raffaele Quasarano, the highest ranking Detroit Mafia official ever to be convicted, was sentenced today to four years in federal prison. Having eluded state and federal prosecution on countless occasions, Quasarano was convicted for illegally seizing control of a Wisconsin cheese factory through intimidation and extortion.

A case of $270,000 tripped up a man who had supposedly raked in millions of dollars as a

conspirator in heroin trafficking. His name has been associated with Frank Coppola, the New York Lucchese crime family, and drug baron John Omentio.

A former owner of the Central Sanitation Services waste disposal company in Hamtramck, Quasarano has long been suspected of being a primary player in the death of Jimmy Hoffa.

CHAPTER TWENTY-TWO

Wearing the same black Nehru shirt and brown sport coat he wore the first time Abby and he had dinner at The Whitney, Clark took her hand and strolled inside. He remembered the dark green sequined cocktail dress from before; she looked stunning. Clark couldn't help staring at her. *She's more gorgeous than I remembered. Her shape and beauty aren't the only reasons I think about her. Conversations with her are the best — she can talk about any subject without being opinionated. It's a joy to be with her.*

The two were shown to a cozy table for two. Abby ordered the Beaujolais they'd had before, except this time it was on Clark's tab. Within minutes the sommelier offered her a taste, and following her nod, poured their glasses part way. Clark gazed at her and raised his glass; he admired *that smile.* "Here's to a most enjoyable dinner."

She tipped her glass to him. "And a wonderful evening afterwards," she purred.

"Sounds better than dessert." He laughed softly. Glimpsing around the dimly-lit room, he recalled the first time he'd spent the night at her place. Actually, he'd thought about it umpteen times. *I'll never forget it.* Coming back to reality, he pulled a Valentine's Day card from his coat pocket and leaned it against her water goblet. "Here's a special welcome back to Detroit."

That smile popped.

"Go ahead, open it."

She took her time opening the envelope, reading each line slowly. Her face melted; a sniffle held back a tear. "You're so sweet, Clark," she said softly, then reread the card. Placing it on the table facing her, she pulled a card out of her purse. "Here, it's your turn."

He opened the envelope and, like her, took his time letting the words sink in. Pausing for a moment, he stood, stepped around the table, and kissed her tenderly on the lips. "Thank you so much."

Watching him return to the chair, she extended her arm across the table and laid her hand on top of his. Her fingers moved slowly from one to another. *That smile* did the talking. "I want you to know, Clark, I'll never do anything to hurt you. I love you more than you'll ever know."

He hesitated. "Abby, I don't know how to respond."

She whispered, "You don't have to say anything, being here is enough."

The waiter refilled their glasses and brought another bottle of wine. She ordered the tenderloin. He had the roasted salmon, as before. Abby suggested they not talk about their jobs so they could learn more about each other. Finding humor and delight in the gentle words of the other one, the two giggled through the evening.

***

"Any more questions for Will?" Clark glanced around the table. Receiving a series of blanks, he turned to officer Robinson. "Thanks again, Will. Great job."

He rose. "I hope this briefing helps you understand the stranglehold black gangs have on our neighborhoods."

Heads nodded their agreement.

Clark asked Clifford to summarize his perceptions of the Washington meeting. He made it quick, knowing Clark had already shared his thoughts.

Woodson's hand flew up. "Do you really believe there is a connection between the 'Gestapo Gypsy' and the murders in Detroit?"

Clifford nodded to Clark. "Go ahead."

"The evidence is overwhelming. The crime scenes are identical. The wounds are in the same places. I have no doubt — everyone in Washington left with the same feeling — and yes, there appears to be a gypsy connection."

A furrow dug into Pag's forehead. "How can that be? Those crimes occurred nearly forty years ago, and now, all of a sudden they crop up in Detroit?"

"Beats me." Clifford shook his head. "Guess that's what we have to figure out."

Kimberly interjected. "I *told* you there was some kind of a cult involved."

Fitzpatrick shook his head side-to-side very slowly. "I'll give you an A+ on this one."

"More like a nutcase if you ask me," Woodson said.

Pag scratched his head. "Anything else we need to know about gypsies?"

"You're a great straight man." Clark picked up a stack of papers lying on the table. "Jack Grimes gave me a twenty-page analysis of their history and culture," he said, handing a copy to each. "You can read the details later. Right now, Clifford and I would like to highlight a few points." He turned to Clifford. "Wanta start?"

"Sure." He laid it on the line. "Gypsies are the greatest *unknown* in law enforcement history. It's estimated that there are ten million worldwide. We have no idea how many are in the U.S., except we know most of them are located in big cities."

"Why's that?" Kimberly asked.

"They tend to cluster in small enclaves where they're not noticed. Cities are the perfect location to gather. They can go unnoticed and disappear into the crowd."

"Makes sense."

Woodson raised his hand. "I heard they function in families. Even their kids are involved in the scams."

"Right." Clifford grinned. "Even unrelated, they're like extended families, each with its own criminal specialty."

Clifford winked at Clark. "Want to carry the ball from here?"

Clark began his history lesson. "Their culture is based on a lifestyle of thievery; it's part of their religion. They're the best con artist of all — fortune telling scams, credit card fraud — they're all talked about in Grimes' report. We can discuss it next time, after you've read through it. Are there are any questions?"

Kimberly raised her hand. "How does fortune telling qualify as a major scam?"

"It may not be for you. You might go once or twice on a lark. However, there are cases where victims have been sucked in and lost their entire life's savings. Wait until you read Grimes' report. He presents several criminal examples for each one of these scams. The real problem is gypsies are seldom caught, rarely prosecuted, and almost never jailed. Now can you see the task ahead of us?"

"I guess," Pag said. Then excitedly, "I can hardly wait to read it."

Kimberly's hand shot up.

Clark nodded. "Go ahead."

"Since we're talking about a small number of people being involved, I'd like to share my findings about numerology, too, that might relate."

"Go ahead."

"Believers in numerology think differently too. I picked the twenty-second of the month for a person's birthday just to see where it would take me."

"Could it be in any month?" Pag asked.

"Yes, the month doesn't matter. Numerology is different than a horoscope, which uses months as a guide. Numerologists focus totally on the actual number and how it relates in the universe and applies to your life." She paused for effect. "For example, a person born on the twenty-second of the month … any month … has great inner strength; he or she can come up with unique solutions, are good at taking care of details, and have the capability to carry out a vision to the nth degree," she said pridefully.

Clark gave her a reassuring grin. "Sounds like the kind of person that would be on our list, except for one thing."

She gave him a confounded frown. "Except?"

"They're experts at false identification and often use January first as their birth date."

She laughed. "Maybe this guy decided to be different."

"Hmm." Fitzpatrick, perplexed, mused again, "Hmm, I don't know how anyone could believe all of that numerology stuff."

Kimberly smiled coyly. "Hey, it isn't much different than you reading your horoscope every day."

Fitzpatrick gave her a sheepish look. He didn't think she had noticed. "Guess you're right."

***

Sliding into *the booth,* Nicole brought a glimmer of excitement to the group. "Thanks for scheduling the luncheon here rather than the Sax Club," she jested.

Carlos nodded; his round face full of expressive support. "Too many distractions there for me too."

Renzo placed a glass of wine in front of her. "Chianti for the lady," he said cautiously. "Unless you want to share our pitcher of Stroh's."

She winked. "Thanks, I'll stick with the wine."

Sitting across from her, Earl took the lead. "Anyone have a thought on how we might combat the tactics of the Mafia?"

Nicole watched the heads shake around the table and heard the grousing roll.

"Hey, I'm good at selling cars," Carlos said hesitantly. "Strategies on how to deal with the mob I-I don't know."

"Same with me," Ted echoed. "If we do anything obvious, they bust up our places. Whatever we do needs to be subtle."

"Makes sense." Nicole studied the group in a thoughtful way. "I like that thought. We ought to start in a low-key way so as not to attract any attention."

"Do you have a thought on how we might do that?" Ted ventured.

She gave him a gentle grin, knowing he'd asked the perfect question. "I've thought about a couple of things."

He figured she had a plan in her head. Earl said, "Go ahead, please share some of your thoughts."

"I'd suggest we establish some guidelines so we can operate with a common sense of direction."

Renzo doubled nodded. "Sounds good to me."

Nicole lifted her shoulders; a sign of her confidence. "Let's say we start with the point we already mentioned; for example, Principle #1: Our actions must be subtle and not obvious."

"Yes," Earl agreed, knowing she was only warming up.

Blood rushed through her veins. "Ever since Alsye was killed, I've had a burning desire to strike back at the Mafia in some way. Everyone has told me 'there's nothing you can do.' Still, I've always believed there was something. As Alsye would have said if he were here today, 'we have to be strong and maintain our resolve.'"

"Sounds like Principle #2 is coming," Carlos said quietly. "We must stand strong regardless of their actions; we can't afford to back away."

She clapped her hands quietly. "Thank you, Carlos. I couldn't have said it better."

Renzo showed a sign of reluctance. "I appreciate your drive and commitment, Nicole, but we're just regular guys — a car salesman, an apartment building owner and me. We don't have the knowhow or power to challenge the Mafia."

She offered a response for every obstacle. "We have power; the power of our spirit. Power of our drive and commitment."

Carlos nodded his agreement. "I'll buy into Principle #3: We may have power, but I don't have a clue of how I might use it to impact the Mafia."

Renzo shook his head. "Nicole, I appreciate your enthusiasm too, but I'm just a contractor."

"I agree." Ted said. "I believe in the power of the people, but there are only a handful of us against the mob. We have no power; and we have no plan."

Nicole paused for the longest moment. "Think about it guys, each of you has something the mob wants."

Earl chimed in, "Principle #4: We have something the Mafia wants."

"Like what?" Renzo said on behalf of the group.

Her brain firing on all cylinders, she glanced at Carlos. "They want cheap cars for their thugs and prostitutes from you, right?"

"Right."

She pointed her finger at Ted, "They want housing for their prostitutes and," she nodded to Renzo, "they want you to remodel their blind pigs." She paused, letting her remarks set in. "Now we're getting somewhere."

Ted jumped on board. "Caroline and I could keep track of prostitutes so we'd know where they're working."

Renzo scowled. "Why would that be important?"

"I don't know right now."

Carlos pointed out. "We'd know which whore houses and blind pigs were open."

"That's something the vice squad could use," Earl said, a second thought lingering. "If we could find out specific details we'd be able to get the jump on them."

Seemingly searching, Nicole probed. "They'll be driving Carlos's cars. Might that help in any way?"

Carlos's face came aglow. "I could install bugs in the cars." He paused, thinking out loud. "They could run off the battery. We could hide a tape recorder between the back seat and the trunk. No one would ever figure that out."

Earl's brain shifted into high speed. "If all of your cars were bugged we could record conversations between their lackeys. That could provide some damaging testimony in a legal case. We might also obtain inside information from a capo or top-tier guy."

Renzo sat quietly, his mind roiling like a calculating machine. "I could plant bugs in the blind pigs."

"Wouldn't that be dangerous?" Earl asked.

"Not really." Renzo said, sounding calm and in control. "I'd do it personally so no one would know. It's the same thing Carlos is talking about in bugging their cars."

Feeling the guys were on a roll, Nicole turned to Earl. "Armed with this kind of information, what is possible on your end?"

"We might be able to shut down a blind pig and nab a bunch of Mafia associates."

"Wouldn't that be something? Do you really think that's possible?" she asked.

Nodding his head, Earl brightened with a thought. "We could take out all ten in one fell swoop!"

"Oh my goodness." Nicole bubbled with excitement. "That'd be wonderful, terrific. Do you really think that might be possible?" she asked again, eagerly.

"It'd take a lot of work from us." Earl spoke slowly, his confidence growing. "It'd have to be a massive, hush-hush operation conducted by the feds. One leak to a department police officer will kill the entire operation; it'd be dead in the water."

Nicole glanced around the table. "Well guys, how about it?"

Renzo gave her a thumbs up. "Nothing to lose, I'm on board."

"Me too," the others chimed in.

***

"Did she offer you a piece of warm apple pie?" Fran asked.

Clark glimpsed at his dad, bundled up on the back porch puffing away on his Corona, and turned toward his mom. "Yes," he said, brimming with pride.

"Well then, when do I get to meet her?"

"Mom, things don't happen that way."

"They did with your father and me."

Clark shook his head, trying to weasel free. "Times have changed; things are different now. I told her your story and she liked the sweetness of it, that's all."

His mom shook her head, confused by his answer. "How much different could it be if two people are in love?"

"Mom, there you go again. Trying to marry me off. We're getting reacquainted that's all."

"Sure," she said. "I know the code words. You're not pulling the wool over my eyes."

The slider opened. "You have something in your eye, Fran?" his dad said.

"A speck of flour. It's gone now."

"Good." Lewis turned to his son. "Anything new on the 'fortune-teller killer?'"

"'Fortuneteller killer, where did you hear that?"

"It's on the streets — all over town."

"That's nice to know." Clark tossed his head in frustration. "Have the media crank up the presses. All they want to do is sell newspapers."

Fran shook her index finger at Clark. "You have to have a sit-down conversation with the editors at *The Detroit News* and *Free Press*. Let them know they're doing the public a disservice."

Clark let out a deep sigh. "Mom, it doesn't work that way. Their job is to sell papers. My job is to catch the bad guys. We just have different objectives."

"Huh." She turned toward the oven.

"Want a Stroh's?" dad asked.

"Yeah, I'm buying." Clark pulled a couple of bottles from the fridge and headed for his dad's den.

Lewis grabbed a beer and took a sip. "How'd your trip to Washington, D.C. go?"

"Fine." Sitting in the straight back chair, Clark ran his hand around his jaw, needing his dad's police force expertise. "You ever hear of the Gestapo Gypsy?"

Dad rubbed his forehead. "Hmm, way back, during the war … a serial killer in Seattle."

"Excellent." Clark sat his bottle on the end table between their chairs. "The crime scenes are identical to our murders.

"Really." Lewis slid forward on his chair. "Do the feds think the same person is involved?"

Clark nodded. "If it isn't the same person, he certainly took a page out of the old playbook. You know much about gypsies?"

His dad's eyebrows drew together questioningly. "I know they're great con artists and run all kinds of scams." He ran his fingers over his lips. "They're good with knives too."

"Really."

"Yeah, but other than the Seattle cases, I never heard of a gypsy being involved in a murder."

His recollection surprised Clark. "You're right. They're mostly noted for their thievery and con jobs." Clark looked at his dad curiously. "I heard way back in history there was a small sect known as killers."

"Don't know much about that." Lewis shrugged his shoulders. "You'll have to talk to your mother about that."

"Good idea." Clark switched his interest. "You hearing anything else on the street?"

"Nothing other than there's a growing amount of anxiety."

"Yeah, thanks. I can hear it now. The media beating the drums for us to the nab the fortune teller killer."

CHAPTER TWENTY-THREE

March poker began on a high note. Clark read part of a letter from Sharon about her successes on the DNA research project in England.

Ted perked up. "Sounds like that'll make it a lot easier for you guys to nail criminals."

"No question," Clark said. "Once we win a court case or two using DNA evidence it'll be a whole new ballgame."

Earl chimed in. "It'll be like adding two and two. We'll be able to put guys away we never thought possible." He laughed. "We might even put Bufalino out of business."

"Wouldn't that be something?" Clark added.

Father Dom stood and recited a few passages from the Bible about friendship and working together before offering a short prayer.

Arriving late, Carlos grabbed a beer and plopped down in the vacant chair. "Sorry, I had issues all day. Finally got out."

Renzo called "Dealer's choice," shuffled the cards once and laid them down, with a little attitude. "Seems like dealing with Carlos's problem might be more important than playing cards right now."

Earl sensed his tension. "What's going on, Carlos?"

Carlos sucked in a deep breath. "When I arrived at the office this morning I was greeted with a flatbed trailer loaded with some of my most expensive cars, flattened like pancakes. Not one of them was more than eighteen inches high."

"I can't imagine." Earl said, his eyes wide with surprise. "How did you handle it?"

"I sat down and cried." There was a long pause while no one spoke. "I don't think I can handle much more."

"We'll work it out," Earl reassured him. "You have to hang in there; it won't be long before we can go after them full bore."

"I hope so," Renzo chimed in. "I had some minor damage on one of my job sites over the weekend. They ripped out the electrical wiring and kicked-in some drywall, nothing major."

Earl nodded. "Sounds like they want you to know they're still around."

"Yeah, probably so." Renzo picked up the deck and tried again to get the game going, "Dealer's Choice," he announced, and the marathon was on.

Midway through the evening Father Dom called, "Break Time." The guys hit the head. Clark filled his plate, grabbed a beer, and eased onto his chair.

Ted glanced his way. "You've been quiet tonight, anything happening with you?"

"I've been thinking about those murders."

"The fortune teller killer ones?"

"Yeah, the twenty-second of March is coming up. I'm wondering if there is going to be another one."

Carlos glanced at him. "Hey, it's on everyone's mind. Rosa Maria says we're staying home and locking the doors."

"No need for that," Ted said. "They're killing bastards who deserve to die."

Clark wiped a scowl from his face. "C'mon Ted, lighten up."

"Peace." Father Dom raised his hand. "No one deserves to die that kind of a death."

Ted bit his tongue; his face red with anger.

"Time out," Renzo called. "Let's change the subject. Clark, anything else happening with you *personally*?"

"Hmm." Clark stalled, then gave the group a sheepish look. "Abby and I are going to Vegas next week."

Eyes rolled around the table.

Earl lifted a brow. "Now there's something to talk about."

"Abby or Vegas?" Renzo joked.

Earl laughed. "You pick it."

"I think we should stick with Vegas."

"Where are you staying," Father Dom asked.

"The Desert Inn."

"That's a fancy place." Carlos said. "Make sure you have a room on the fifth floor or lower."

"Why's that?"

"The fire department ladder trucks in Vegas only go up that high."

"Right." Earl interjected. "That was a big issue in the MGM fire last year. The fire spread through the casino like it was a wind tunnel. Good thing it happened in the morning rather than later in the day when the casino would have been packed. Almost all of the eighty-five people died of smoke inhalation."

"Good luck my son. I wish Abby and you well," Father Dom raised his hand as if giving a blessing, then dealt the cards. "Read 'em and weep."

***

Detroit Free Press
March 22, 1981

FORTUNE-TELLER KILLER
SLICES FOURTH VICTIM

The body of Mafia caporegime Joey Naples was found this morning in the spacious bathroom of his upscale home in Grosse Pointe Farms. The top lieutenant for the newly named Street Boss Blackie Giardini, Naples had established himself as one of the up-and-coming men in the Detroit Partnership.

Handcuffed in front of a full-length mirror, he suffered through a series of precisely located punctures and wounds, placed exactly like the three previous murders by the fortune-teller killer.

This is the killer's fourth murder on the 22nd of the month and each one has been three months apart.

***

At nine o'clock that morning every Mafia capo and high-ranking lieutenant lined the walls around the walnut conference table in Jake Nicolette's Grosse Pointe mansion. Wasting no time, he called the meeting to order and signaled the priest to deliver remarks.

"Please stand and bow your heads," the elderly man said, starting the prayer. He went on to pay tribute to the man they had lost — a devoted husband, loving father of three, a soccer coach — a man they'd come to know as a future leader in the organization.

Jake's nod dismissed him.

Blackie collapsed onto his chair.

The other high-ranking officials took their places around the table. The rest of the group stepped back against the walls.

Taking a seat at the head of the table, Jake gazed around the room; his face soured, his cold eyes piercing the souls of the mortals around him. "It could have been you." He pointed at each man, one-by-one, around the table. "It could have been you … you … you …" he steered his finger around the room. "… you, you, and you."

A subtle moan trickled through the room.

"We've reached a crossroads in the life of our organization." He paused for effect. "We can do nothing and watch our influence diminish. It'll be a slow death, none of us would notice; slowly our way of life would drift into the past. Our children would be left with nothing; we'll be old men on the outside looking in." Jake paused, letting his words sink in. "Or, we can stand up and take action against the bastard who took Joey's life." He stood and shouted with resolve. "It's our responsibility, *our obligation*, to seek out and punish the ones who have committed this dastardly act. We cannot. We must not turn our back on Joey."

Roaring their approval, the men beat on the table and stomped their feet.

Blackie rose slowly, braced himself with both hands on the table. "Men, you know how important Joey was to me. It's the same feeling your boss has for you. We are one — a family — we must do everything humanly possible to hunt down and kill those responsible for Joey's death."

"I'm ready," someone shouted.

"I'm with you," Blackie reiterated then fell back into his chair.

Applause filled the room.

Jake raised his fist over his head. "Joey's death is a personal affront to all of us. We cannot and *will not*, let an outside action of this type go unpunished. We must stand strong. We stand for Joey. We must stand strong for Joey!"

The men sprang up from around the table. "Stand strong for Joey," reverberated through the room. "Stand strong for Joey!"

***

Kimberly held up two fingers on each hand in front of her. "Didn't I tell you? It's twenty-two. We find the meaning of twenty-two and we find the killer."

Seeing Clark enter the room, she closed her mouth.

Seeing everyone's eyes on Kimberly, Clark glanced at her.

No one made a move.

He sensed the tension. With an inquisitive look he said, "Okay, what's going on?'

Dick Woodson smiled at Kimberly, raised his arms and conducted the chorus. "It's twenty-two. When we find the meaning of twenty-two, we'll nab the killer."

Clark laughed.

The guys roared.

Kimberly's face turned red. "It isn't funny," she squeaked out.

Clark pulled out a chair. "Fact is you may be right."

Fitzpatrick, her biggest skeptic ate crow. "Thanks for hanging in there, Kimberly. Did you learn anything new from your recent investigation?"

"Not really, but the more I read about numerology the more I'm convinced there is some kind of a connection. Maybe it is his birthday, the year he was born … I don't know, but there's some particular meaning."

Woodson's scowl turned blank. "The year he was born, huh? If he was born in 1922 and the murders happened in '42, he would have been twenty. That would make him close to sixty now, hmm, could be."

"That's certainly an angle … the best one we have so far." Clark winked at her. "Keep digging. We're looking forward to hearing more next time."

She grinned ear to ear and thumbed her nose at Fitzpatrick.

"Okay, okay, you win." He grinned back.

Pag raised his hand. "I'm still stuck on Grimes's thought that we're wasting time following up on the leads dealing with the mob and gangs. That would eliminate most of our options, except for the gypsies."

Woodson rolled his shoulders. "How about a vindictive nut?"

"Maybe it's a vindictive gypsy."

An inquisitive look crossed Pag's face. "That's an interesting thought. I need to know more about them."

"Me too," Woodson agreed. "Any ideas?"

Nods floated around the table.

"I have a friend who's a gypsy," Clark said. "Give me your questions and I'll have a conversation with him."

***

Clark slid into a club chair along the wall at the Ghostbar. Ted settled in across from him. "Thanks for agreeing to answer some of the questions from my team members."

"Hey, I'll be glad to help in any way I can," Ted said, looking around the upscale bar in awe. "You come here often?"

"Hmm, maybe once a month. I like the 1890s' atmosphere and the rich ambiance of the past. It's a good way to slip away from the hustle-bustle."

"I can see why. I'll have to bring Laverne here for a special occasion."

"The restaurant is even better," Clark puffed up a bit, remembering his dinner with Abby. "A little expensive, but worth the extra."

Ted laughed. "I'll let her buy."

Clark ordered his regular, a Tanqueray on the rocks with three olives. Ted went for his standard Scotch on the rocks. The two chit chatted for a few minutes before Clark pulled out a slip of paper with some notes on it. "I have a few questions about gypsies from my colleagues, I'd like to ask."

"Fire away. Ask as many as you like," Ted said politely. "Everyone at the newspapers seems to have their own opinion. Last I heard not one reporter had interviewed anyone from the local gypsy community."

"That relates to one of my questions."

Ted nodded and gave him his full attention. "Go ahead."

"How many gypsies are in the Detroit area?"

Ted thought for a moment. "It's hard to say on a day-to-day basis. A lot of people come and go. Regulars … I'd say a few hundred."

"Could you provide a half dozen names and addresses so we can interview a few of them?"

Ted grunted. "Hmm, I don't know. Most of them don't talk to outsiders. I might come up with a name or two. Maybe you could interview them and see how it goes."

"That'd be a good start. How about their phone numbers too?"

"Hmm." Ted smiled broadly. "It's not likely any of them have a phone. I'll try to arrange a meeting in a neighborhood café. Would that be okay?"

"Sure." Clark gave him a thumbs up.

"Two women come to mind. Do you have a female officer who could meet with them?"

"Yes, one of our best."

"Good, and no uniforms. Ask her to wear civilian clothes, jeans and a sweatshirt; otherwise there'll be no one in sight. Our people don't trust people in uniform or government officials."

"Got it." Clark took a sip of gin. "How is the gypsy community reacting to the news about the fortune teller killer?"

A scowl crossed Ted's forehead. "Don't use that phrase." His voice hinted at anger. "Our people are pissed off. Not only does the characterization cast a negative image on fortune tellers, it is very upsetting to all of us." Cruising on his Scotch, Ted sneered. "Clark, we've been persecuted throughout history. The Nazis killed hundreds of thousands, probably a million if the truth be known. Your officer has to be aware of our past. She needs to treat our people with dignity."

"Of course, I understand."

"Just because we have different beliefs doesn't mean we are bad people. Right now the level of trust and respect for outsiders is extremely low."

Clark nodded, positively. "Understandable. Thanks for putting it that way. The person I send will fully understand the points you've made."

"Clark, it's critically important," Ted emphasized as his tone rose. "I don't need egg on my face."

"Don't worry," Clark said, his voice calming and reassuring. "Kimberly is our best."

Ted gave him an unconvinced look.

"Ted, I promise … there won't be a problem."

Ted's patience seemed to be wearing thin. "Anything else?"

"No, my officer will cover the rest during the interview." Clark paused in long thought. "Yes, there is. One of my officers is studying numerology. Do you know anything about that?"

"Not personally. Some fortune tellers are into it big time." Ted hesitated. "You know the way *you* use numbers is not important to us, don't you?"

"Ah yes, I think so." Clark stroked his jaw. "Maybe you ought to explain the use of numbers from your perspective."

"To begin with, we don't have different birthdays …"

Clark interrupted, "I read that many gypsies use January 1st as their birthday so they can't be traced."

"No, that's not the reason," Ted said forcefully; his face reddened. "We use the same birthday, so as not to differentiate or place emphasis on any one person. We all celebrate on the same day."

"That's good to know." Clark showed a little surprise. "Thanks for clarifying it."

"Our family is a little different. We use February 22nd."

"The 22nd?" Bells rang in Clark's brain.

A deep furrow crossed Ted's forehead. "Is there something wrong with having birthday on the 22nd?"

"No, it surprised me." Clark said uneasily, trying to cover up his gut-level instinct.

Ted perked up. "If you're into numerology, try this on for size. My dad has the perfect birthday … 2-22-22."

Clark's jaw dropped. "February 22, 1922."

"Yes, that's what I said."

Clark ran his fingers through his hair. "Do you see him often?"

"Hmm, every three or four months, sometimes for a day or two, sometimes for a week. He lives in Seattle and travels a lot.

CHAPTER TWENTY-FOUR

Abby made her way through the dimly lit maze of tables to the elevated booth, as she had many times before. Blackie sat alone, staring into another world; his face somber, his forehead wrinkled. Rather than watching her graceful body, he gave her a forlorn glance.

"You okay?" she asked.

"I guess," he said without thought. "I can't believe anyone would want to kill Joey. He was a super guy. He'd been my right arm for nineteen years. I don't know how I'll replace him."

"He must have done a lot …"

"A lot?" Blackie interrupted. "He did it *all*."

Knowing she had to change the subject, Abby paused. "Being the new Street Boss, I guess congratulations are in order."

"Huh." He rubbed his jaw. "Funny. I worked all of my life to become the Street Boss and now, all of a sudden, it isn't important."

"Your call sounded urgent," Abby changed the topic again.

Blackie took a sip of his lukewarm beer. "I want to know everything you can find out about Joey's murder. I'll pay you double if you identify the culprit. I want to strangle the bastard myself."

"Clark's group is working night and day. So far they haven't come up with anything."

"Nothing or not, I want every piece of information Clark turns up." he said with strong conviction. "Do you understand?"

"Yes sir."

Blackie sighed. "What angle is Clark working on now?"

Abby didn't pause; she spoke freely. "He's focused on gypsies. Forty years ago, there was a series of murders in Seattle that were identical to the ones here. Seven gang and mob members killed. They called him the 'Gestapo Gypsy.'"

Blackie perked up. "Are you positive?"

"Absolutely, everything was a perfect match."

"Huh. I'll call the boss on the West Coast and see if he can dig up something." Blackie looked her in the eye. "Has Clark dug up any clues around here?"

She shook her head. "Not that I'm aware of, why?"

"My boys are scouring the city. Someone has to know something. Somebody will talk."

***

Earl took a sip of Stroh's. Clark rushed into T. J's., and headed his way. Earl pushed a cold bottle across the table. "Have a Stroh's. I've ordered onion rings to get started."

"Sounds good." Clark motioned to the waitress and ordered. "Ted said he would identify a couple gypsies who might talk with us."

"After all of this, I doubt if anyone will talk."

Shifting uncomfortably, Clark glanced distractedly at the eclectic wall décor.

Earl gave him a peculiar look. "I know that reaction, something else wrong?"

Clark sat silently; his mind whirling, unsure of how much to tell Earl.

"C'mon man, did Ted say something that bothers you?"

"Everyone in Ted's family has the same birthday — February 22 — his father's birthday is February 22, 1922."

"2-22-22!" Earl's eyes bugged out. "Wait till Kimberly hears that."

"And listen to this, his dad has lived most of his life in Seattle."
You gotta be shittin' me."

"Wait, there's more. His dad visits Detroit three or four times a year."

"He could have been in town when the murders occurred," Earl muttered as his face went blank. "Do you think ...?"

"Don't even go there," Clark cut him off. "Right now that's a leap from where we are."

"If he was here, how could his dad be connected with the murder?"

"It'd be nothing." Clark shrugged. "It could have been a casual thing, maybe chatting over a beer."

Earl frowned. "How about the two black guys?"

"Revenge for them beating up Nicole maybe, I don't know."

220

"I suppose, Laverne and Ted could have spilled the beans over dinner and never gave it a second thought."

"Remember Ted's reaction at poker, when we talked about her? I thought he was going to go berserk." Clark shook his head, trying to shake an ominous feeling.

"Yeah, he was really anxious. If he told his dad that, who knows?"

"Yeah, and remember when I said we were moving slowly. I thought Ted was going to lose it. Clearly, he wanted action, right away."

"Yeah, he got red in the face," Earl recalled. "How about the killing of the bar owner, Narduzzi?"

"That could have been because of Renzo, remember him talking about the hard time Narduzzi was giving him."

"It all fits," Earl said. "You ought to call Jack Grimes and have him run a search on Ted and his family."

***

Caroline paid the cashier, grabbed a paper cup and poured in the coffee. Spotting Feliciana at the far table in the college snack bar, she weaved her way past the scattered chairs and empty tables.

Feliciana cracked a partial grin; her eyes swollen, her mascara streaked.

Caroline hurriedly placed her cup on the table.

Feliciana stood and hugged her. "Thank you for coming," she mumbled in Caroline's ear. "I had no one to call."

"I'm glad you did." Caroline squeezed her harder, stepped back, and brushed the hair away from her face. "It's going to be all right. Sit down and tell me what's bothering you."

Feliciana pulled a tissue from her pocket, blotted the moisture from her cheeks, and eased back into the wire-back chair. Blowing her nose, she lowered her head. "I think I'm pregnant."

Collecting her thoughts, Caroline paused for a moment. "It's okay, it's okay." She extended her hands across the table and clasped Feliciana's. "Tell me the rest."

"I shouldn't have …" Feliciana bit her lip. "Arturo and I have been sleeping together for the last three months. I missed my period and feel kind of strange. I don't know where to turn."

"Do you feel ill or have any nausea?"

"No. I'm scared. I had the apartment manager call James. He said James was about to leave for Mexico. I couldn't talk to Arturo's parents; they are extremely strict. You were the only one left."

Caroline's grin broadened. "I'm glad you did. First things first, I'll call my doctor and make an appointment."

"I don't have money for that. I can't ..."

Caroline raised an index finger to Feliciana's lips. "Don't worry about it. I'll take care of everything."

"Oh, thanks so much. I ..." she burst into silent tears.

"Hush, you're here now." Caroline said. "It's something I want to do. Did have you have breakfast this morning?"

"No. I was so upset I couldn't eat."

Caroline rose and extended her hand. "Let's get something to eat before we talk more."

Feliciana gave her a half-grin, grabbed Caroline's hand, and the two headed for the cafeteria line. Feliciana filled a large bowl with oatmeal and picked up a carton of milk. Caroline toasted a bagel, placed two containers of cream cheese on her tray, and paid the bill.

Munching slowly on her bagel, Caroline watched Feliciana shove in the cereal, taking several bites before glancing up. "Guess I was hungry, huh?" she said politely. "I don't know how I would have handled this without you."

"It's okay, really. That's why I gave you my phone number." Opening the second container of cream cheese, Caroline changed the subject. "Tell me about James."

Feliciana's grin grew. "He's a nice man. He takes care of me."

"Can you describe him?"

"He's in his early fifties, medium height and, maybe a little overweight."

"Does he have any distinguishing qualities or characteristics?"

She rolled her shoulders. "Hmm, he wears an old Detroit Tigers' baseball cap; it's black with an orange 'D'."

"Anything else?"

"Ah ... yes, he carries a black bag."

"A bag, like a satchel?"

"Yes, kind of like a large purse."

Caroline stopped, figuring she'd gotten as much information as she could, "Are you feeling better now?"

 ***

Caroline made the doctor's appointment and within the hour she was in Clark's office, briefing him on her meeting with Feliciana.

"Sounds like a real break," he said. "I'll tell Father Dom to see if he can find out anything from his end."

"Has your team come up with any suspects yet?"

"Not really."

"Where to now?"

Clark stood. "I'm heading back to the McNamara Building. We have to tell Clifford. If we're lucky, an FBI agent might see your Tigers ball cap guy at the airport."

"James could be leaving for Mexico any time."

"Don't worry, Clifford will move quickly. He'll have a team at Metro before noon checking the flights departing for Dallas and Houston."

"I can't believe this. It sounds like a movie scene. I'm so excited."

Clark winked at her. "Would you like to be at Metro in case it happens tomorrow?"

"Yes, of course. I'd love to see the Tigers cap come my way."

Clark flashed a broad smile. "I'll check with Clifford to see if you can be a part of his surveillance team."

"Really?" Caroline jumped out of her chair. "I can hardly wait."

***

Father Dom paced in front of the eighth-floor window of the Gabriel Richard Building at 305 Michigan Avenue, stopped, and gazed at the skyline of Windsor, Ontario. Having carefully reviewed the people named James working in the central headquarters, he'd come up with nothing. *Okay, who are the other people who come into the building on a regular basis that might be transporting information — repairmen, custodians, part-time security officers, mailman — who else?* His mind wandered. "Maybe," he thought out loud. "Maybe, James is a middleman, a courier, why not? It's worth a try."

He bolted from his chair, hurried down the hallway, and took the elevator to the first floor. Stepping into the director of security's office, he winked at the secretary. "Is he in?"

She pointed to the half-open door. "Go on in."

Father Dom knocked softly on the door frame and poked his head inside. "Do you have a minute, Chief?"

Knowing the voice, the heavyset director answered without glancing up. "For you, of course. Have a chair." He pointed to the straight back ladder chair in front of his modest size oak desk. "How may I help you?"

"Do you keep a list of visitors who come into the building?"

"Yes, by the month. Which one do you need?"

"How about the last two or three months."

"What are you looking for?" the chief asked.

"I'm playing a hunch."

"Oh-Okay." The chief swiveled around, pulled open the bottom file drawer and sorted through the files. Pulling out three folders near the rear, he turned and tossed them in front of Father Dom. "Here's February, March and April. That okay?

"It'll be fine for now. I'd like to take them to my office, do you want me to sign something?"

"Hah, I know where to find you."

***

Father Dom walked into the archdiocese personnel office, past the clerk, and went straight into the human resources director's office.

Hearing the door creak open, she glanced up. "I get uncomfortable when someone comes in and closes the door."

Father Dom laughed. "It isn't that bad. I'd like to review some travel authorization forms. Think you can help me out?"

The Spanish-American woman contorted her lips into an odd grimace, and stood. "I'll try."

"I'd like to see the travel forms for our Most Reverend Raphael Orlando, head of Evangelization, Catechesis and Schools."

"Dr. Orlando …?"

"Don't ask, right now," he interrupted.

"Okay, I'll pull his file." She walked across the room, opened the middle drawer of her file cabinet, and sorted through the manila folders. Grabbing a thick one, she placed it on her desk, and eased into the chair. Leafing through the file, she pulled out several sheets of paper, and aligned them in perfect order. "Here's the last two years." She handed them to him. "If you need more I'll have to go in the back room."

"This will work for now." He paged through the stack. "The purpose states he went to 'extend our missionary commitment.'"

"So?" The HR director gave him a strange look. "That's part of his assignment. Did you expect something else?"

"Oh, nothing," he said, jotting down a few words on a notepad.

After filling a page with notes, he grinned. "Thanks, I have everything I need."

"Take your time. I have a meeting to attend. When you're finished, leave the forms on my desk."

"Thanks."

Sorting through the travel forms, he slipped a handful inside his robe and walked into the reception area. "I'm going to the restroom. I'll be right back."

She nodded.

Stepping into the hallway, Father Dom walked briskly to the copy center, made copies and returned to the director's office. Checking a few more forms, he heard the door and glanced up. "You back already?"

"Yes. It was a short meeting; can you believe that?"

"A rarity." He laughed. "I have a couple questions."

She settled into her desk chair. "Go ahead."

"I noticed Father Orlando made several trips to the archdioceses in northern Mexico. In all of them, except Monterrey, he stayed in a hotel. That's kind of strange, don't you think?"

"I don't know, maybe he has a friend there." She shrugged. "Maybe that archdiocese has its own living quarters."

"Hmm, could be." Father Dom wrinkled his brow. "Where did he obtain his degrees?"

"Just a minute I'll check." The director opened a second file and pulled out a stapled packet. "Here it is on his resume. His masters and doctorate degrees are from the University of Mexico in Mexico City."

"I wonder why he never went back there. He could have had his old friends help extend our missionary efforts. Huh, interesting."

***

Father Dom pulled up a chair in front of Clark's desk. "I've found our man." He chuckled. "One confirmed for you and one for me to investigate."

A startled expression crossed Clark's face. "I don't understand your point."

Father Dom laughed. "I went through the list of visitors to the archdiocese offices for the past ten months. Your "James" is a busy man. He visits two or three times a month."

"Really, that ties up one loose end." Clark stroked his jaw. "Who does he meet with?"

Father hesitated. "I can't tell you … it's church business."

"C'mon Father, after all of these years."

Father Dom scrunched his mouth. "Mm, I'm not allowed to give you his name."

"There must be something. Could you give me a hint?"

The father glanced around the room as if making sure they were alone. "He's tall and slender, dark hair, handsome, speaks with a Spanish accent, and has unlimited opportunity for international travel."

"Thanks," Clark said in a disappointed tone, finding the information useless. "How will the archdiocese handle this matter?"

"I'll do my due diligence and share the information with the Bishop. It'll be his decision how to deal with whatever I find."

"That's it?" Clark frowned. "Will the matter be totally closed within the church?"

"Probably, if the Bishop finds significant criminal action that has outside implications, he could turn it over to you." Father wiped his forehead. "I'd say that would be highly unusual."

CHAPTER TWENTY-FIVE

MONTERREY, MEXICO

Two Mexican-American FBI agents waited in the Monterrey International Airport in hopes that only one Detroit Tigers' ball cap would appear. Watching the line of passengers unload from the American Airlines flight from Dallas, the stocky agent spotted the ball cap guy carrying a small shoulder bag. He nodded to the other agent and the two tailed him outside.

Lingering by the taxi stand, the two agents watched the suspect slip into the lead taxi. The agents hopped into the next one in line and directed the cabby to follow the taxi pulling away. Speeding southwest out of Apodaca on Road 54 toward Monterrey, the taxis zipped past the Whirlpool and General Electric plants, then motored through the countryside before entering the central part of Monterrey.

Traffic slowed to a crawl.

The lead taxi turned down Zuazua Street and pulled to a screeching halt in front of a small cantina. The agents pointed to a vacant spot just beyond the restaurant and asked the driver to pull in and wait. The suspect stepped out of the back door of the taxi and walked briskly into the non-descript hole-in-the-wall bar. Following his path, the stocky agent headed for the front door. The tall agent turned down a side street and hustled around back.

Dawdling outside, the agent gazed down to a long city park at the end of the street — loaded with trees, walkways and park benches. Noticing a sign pointing to the Archdiocese of Monterrey, he saw a heavyset robed man stroll his way. The agent acted as if he was window shopping in the small store next door. Following the priest out of the corner of his eye, he watched him continue down the street and into the cantina.

Delaying for a minute, the agent went inside and waited for the hostess to seat him. Seeing the ball cap and priest sitting in a booth on the left, he pointed to the other side and followed the hostess to the booth across from them.

The two men ordered luncheon.

Leaning over the table, the guy from Detroit did most of the talking. The priest nodded several times, then assumed the lead. He pulled an envelope from inside his robe and pushed it across the table.

The ball cap nodded.

Finishing half of his lunch, the priest said something to the man, slid out of the booth, and headed for the front door.

Observing from the back doorway, the second agent stepped in and ambled through the restaurant. Following the priest outside, he stayed at a safe distance and crossed behind the cleric, into the park. He trailed the robed man up to the archdiocese complex, waited a couple of minutes, and hurried back to the cantina.

The Detroiter cleaned his plate, ordered a second beer and another bowl of chips and salsa. Kicking back, he took his time, munching his way through the chips.

A thin, sleazy Mexican walked in and glanced around. Spotting the ball cap, he ignored the hostess and headed for the door. He ordered a beer and grabbed a handful of chips. The two men talked for fifteen or twenty minutes before the Detroiter pulled an envelope from his bag and slid it across the table. The Mexican stuffed the envelope in his pocket and left.

The Detroiter chugged his beer, paid the bill, and hailed a taxi. The two agents slipped into their taxi, told the cabbie to make a U-turn and followed the cab.

Two hours later, the guy boarded an American Airlines flight headed back to Dallas.

* * *

DETROIT, MICHIGAN

Waiting at Detroit Metro, an FBI surveillance team member spotted the Detroit Tigers' cop disembarking from the American Airlines flight. Giving his colleagues a nod, the lead man followed the guy outside to the taxi stand. Seeing him jump in a cab, the agent followed suit and directed the cabbie to follow the yellow cab ahead.

The taxi sped toward downtown, then headed north on Southfield.

Slowing down at a west side apartment building, the agent pointed to a parking spot to the side of the building, behind a large old oak. He watched the suspect get out of the cab and go inside.

The agent called for a backup team.

Early the next morning the guy walked outside to the parking lot, got in an old Chevy and drove up Southfield to the Big Boy on Six Mile Road in Livonia. An agent followed.

A tall, stately man sat in a small booth. The ball-capped guy spotted him and slid in on the other side. The agent following him slipped into the booth next to them, his back to the tall man.

The handsome, tall man spoke with a Spanish accent. "Did your assignment go smoothly?"

"Yes. Father Menendez gave me the money and I passed it on to the guy from the Cali Cartel. He'll take care of the baggage."

***

Ted walked into the poker game late; it'd been a tough day, and tensions were high in the gypsy community. The others sat quietly around the table waiting for him to grab a beer. He tossed his jacket on a chair in the corner, slicked back his hair, and settled in at the table. Appearing tired and drawn, he mumbled something to Renzo.

Renzo set the deck on the table. "One of the things we've always done is to take time to talk, when someone needs it. It seems like this is one of those times." He gave Ted an understanding grin. "Is there something you want to say?"

Ted sucked in a deep breath and glanced 'round at his buddies. "I guess, maybe it'll help to get it off my chest." He spoke slowly and deliberately. "Several Mafia thugs have been snooping around the gypsy community, asking questions about Joey Naples' murder, and threatening people."

"How long has that gone on?" Earl asked.

"A week, maybe ten days. They've been harassing everyone — little kids and old people — it doesn't seem to matter to them."

"That's not right." Clark's shoulders sagged. "Has anyone been hurt?"

"Not really. A little pushing and shoving, and lots of intimidating shit. One lady fell down and bloodied her elbow. You know how the thugs work."

Earl sympathized aloud. "Is there any way we can help?"

"Hmm no, I'm just afraid something is going to happen that will create an incident."

Clark's focus sharpened. "Why do you say that?"

"Mob tactics won't work in our community." He gave it to them straight. "Members of our community have been persecuted, mistreated, and wronged throughout history. Our people will simply cut off all communication with outsiders."

"How do you deal with things if something bad happens?"

"If there's a substantive issue the community has its own ways of dealing with such matters," Ted said, matter-of-factly."

"Sounds like the Catholic church," Father Dom said, in a joking manner.

Ted chuckled. "I think our actions are more exacting." He pointed to Renzo. "How was *your* week?"

Renzo gave him a disgusting grunt. "Shit city. They bulldozed one of my job sites — leveled everything; not a two-by-four left standing."

"I can't believe that," Clark said.

Renzo bristled. "Hey, come and look for yourself."

"No, no." Clark raised his hands. "I didn't mean it that way. I was talking about the level of destruction." He gave Renzo a quirky smile and turned to Carlos. "Anything new with you?"

"They banged up a couple of cars, guess I got off easy."

***

THE DETROIT NEWS

May 11, 1981

FORTUNE-TELLER KILLED—
TABLES TURNED

This morning the severely beaten body of Molly Maeve Tuesday better known as "Molly Dolly" was found in her north side parlor. For nearly a year the police have pursued the fortune-teller killer. The murder of Ms. Tuesday has turned the tables on officials.

Authorities would not comment on Ms. Tuesday's killing.

THE DETROIT NEWS

May 11, 1981
Section C, Page 1

POLICE HAVE NO ANSWERS

Chief Hart was not available at today's press conference. A spokesman for his office indicated they had no clues or leads in the death of fortune teller Molly Dolly.

THE DETROIT NEWS

May 11, 1981
Section C, Page 4

GYPSY COMMUNITY SILENT

The murder of Molly Dolly sent shock waves through Detroit's gypsy community. Shops were closed. Street vendors were no where to be seen. No one was willing to be interviewed.

***

"Did one of your thugs kill the fortune teller?" Abby asked.

Blackie stared across his favorite bar; his eyes drifted over her décolletage. "Bastards didn't know when to stop. They acted like Abbott and Costello — dim wits."

"Why were they sent to her place?"

"Everyone knows Molly Dolly. The boys were supposed to put a little scare in her."

"From my limited knowledge about gypsies, your boys may have just closed the door," she said, repeating her conversation with Clark.

"So I hear," Blackie said, sounding remorseful. "Any ideas on how we might fix it?"

"I can tell you one thing; more of the same won't get you anywhere." She paused, trying to come up with another suggestion. "Everyone is in the same boat. Clark is leaning on his friends to see if he can crack open the door from his side. Your boys probably closed that door too."

Blackie frowned; his expression less than encouraged. "If Joey were here, he'd figure out a way. Now I'm stuck with a bunch of bumbling idiots." Fiddling with his sunglasses, he took his time, thinking about Joey. Finally, he looked up, "Anything new to report on Clark?"

"It may sound crazy, but they're following up on the numerology angle."

"Numerology? What the hell is that?"

Abby told him everything she knew. "It's a system that some people believe in. Kind of like the horoscope except it's based on numbers."

"I don't get it." Blackie shook his head. "How does that connect to the killer?"

"Since all of the murders have occurred on the 22nd, his team is trying to determine if twenty-two has any special meaning to the killer. Maybe it's his birthday, the year he was born or who knows?"

"Huh." Baffled, Blackie muttered, "They gonna check out everyone in Detroit with a birthday on the 22nd? I don't think so."

***

"Gees Dad, put out that Corona," Clark said, opening the slider to the back porch. Waving his hands to clear the smoke, Clark made his way to *the chair*, the wicker one across from his dad's. "How's it going?"

Lewis leaned back; a smile crossed his face. "Figured I'd ask *you* that."

"Like I said last time. The media has gone bananas," Clark said in a low harsh tone. "They're on my case every step of the day. It's like they're pointing a finger at anyone I talk to."

"Been there," his dad said calmly.

"God damn Dad, I'm getting hammered."

The old man took a long drag and released a perfect smoke ring. "See that son? Take a lesson."

Clark folded his hands behind his head. "A smoke ring? C'mon Dad, I've heard it all. You've never said anything about a smoke ring."

"Think about it." Lewis snuffed out the stogie. "The smoke ring floats upward until it disappeared into the hot air. It's the same with the reporters; they're blowing smoke, a lot of hot air."

Clark cocked his head to the right, a slow grin forming. "Did you just make that up?"

"Kind of," his dad confessed. "I was thinking today about the comments Jack Grimes made to you about the Seattle newspapers … remember?"

"No, not exactly."

"He said something about when the shit hits the fan don't worry, it's part of the process. They're out to sell papers; your job is to find the crooks. It's a game, son, play it that way."

***

The team members eased into the chairs that had become their assigned seats and waited for Clark — question marks plastered on their faces.

He strolled in with a mug of steaming coffee and set in on the table in front of his chair.

Holding the Grimes' report in his hand, Pag slammed it down. "I've read this sucker a dozen times trying to find something he missed or did wrong. There's nothing; he did everything right."

Mystified too, Kimberly nodded her head. "I've come to the same conclusion."

"Where to now?" Pag spouted on behalf of the group.

"Back to square-one and go through every detail again." Clark picked up an eraser and wiped the chalkboard on the sidewall. "Woodson, would you list the primary elements?"

"I'd be glad to," the flattop said, sliding out of his chair and picking up a piece of chalk.

"Who's first?" Clark asked.

Kimberly led off. "There's some kind of a connection with twenty-two."

Woodson scratched 22 on the board.

Others chimed in:

- There's a connection between Seattle and Detroit

- All crime scenes are identical

- There's a gypsy connection

- The killer has a vendetta against criminals

The flow of thoughts stopped.

Clark took a sip of coffee. "Well, who has another thought?"

Blank looks peered back at him.

"C'mon, we have to dig deeper."

Kimberly raised her hand, slowly, ever so slowly. "Grimes said there are countless unsolved murders around the country that may relate. Anything we might gain from those?"

"Hold on there," Pag said. "What he's talking about may relate."

"I took it to mean, unsolved murder cases that have a strange twist to them."

"Mutilated?"

"Could be, I think it might include other things like killings by suffocation, hanging, torture… I don't know.

"Good question." Clark stroked his hair in thought. "I'll give him a call."

Woodson perked up. "Ask him if he knows any experts on gypsy heritage and culture. There must be someone in one of our universities who's researched them and we may be able to gain some insight from them."

"Excellent point." Clark stood. "If you have any further thoughts, let me know. I'm calling Grimes at eleven this morning. He should be on his third cup of coffee by then."

***

Sipping on a Stroh's, Earl waited in *the booth*. Clark rushed in, picked up the bottle Earl had waiting for him, and took a sip. "Man, that's good. It must be ninety-five outside."

"It's supposed to be like this all week. No rain until next Sunday." Earl shifted to the agenda. "Get anything from Grimes?"

"Yeah, that's why I'm late. I just got off the phone."

"Is he aware of any similar cases?"

"He's documented six other cities where there have been two or more killings." Clark sighed. "Grimes said he's spent most of his time since retiring tracing murders in other states."

"Did he mention where the others were located?"

"Yeah, Cleveland, Pittsburgh, Chicago, New York, Philadelphia and Los Angeles."

"Interesting." Earl counted on his hand. "With the addition of Detroit the killer has covered all of the major mob cities."

"I wonder if that connects."

Earl collected his thoughts. "If he has a vendetta against the syndicate, where else would be more logical? It'll be interesting to see if the other murders were in hotbeds of criminal activity."

"We'll know soon." Clark took a gulp. "He's sending me a map of the other confirmed locations and those where he has a strong inkling the killings may be connected."

"Did he identify any university experts we might draw upon?"

Clark shook his head. "He's not aware of a reputable researcher in the country who's studied gypsies."

"That's surprising. Why not?" Earl asked.

"He didn't know. Almost all of the research has been done in England and Europe. The only material he's found in the U.S. was in the Holocaust museums."

Earl's interest zeroed in on Clark's comments. "Why's that?"

"The Nazis treated gypsies the same as the Jews."

"Huh." Earl sighed. "When Ted said they had been persecuted I had no idea it was that bad."

"He told me about Dr. Robert Ritter, a racial German scientist who tried to find a link between heredity and criminality. In 1937 he began systematically interviewing all of the gypsies residing in Germany. In cooperation with the Gestapo, they rounded up the entire gypsy population and forcibly moved them into municipal camps — eventually sending them to Auschwitz."

"I thought Hitler was the driving force behind Germany's 'super race' concept."

"Most people do." Clark emptied his bottle. "Ritter's work began in the early '30s and simply provided justification for the Nazis to isolate gypsies and killed over 90 percent of them."

"Wow. That's unreal. So Hitler was part of a movement. He used Ritter's radical research and the Gestapo to achieve his goals."

CHAPTER TWENTY-SIX

Clark and Earl walked painstakingly down the hallway of Henry Ford Hospital — their hearts heavy with grief — neither knowing how he'd handle the situation behind the closed door. Pausing outside a private room, Earl nodded for him to lead the way. Clark stood stoically; his hand fumbled for the doorknob.

Sucking in a deep breath, he tightened his grip and reluctantly turned the knob. An unpleasant hospital odor rushed out; moisture filled his eyes as he searched a plethora of guidewires suspended from a chrome bar above that formed a grid-like maze. Clark's attention shifted to the two arm-casts locked in place — forearms pointing straight up, thumbs inward, little fingers protruding to the side. Bandages wrapped the space where the three middle fingers on each hand used to be.

His heart sunk.

Knowing he'd choke up if he caught Earl's eye, he continued making his way to the bedside. Jimmy Fender cracked open an eye toward Clark. Neither man said a word. Clark swallowed hard, trying to maintain his composure. Earl glimpsed at Jimmy then turned away and covered his face with his handkerchief. Clark leaned over the bed and spoke softly, "Hey buddy, you're going to be fine."

Shifting his glazed eyes to the ceiling, Jimmy mumbled, "Guess my piano playing will be limited to 'Chopsticks.'"

"Well, you'll be the best goddamn 'Chopsticks' player in the world."

Jimmy tried to grin; his lips barely moved.

Earl stepped closer and placed his hand on Jimmy's shoulder. "We'll hunt down the bastard who did this."

Staring at the ceiling, Jimmy asked, "Will he give me my fingers back?"

"No, but I know Jimmy Fender will reinvent himself. In a couple of years, you'll be on top of the chart, you wait and see."

Staring at the ceiling, a smirk was the best Jimmy could muster.

Trying to humor him, Clark and Earl reminisced about the good ole' days — trying to take Jimmy's mind off the here and now, they talked about the things they had done in high school, the places they had gone, and the girls they'd had. Nothing changed; Jimmy lay motionless, staring at the ceiling.

A nurse appeared in the doorway and asked the two men to leave. Clark and Earl took turns squeezing out a polite goodbye and left.

Two doctors and a nurse came in and closed the door behind them.

Clark took a few steps and broke down in tears. "I can't believe the bastards did this to him just because of me. Tell the guys to crank up the process. We're going to shut down every goddamn blind pig in town."

Earl placed his hand on Clark's shoulder. "It isn't your fault. You can't carry the blame."

"That's bullshit, Earl. Don't try to placate me. They're turning up the heat on all my friends. Jimmy paid the price. If it weren't for me he'd still have all of his fingers."

Knowing he was right, Earl changed the subject. "Any ideas of who did it?"

"You bet I do," Clark said emphatically. "Thomas 'Tommy Gun' Lewis has been cutting off three fingers as a trademark. He's one of the most-used strong-arm enforcers of the Mafia; works under crime family captain Dominic 'Fats' Corrado. You know, the guy whose office is in the St. Antoinette Coffee Shop."

"Yeah, I remember the place … the coffee shop that doesn't sell coffee. Oscar told us the story about that place. Back in '75 when the FBI had bugged the place and the refrigerator kept drowning out the sound."

"Right, they were hoping to obtain some inside scoop on the disappearance of Jimmy Hoffa." Earl asked a question he knew was hopeless, "Do we have enough on 'Tommy Gun' to put him away?"

"Hah!" Clark threw his hands up in dismay. "He has a record a mile long. I've checked him out with the state's attorney. Bufalino will have him out in an hour. There's no way we'll be able to convict him."

***

Sitting in the doctor's waiting room, Feliciana turned to Caroline. "Last night there was a horrible fire in the Los Herreras Parish House near my parent's home in Mexico."

"Oh, how did it happen?" Caroline asked.

"The authorities aren't positive. It'll be some time before the fire marshal submits his report. When the firemen arrived they saw Father Gonzales on fire, struggling to remove his robe. It was too late; he died in the fire."

"I'm sorry to hear that."

"The parish house was a total loss. All of the records were destroyed. I'm afraid our program may not continue."

Shocked, Caroline frowned, "Why do you say that?"

"Father Gonzales handled all of the details. No one else knew anything about the program. I don't know if the other girls will be able to return."

"How about you?"

"Arturo and I have talked to his parents. They were especially kind and want us to move in with them."

Caroline gave her an approving nod. "That's wonderful, Feliciana."

"It's all because of you." Feliciana stood and wrapped her arms around Caroline and squeezed her. "You gave me the confidence I needed to do it."

***

Detroit Free Press
June 22, 1981

FORTUNE-TELLER KILLER STRIKES AGAIN

BODY OF ERNESTO COSTELLO MUTILATED

Early this morning the body of Ernesto Costello was found in an eastside apartment.

Responding to a call about a disturbance in the building, the police found Costello stripped to his shorts and handcuffed to a chair facing a mirror.

Like other murders by the fortune-teller killer, Costello's body had a series of punctures and slices, each executing severe pain before his death.

Costello's death is the fifth by the killer, all four months apart, each occurring on the 22nd of the month.

Informants confirm that Costello was an enforcer for the Mafia.

***

Later that morning Underboss Angelo Travaglini, Street Boss Blackie Giardini, and Consigliere Tony Minelli huddle around Jake Nicolette at the end of the conference table in his Grosse Point mansion. Jake had received the call about Costello's death at four thirty — less than thirty minutes after he'd been found dead.

He downed the last of his coffee. "Blackie, any idea why someone would carve up Costello?"

Blackie shook his head. "The only thing I can come up with is he was one of the boys who messed up by killing fortune teller Molly Dolly."

A frown raced across his face. "This is out of hand. We have to stop these killings."

"Hell!" Angelo exclaimed, out of frustration. "Any one of us could be next."

"Exactly," Jake responded, driving his point home.

Blackie spoke up, "Yesterday I received a tip from 'Red.'"

Heads turned his way, waiting for more.

"She said the feds have found similar murders in the home cities of the men seated around The Commission table."

"All six?"

"Yes"

"That's not possible." Consigliere Minelli reacted. "I can't believe someone has coordinated that many killings without our knowledge."

"They've been spread out over a period of time — under the radar I guess. There has been at least one murder in each of the five Burroughs of New York and two more in Chicago. The same is true for Boston, Philly, and L. A. Add ours into the mix and we're over a dozen of our guys, killed in our biggest locations."

"Were they all mutilated?"

"Apparently not, but in each city the killings there followed a similar pattern."

"It's hard to imagine no one has noticed." Jake's face reddened for a rare moment. "Do we know anything else?"

"Yes," Blackie chimed in. "Phillips is studying the possible connection with some of our smaller affiliated cities."

The Consigliere's finger traced the fuzzy gray fringe around his head. "I recall hearing about one in Providence. Hmm, maybe three or four years ago."

Jake nodded. "Now that you mention it, I remember one in Atlantic City. They found the guy under the boardwalk; he was bloated, a real mess."

Consigliere Minelli's tone elevated with his revelation, "There's a big problem out there."

"Any thoughts on how we might deal with this?" the frustrated Boss asked.

"We've never asked for a special meeting of The Commission. I think it's time to call 'Big Paul' Castellano in New York," the Consigliere proposed. "He can talk it over with the Families there and decide the kind of action that should be taken."

"Good suggestion." Jake's face relaxed with relief. "Yes, I like that."

***

Abby opened the wooden gate to the Ricciuti's backyard and held it for Clark. He winked at her and headed for the covered patio. Lugging his old Detroit Tigers cooler chucked full of ice and bottles of Stroh's, he shouted to the group, "Sorry we're late."

"Better late than never."

"You can put it in the empty spot on the table over there." Wendy pointed to the left hand corner. "Hi Abby, how have you been?"

"Great. In fact, wonderful." She flashed a smile toward Clark, secreting the reason why they were late.

With a grin on his face, Clark sets the cooler on the table and pecked Abby on the cheek.

"Don't start that now," Wendy joked, nodding over her shoulder at Nicole and Earl — deep into their conversation. "We already have two lovebirds."

"C'mon Earl," Clark called. "It's time for the two of you to join the party."

With a sheepish smirk like a teenager coming home late, Earl stood and headed for the cooler.

Renzo fired up the grill — large flames jumped from the coals. "Earl, wanta help me with the burgers and hot dogs?"

"I'm on the way."

Earl grabbed a beer. "I like my dogs burnt."

"You'll get them the way they come off the grill." Renzo unloaded a package of Ball Park franks. "It won't be long for the dogs, five more minutes for the burgers."

"Let's fix the kids' plates first so we can enjoy ours," Nicole said, picking up two plates and placing a scoop of German potato salad on each. "J.D. and J.J., wash your hands and sit down at the table over there." She pointed, in a directing fashion, to the small table in the corner.

Carlos opened the kitchen door for Rosa Maria and Laverne. The two women carried a hot dish in each hand.

"We're ready to eat." Wendy motioned for the group to take their places at the long table set for ten.

"Please join hands," Renzo said and gave a quick blessing.

The plastic plates were filled, the men dug in and started talking about the Tigers. Within minutes the women were munching and engaged in their own idle chitchat. Sitting in alternative fashion around the table — man/woman, man/woman — it didn't take long for the couples' conversation to turn to the issue on all their minds.

"The fortune teller killer is a nut if you ask me," Renzo spouted.

"Punch and slice, I don't understand why," Wendy said.

"How does he pick his victims?" Nicole asked.

"I bet he has the attention of the mob now," Abby said with full knowledge she was right.

Renzo raised his hand to get Clark's attention. "Clark, anything you can tell us?"

He hemmed and hawed, putting his thoughts in proper order, his words leaving no doubt about his frustration. "We're into something that may be beyond our wildest thoughts."

Smiles around the table turned into frowns.

"What's that mean?" Carlos asked.

Calm and in control, Clark said, "We have indications that Detroit may not be the only place in turmoil."

A furrow crossed Renzo's forehead. "In real words, can you give us a hint?"

Knowing he couldn't say more, Clark covered his mouth with a napkin and clammed up.

Renzo pushed further. "Looks like Clark is up to the same old stuff — teasing without telling. Earl, how about you?"

Heads turned to the other end of the table.

"Take it easy on Clark, be cool," Earl suggested. "We're having a picnic. Let's just have fun."

"Sounds like the same ol', same ol'," Carlos echoed.

"Hey, Clark made it perfectly clear," Earl said, trying to end the discussion. "Pass the pasta, please."

"Perfectly clear," Laverne exclaimed. "Can anyone tell me *anything*?"

Nicole came to Earl's defense. "It's clear to me. Detroit may not be the only city with the problem."

"Shit," Renzo said. "All we get is gobbledygook." He flipped a hand up and turned to Laverne. "How much longer before Ted will be here?"

She glimpsed at her watch. "Should be any time now."

"Where the hell is he?" Earl asked.

"He took his dad and uncle to Metro. They've been staying with us for the last two weeks."

"Do they do that often?" Clark asked.

Laverne scrunched her shoulders. "It's hard to tell; they're unpredictable. Sometimes they stay two or three days; sometimes two or three weeks."

Rosa Maria grimaced. "How do you handle that?"

"They're not a problem. They're on Pacific Time all day." She chuckled. "They stay up half the night and sleep in all morning. They fix their own lunch while I'm at work. So I only have to prepare dinner and half the time they take us out."

Carlos gave her an inquisitive look. "Do they watch late-night television?"

"Nah, they're out carousing. I guess they'll never grow up."

"Where do they go?"

"Who knows," Ted said, having heard the tail-end of their curiosity. He closed the gate and walked toward the group. After giving Laverne a peck on the cheek, he grabbed a plate.

"I'll get you a beer," Wendy offered on her way to the cooler.

"Thanks." Ted heaped his plate and joined the group. "Did I miss anything?"

"We were talking about the schedule of your dad and uncle," Laverne said.

"Crazy, huh." Ted shot the group a strange expression. "I think they've hit every blind pig in the city this time."

Clark's brow shot up. "How did they find them?"

Ted rolled his shoulders. "They're in the network, I guess. Apparently they find someone in each place who knows about another location. They bounce from one to another."

Earl's slight frown turned more serious. "Aren't there any after-hours places where they live?"

"In Seattle?" Ted laughed. "The neighborhoods are tighter than a drum at midnight. The harbor side is wild as hell, though. It's been that way since large numbers of sailors started porting there during World War II."

Earl's interest peaked. "Wild? Like, what kind of wild?"

"You name it — prostitutes, drugs — Chinese gangs running the place."

"Hmm," Clark said, trying not to appear overly interested. "Were they going back to Seattle?"

"Yeah, I dropped them off at the airport curb."

Laverne shook her head. "The two of them are a real hoot. You should have seen them when they were here in March …"

Ted interrupted. "C'mon sweetie, they're not interested in all of that."

Earl picked up on the date. "Yes, we are. Let's hear it."

"Fine, tell them everything." Ted waved a hand in surrender, picked up a handful of chips and munched into a burger.

Laverne gave him a questioning glance. "Is it really okay with you?"

"Sure, I was just joshing."

"Okay, I had a birthday cake for the three of them on March 22nd..."

Clark interrupted. "I thought his dad's birthday was February 22nd."

"It is." Her glance caught Ted's nod. "They celebrated a month later. It doesn't matter to them. All of the dates are the same."

"That's a real coincidence," Rosa Maria said.

"It isn't, really," Laverne said, politely. "It's a family tradition; they treat everyone the same. Their birthdays are all on the same day and their names are the same or similar—Ted's dad's name is Ned; his uncle's name is Ed."

Interested curiosity marked the faces around the table.

"Nah … c'mon," Wendy said in mock disbelief. She turned to Ted. "Is that true?"

"Yep. I celebrate February 22. My dad's birthday is February 22, 1922, and my uncle's birthday is February 22, 1918."

"Is it like that in all gypsy families?" Wendy asked.

"Some families have an alternative date like ours. Most gypsies use January 1st as their birthdate."

Renzo's interest peaked. "One of these nights before poker I'd like to hear more about gypsy traditions."

"Sure, I'd be glad to share more." Ted smiled. "Anything new with you?"

Laverne raised her hand. "We went over all that before you came in."

"It's okay." Clark grinned softly. He shared another frustration. "I feel like I work in a glass office. There are TV cameramen and newspaper reporters all over the place. They're even in the restroom."

"Maybe you should take Ted in with you; that way they'd have something else to write about."

"Renzo!" Wendy said, reprimanding him. The guys wiped their faces to keep from laughing. "I can't believe you'd say something like that."

Renzo mockingly covered his mouth.

Carlos saved the day. "Renzo, wanta help finish up the homemade ice cream?"

"Yeah, I'm with you." Renzo stood and followed him to the garage.

"Hey, wait for me," Ted said. "I want to see how you do it."

A nod from Clark's head shot Earl's way; they each grabbed a beer and headed for the lounge chairs parked in a quiet corner.

"What is it?" Earl asked.

Clark checked out the area around them to make sure no one could hear. "First thing Monday I'm asking Pag and Woodson to go to Metro and review today's manifests for departing flights to Seattle."

"Do you really think they …?"

Clark cut him off. "Hell, I don't know what I think. I'm calling Grimes to see if he can dig up anything on the Seattle murders in the early forties and late thirties."

Earl looked baffled. "*Before* the string of murders started? You think someone has a vendetta?"

"Who knows, we don't have anything right now. We have to explore every possibility."

***

Father Dom waited with a file folder in hand, outside the office of newly installed Archbishop Peter Dooley. Exactly at the appointed hour, a tall, robed man appeared in the door and extended his hand. "Father Dom, come in," he said pleasantly.

The two men greeted each other and entered into the richly appointed room — handcrafted furniture, heavy red drapes, an overpowering desk with a large portrait of Pope John Paul II hanging on the wall behind.

The archbishop pointed to the small gathering area to the right with four red, padded armchairs precisely positioned around a coffee table. "Would you like a cup of tea?"

"No, thank you."

Archbishop Dooley poured himself a cup and took a seat across from Father Dom. "Tell me about this important matter you'd like to discuss."

Father Dom slid to the edge of his chair and spoke softly, deliberately, as if someone might hear. "I have some distressing information about The Most Reverend Raphael Orlando."

246

The archbishop took a long sip of tea. "What might that be?" he asked, casually.

"I believe he is part of a Mafia-controlled prostitution ring."

"A prostitution ring?" the startled Bishop questioned, his tone sharpened. "How can that be?"

Father Dom took his time describing the information he'd gained from Caroline and Clark, and his internal investigation. "The FBI followed James to Monterrey, Mexico, where he met with a priest from the Archdiocese of Monterrey."

"Does the FBI know about Raphael Orlando?"

"I don't think so," he stretched the truth. "I have not shared any information about our inner workings."

"Good. It's important that nothing be shared with them."

"Yes, I know."

The archbishop paused for the longest moment. "May I have your file?"

Father Dom handed him the manila folder of evidence.

"I will review these materials and determine if any action need be taken," he said, calmly. "If anything else comes to your attention, please bring it to me immediately. In the meantime, this matter shall remain between the two of us. Do you understand?"

"Yes, of course."

CHAPTER TWENTY-SEVEN

THE DETROIT NEWS
July 30, 1981

CARLO LICATA FOUND DEAD

Six years to the day, the man speculated as having the closest ties to Jimmy Hoffa's murder, Carlo Licata, was found dead in his Bloomfield Township home, less than five minutes from the Macchus Red Fox restaurant where Hoffa was last seen.

Born on December 29, 1924 in Detroit, Licata was found in his bedroom with two gunshot wounds to the chest. Over the years, Licata had been in and out of favor with the Detroit Partnership. In the early '50s, he moved to Los Angeles and became connected with the mob there.

His father, Nicolo Licata, became boss of the L.A. Family in 1964 and smoothed connections over with the Detroit Mafia, making it possible for Carlo to return home. Known as a dealmaker, authorities speculate he was killed

because he knew too much about Hoffa's disappearance.

***

Sliding in across from Clark, Earl raised two fingers to the waitress standing nearby. "We'll have an order of onion rings too." He turned to Clark. "Do you think we'll ever find out who killed Hoffa?"

"No way." Clark shook his head. "I can't tell you how many times dad and I have talked about that. It's like the Kennedy assassination. There are hundreds of theories and thousands of rumors. Truth is, the whereabouts of Jimmy Hoffa is buried high up in the elite Mafia minds."

"Do you think the Mafia had a role in the killing of President Kennedy?"

Clark rolled his shoulders. "That theory is as good as any. There's no question Hoffa had a vendetta against Bobby Kennedy." His voice sharpened. "I'm positive Licata knew who took care of both of them."

"Sounds like Hoffa got too big for his pants." Earl crunched into an onion ring. "Did you learn anything new from your meeting with Father Dom?"

Clark pursed his lips. "He's between a rock and a hard place." His words stirred apprehension.

Earl shot him a serious glance. "What's that all about?"

"I could tell he wanted to give me the man's name, but he couldn't because he was bound by Church code."

"How did he handle it?"

"He was coy, as you might expect." Clark grinned. "He described the person in great detail."

Earl stopped smiling. "I don't get it."

"He knew I'd stake out the Dioceses' offices and find out on my own."

"Pretty smart, I'd say."

"I gave the assignment to Pagnozzi to bring in pictures and anything else he finds, to our next meeting."

A several-minute lull passed as they munched on the onion rings, both in deep thought.

Clark glanced at the Vernors' clock hanging from the ceiling on its slender silver rod, and back to Earl. "You hear anything from Woodson?"

"Not yet, he's bringing his report to Monday's meeting too."

"Wait 'til you hear what I got from Grimes." Clark paused, finishing off an onion ring. "There is no one by the name of Moomau living in Seattle. No Ted, Ed or Ned Moomau has ever had a state driver's license. Not one of them have ever been in an accident; they never attended a school or gone to a hospital. Weird, huh?"

"You're telling me. Did he check Social Security?"

"Yes and got the same thing. No record of them. It's like they don't exist."

"Another dead end." Earl rubbed his shaved head, a habit when thinking. "Was he able to come up with anything else?"

"Hmm, maybe," Clark said with a hint of hope. "He was surprised when I asked if any of the victims were Chinese. Turned out five of the seven victims are Chinese and one was the number two man in a big gang on the Seattle harbor."

"I wondered about that when Ted mentioned Chinese gangs ran the drug and prostitution rings at the seaport."

"Grimes is going to pursue that angle to see where it goes."

"Was he able to do any digging in the towns where similar murders occurred?" Earl asked.

"He's sending a map to Clifford that depicts the locations and dates of each killing."

***

Monterrey, Mexico

Seeing the stately man pictured in the FAX from FBI headquarters in Detroit, the two agents waiting on a bench in the International Airport scrambled to their feet and followed him through baggage claim to the taxi stand outside.

He stood by the curb, near the pedestrian crosswalk, and watched the cars zoom by. A black Mercedes Benz pulled into the loading zone and stopped. The back door opened and a tall, very attractive woman slid out — her mini skirt couldn't have been higher; her plunging neckline couldn't have been lower.

The suave, dark-haired man set his bag down, and with one hand well under her skirt, embraced her. She planted a heavy kiss on his lips and tugged at him, pulling him toward the backseat. He grabbed his bag, slid in with her, and closed the door.

The large slick auto motored slowly away.

The two agents jumped into the next available taxi and followed the Mercedes, at some distance behind. The sleek car weaved through the city, passing several poor neighborhoods before entering an extremely exclusive district. Reaching a gated, two-story Georgian mansion, the limo stopped and waited for the iron gate to open. The car pulled into the circular drive and halted. A man jumped out the front door and opened the back one where the two passengers were entangled.

"Drive by the gate slowly again so I can see the address. I need to call in a stakeout," one of the agents ordered.

***

DETROIT (THREE WEEKS LATER)

Clark sat patiently with his team in the twenty-fifth floor conference room. Clifford McGill popped into the doorway, a short Mexican man close behind him.

The two eased in at the end of the table. Clifford introduced Jose, the team captain of the surveillance team in Monterrey, and nodded. "Jose, the floor is yours."

The short, dark-complected man tried a smile; a slight grin appeared. Nervously, he shuffled through his notes and placed a stack of photos in front of him. "This is my first time to the USA. I thought maybe I'd see snow. It's much warmer here than I thought."

Trying to settle the man's nerves, Clifford jested, "You'll have to come back for Christmas we'll have plenty of snow."

The fiftyish man cracked a smile. "Maybe I bring my wife so we can have a snowball fight." He laughed heartily.

"You certainly will be welcome guests at my house."

"Gracias, I'll tell Camila." He pulled a folded sheet from his file. "I have a brief presentation, like you say 'dog and pony.' Please feel free to ask questions."

Pag shot his hand in the air.

Jose's face went blank. "You have a question?"

"No." Pag laughed. "I was just joking."

"Phew." Jose wiped his brow. "I thought I was in trouble, before I started."

A grinning Pag motioned to him. "Go ahead."

Jose placed a set of three photos on the table in front of him and turned them toward the group. "These are pictures of the mansion where your man stayed."

Hems and haws followed as he circulated the photos around the table.

"This is one of many estates owned by the Cali Cartel in our country."

"Many?" Pag asked. "How many?"

Jose raised his thick eyebrows. "It is hard to say. In cities like Monterrey, maybe two or three. In Mexico City, maybe one hundred. And in the countryside, many, many more."

Dick Woodson, the flattop agent from Valparaiso jumped in. "That's hard to imagine."

Jose laughed. "When it comes to Cali nothing is hard to imagine. They control everything; do whatever they want."

Eyes rolled around the table.

Jose spread four more photos in front of the group. "This is the woman he stayed with for the week. Not bad, uh?"

"Not bad!" The older Fitzpatrick wiped his mouth. "Talk about being over the top, she's stunning!"

Kimberly picked up the photo nearest her, studied the woman for a long moment, and pointed to her own breasts. "I thought mine were something. I've never seen a slender woman built like this — look at her legs. Goddamn, they're out of sight," she blurted, then covered her mouth.

The men's eyes bugged as Kimberly passed the photos around the table. No one said a word.

"No one can top that pair," Kimberly said, stating the thoughts running through the minds of the men.

Jose cocked his head to the side. "Here's your man," he said, passing out another set.

Pag held his picture at arm's length. "This is The Most Reverend…"

Jose interrupted. "He's a priest?" His voice raised in shock.

Pag nodded. "I've been on stakeout watching him come and go. He's one of the top men in the Detroit Archdiocese."

"Holy crap. Wait until Camila hears about that." Jose glanced at the photo of the man. "He's pretty slick, don't you think? A multi-colored ascot, his dark hair combed back; he could play the role of the Godfather."

Nods followed.

"Any questions before I move on to his itinerary?"

"You mean there's more?" Kimberly said, without thinking. "Sorry."

"Not a problem." Clark winked at her and nodded to Jose. "Let's hear about his travels."

"He went to the archdiocese's headquarters in Monterrey on a daily basis. We don't know who he spoke with, but we have pictures of him with this man." Jose sent a copy of the photo down each side of the table. "Here he is in the back courtyard of the archdiocese with a short, robed priest." He circulated a second picture. "Here they are having lunch in a nearby cantina."

"Do you know who the priest is?" Clifford asked.

"Yes, he's the assistant to the archbishop in Monterrey."

"Anything else?" Clifford asked.

"Only the extracurricular activities of your man and the Cali call girl." He handed out another sheet. "Here's a list of the places they went to eat. We have more detail on each location if you want. They were home each night by ten and lights were out by ten thirty. Early to bed and early to rise." Jose laughed.

***

September lunch at the Roman Village served as a break from the hustle-bustle of the hot summer. Wendy waited at the door to greet the newest member. Seeing Abby park her five-year-old red Camaro, she waved and extended her hand. "All of us are looking forward to getting to know you."

"I'm excited, too. It's great to be a part of something like this."

Nicole stood at their corner table and motioned Abby her way. "Here, come sit by me."

Abby nodded and pulled out a chair between Laverne and her. Nicole picked up a glass of Chianti and toasted, "Here's to our newest member. Welcome aboard!"

Abby blushed. "I'm so glad Clark recommended me. I'm excited about having fun with all of you."

"Wait till you see the results of my latest project." Nicole rose, walked into the hallway and lugged in a four-foot octagon-shaped piece of aluminum. Standing behind it, the blank side to the group, she said, "Mark your calendars. One week from today at ten o'clock in the morning, you're all invited to our opening ceremony."

"Ceremony?" Laverne questioned. "What kind of an announcement are you making?"

"Kind of." Nicole's face glowed. "We're opening the city's first Crime and Drug Free District. It's a six-block area around our main store. Mayor Young will be there to make the announcement. Signs like the one I'm going to show you will be posted at each pedestrian entry."

"C'mon, let's see it."

"Yeah, turn it around."

"Hold on, I have one more thing to say. The mayor is going to use the opportunity to stress the main elements of the zone. He wants all crooks, big-time and penny-ante, to know they are *not* welcome; and if they try something they'll be slapped with severe penalties. He signed the City Council's action that says there'll be no plea bargains. If they are caught, they'll receive a five-year minimum sentence for any offense and fines will triple the normal amount. And, for the young kids walking down the street there'll be a reminder 'don't even think about it.'"

"That's outstanding!" Wendy shouted. "Let's see it."

A smile exploded across Nicole's face as she turned the sign with a flourish and held it waist-high. "So here it is."

Rosa Maria jumped up. "It's terrific. How did you ever come up with that idea?"

"Let's hear it — three cheers for Nicole," Wendy shouted. "Hip, hip, hooray!" The others chimed in, "Hip, hip, hooray … Hip, hip, hooray!"

Laverne grabbed her wine glass and held it high. "A toast to our own thorn bird."

"Hip, hip, hooray!" the group repeated before taking their seats again. Other diners in the restaurant smiled and nodded approval.

"Tell us more," Abby asked.

"Yeah." Laverne refilled the other glasses.

Speaking with pride, Nicole took her time. "The three blocks on each side of the store have been closed off and converted into a walkway with park benches, flower pots, and flowers hanging from the lampposts. New or renovated stores are open along both sides of the street."

"That's really impressive," Abby said. "This could be a model for cities across the country."

"I'd love that. We received special dispensation from the state police to use the image of the stop sign. The use of the shape is protected by law."

"Wow. How did you ever think of that?" Laverne asked.

"It just popped in my mind." Nicole's smile broadened. "There is parking around the perimeter and the streets continue in a one-way direction around the district. City planners did a great job of pulling the concept together. We had a citizen's committee help on each phase."

"Speaking of goals, how is your foundation going?" Rosa Maria asked.

"It couldn't be better." Nicole's face lit up. "We're up to three hundred thousand dollars. Some of the big-hitters downtown have stepped up. We're getting checks for five and ten dollars, and it really adds up fast. We even received thirty-eight cents from one little boy. It's really heartwarming to read the notes that come with some of the donations."

Rosa Maria shook her head. "I can't imagine."

The waitress arrived to take their lunch orders. As she left, the conversation continued amiably.

Munching their way through lunch, the women learned more about Nicole's project.

"I don't see how you can accomplish all of this and still find time for your boys," Rosa Maria said, speaking on behalf of the other women.

"It's a challenge." Nicole got the point. Earl had mentioned the same thing to her several times.

The conversation slowed to a few words as they ate.

Wendy raised her hand. "I'd like to change the subject. Does anyone know how Jimmy Fender is doing?"

The faces around the table turned solemn.

Her voice weepy, Rosa Maria offered, "Carlos saw him recently and said it is a sad situation."

"Is there anything we can do?" Laverne asked.

Wendy raised her hand again. "The guys have to reconnect with him. Sitting around feeling sorry for Jimmy won't help."

"It's even worse for Jimmy to be sitting around," Nicole reminded them. "The mind can play horrible games with reality when you're depressed and no one to talk to."

THE DETROIT NEWS

September 7, 1981
Section C, Page 7

HIGH RANKING PRIEST COMMITS SUICIDE

The robed body of The Most Reverend Raphael Orlando was found this morning slumped over his desk in the Catholic Archdiocese of Detroit offices at 305 Michigan Avenue. A half-bottle of pills was spilled on top of a bible.

As the Head of the Evangelization, Catechism, and Schools Division, The Most Reverend Orlando had received numerous awards and Papal recognition for international activity. He was also a vital person on the Bishop's leadership council for the archdiocese.

CHAPTER TWENTY-EIGHT

A mild 82-degree breeze ruffled Clark's Robert Redford hair as he strolled into T. J's. The guys were huddled around the table talking about Jimmy Fender.

Walking through the maze of chairs, he motioned for two pitchers of beer, slid into the corner booth, and winked at Father Dom. The father raised his hand and offered a short prayer of hope for an improvement in Jimmy's health and attitude.

The waitress placed the mugs on the table and filled them, emptying one of the pitchers.

Earl took a sip. "We have to do something about him. He sits on the bench all day and stares at that goddamn piano. His mother says he hasn't played a note since he came home from the hospital."

"I can't imagine the kind of thoughts that are going through his mind," Carlos said, in a sympathetic tone.

Renzo's brows came together as he spoke his thought. "We need to do things that will get him more involved in our activities."

"I agree. Besides, it'll be good for all of us, too," Carlos replied. "I haven't been to a Tigers' game all year. That's a thought."

"Neither have I," Ted said. "How about Carlos and I take him this week?"

"Perfect." Clark picked up his mug and led the clinking of their mugs. "We have to get him out of the house and back on the road to recovery."

"Here, here."

Father Dom's face lit up. "I'll set up a schedule with him to play chess every other week like we used to. At first it'll be a challenge for him to move the pieces; but he'll get into it. It'll be a good step forward."

"Great idea," Clark said.

Father Dom ignored the compliment to change the subject. "I'd like to hear more about how you plan to close down the blind pigs. And anything else new to report?"

The guys glanced around waiting for someone to take the lead.

"I'll start," Ted said, his head nodding up and down. "Nicole is an absolute dynamo. She's enthusiastic, organized, and ready to go. We'd be at ground zero if it weren't for her."

"You can say that again." Renzo said sharply. "Somehow she stays one step ahead of us."

Clark mused. "I'm not surprised. I remember Alsye saying when she was on a mission, all he did was step back and stay out of the way."

"It's more than that," Carlos said. "She has an amazing ability to put the pieces together and come up with a plan. I'm confident we're going to pull this off."

Earl couldn't hold back his enthusiasm for the group's progress on the blind pigs. "Clark, wait until you hear the things they've accomplished."

Clark grabbed the second pitcher and filled the glasses. "Let's hear it."

Earl nodded to Renzo. "Want to go first?"

"Okay." He spoke deliberately. "I've completed my work on seven of the blind pigs and will finish up the other three before the end of the month."

"Right on schedule," Earl reminded the group.

"Hey, when I have a due date I'm on time." Renzo stated with pride. "I'm installing twelve to fifteen bugs inside the electrical receptacles in each of the blind pigs. The bugs are the latest design so we don't have to worry about backup batteries." He took a short sip. "Damn things never lasted before."

"How do they work?" Ted asked.

"That's the best part," Renzo said. "The recording equipment is outside in an electrical box attached to the main power box with an official-looking padlock. No one would ever think about trying to open it."

"You're smarter than you look," Clark quipped.

"Hey you, be quiet." Renzo pointed at him. "You're supposed to be listening. I'm in charge of the remodeling."

Clark backed off with a half-laugh, not knowing if Renzo was serious or not.

"Ha, ha." Renzo chuckled. "Got you on than one."

Clark exaggeratingly wiped his brow as if he'd been sweating it. The guys laughed and poked fun at him.

"Okay, okay. You got me on that one." Clark sealed his lip with a mocking gesture and nodded to Renzo to continue.

"The bugs can pick up conversations ten to fifteen feet away. There is one in the office and under the main gaming table. I even put one in the bathroom."

Clark gave him an approving nod. "You'd be surprised about the things a guy says when his pants are down."

"Are you speaking from experience?" Ted asked.

Clark's face reddened. "Ah, no. I've heard that from others."

"Surrre …" Ted smirked.

Renzo spread his hands a foot apart. "How do women react when they see the size of your tool?"

"Enough." Father Dom raised a hand above his head. "It's time to move on."

Renzo laughed. "You can even hear the guys upstairs banging a prostitute if you're into that kind of stuff."

Carlos took center stage. "We're in good shape on my end too. I've bugged at least thirty cars. Almost all of them are driven by the capos — mostly captains and lieutenants and other top soldiers — we're collecting information every day."

"Do you think we'll be able to nab one of the higher ups?" Clark asked.

"Hmm, probably not. The big guys get new Buicks or Caddies every year and pass them down to their assistants."

"How did you bug them?" Ted asked.

"I had some special training by an FBI bug expert. He flew in from Washington for the day and walked me through the process."

"Sounds impressive," Earl said.

"Yeah, he had the schematics for each car model and knew how to wire them. Before I knew it, he'd installed one up under the dashboard and had run the wire to a recorder inside a panel in the trunk."

A questioning frown crossed Father Dom Face. "How does it work?"

"It's simple. When a person turns the ignition key, the recorder kicks on and runs off the battery. When the car is turned off the recorder goes off. When they bring the car back for a checkup, I put in a new tape and take the old to the feds."

Ted caught Carlos's attention with a wave of his hand. "Do you do the installations?"

"Absolutely, none of my employees know anything about the bugs. I didn't even tell Rosa Maria."

"Hmm." Father Dom nodded. "Slick I'd say."

Clark turned to Ted. "How are Caroline and you coming along with your project?"

"Hey, I'm just the maintenance man; Caroline is carrying the ball. She's like Nicole, has the place running like a professional charm school."

"A charm school?"

"Yeah, she has them speaking English, practicing proper etiquette skills, and sitting at the table, eating properly. Best of all, the women are happy. They love her." Ted paused. "Caroline has a weekly schedule for each woman. She knows where they work, the days and hours — everything. She has it all on a big sheet of graph paper; she can tell you anything you want to know about the ten major blind pigs."

***

Clark and Clifford lingered outside the McNamara conference room, taking a moment to end their conversation. Clifford nodded and led the way into the room. Clark followed him in, took his time refilling his coffee mug and slid onto the swivel-rocker at the other end of the table.

Joe Pagnozzi, the graduate from Denby had a five o'clock shadow already, at nine in the morning. Dick Woodson, the clean cut agent from Valparaiso missed a button on his shirt. Fitzpatrick downed his third cup of coffee.

A prim and proper Kimberly smiled, "Morning," she said softly.

Clark acknowledged her with a half grin, and then glanced at the men's solemn faces. "Why do you guys look so glum?"

"Things didn't go well at the airport," Pag mumbled.

Clark cocked his head slightly left. "Okay, what do you have to share with us?"

Woodson straightened his shoulders a bit. "We followed up on your hunch about Ted Moomau dropping off his dad and uncle at Metro."

"Yeah, so what's the big deal?"

Collecting his thoughts, Woodson took his time opening his notebook. "Airport officials helped us identify all of the possible connecting flights to Seattle. Pag and I went through the passenger list for each one." He paused, peaking the group's interest. "We came up with nothing — no Ed or Ned Moomau — nor a name that resembled their names."

Kimberly's face flushed. "Where did they go?"

"Who knows?" Woodson scrunched his shoulders. "We checked Sunday too, just in case they decided to stay a day longer. We checked all of the airport hotels and all of the rental car agencies — nothing!"

"They couldn't have disappeared just like that," Kimberly said.

Woodson scratched his head. "Well, all I can say is they didn't take a flight; they didn't stay overnight at Metro and they didn't rent a car."

"Huh." Clark sucked in a deep breath. "Sounds like the same thing they've learned on the Seattle end." He let that sink in, to take a sip of coffee. "Jack Grimes searched every database in the State of Washington — driver's licenses, school graduation, hospital claims — for every Moomau he could find — Ted, Ned, Fred, whatever."

"And?" Kimberly asked anxiously.

"Nothing."

"Nothing, mean your friend Ted didn't come from Seattle and his dad …"

Clark cut her off. "He could have. All I'm saying is there is no official record that he ever lived there."

"Weird, huh." Pag rubbed his stubble. "Sounds like were going down the same road Grimes did in the past; one dead end after another."

Fitzpatrick looked around the room. "Remember the Grimes' report — gypsies are extremely hard to chase down — they're experts at disguise and deceit."

"I need another coffee." Clark stood to fill his mug, stared out the window for a moment and turned. "Anyone have an additional thought before I turn the agenda over to Clifford?" Seeing no takers, he nodded to him. "Want to update them on the findings from Washington?"

Clifford cleared his throat. "After analyzing all of the murders he'd connected to gypsies, he came up with forty-eight similar cases. Most of the victims were not mutilated, but they we all tortured in some fashion with a knife."

"Forty-eight killings over forty years," Kimberly blurted. "That's more than one a year. How is it possible that no one made the connection?"

"Well …" Clifford rolled his shoulders in a slight shrug. "A couple of things come to mind. Forty years ago the level of communication was nothing compared to today. Second, we didn't have the type of databases we have today. And the killings occurred in twenty-two cities spread across the country. At the time, I'm sure they were isolated cases. No one ever connected the dots."

"Twenty-two cities." She laughed. "You're putting me on."

Shaking his head, Clifford gave her a peculiar look. "No, I'm not."

Kimberly was flabbergasted the others didn't see it. "I can't believe it. Twenty-two keeps popping up. How can that be?"

"Good question," Clark noted.

Clifford picked up a stack of papers and slid a sheet to each one around the table. "Here's a national map. Grimes placed a star on each of the twenty-two cities."

The team members studied the starred locations, with interest.

Breaking the silence, he asked, "Notice anything?"

Kimberly's look of surprise caught Clifford's eye. "Kimberly?"

A dark shadow passed across her face. "They all have strong underworld connections."

"Right and I bet all of the victims were associated with the mob." Clifford spoke deliberately. "I'd say our killer has a vendetta against the Mafia."

"Are you positive?" Woodson asked.

"Hmm, right now I'd say 95 percent. These are not random murders." He stood and passed out stapled sets of paper. "Here's a list of the killings. I've listed them by date and city. It's possible that the same person could have killed all of the victims."

Pag looked astonished. "A forty-year serial killer."

Jimmy flung the back of his hand across the chessboard scattering the pieces over the floor. "I quit; I can't do it!" he shouted and bolted from his chair. He stormed into the kitchen.

Father Dom didn't say a word.

Getting down on his hands and knees, he crawled around the dining room floor picking up the pieces and placed them on the table. Sliding back on his chair, he took his time systematically arranging the chess pieces in their assigned locations.

He waited five minutes. "Hey Jimmy, bring me a Stroh's too."

Silence.

Minutes passed.

Jimmy poked his head through the doorway. "Do you want a glass?"

"Nah, a bottle will be fine."

Time passed in slow motion while Father Dom waited patiently.

Jimmy walked in, a bottle in each hand, as if nothing had happened. "Sorry, for all of that."

"No problem." The father motioned to the chessboard. "I believe it's your turn to start."

Jimmy nodded, sat down and moved a pawn.

Father Dom wrinkled his brow. "Don't tell me you're going to use that strategy, again?"

Jimmy smirked. "Why not, it's worked the last three times."

"Well, it isn't going to work this time." Father Dom took a sip of his beer. "You have anything special going on this week?"

Jimmy grinned. "It was the best ever. Monday I went with the guys to Renzo's place and watched the All-Star game."

"That was some game, wasn't it?"

"Yeah, it was the largest attendance ever. The pundits had been pooh-poohing the game because of the players' strike, serves them right."

"I get tired of those talking-heads spouting off about things when they really know nothing."

"You're not the only one. Can you imagine one of them being in Mike Schmidt's shoes when he came up in the eighth? He would have crapped his pants."

"And he hit a two-run homer, wasn't that something?" Father Dom captured Jimmy's knight. "Do anything else?"

"Yeah … Carlos, Ted and I went to the Tigers' game Friday night. Carlos is a real goofball; he hasn't changed a bit since high school — still the life of the party. And Ted, I've never seen him like that. He was a real hoot and was on the home-plate umpire all night."

"How'd the game go?"

"A great pitching duel — May vs. Wilcox. Wilcox tossed a three-hitter. Trammel drove in Whitaker in the third for the only run. We beat the Yankees one zip."

"Wow."

"I'm going with Clark and Abby to the game on Sunday."

"Don't you ever stay home?" Father jested.

"My mother asked that the other day."

"Guess that can't be all bad … keeps you out of trouble."

Jimmy's mouth turned down at the corners. "It isn't likely that I'd get in much trouble — a little finger and a thumb won't get you to first base."

***

Abby planted a friendly kiss on Jimmy's cheek.

"Hey, what was that for?" he asked in surprise.

"For all the times you performed for us."

Jimmy's face soured. "Guess that won't be happening again."

Abby swallowed hard, knowing Jimmy had taken her compliment the wrong way.

Clark saved the day. "I'm making a beer run. Anyone want something to eat while I'm up?"

Jimmy glanced at her. "Ladies first."

A little startled, she paused. "Ah yes, thanks. I'll have a bag of peanuts. How about you, Jimmy?"

He smiled at her lovely face. "A hot dog with mustard and double onions."

"Perfect, I'll have a hot dog too." Clark winked at Abby. "Want to change your order?"

"Why not? I'll have one like Jimmy's. I can restart my diet on Monday."

Clark stood and headed for the concession stand.

Jimmy poked Abby with his thumb. "The two of you are really in love, aren't you?"

Taken aback, she hesitated for a moment, her face aglow. "He's the most special person I've ever met. I love him more than he'll ever know."

"He knows. He feels the same way. I can tell. I've never seen him act like he does when he's around you."

"I guess I'm the lucky one."

"Maybe, I think he's the lucky one."

Clark returned with both hands full — three beers, three hot dogs and a bag of peanuts. "Hey, I left you in charge, the Yankees are ahead four to one."

Jimmy dipped his shoulders. "We had things to talk about."

"I hope you can get us back in the game."

"Ha." Jimmy pointed to the scoreboard. "That won't happen unless Kirk Gibson comes up. He's the only one who's hitting a lick."

"That might happen," Abby suggested. "If we could get a couple guys on base, Sparky could bring Gibson in as a pinch hitter."

"Yeah, if I could get six new fingers I could be a world-class pianist," Jimmy said sarcastically.

Lance Parrish walked.

Abby jumped up and shouted, "We have a chance. Let's go Tigers!"

Jimmy motioned for her to sit down. "One on, no big deal."

"I'm not sitting down. We can pull this one out."

"Right." Jimmy rolled his eyes.

Rick Leach walked.

"One more runner and we have a chance." Waving her arms excitedly over her head, she shouted, "C'mon Fahey, get a hit!"

Clark stood and echoed her, "C'mon Fahey!"

Catcher Bill Fahey singled, scoring Parrish — Yankees 4 and the Tigers 2.

Abby tugged on Jimmy's shoulder, trying to get him in on the excitement. "C'mon, stand up, Gibson is swinging a bat in the on-deck circle."

The PA blasted through the stadium, "Now pinch-hitting for the Detroit Tigers … K-K-Kirk Gibson!"

The crowd roared.

"C'mon Gibson, you can do it." Abby pulled Jimmy to his feet. "You have to *believe*."

He stood reluctantly and stomped his feet lightly; then got into the rhythm of the twenty-one thousand fans.

"Here comes the pitch," the announcer's booming voice filled the stadium.

"There it goes," the PA shouted out for all to hear.

"Oh my God, Gibson slammed a three-run homer," Abby shouted. "Tigers win 5 to 4. She grabbed Jimmy. The two jumped up and down. "See I told you. You have to believe!"

"I can't believe it. I can't believe it." Jimmy stammered; he choked up and tears moistened his cheeks.

Abby held him tight and the two embraced for the longest time while she whispered in his ear, "You have to believe."

CHAPTER TWENTY-NINE

Glancing around the Ghostbar, Ted cracked a grin. "You come here often?"

Embarrassed, Clark joked, "Only when I'm slumming."

Sliding into the dark mahogany club chair, Ted took a look around the glossy bar and the indirect lighting showing off bottles of booze stationed on the backbar. Wondering why Clark had asked to meet him for an impromptu drink, Ted raised the point. "Something special on your mind today?"

"Want a drink?" Clark asked, trying to postpone the inevitable.

"Make it the usual, a double Scotch on the rocks."

Clark motioned to the barmaid. She pranced over in a flash. "What can I do for you?"

"A double Scotch on the rocks." He nodded to Ted. "My usual and a bowl of mixed nuts." Waiting for the drinks to arrive, Clark grabbed a handful of nuts. "Anything new with you?" he asked in a make-do fashion.

"Hah, same ol', same ol'."

The waitress sat Ted's drink on a classy pewter coaster and followed suit with Clark's. "Anything else you'd like," she said sensually, making sure Clark noticed her half-buttoned blouse. He shook his head; she turned and flaunted her ass all the way to the bar.

Ted raised an eyebrow. "Guess I know why you come here."

A blushing Clark spoke innocently. "It isn't like that. She's ready to go to bed with anyone."

Ted gave him a questioning look. "Okay, if you say so."

Clark jutted his jaw. "I feel awkward, but I have to ask some questions about your past."

"Huh." A partial grin broke Ted's lips. "I'm not surprised; figured it was coming sooner or later."

A little relieved, Clark smiled timidly. "I thought maybe I wouldn't have to; as it turns out I don't have a choice."

"Hey, no problem," Ted said; his mood optimistic. "I could have saved you a lot of frustration."

Clark looked perplexed. "Why do you say that?"

Acting as if he didn't have a care in the world, Ted said, "I would have told you there's nothing to find out. I haven't done anything wrong. You need to remember my background is different from yours — you were raised in a family built on trust — my culture assumes mistrust."

Clark couldn't hold back any longer. "How can you live your entire life without a driver's license, social security number, and not be in any state or national databases?"

"There are alternatives," Ted said casually. "As I mentioned, your systems are built on trust. I don't trust your systems so I don't use them. That way I don't have to worry about the kind of problems they may create."

Clark flipped a cashew in his mouth. "It's really hard to understand; our backgrounds are so different."

Ted motioned to the barmaid for another Scotch. "You want another one?"

"Nah, I'm fine."

Leaning back in the club chair, Ted bit his lip. "Here's a peek into my youth. Maybe it'll help you understand our culture."

"The waitress eased his drink in front of him, her cleavage hanging free. Taking a long sip, he glimpsed at her come-on look. "Guess you're right." Ted laughed. He turned back to their conversation. "Okay, here goes. I grew up in a small gypsy neighborhood in Seattle — people were coming and going all the time. Our family was one of the few permanent residents. My dad and uncle ran a used bicycle shop. I learned how to do everything from my mom and dad. Mom taught me academics; I learned about life from dad. I didn't have to go to school."

"I learned a lot from my parents too, but…"

Ted cut him off. "Of course, we all do, but you can't understand me by comparing to your values."

"I'm starting to get it."

"I worked odd jobs, made good money." Ted wound down, his demeanor soured. "One time this guy from the mob came by and wanted my dad to pay five dollars a month for protection. It wasn't much; it was the principle. Things changed after that."

Clark wrinkled his forehead. "How so?"

"Dad wouldn't pay," Ted said in a sharpened tone. "It seemed like every day was another adventure, another problem, harassment and more harassment. They busted-up the place a couple times. My mother died of a heart attack, and then the worst thing in the world happened."

"Want to tell me?" Clark asked sincerely.

Ted paused; his eyes moistened. "They kidnapped my sixteen-year-old sister. She was beautiful with long black flowing hair. They sold her to one of the Chinese gangs down by the shipyards. They drugged her up and sent pictures to my dad of her doing horrible things."

"Doing things?"

"First, she was dancing naked; next, guys were performing sex acts with her. It was awful." Ted wiped a tear from his cheek. "My uncle went bananas and hit the road — he'd be gone for months at a time. My dad gave me his life savings, three thousand dollars, and told me to leave."

"How old were you?"

"Seventeen."

"Where did you go?"

"I hit the road, bouncing from city to city. I heard about the problems in Detroit so I came here and started buying dumps for cash and fixing them up. It was a gold mine."

"How about your dad?"

"One day he got a dead fish in the mail — the final warning —, he went after them. They caught him in an alley and beat him up so badly he had to crawl home. After that he got the next to last picture of her." Ted choked up. "She had been beaten badly; her face was swollen beyond recognition." Ted hesitated for the longest time. "Then comes a picture of a butcher knife plunged into her…" Ted stopped, unable to speak, tears streamed down his cheeks. Slowly he pulled a handkerchief from his pocket, mopped the tears, and took a fortifying sip of his drink. "My dad went berserk and left with my uncle." Ted sucked in a deep breath. "Maybe that gives you a little better picture of me."

Clark reached across the table and squeezed Ted's forearms. "I'm so sorry. You're the best."

***

THE DETROIT NEWS

August 21, 1981
Section F, Page 1

PRIEST TO BE BURIED IN CATHOLIC CHURCH

In a startling reversal of Catholic Church doctrine, the Bishop of the Archdiocese of Detroit today announced that The Most Reverend Raphael Orlando would be buried in the Catholic Church.

The Bishop acknowledged, in a ten-page statement, that the Church had traditionally considered suicide a grave moral action — a mortal sin. Quoting major sections of the Catechism of the Catholic Church, he wove together traditional Church doctrine and the psychological well-being of the individual, and concluded, "Cases of this type almost always result from the effects of an imbalanced mental state and, as a consequence, it's no longer forbidden to hold a funeral rite for a person who has committed suicide, although each case must still be studied on its merits."

***

Glancing at the red, yellow, and green traffic lights alternately beaming, Earl headed for *the booth*. He noticed Abby's hand halfway up Clark's thigh, the two so deep in conversation their noses nearly touched.

"Hey, how you doing?" he called.

The two broke away like a pair of teenagers caught dead-to-rights.

"We were talking about *you*," Clark jested.

Earl laughed. "I think more than that was going on."

The waitress placed three bottles of Stroh's in front of them. Abby picked up one and clinked Clark's and Earl's bottles. "Here's to my two favorite guys."

Earl took a swig and winked at Clark. "Sounds like I just got promoted."

"Get out of here." Clark gave his shoulder a teasing push. "Did you bring a copy of the map and the list of murders?"

"Yes." He tossed two sheets of paper on the table and slid the list toward Abby.

Clark unrolled the map in front of her. "This is the map I was telling you about. You need to find a way for it to end up in Blackie's hands."

Baffled, Earl looked at him questioningly. "Why are we doing that?"

Clifford and I decided that after forty years of dead ends, we had nothing to lose. Based on the pattern of the killer or killers, we're positive the Mafia would have added motivation to get to the bottom of this."

"I hadn't thought about it that way." Earl glanced at his watch. "I thought Father Dom was supposed to be here."

"He called before I left the office, said he was running a little late and for me to order him a burger and fries."

"Let's order." Earl waved to the waitress. She hustled over.

Clark placed Father Dom's order, and added a Reuben for himself. Abby ordered a Cobb salad and Earl asked for a deluxe burger. "I'll have another beer, too," Earl said. "How's Jimmy doing?"

Clark gave him a thumbs up. "I think he has turned the corner. He's playing chess on a regular basis with Father Dom. The guys are involving him in as many activities as they can."

Abby swung her head from Clark to Earl, clearly disturbed. "I'm not as optimistic as Clark." Her mouth settled into a frown.

"Why not?"

"Hmm, I don't know, he says the right things, but I don't think his heart is in it."

"Abby, the two of you were jumping for joy when Gibson hit the home run."

"I know, but it didn't feel right. Maybe it was just me."

The waitress placed a tray on a serving stand and slid the plates around the table. Father Dom appeared at the door and headed their way.

"Perfect timing," Earl called.

The older priest walked slowly their way; spotting a Stroh's waiting, he picked it up and took a sip. "Man, I needed that."

"Had a rough day?" Abby asked.

"Ah …" Father hesitated slightly. "Not so rough, more like complex."

"Complex?" Abby poured a small portion of blue cheese dressing on her salad. "I'm not sure if I should ask or not?"

"No problem. It's why I wanted to talk to Clark." He sliced his burger in half, loaded ketchup on his fries, and stabbed a couple with his fork.

Clark couldn't hold back any longer. "Have you been dealing with the Mexico connection?"

"That's part of it." Chewing on a couple of fries, the priest nodded. "The more questions I answer, the more questions I come up with."

Clark laid his burger down. "Go on, let's hear about it."

Father Dom took a short sip of beer. "I was concerned when you told me about Father Gonzales' passing in Mexico. When his death was ruled accidental, I felt better.

"Accidental, ha," Abby interjected. "I bet it's connected with the Mafia."

He ignored her for the moment. "Next, you told me about The Most Reverend Orlando's hanky-panky. He commits suicide."

"I'm beginning to wonder?" Father Dom pressed his lips together before continuing. "And now, Orlando is being buried in the Church. I'm questioning now, how high does all of this go?"

Earl asked hesitantly, "I hate to interrupt, Father, but why is it such a big deal where The Most Reverend is buried? Why did the bishop prepare a ten-page pronouncement? I don't understand."

"That's part of the complexity." Rolling up his sleeves, Father Dom took his time while he enjoyed his meal. "In order for Orlando to

274

be buried in the Catholic Church, the bishop must, in effect, establish new policy."

"He knew some funny stuff was going on. So why did he do it?

"That's one of my questions." Father Dom turned to Earl. "Policy is rarely made at this level. Someone higher up had to be aware of the situation."

"Do you think someone in Rome signed off?"

Father Dom shifted uneasily. "Hmm. If not a sign-off, maybe someone gave a *nod* or a *looked the other way.*"

Earl gasped and whispered, "The Pope?!"

Father Dom covered his ears. "You didn't hear me say that."

"Maybe some big mob money has come through The Most Reverend," Abby interjected.

"That's a possibility." Father Dom looked perplexed. "Whatever, whoever, someone tossed a log onto smoldering coals."

Confessing his confusion, Earl stated the obvious, "I'm still lost."

Father Dom finished the first half of his burger. "I'll start at the beginning."

The three leaned back, assuming a long explanation.

"I'll make it brief," he jested and went on not to disappoint them. "Throughout history, suicide has been defined as a mortal sin in the Catholic Church. Anyone who committed such an act was destined for hell; it was plain and simple. There are countless passages in the Catechism that reinforce this position. For example: 'suicide violates a genuine love for oneself … suicide contradicts the natural inclination of the human being to preserve and perpetuate one's life … suicide is contrary to love for the living God.' I could go on and on. That's the way it's been for hundreds of years."

"So I'm back to why?" Earl repeated.

Father Dom nodded. "That's the part that bothers me. It doesn't smell right."

"Is there something I can do?" Clark asked.

Father Dom pursed his lips. "Not much. The Church has its own codes and procedures. I'll have to do a lot more snooping around."

"Father?" Abby shook her head.

He winked. "Forgive me my child. I checked Orlando's travel authorization forms. The bishop signed off on them."

Clark mulled that over. "Is that a routine procedure?"

"Yes. He has to approve the travel for everyone on the Administrative Council."

"So it's no big deal."

"On the surface, but…" Father Don rubbed his jaw. "Bishop is extremely particular; he checks every detail."

Abby eased closer to the table. "Do you think he is in on …?"

Father Dom interrupted "Don't say it. I have to do a lot more searching."

***

"How long before Father Dom will be here?" Earl asked.

"Ah." Clark glanced at his watch. "Fifteen, twenty minutes. He said he'd be here at 12:15. Want to have a beer while we wait?"

"Might as well." Earl's two fingers motioned to one of the longtime waitresses at T.J.'s.

She nodded and delivered a couple of Stroh's in a flash. "So whataya think … two or three weeks before we bust the blind pigs?"

"That sounds about right. Clifford has everything he needs from the tapes provided by Renzo and Carlos that will put most of the Mafia's capos away."

"That ought to make a real dent their operations."

"I guess so. Cutting off a major revenue and taking out most of their mid-management, it'll be a real hit."

"I can't wait.

Clark took a slug. "Kimberly and you will function as operations central."

"It'll be like a phone-a-thon on one of those fundraising shows," Earl said enthusiastically; his thoughts wandering elsewhere. "How about that Nicole, isn't she something?"

Clark gave him the eye. "You better work hard to stay in her good graces."

"That won't be a problem. She's the most spectacular woman I've ever known — she has it all. I love her so much." Earl took a sip. "Did you hear that Ted's dad and uncle are coming in October?"

A questioning expression fell over Clark's face. "Not around the 22nd?"

"I don't know. Nicole said Laverne was talking about her quarterly ordeal coming up."

"Ordeal?"

"Yeah, Nicole thought she was half joking. You know Ted's dad and uncle are out drinking and carousing most of the night. They come home about the time Ted and she are having breakfast." He curled his brow. "She says they're a lot of fun and take them out to eat almost every night."

Clark's thoughts ran wild. *I'm not positive she feels that way. Maybe she thinks that's something she has to say. Or there is something she can't tell us. There are too many coincidental things happening.*

Earl spoke his mind. "You think they might be connected with the …?"

Clark cut him off. "I don't want to go there, but I must admit circumstances seem to point in that direction."

"Nicole said the same thing; her insights are always right."

Father Dom slid into *the booth*. "I assume you're talking about your Nicole."

"You bet."

Father Dom grinned. "Good for you my son. The two of you seem like a perfect match." He turned to Clark. "You guys order yet?"

"No, we're ready," Earl said, motioning to the waitress. The three placed their orders.

Father Dom acted like he wanted to say something, but didn't open his mouth.

Clark picked upon on his body language. "Okay, you want to spill the beans?"

Father Dom sighed and spoke softly, almost in a whisper. "I'm not positive where my investigation is going. Each time I open up another file it seems like I find another can of worms."

Earl scowled. "I thought you had a handle on the Mexican connection?"

"Hah, that's the least of my worries." Father Dom shook his head. "The escapades of Raphael got me snooping into other financial matters. I recalled how a priest at the St. Monticello bragged about the million dollar donation from Jake Nicolette, so I decided to check it out. Sure enough, the parish recorded a million dollar donation."

Earl spoke up, unable to wait. "So, what did you expect?"

"Right now, I don't know." He spread his hands four feet apart. "When I take an inch forward I go back a foot. When I'm searching for a hundred dollars I find ten dollars." He cleared his throat. "When the money was deposited with the archdiocese, the million dollars had shrunk to $250,000."

"What happened to the rest?" Earl asked.

"It disappeared, vanished."

"Sounds like money laundering to me." Clark's interest peaked. "Are irregularities like that common in the Church?"

"Huh, the Catholic Church loses millions of dollars every year. And that's only the big stuff. I've long felt that the parish level is where no one knows how many dollars are lost."

Clark stared hard at him. "Why do you say that?"

"There are no checks and balances at that level. The system runs on faith. If the priest records ten dollars, it's ten dollars. If he records ten thousand dollars, that's what it is. No one ever questions."

"How are you going to handle this?"

Father Dom shrugged his shoulders. "One more can of worms, I guess."

CHAPTER THIRTY

Paul Castellano, known as "Big Paul," stood on the expansive portico of his lavish seventeen-room mansion perfectly situated on a ridgeline in Todt Hill — one of the more exclusive areas of Staten Island and the highest natural point in the five boroughs of New York City. He'd had his home designed to resemble the White House in Washington, D.C. and tonight was the inaugural occasion to open it to his comrades.

Towering at six feet two and two hundred seventy pounds above the granite half-wall, he proudly welcomed the arriving Mafia bosses from the rest of the country. For the last five years he'd been the Don of the Gambino family, one of New York's Five Families, and today was acting in the prestigious role as the "boss of bosses." He'd called a special meeting of The Commission.

A close affiliation of mob bosses across the country, The Commission had met on a regular basis since its formation in1931 — today was different — a specially called meeting, a rarity for the group. While its membership had changed over the years, the leaders of the Five Families of New York and the boss of the Chicago Outfit remained in control; each would be stationed at the conference table. Positioned in secondary chairs around the most powerful bosses in the nation, were the heads of the sixteen other major areas of the country.

Dressed in a dark blue pinstripe suit and blue and white striped tie, he waved to each boss as he exited the limo. Watching the men climb the marble steps, one-by-one to the main level, he greeted each with a few words, embraced him, and kissed him on the cheek. Knowing the personal preference of each man, he nodded to the female hostesses behind him, lining both sides of the Carrara marble-floor. The glossy, blue-gray tile attractively reflected the dark blue, red and green dresses of the ladies.

Pointing their way, he suggested an escort for each attendee so he could have a more relaxing afternoon around the English gardens and an Olympic-size swimming pool. Located on the lower level, the gardens to the left complemented the huge turquoise pool on the right. Between the two stood a huge ice-sculpture of Caesar, surrounded by layers of seafood — jumbo shrimp and lobster; calamari, scallops and clams; smoked salmon, herring and cod. And of course, layered below them — trays of olives, cheeses and Italian hors d'oeuvres — mini calzones stuffed with pepperoni and toasted pistachio/cheese arancini, the size of tangerines.

With nearly a hundred in attendance, including personal body guards and advisers, the bartenders at each end of the enormous compound poured a continuous supply of booze delivered by scantily dressed women.

A band stationed above the gardens to the right, played traditional Italian songs — "Ciure Ciuri," "Mamma MIA dammi cento lire," and repeatedly, "La Luna Mezz' o' mare" (Godfather). The party-like atmosphere continued into the evening — cigar smoke swirling above the crowd.

At seven o'clock the music stopped. Drums rolled, the lights flicked off and on; trumpets sounded the arrival of Paul Castellano.

Appearing on the main floor balcony, he held Nina's hand, his attractive wife of forty years, and mother of his children. His left arm wound around the arm of his mistress, Gloria Olarte.

Nodding to the applause of those below him, he squeezed Nina's hand. She placed her hand on his forearm and dug her fingernails into his arm, drawing blood, and stepped forward.

Walking gracefully toward the ten-foot wide marble stairs leading to the entertainment level, she carried herself like a queen, while caked mascara covered her swollen eyes. Nina flowed eloquently down the stairs, smiling and waving to all.

Castellano turned to Gloria Olarte, his live-in maid, a striking thirty-two-year-old Columbian with straight black hair and thick eyelashes. The two had been lovers for the last two years. Nina recently discovered Paul's infidelity. She'd exploded in rage, but following several arguments, Gloria won out.

Tonight Paul demonstrated his power by defying one of the Mafia's most important sacraments — present the image of a loving couple, show off a wife who prepares the pasta sauce and lives with him, and make sure the mistress never appears under the same roof.

In front of the nation's other bosses, he pridefully presented Gloria to the other women. She turned and paraded haltingly down the steps.

Raising his hand, a hush fell over the crowd. Castellano complimented his wife and made it clear he'd be sleeping with Gloria tonight.

No one blinked. Not a word was said.

The Don raised his hands, like a Pope giving a blessing, and greeted the group, "I'm pleased to formally welcome my friends and colleagues to my home. Tomorrow we will address a very important issue, but tonight is a time to relax and unwind."

Soft applause followed from the legions below.

Trumpets sounded.

Standing erect, Paul pointed to the bandstand. "Tonight we have a special treat." Gesturing toward the twenty-foot stage for the band now rotating into view, he paused. The skyline of New York City appeared on the back panel, a Steinway piano positioned in the center of the platform. "It is my pleasure to introduce Vinnie Falcone, the touring pianist for you-know-who."

Stepping forward, Vinnie nodded to the group, slid onto the bench and hammered out introductory chords of "New York, New York."

With that, Frank Sinatra stepped from behind the backdrop and onto the stage. The guests applauded and cheered wildly.

Sinatra smiled graciously, picked up the mike, and eased onto the stool in the front of the stage. He winked at Vinnie and began to croon his song, "Start spreading the news I am leaving today. I want to be a part of it — New York, New York."

Frank sang and joked with the audience for the next hour, belting out his best — "Just One of Those Things," "I Get a Kick Out of You," "I've Got You Under My Skin," and honored a long list of requests, doing one more encore and another. Ol' Blue Eyes ended his performance with another rendition of "New York, New York."

The audience stood and shouted enthusiastically, cheers bounced off the marble walls.

Sinatra bowed to the group, came down from the stage, and signed autographs for the bosses and their colleagues.

***

Following a hearty family style breakfast, the group assembled in the ballroom — a large, well decorated art museum with three handcrafted French chandeliers hanging over a fifteen-foot walnut conference table. The bosses with permanent positions on The Commission, along with their Consiglieres, took their seats on each side of the vacant chair at the head of the table — they constituted the remaining bosses of the Five Families of New York — Anthony "Fat Tony" Salerno, Carmine "Junior" Persico, Anthony "Tony Ducks" Corallo, Philip "Rusty" Rastelli — and Tony Accardo of the Chicago Outfit.

Sliding onto the straight back chairs in a U-shaped arrangement around the head table were the other bosses and their Consiglieres — Carlos Marcello from New Orleans, John La Rocca from Pittsburgh, James Licavoli from Cleveland, Peter Milano from Los Angeles, Jake Nicolette from Detroit, Santo Trafficante, Jr. from Tampa, and Nicodemo Scarfo from Philadelphia.

Along the other side of the table were Raymond Patriarca from Providence, Joseph Todaro from Buffalo, Joseph Campisi from Dallas, Nicolas Civella from Kansas City, Peter Balistreri from Milwaukee, Russel Bufalino from Scranton, Anthony Giordano from St Louis, and Angelo Marino from San Jose.

Not to the surprise of those in attendance, John Gotti was conspicuously missing. Castellano had repeatedly said he would kill anyone known to be selling narcotics; having full knowledge, Gotti became deeply involved in heroin trafficking. Unbeknownst to the group, Castellano was not as saintly as he professed, either. He personally accepted large drug payoffs from the Cherry Hill Gambino family.

Castellano raised his hand for silence — a hush fell over the room. "Gentleman," he started, "Again, I want to thank you for your attendance. We have a grave situation that requires our utmost attention and deliberation." He paused while an assistant handed out enlarged copies of the FBI map of murders and the list of the cities where the killings had occurred.

Following the script Abby had shared with Blackie, Castellano laid out the gravity of the situation. As they read, scowls crossed the bosses' faces, followed by mumblings.

"Goddamn!"

"Son-of-a-bitch!"

"Bastard!"

Jake Nicolette raised his hand. "What do you propose?"

"There's a nut out there with some kind of a vendetta against us. He must be stopped. We must find out who he is and kill the son-of-a-bitch."

"Here, here," the men shouted in unison.

"The FBI has worked on this case for nearly forty years and come up with nothing."

"I'm not surprised," one of the bosses down the table said. "They don't give a damn about us."

Nods followed.

"We have to take aggressive action," Paul stressed, his voice strong and powerful. "Rather than pursuing the loose leads, we have to focus on the causes."

"Makes sense," his friend Phillip Rastelli from the New York Bonanno family said.

Castellano's voice rose, almost to a shouting pitch. "I want to know who, what, why and where; everything about the killing of our men." Wetting his lips, Paul's eyes pierced those around the table, landing on the Boss of the Chicago Outfit, he asked, "Tony, whataya make of this?"

Tony Accardo stroked his jaw and spoke deliberately. "I'm troubled by the fact that the FBI is ahead of us. How could we not know about all of this for so long?"

"Yes," Paul agreed. "It's hard to imagine."

Tony cast a cold, arrogant stare across the room. "I'm deeply concerned by the fact that we lost thirty-eight men and no one noticed. Who's responsible for this oversight?"

"Indeed," Carmine Persico, Boss of the New York Colombo Family said. "Two of them were our boys."

Anthony Salerno, Boss of the New York Genovese Family and most senior of the group, spoke with a growl, "I've not seen anything like this since Mussolini tried to annihilate the Italian Mafia."

Paul waited, giving his colleagues plenty of space and time to think.

They grumbled, cursed, and complained.

He let them air their feelings.

Building upon their frustration, he slowly raised his hand. "Anyone have a thought as to how we might proceed?"

The old men around the table glimpsed their Consiglieres and said nothing.

Making sure nothing more was coming from the bosses around the table, Jake Nicolette slowly raised his hand slightly over his head. Paul missed his hand the first go around, then looked in Jake's direction. "Jake Nicolette from Detroit," he announced for the benefit of the newcomers, "has something to say."

Jake rose and nodded to his Consigliere Tony Minelli. "As you know, this has been a most troubling problem for those of us in Detroit. Paul's comment last night about pursuing the causes got me thinking down an entirely different line. With your permission Mr. Chairman, I'd like for my Consigliere Minelli to share our thoughts."

"Yes, yes, go ahead. Paul nodded. "Permission granted."

Jake motioned for Tony to stand.

The short man with sharp features and wavy black hair stood with the help of a cane. Folding his wire-rim glasses, he slid them into his suit coat pocket and nodded to Paul Castellano. "Mr. Chairman, I am honored to speak before this distinguished group. Jake is right, we are convinced that doing the same thing the feds did for the last forty years will not produce anything different. The killer will continue to attack our men at will. We must take a different approach."

"Here, here," rumbled through the room.

"I suggest we take two actions." He paused for effect. "First of all, the men killed in our cities were not random murders. They were targeted. Thirty-eight killings. We must find out why."

"Makes sense," Paul said, his voice booming across the room.

"We must retrace theses killings back to their origins and find the circumstances that led to each man's death — did he have a fight, was he in an argument, maybe with his wife or girlfriend. Someone got crossed — the killer got crossed. It could have been a minor offense. Something made his name pop up; something pissed the bastard off."

"Yes, I agree," Big Paul affirmed.

"The next time we meet I'd suggest that each boss present a detailed report on the men he lost. After that will come the difficult task. We must piece together our findings to form a mosaic of common ground that leads us to the killer."

"Agreed," Castellano boomed.

"Second point." Tony Minelli turned to Angelo Marino, the San Jose boss. "Those of you on the West Coast have a special burden. While we are working on the more recent killings, you must go back in history to find the root of the problem."

Marino nodded. "We're on it."

"Good. Since the murders started in the early forties, your boys will have to search the records in Seattle for the years prior to the first killing. Something happened — maybe it was a rape, a brutal killing or simply a small incident with one of our men. Someone out there knows something; it's your task to find out who and why." The old man set aside his cane and plopped down in his chair.

Jake stood in his place. "Mr. Chairman, I'd be pleased to hear other suggestions you or anyone else may have."

Castellano rose and gazed around the room. "Impressive — an excellent game plan. You've given considerable thought to this matter." He glanced around the group. "Anyone else?"

Seeing no other hand, he slammed his fist onto the table. "Done. We'll meet here, three months from today."

CHAPTER THIRTY-ONE

October poker began on a sober note, much like it had three years ago when Alsye Weatherspoon died at the hands of the mob. Gathering around the table, the guys mumbled a personal prayer. Father Dom rose, wiped the tears from his cheek and began, "We are gathered to pay respects …"

The guys barely heard the rest of his somber words — their hearts heavy with grief — their minds recalling the good times they'd had with Jimmy Fender; each one asking why?

Father Dom sat down.

The room remained quiet, the men dealing with their sadness in silence.

Earl glanced up; his eyes blurred with sorrow and said softly. "How can these guys be so dumb? Do they really believe messing with Clark's friends will stop him from doing his job?"

White-faced with rage, Ted spoke up angrily. "If it was me, I'd kick some ass. I wouldn't take that kind of shit."

"Me too," Renzo barked, glancing over at Clark. "How can you sit there and be so calm?"

Clark's mouth curled into a grimace of distaste. "It's eating away at me. I'm pissed off like the rest of you." Speaking deliberately, Clark picked up the cards and tossed them across the table. "If I lose my cool, they'll be in control. I can't allow that to happen."

"He's right," Carlos said in a calming tone. "Striking back will not make things better."

"I'd like to see how Jake Nicolette's tennis game would fair if he had three fingers missing on each hand," Ted said impatiently. "He wouldn't be bragging about winning another championship at Hillcrest Country Club or the Warren Tennis Club."

Earl cocked his head to the side. "Where did you hear that?"

Ted broke into a sardonic smile. "His name is in *The Macomb Daily* sports page all the time. He's been the Men's Singles Tennis Champion at Hillcrest for the last four years."

"Since when have you been reading that paper?" Earl asked.

"Since I bought 30 percent of an apartment building in Roseville."

"When did you do that?"

"Two years ago." Ted grinned excitedly. "I kept it quiet until last week when I assumed another 30 percent option."

Father Dom stood, walked around the table and placed his hands on Clark's shoulders. "You can't take it so hard, my son. It isn't your fault."

Clark sniffled, his eyes filled with tears. "Father, if it wasn't for me Jimmy would be playing at T.J.'s tonight."

"Maybe so my son, but the Lord has peculiar ways of dealing with matters like this. You're not the one responsible for his death."

"You can't say that." Clark pulled out his handkerchief and blew his nose. "Had it not been for me Jimmy would have all of his fingers. He wouldn't have become so despondent and hung himself."

"You have a job to do, Clark. It happened," Father Dom consoled him. "You can't change that. I can't change that. We must draw upon our inner strength and ask God to show us the way."

"I know, Father," Clark said, wiping a tear from his cheek and slipping his hanky back in his pocket.

Renzo picked up the deck and dejectedly tossed the cards around the table, "Dealer's Choice."

***

Fran wiped her hands on her apron and hung it on a hook in the pantry.

The front door opened and slammed shut. "Mom, do I smell something special?" Clark called.

"Brownies … they're cooling right now. Grab a plate and take some out to your dad. He's been bugging me for something sweet all day."

"Sounds good to me." Clark gave his mother a big hug and kiss on the cheek. Loading a plate with brownies, he turned for the slider. "Anything new with you?"

"I keep thinking about Jimmy Fender — the occasional nights your dad and I watched the fun times you had — Renzo playing backup on the guitar, Carlos, and you trying to sing."

"Mom it didn't matter how poorly I sang, everyone was listening to Jimmy. Once in a while Earl would pipe in on the harmonica."

"He was pretty good."

"Yeah, I can still see him standing by the piano while Jimmy played one of James Taylor hits."

"I remember too — *Country Road, Carolina on My Mind, and Something in the Way She Moves* — those were the days." Her face sobered. "It's certainly better than waiting for October 22nd to see who's next on the mutilation list."

"Don't let it bother you, mom."

"Clark, everyone is talking about it. It's like the city is on the clock — a countdown. It's getting under my skin."

"It's insane. I'm stressed too."

"How are Abby and you doing?"

Clark's demeanor blossomed. "She's like the Rock of Gibraltar. Nothing bothers her. It doesn't matter how I feel, she finds a way to make me forget about it. I've never known anyone like her."

"Good for you." His mother winked. "That's a good sign. When two people are drawn together, it works best when one picks up the other and vice versa." Fran hesitated a moment. "You ever hear from Sharon?"

"Once in a while." A sentimental smile crossed his face. "She's into that DNA research — DNA fingerprinting and DNA profiling. Professor Jefferys has changed everything. Once we get a court case that uses DNA in the prosecution it'll be all over."

"Wouldn't that be something?" Fran's excited tone coming from a lifetime of family police work. "You'd be able to confirm someone committed the crime without having any witnesses."

"I can't wait to hear from her this December. She's assisting Professor Jeffreys in a major presentation in New York City."

"That's really something. Too bad you couldn't use some of her DNA research to help identify the Fortune-teller Killer."

"Yeah … it is," Clark said slowly, giving her a curious look; his mind shifted to that possibility. "I'm taking these brownies out to dad while they're still warm."

Opening the slider, a puff of smoke swirled up his nostrils. Waving his hand frantically, he coughed. "Dad, put that Corona out. I have a plate of brownies."

"Brownies!" Lewis' brain cells responded to the thought. "Right away." He stuffed the stogie in a handy ashtray. "Good to see you, son. How have you been?"

Clark shoved the plate in front of his dad. "Not so good." He grabbed a brownie and sat the plate on the end table between them. "I can't forgive myself for Jimmy's death."

Dad gave him a sympathetic smile. "You're not the first person to lose a good friend."

"I know dad, but it was because of *me*. The mob is trying to force me to back off."

Lewis took a bite and chewed slowly, enjoying his brownie. "Maybe."

"Maybe?" Clark responded in an elevated tone. "How can you say that?"

"Maybe they're upping the ante."

Clark eased back into *the chair*; his mind recalling the advice he'd received there many times before. "Dad, I'm stressed, the killing of Jimmy was the last straw. I'm going to …"

Raising his hand, Lewis asked, "You're going to do *what*?"

Startled by his dad's question, Clark paused, reconsidering what he had first thought to say. "Hmm." A frown raced across Clark's forehead.

"You gonna bring Tommy Lewis in for questioning?"

Clark scrunched his shoulders. "Probably not, he'll just sit there and smile until Bufalino shows up."

"Absolutely. He knows you don't have enough on him. Bufalino will have him out of jail before you can ask a question." Lewis grabbed another brownie. "So what's the game plan?"

"We're trying to determine the basis for the killings. Ted told me about some of the horrible things that happened to his sister in 1939. We've been considering that maybe there's a connection. Maybe there was another event that triggered all of this. Maybe all of the similar murders across the country are connected in some way."

***

Sitting in Clifford's office, Clark twiddled his thumbs, waiting.

The phone rang. Heads popped up around the room.

Clifford picked up the receiver and listened — his face brightened as he let the caller speak — he hung up. "The ball is in our court. Washington has approved our plan to conduct an orchestrated, simultaneous hit on ten blind pigs. When I say 'go' we're on our way."

"Terrific! I can hardly wait."

"You have to hold your horses," Clifford cautioned. "I have a lot more preliminary work to do."

"It can't go fast enough. I want to avenge Jimmy Fender's death."

"That was a really cruel thing to do, wasn't it?" Clifford said with frustration. "I can't believe the mob would do something like that to an innocent, law-abiding young man."

"I should bite my tongue, but …" Clark grimaced. "Sometimes I feel like we should close the book on the Fortune-teller Killer and let whoever it is kill off the bastards."

"You don't know how many times I've said the same thing to my wife. Sometimes I wonder if going by the book doesn't make sense."

Clark nodded. "You got that right."

Clifford changed the subject. "How's your double-agent doing with Blackie?"

"Abby is doing great!" Clark exclaimed with pride. "She has Blackie eating out of her hand. The Mafia swallowed our bait, hook-line-and-sinker. She passed the script on to him. He sent it on to Paul Castellano. Apparently, Castellano used it word-for-word at The Commission meeting last week, at his place in Staten Island."

"So that's why there was so much commotion out that way. I read the report from the FBI in New York, but never made the connection."

Releasing an exaggerated sigh, Clark said, "It was some kind of a lavish event — Champagne, lobster, caviar — Frank Sinatra even showed up."

"Sounds like Castellano alright; he pulls out all of the stops."

"He's charged the bosses across the country to search every nook and cranny. Apparently, he really laid it on them."

Clifford grinned. "Maybe our strategy is working out."

"I hope so." Clark paused and shifted to his priority. "How do we move forward on closing down the blind pigs?"

Clifford took a reflective moment. "Staff has finished analyzing the tapes your guys provided. We have the capos and lieutenants, up and down the gambling and prostitution chain, dead to rights. When we get them alone, we expect several of them will sing like canaries."

"Hah." Clark nodded. "For some reason it seems natural for people to talk about other people's secrets."

"I'd wager a month's check that more crooks have been apprehended because of their buddy's big mouth than for any other reason."

"No question." Clark paused. "So what happens when we close down the Mafia's 'big ten' blind pigs?"

Clifford winked at Clark. "It'll be a big-time hit on the mob. Our guys figure we'll be able to cut the revenue from the blind pigs down to a trickle."

"Wow." Clark cast an encouraged glance. "It could take some time for them to recover."

"That's why our logistics are so important."

"I agree." Clark's interest in the plan grew. "What are you thinking?"

Clifford hemmed and hawed. "Washington has released the entire Detroit FBI contingent to me for one month. That's one hundred and fifty agents. They're bright as hell. Still, pulling off ten stings at the same time will be an enormous task."

"Anything I can do to help?"

Clifford shook his head. "Remember when we hit Freddie Salem?"

"Sure do, it was one of the most exciting days of my career."

"Remember anything else?"

"Ah … yeah, Oscar took the guys through the drill day after day."

"Right." Clifford looked him in the eye. "Learn anything from that?"

"Sounds like we have a ways to go."

"Timing is critically important." Clifford paused deliberately. "And one last point, keep reminding your team, *mum* is the word. One slip of the tongue and we'll lose it all."

Clark laughed. "We're good. Earl and Kimberly are ready to go."

"We'll maintain silence throughout the entire raid until every place is secure. At that time Earl can call the Detroit PD for transportation. By the time they arrive at the blind pigs it'll be over."

"Sounds like a plan."

"That's just the half of it." Clifford stated pungently. "It'll take another week or so to implement. We'll practice with one team and then another until we have worked out all of the logistic kinks."

"This is going to be spectacular. I wish Nicole could get the news first-hand. She's been on a mission to get even with the Mafia ever since they killed Alsye. Fact is, without her thorn bird efforts, we'd still be at square one."

Clifford hesitated; his brain clearly working overtime. "We'll have an hour or so before the television stations interrupt the regular programming. You won't need to be at the station. There'll be time for Earl and you to have an early Saturday morning coffee at her place. After a little chitchat, Earl can turn on the morning news and the three of you can watch the events unfold."

***

Clark carried a freshly baked coconut cream pie into the kitchen and placed it on the counter.

Fran wrinkled her nose. "What's this for?"

He leaned over and whispered in her ear. "A celebration."

"Don't tell me you're getting …"

Clark cut her off. "No mom, we're celebrating something else. I can't say. You can have a piece. Dad and I are going to talk."

"Fine with me. I'm on the last chapter of *Follow the River* anyway."

Clark pulled a knife out of the rack and sliced the pie into large pieces; he headed for the door, a plate in each hand.

Fran opened the slider for him and he grinned tenderly at his mother as he slipped by her.

Clark eased onto the porch and nudged his dad's foot. "Wake up, we're going to celebrate."

Opening his eyes, Lewis zeroed in on the pie. "Did the Tigers win?"

"No, though it's about time."

The old man pushed himself up in his wicker chair and reached for the pie. "Can you say anything about what we're celebrating?"

"We've finished our training just like we did when we hit Freddie Salem's place."

"Good enough for me. Coconut cream is my favorite. Good choice." Lewis cut off a large piece and shoved it in his mouth. "Mmm, this is the best."

His dad cleaned the plate and handed it to Clark.

"Want another piece?"

Lewis leaned forward to look through the screen and see Fran dozing in her chair. "A small one," he whispered. He paused. "Will it happen before October 22nd?"

"Can't say." Clark winked. "I'll cut you a big piece."

***

WXYZ DETROIT

ABC Channel 7

October 17, 1981

—Breaking News—

FBI BUSTS TEN BLIND PIGS CITYWIDE

OVER FIVE HUNDRED JAILED

Reading the words from the rolling screen, the commentator announced:

At three o'clock this morning the FBI conducted the most highly coordinated, simultaneous crime bust in Detroit history. One hundred and fifty FBI agents hit ten of the Mafia's blind pigs, the common name for illegal gambling establishments.

By four o'clock calls were pouring into police headquarters at 1300 Beaubien. Within the

next two hours over five hundred individuals had been transported to the Wayne County Jail.

Clark Phillips of the Detroit PD and FBI head Clifford McGill have scheduled a joint press conference at ten o'clock this morning to provide complete details of the raid.

"Oh my God." Nicole covered her mouth. Tears ran down her cheeks. "I had no idea you were so close." She patted the moisture from her face with a tissue. "I can't believe it. You guys are wonderful — you're the best!" She jumped up from the sofa to hug and kiss Clark, standing a few feet away.

Flopping down next to Earl, she planted a wet one squarely on his lips. "You never said a word."

He grinned. "Well, *you* can't be in charge of everything."

"It's my dream since Alsye's death. I'm so happy to be part of something like this. Hallelujah!" She pointed upward. "This one is for you, Alsye!"

GET EVEN

CHAPTER ONE

Sitting beneath a large, lime green umbrella, Clark Phillips gazed at the wrought iron fence surrounding the Side Street Diner's patio on St. Clair Street, a block south of Kercheval. A garden-like area outside the crowded Grosse Pointe eatery offered a comfortable place for locals to relax and unwind.

Small, with only four other outside tables, the place was a beehive of activity with a wide range of people. Obvious church-goers crowded around one table; two women dressed to the hilt and men in suit and tie. At another table, two younger couples savored the restaurant's famous homemade breakfasts. In the center, two couples chatted over the September 5, 1982, Sunday Edition of the *Detroit Free Press*.

Flipping open his copy of the paper to the sports page, Clark's head snapped up at the sound of machine-gun fire clanging against metal. Instinctively, he pushed the table as he lunged out of his chair, hitting the pavers with full force.

Pandemonium struck the courtyard: Customers scrambled to the ground… chairs flew helter-skelter, as overturned tables blocked escape paths and scattered food mixed with shattered glassware.

A screaming woman fell against the hard metal fence as she and her flowery straw hat landed on the pavers.

Tires squealed.

Raising his head slightly, Clark peered over the table's edge and saw a late model black Buick peeling around the corner. He pulled his weapon, jumped up, and ran into the street, hoping — to no avail — he'd be able to obtain a license plate number.

Looking *across the street,* he stared at the bullet holes riveted along the driver's side of the blue Chevy parked in front of his Mustang. One bullet hole centered on his windshield had shattered it into a thousand pieces. Seeing the disparity between the two cars, left no doubt in his mind the incident was meant to send him a message. *How in the hell could they know I'd be here? It was a private call. I didn't tell anyone.*

Turning slowly toward the garden café, he holstered his Beretta, and walked back into the courtyard. "It's all clear," Clark shouted. "I'm a Detroit police detective."

Not a head appeared.

The door to the restaurant cracked open and a bearded man peeked out.

"It's okay." Clark waved to him. "A random drive-by shooting," he lied, for the benefit of the customers.

"Are you positive?" the bearded man asked, hesitantly.

"Absolutely." Clark turned to the side and extended a hand to the lady lying by the fence. "Are you alright?"

"Yes, I think so." Shakily grabbing his hand to stand, she threw her arms around his waist. "I'm so glad you were here. Anything could have happened."

Clark looked around the garden area. "Is everyone okay?"

Hands and heads slowly appeared.

"We're alright," came from a man huddled with his wife behind a tabletop.

"We're good," an older man called out.

A timid chorus of "We're okays," filled the air.

Sirens blasted in the distance.

Clark motioned to the bearded man in the doorway, his starched white toque cockeyed on his head. "Your staff can straighten up. The police are on the way. I'll take care of the situation."

***

By the time Clark finished with his law enforcement colleagues huddled around the two cars, the tables and glassware had been restored to their original locations. Still, patrons sat nervously, talking about the gunfire, questioning each other as to whether they should stay.

The chef burst through the doorway with a tray of Bloody Marys. "Breakfast is on the house," he declared in a jovial manner, trying to calm everyone's nerves.

Hands gladly grabbed a glass; one customer took two.

Patrons buzzed about the shooting — leery of the situation — they talked about pent-up anxieties concerning public safety and the drug gangs who were raping the city.

Swinging open the front gate, Clark stepped into the café's garden again. His appearance generated a sense of security.

Spontaneous applause erupted.

He gave the group a half-salute, walked slowly to his table, and sank into the wire chair.

A sigh of relief spread across the courtyard.

The scare tactic for the young police detective, who'd become one of the few symbols of law and order in Detroit, had become a way of life. Five years ago, Police Chief Hart had named him to head up a joint team of Detroit's finest along with a group of FBI agents. Since then, off and on, he'd been *under surveillance by the Mafia*, and some of his closest friends had been roughed-up.

At the time, such joint efforts were unheard of — FBI officials always dragged their feet, and for good reason — police officers *talked too much; often spilling the beans.* FBI agents couldn't trust them — the Detroit police department had a national reputation as the most corrupt force in the nation.

Earlier in the week, he'd received a mysterious call from a woman asking him to meet her for breakfast at the restaurant around 9 o'clock. Initially, he'd been inclined to say no... yet, there was something compelling in her words — her voice stern and somber, she seemed far more serious than most crank callers — *Hell, why not see what it's about?* He'd thought to himself.

Picking up the water-spotted sports page, Clark glanced at the headlines — "A's Ease Pass Tigers." He'd watched the Tigers lose yesterday's game with his dad. Stopping by his parents' home on Saturday or Sunday every weekend had become a tradition. Best of all, his mother, Fran, always offered something hot and yummy from the oven. Huh, he thought, some things never change.

Dad was always there, sitting in the screened porch on that old wicker chair, puffing that damn Corona, and releasing smoke-rings like an old-time steam locomotive. It's been like that since I was a kid.

A petite blonde refilled Clark's white porcelain coffee mug, gave him a flirtatious wink, and darted away. Recognizing the come-on sign, he smiled to himself and brushed back his thick, sandy brown hair. Things were different now; his love for Abby had become greater than he ever thought possible.

***

Hearing the creak from the courtyard gate, Clark laid the paper aside and glanced that way. Seeing a shapely woman step in, his glance turned into an appreciative stare. She had the look — stylish and well put together — wearing large-framed sunglasses with a black crystal Gucci handbag hanging from her shoulder.

Dressed in a brightly colored — red, purple, and yellow — floral print, she pushed her large, floppy straw hat back on her forehead and slipped off her sunglasses. Standing just inside the gate, she searched the customers at each table before her blue eyes settled knowingly on Clark.

With a flick of the wrist, she sent him a subtle wave.

He gave her a thumbs-up and shifted his eyes away from her trim body, trying not to gawk.

The woman sashayed toward him in an ostentatious yet causal way. Appearing like a model out of *Vogue,* the exaggerated movement of her hips and shoulders demanded attention — her red heels clicked the brick pavers.

Heads turned her way.

Clark couldn't take his eyes off the diamond-studded red broach nestled in her décolletage. Exactly as she had described herself — long blonde hair, Swedish descent, 5' 8," — except she hadn't mentioned she could have passed for the younger sister of *Anita Ekberg.* How could he forget those *sexy eyes*? He'd just seen Ekberg play the role of Dr. Elsa Biebling in "S*H*E: Security Hazards Expert."

Nearing the table, her lips parted in a soft, pleasant smile. "Are you Clark Phillips?"

He stood and responded, instinctively, "Detective Clark Phillips, Detroit PD." *Damn, why did I say that? She knew my rank when she called last week.*

"A friend." She extended her right hand.

"A friend." Figuring she wasn't going to give him her name, he held her hand in a firm handshake.

"May I?" She gestured toward the wireback chair next to him.

"Yes, of course," he voiced in an apologetic tone. "Would you like a cup of coffee?"

"That would be nice, black please."

Clark motioned to the waitress.

The blonde hustled their way, made a note, and flitted away.

Zeroing on his clean-cut shave and newly pressed shirt, the woman asked, "Are you always so prim and proper?"

"Usually." He shrugged. "Guess it's the result of growing up in a household with two hardworking parents."

"Yes, so I've learned. And both highly successful, I might add."

Turning his head to the side, Clark's inquisitive stare revealed his thoughts. *So I've heard? Where? How would she know that?* He considered pursuing the point then elected to let it slide.

The waitress reappeared with a mug of coffee and left without a sound.

"Thank you for taking time to meet with me," she expressed sincerely. "I hope being late didn't inconvenience you."

He chuckled. "As a matter of fact, you missed the excitement."

Her face turned into a questioning glare. "Excitement?"

"There was a drive-by shooting across the street. The Chevy parked in front of my car got riddled with fourteen bullet holes."

Sliding to the edge of the chair, her pensive frown revealed anxiety. "It was the Mafia, wasn't it? How did they know we were meeting? Are they here, now? Maybe they're watching. I have to leave."

Clark placed his hand on her wrist. "Hold on."

"I can't take any chances. I've worked too hard to prepare for this moment," her voice had an edgy tone. "I must leave."

Clark tightened his grip on her wrist, and pointed out reassuringly. "There's no way they could know about our meeting."

"They had to know." She pulled her hand away and stood.

Clark eased up next to her. "It was probably a random drive-by shooting," he fibbed, trying to settle her nerves.

"Fourteen bullet holes, I don't think so."

"Well…" he spoke honestly, "They probably tailed me. It has nothing to do with you." He inched closer and spoke softly. "Trust me. I didn't tell anyone. At most it was a couple of thugs ordered to send me a message. They're long gone."

She released a heavy sigh. "You're positive."

"Yes." He winked, reassuringly. "Relax, and have some coffee."

Studying the individuals at the other tables, all deep in conversation, she gracefully slid back into the chair. "Thanks." She took a short sip. "The coffee is as good as ever."

"Would you like something to eat?"

Shaking her head, side-to-side, she motioned to him. "No… but feel free to do so. The stuffed French toast used to be wonderful."

"No, I'm fine."

The *Vogue*-worthy beauty brushed strands of blonde hair away from her face. "I'll get right to the point. My schedule is really tight; I have to be in L.A. tonight."

He tried to come up with an appropriate remark. "How'd you find this place?" he asked as a last resort.

Hesitating for a moment, she responded guardedly. "I used to come here, a long time ago."

"Did you grow up in Detroit?"

"Ahh…" Pausing, she rubbed her fingertips slowly over her lips, as if evaluating his question. "Sort of…" She hesitated again for the longest moment before opening up. "I was raised in a very nice part of the city and had a wonderful family… I went to a boarding school out east and spent the summers boating on the river."

"I enjoy that too…" Clark hesitated, and shifted the conservation. "Have you lived in California long?"

"Almost ten years. I spent my college years there and fell in love with the place."

Figuring he might as well move into the agenda, he asked, "You mentioned on the phone we had some things in common, so why are you back in Detroit?"

"Unfinished business."

Feeling she might say more, Clark waited.

She changed the topic. "Your father had a distinguished career as a patrolman on the southwest side. How is he doing?"

Question marks plastered Clark's brain; his face remained placid. *That was a strange thing to say. How did she know about dad? Has she been investigating me? Why would she do that?* His mind wandered before he decided to play it her way. "Thank you, so much." A special feeling of admiration for his father came over him. "He retired seven years ago and is doing quite well."

"Good for him." The woman watched a black car cruise by.

"Do you know my father?" Clark asked, trying to decipher how her words connected.

"Not really. A family acquaintance from long ago."

A family acquaintance... how does that connect? Rephrasing his question, Clark asked, "Why are you here?"

"Some unfinished business."

Crap, that's the same as before. Hiding his frustration, he paused with a chuckle. "There's a lot of unfinished business around here."

She gave him a casual gaze and spoke slowly. "You've established a remarkable record in a short period. I've been impressed with the thoroughness of your investigative work, particularly sorting out the issues in the Huston Nash case, and connecting his wife to the mob — that was really something."

Clark's mind twirled. *Nash? That was four years ago. How does that relate?*

Swirling the dregs of her coffee, she tipped her mug side-to-side.

"Would you like a refill and a Danish?" he asked, hoping she'd agree. "They have apple, cherry, and cream ones."

"Yes, a cherry one would be fine, thank you."

Clark motioned to the waitress standing by the gate.

She hustled over and took their order for two cherry Danishes.

Sliding her chair closer to him, she returned to the subject, "I was captivated by the way you determined the mobster was hiding in Miami. And putting away those scumbags at the DRC was quite an accomplishment." She flashed a subtle grin. "And all in one fell swoop — that was spectacular!"

"Thanks, that's nice of you to say," he replied, impressed by her insights, yet wondering where all of this was headed. "Those were team efforts. Without the hard work and commitment of countless individuals, none of it would have happened."

"Somehow, I figured you'd say that." She gave him an unconscious nod. "Fact is, every successful team has a strong leader."

Unable to hold back any longer, Clark waved his hand. "I appreciate your most gracious comments, but I assume our meeting is about more than my career."

Her penetrating stare revealed a sign of relief. "Yes, it is."

The waitress slid two plates in front of them — a large cherry Danish on each — and refilled their mugs.

Clark sliced into his and took a bite.

Clearly uncomfortable, she gazed off. "I've reflected on this moment countless times. Last night, my thoughts were clear in my mind, now, somehow, it's difficult to say."

"Things happen that way." Clark grinned, trying to reassure her.

She shook her head. "Maybe for some, but not for me; it's usually easy."

Clark eased back in his chair and flicked his hand. "Why not start at the beginning and we'll go from there. No big deal."

"That's part of the problem." She looked him in the eye. "I can't share all of the details. I don't want to compromise your work."

"Compromise?" Confused, Clark pushed forward. "Okay, pick one point, any point, and we'll go from there."

"Fair enough." She shifted uneasily in her chair. "I'm sure it's obvious… I hired a private detective to check you out."

Clark's lips moved slightly.

She raised a hand before he could say a word. "Wait, I want you to hear me out."

"Okay." He gobbled the last piece of his Danish and rocked back on the wireback chair.

"My research was well intended," she declared in all honesty. "I simply couldn't afford a slip-up or a false step. I had to be absolutely positive you were the right person and I could trust you. With that accomplished, I'm ready to share with you my sole mission in life."

A mystified expression crossed Clark's face. *At twenty-nine/thirty, she has a sole mission in life. It must be a real cause.*

Her voice stayed calm as the words rushed out. "I was going to say this in a pleasant manner, but there's nothing nice I can say about the two of them. They are the most despicable… ruthless… callous men on the planet. They're conniving. They have no concern for human dignity. They play the role of Mr. Nicey, Nicey; goody-two-shoes — you name it — the two bastards atop the Mafia must be stopped."

Hearing the shocking description, Clark's face looked perplexed; he talked slowly, softly and deliberately, "Are you talking about the top guys in the Mafia — Boss Jake Nicolette and Underboss Angelo Travaglini?"

Her piercing eyes revealed her thoughts. "You're damn right, I am," she whispered with a quiet snap; a sneer reddened her face. "I can't even say their names."

Clark edged his chair against hers. "Why them?" he asked in a comforting voice. "If you have an issue with the Mafia, it's likely one of their lackeys who did the job — there're layers of soldiers below the two of them. The Mafia is a large, complex organization. You just can't walk up to one of them and say…"

She touched his wrist, cutting him off. "I have a vendetta to settle with each of them and I won't stop 'til I've accomplished my goal."

"That's insane. The top dogs in the mob are virtually untouchable. We've tried to nail them for years." Collecting his thoughts, Clark inquired, "Maybe if you could tell me why you're so insistent, I could help."

"I can't." she replied sharply. "It's personal."

"So you're not going to tell me anything more."

"Clark, I have confidence in you, but I can't… I can't disclose the specifics." She slid her fork into the last piece of Danish, eased it into her mouth and chewed slowly. "I know this is hard for you to understand, but I know exactly how I'm going to do it." She rose, took a few steps toward the gate, stopped, and turned halfway around. "I know our paths will cross again."

"Wait," he called. "Where? When?"

She took a step back, toward him. "I'll tell you more when the time is right." Her smile broadened. "I'll let you know when that time comes."

Closing the gate, she headed for a dark blue Porsche, and slid in. Sitting there for at least a minute or so, she turned on the ignition, and squealed around the corner, down Kercheval.

Clark sat dumbfounded. *I don't understand. Unfinished business? She can't say anything. Our paths will cross. What's that all about?*

The waitress refilled his coffee.

He picked up the hot simmering mug, stared at the steam, and placed it back on the table. "Damn, that's hot," he mumbled, his mind a blur. *I've had countless experiences... this takes the cake. I'll let you know. Shit, I can't grasp the meaning.*

He motioned to the waitress, ordered stuffed French toast, and picked up his mug.

In seemingly no time, a plate heaping with the restaurant's specialty was in front of him. He automatically covered the double-thick bread with a heavy dose of maple syrup and dug in. *Compromise me... how in the hell would she do that? Unfinished business; like what? An acquaintance of the family; how does that fit? Our paths will cross; when, where? I'll let you know when the time comes.*

Shaking his head, he shoved the last piece of French toast in his mouth, his mind still unwilling to stop. *Our paths will cross... when, where? That doesn't connect. I don't get it!*

Steve Schilling, a university president, is loved and respected by all. He's successful and ingenious; he's thoughtful, caring, and loving. And then, the next moment, he is self-satisfying, egotistical, and narcissistic.

Although Steve is very likeable, he not your conventional character—he's both awful and empathetic—you'll find yourself rooting for him to conquer his addiction and then you want to kick him in the butt when he fails and slides backward.

The type of addiction doesn't matter—alcohol, drugs, gambling, sex, shopping, smoking—the results are the same. Addicts lie and cheat; they deceive those closest to them, and often hurt the ones who love them the most.

Certified Addiction Professional, Dr. Francis R. Valenti, called the work, "An excellent portrayal of the double-life of a sex addict—his trials and tribulations, and struggles against all odds."

The real-to-life situations in the trilogy make it easier to understand their actions and how they affect friends and family members.

www.ingramcontent.com/pod-product-compliance
Lightning Source LLC
Chambersburg PA
CBHW060946120726
47910CB00002B/506